Curse of the Blood Moon

Blood Moon's Fury

D1805880

LEAH KINGSLEY

Blood Moon's Fury

Published internationally by Foxfire Press
88 Captain Morgans Blvd. Nanaimo, BC V9R 6R1

Copyright © 2019 by Leah Kingsley

One

DARKNESS SHROUDED HIS surroundings as Charles Banks crept into the shadowy room. He groped along the wall for the light switch but froze as someone breathed. A hand clamped around his wrist. He wrenched himself free on a jarring jolt of shock. There was an intruder in his home. He turned to run. His shoes skidded on something slippery, and he fell face-first into a pool of blood.

The light clicked on. He recoiled in horror, his mouth falling open in a silent scream. There, right in front of him on his living room floor, lay the body of his father.

The piercing shriek of his alarm yanked him from sleep. He bolted upright and flailed free of his blankets, his heart hammering against his ribs in a frantic struggle to escape his chest. He fumbled for his glasses and rammed them onto his face. His bedroom swam into focus with the harsh certainty of reality. Charles was seventeen, too old for nightmares, yet the memory of his father's murder still haunted his dreams.

The killer had never been arrested. Charles had seen the murderer with his own two eyes, but the officials had refused to believe him. They had labeled him traumatized. They had called him naïve. None had accused him of lying, but all believed he was mistaken. No one wished to imagine a beloved senator capable of murdering a journalist in cold blood. It was easier to ignore the words of a child. But Charles had never forgotten that night or that man's face. How could he while enrolled at the same school as the senator's son?

Charles dragged himself out of bed and braced himself for another day of high school hell. He was unpopular, short, and clung precariously to the bottom of every social ladder. His school was unusual in that it had two hierarchies: standard popularity and supernatural power. Charles was supernatural but had no power.

The paranormal pecking order mirrored a high school popularity pyramid with the most influential supers at the top, like the cheerleaders and jocks, and the least influential at the bottom, like the losers and outcasts. His human classmates had no idea they went to school with supers, or that supers lived among them throughout their entire world. Charles didn't blame them. Humans were naturally oblivious.

The supernatural world was fragmented into factions of warring species, most notably mages, demons, angels, and Darks. Angels resembled kindhearted cheerleaders. They wielded a lot of influence in the supernatural community and were flawless in every way. Demons had serious anger management issues. They acted like trashy rednecks, killing first and asking questions later.

Charles's species, the mages, were at the bottom of the supernatural class structure and represented the average student. They used magic to shape the world around them and emphasized blending with human society. Other supers mocked their powers and ridiculed them for respecting humans.

The last main group of supers, the Darks, were the entitled rich kids, the snobbish queen bees, the crème de la crème of the supernatural world. They were ruthless and smart and delighted in destroying their enemies. Darks had a heightened understanding of emotions and psychology and wielded insane amounts of power that lesser supers could barely comprehend. They ruled the supernatural world because no one had the means to oppose them.

Darks looked down on mages like jocks looked down on nerds. This meant that Charles was bullied by everyone. His entire appearance screamed geek. He was short and skinny with a thin, pale face and closely cropped strawberry blond hair. He had eyes the color of blue forget-me-nots, a long, narrow nose, and always wore a pair of oversized glasses. A girl in his class had once insisted his eyes were gorgeous and suggested he switch to contacts, but Charles had stuck with the glasses to save money.

The Banks family had never been rich or even comfortable. They lived in a shabby neighborhood with a high crime rate, where gang violence and drug deals were everyday occurrences. Their two-bedroom home was 900 square feet, and compared to the other houses in the neighborhood, in amazing shape. They had laminate floors throughout the living room and kitchen, plush carpeting in the bedrooms, and fresh paint on the exterior.

Charles and his mother made the best of what they had because recent redistricting had placed their neighborhood on the fringe of a top-notch school district. Charles's education was his mother's top priority, and she struggled tirelessly to save for his college fund. She had gotten a second job at the beginning of September, writing for the *Toronto Times* in the early mornings before spending long hours at her day job as a rehabilitation counselor.

Charles was a straight A student and hoped to win several scholarships. His mom claimed he was a natural-born intellect. He knew better. His good grades were the byproduct of a nonexistent social life. Studying to get into a college far away was his only chance of escaping Toronto and his tormentors.

He glanced at the clock on the microwave and leapt to his feet on an electric shock of panic. His bus was due at any moment. He swiped his backpack off the couch and raced out the door. His bus was pulling away from the curb. He charged down his sidewalk, waving like a maniac to get the driver's attention. His mom always used to get him out the door. He never thought he'd miss her nagging.

The driver smiled kindly and waited at the corner. He scrambled aboard with a couple dark-haired girls and found an empty seat near the back by a sputtering heat vent. A group of boisterous jocks turned their attention to teasing him, peppering him with insults and mocking his shabby appearance. Their words formed a monotonous backdrop of noise that he did his best to tune out. He gazed out the window and wished he were anywhere else. Charles ditched his tormentors at school by charging headlong into the crowd shoving their way through the front doors.

The bustling entrance hall was even more congested than usual with a group of guys clustered in front of the doors to the auditorium. Their collective attention was focused upon the school flag, a cerulean and gold banner depicting a roaring tiger. It hung majestically above the auditorium's double doors albeit with a lacy black thong dangling from its top left corner. A jock jostled the flag to dislodge the underwear, while his friends bet each other on who was going to catch it.

Charles huffed out a disgusted sigh. His classmates had no respect for their school, their peers, or themselves. Yet they attended Toronto's finest high school and walked the halls as if entitled to everything. The patronizing teachers and tastefully decorated building encouraged their upper-class mindset. From its perfectly manicured lawn to its enormous library, the institute screamed snobbish pretense. It also shrieked by-the-book conventionality. Toronto High School, a.k.a. THS, was the largest and most prestigious high school in the city. Charles gave a disdainful shake of his head. THS's lack of originality never ceased to amaze him.

He plodded through the halls and hesitated in the doorway to homeroom. Students in his class divided themselves into acutely distinct friend groups such as cheerleaders, stoners, nerds, gangsters, and football jocks. Choosing the wrong seat meant social suicide. He usually played it safe and sat with the nerds, but another day of Mathletes and chemistry jokes would melt his mind. That left him with the gangsters, a dangerous hangout for the shortest guy in class.

This group of four had a nasty reputation. They vandalized property, dabbled in illegal drugs, violently targeted minorities, and called themselves a gang by the name of Assassin's Honor. Each wore motorcycle attire, tall boots and black leather jackets. All four made his life a living hell.

Nathan Johnson, the gang's leader and the most obnoxious of his crew, was loud and opinionated and spoke with a thick Tennessee drawl that made everything he said sound vaguely inappropriate. He was a burly six foot two with a square face and deep-set brown eyes the color of chestnuts. His spiky russet hair and unkempt facial stubble gave off dangerous vibes, and the jagged scar running the length of his right cheek confirmed the assumption.

Alexander Cardelle, the member of Assassin's Honor whom Charles loathed most, had one favorite pastime, torturing Charles. Alex was six feet of muscle with a cruel mouth and stormy blue eyes. He had thick mocha brown hair, a strong jaw, and according to all the girls, the sculpted cheekbones of a Greek god.

Ashton Jones, the dumbest member of Assassin's Honor, had white blond hair and dopey hazel eyes. Ash was five or six inches taller than Charles and skinny as a rail. His round, freckled face and gap-toothed smile gave the illusion of innocence, an odd incongruence for a gangster.

Peter Jenkins, the quietest of the group, was six foot four and built like a rock. His broad shoulders, huge forearms, and impressive

4

eight-pack were reminiscent of the Hulk. He had curly dark brown hair and an eternally serious expression. His chiseled features and almond complexion accentuated his gentle sea green eyes.

Charles had a secret fascination with Assassin's Honor. They were led by a human, even though one of their members was a Dark. Why would such a powerful being let a mere mortal tell him what to do? Perhaps the human was the Dark's built-in safety, a convenient scapegoat for every crime.

The infamous four were sitting in the back-left row with two empty seats to Ash's right. Charles took the desk by the aisle, leaving one empty chair between himself and the four horrors.

"Dork at three o'clock," Alex alerted the others.

Charles set down his books and stared straight ahead at the blank whiteboard.

"What you studying, Banks? Your social calendar for the next month?" Nathan laughed at his own joke.

"How's your mommy?" Alex's cold blue eyes flashed with malice. "Bet it's hard now she works all the time. You must never see your best friend."

Charles kept his face expressionless but clenched his fists under the desk. It pissed him off when they brought up his mother.

Nathan snickered. "His mom probably got that second job so she could have more time away from him."

Charles bit his tongue and studied his polished wooden desktop. Three faint scratches marred its smooth surface. He made out the letters $A + J$.

"What's it like being a loser?" Ash leaned across the empty desk, invading Charles's personal space. His shaggy hair fell into his bloodshot eyes.

"Why you asking me? You have a lifetime of firsthand experience." Charles smirked. Ash had made that comeback way too easy. His stoner reputation won no popularity points. The insult hit its mark, but so did Ash's fist. Charles rubbed his jaw. Why did annoying Ash bring him such inexplicable glee?

An attractive blonde entered the classroom. Alex tossed her a note, imitating an overdramatic football pass. She laughed as she read his message and flipped her honey blonde curls. Charles fought his gag reflex. What did girls see in shady guys?

Two

"AMY! AMY! WAKE up!"

Amy Evans startled awake as her nine-year-old sister catapulted into her room and bounced up and down on the end of her bed. Susan was already dressed for school despite the fact it was barely light outside. She wore a pink V-neck shirt with navy blue skinny jeans and had accessorized her outfit with a pair of Amy's favorite earrings. The tiny silver bobbles tinkled cheerfully as she bounced.

"Susan." Amy put her pillow over her head to muffle her sister's shrieking. "What time is it?"

"Six twenty-two and wake up to you!" She giggled at her rhyme.

Amy groaned. "Sue, I sleep until six forty-five."

"But Amy." Susan pouted. She had the best pout in the entire world. No one could resist those dove gray eyes or that adorable little head tilt, and when she puckered up her rosebud lips, her sweet face just about melted your heart. "Are you really gonna be able to fall back asleep?"

Amy sighed. She crawled out of bed and instantly regretted leaving its cocoon of warmth. Her bare feet came into contact with the cold laminate floor as the draft from her single-pane window cut through her fraying T-shirt and sweats. She shivered and hunched her shoulders against the damp, chilly air. The heat had flaked out again. How much would it cost to fix this time? She longed to slip back beneath her covers and sleep the day away.

Amy loved her twin bed. She had rescued a pillow-top mattress from a garage sale a year ago and had spent months saving up for a lapis blue bedspread. She had topped it off with a collection of velvet and faux fur throw pillows, creating a nest-like haven of comfort.

The rest of her dingy room depressed her. Its artichoke green walls resembled the inside of a genetically modified vegetable. Susan had taken one horrified peek at the room on move-in day and run screaming down the hall to her smaller but favorably painted burgundy bedroom. The rickety nightstand by Amy's bed bore nothing but a broken lamp, and a shaggy violet rug in the center of her floor hid a large chip in the laminate. She didn't even have a dresser, since the clothes she owned barely filled her closet. Money had been tight since their dad had walked out on them, but they had all managed to survive. Amy was determined to survive for Susan's sake. Her little sister deserved better than their trashy neighborhood.

Susan dumped the contents of Amy's makeup bag onto her bed and applied sparkly bubblegum lip gloss to her eyelids. Amy had tried a similar look in her preteen, Kesha-obsessed phase. Glitter-zombie much?

"What are you doing?" She laughed.

"Using your makeup," Susan chirped, checking the effect in the mirror. The glitter clashed horribly with her long, dark lashes.

"That goes here." Amy pointed to her lips.

Color bloomed in Susan's already rosy cheeks. She darted into the washroom to remove the offending pink sparkles. Amy closed her eyes, shuttering her soul to its constant pain. Susan looked exactly like her when she blushed. The little girl was Amy in miniature. Everything about her, from her petite features to her trusting smile, reminded Amy of her traumatic past.

Splinters of memories skewered her mind. A baby girl's smile. A photo of her father. A washed-out watercolor of a casket in a grave. Each image twisted its own unique knife, tattooing a special scar upon her broken, bleeding heart.

She picked up her hairbrush and twirled it in her fingers as she studied her reflection in the mirror by her door. Amy was five foot two and fine boned with high cheekbones and a delicate nose. Her fair complexion contrasted her soft, ebony hair, and her haunted misty gray eyes gave her an air of sorrowful mystery. She used this to her advantage, cloaking her thoughts and feelings behind layers of cynicism and snark.

Amy set aside her brush and dropped her head into her hands. She had bags the size of Texas under her eyes and tangled hair flopping limply to her shoulders. She desperately needed a shower and a good night's sleep, but neither goal was achievable before school. She rubbed her eyes and stifled a yawn. Making herself halfway presentable was pointless but mandatory. She retrieved her makeup from where Susan had left it strewn on the bed and rooted through it for supplies. She applied eyeliner and mascara and assessed her pale reflection. Foundation and bronzer completed her look and marginally concealed her exhaustion. Juggling school, a part-time job, and caring for her sister left little time for such luxuries as sleep.

"Amy!" Susan called over the water running in the bathroom. "Will you help me do my makeup?"

"Keep that out of your eyes," Amy said, shooting a look across the hall. Susan stood at the sink, exuberantly splashing water onto her face. Her pink shirt and silky onyx hair were soaked, and her eyes were still rimmed with glitter.

"Yeah, yeah." Susan hummed a show tune as she danced into Amy's room and exited seconds later with Amy's favorite hairbrush.

"Hey!"

The washroom door slammed on another high-pitched giggle. Their mother banged on the adjoining wall for quiet. Erica Evans worked the graveyard shift at 7-Eleven and went to bed at the same time the girls woke up.

"Shh," Amy hissed. "Mom's trying to sleep."

"Okay!" Susan said, just as loudly as before.

Amy opened her closet and threw her head back on a moan of despair. What was she going to wear? She and her mom each worked thirty hours a week. They scraped together enough cash to pay the bills and spent what little was left over on groceries. There was never a cent to spare on new clothes. Even outfits off the clearance rack at Walmart were out of their price range. Amy had three pairs of jeans, a few old T-shirts, and four tops that were barely presentable enough to see the light of day. Her outfit options filled a third of her tiny closet. She had been too tired to do laundry after work last night, and now she was paying the price. A single lonely T-shirt hung in a barren expanse of empty wardrobe. She dug some jeans out of her hamper. "Guess I'm wearing these again."

"What?" Susan shrieked from the depths of the washroom.

"Nothing."

"What?" Susan said at greater volume still.

Their mother pounded on the wall. Amy strode across the hall and kicked the bathroom door to get her sister's attention. "Susan, be quiet!"

"Sorry," she replied in as close to a whisper as she ever got.

The girls trotted downstairs for breakfast. Their dimly lit living room was shrouded in foreboding clouds of doom that reeked of cigarettes and booze. Rex Kastel, their mom's latest deadbeat boyfriend, lay sprawled on their overstuffed sofa. Rex had a wide, pudgy face and an enormous beer belly. His receding graying hair accentuated his prominent forehead, and his watery blue eyes were beady like an insect's. He slept fully dressed in drab brown cargo pants and a canary yellow shirt stained with sweat. His muddy boots dangled off the end of the sofa, and a thin dribble of drool leaked out of the corner of his drooping mouth. Amy screwed up her face. No wonder her mother refused to let Rex join her in bed.

The girls tiptoed past the sofa and slipped into the kitchen. Amy eased shut the pocket door and theatrically pinched her nose. "Good God!"

Susan pretended to retch into her hands. "That dude gets smellier by the day. Did you see his gross, sweaty T-shirt?"

"Did you see the drool?" She and Susan mocked their mother's steady parade of boyfriends to avoid thinking about how uncomfortable they made them.

Susan took a seat at the kitchen island to finish some last-minute homework. The average-size counter consumed most of the tiny room, leaving nothing but a three-foot-wide stretch of floor around the kitchen's perimeter. The limited space made it difficult for more than one person to move about, so the girls had jokingly termed it a "one-butt kitchen."

Despite its diminutive size, the kitchen was Amy's favorite room in the house. It had periwinkle walls and a large window overlooking a busy Toronto street. The honking horns and rumbling trucks formed a cacophony of background noise in the summer when they had to open the window or die of heatstroke. But this morning, they had no need for the chilly November air and resided in peaceful, brightly lit silence.

Amy prepared Susan's less than gourmet meal of cereal and toast but skipped breakfast herself. It made her day even worse whenever PTSD-induced morning sickness had her puking between first and second period. Guilt knotted in her stomach as the terrifying question nagged at her subconscious. Had it been her fault? She took a deep breath and blocked out the memories. Freshman year had happened a long time ago. Never eating breakfast again was a small price to pay to avoid thinking about that summer.

Susan's brows dipped together in concern. "Amy, you okay?"

"I'm fine." Amy forced a smile. Her little sister missed nothing. She slid toast onto Susan's plate and plastered it with honey.

"Hey, hey! I'm not going to drink my toast."

Amy dropped the bottle with a dull plastic plunk. "Sorry. I'm tired, thanks to you. Why the big hurry today?" She changed the subject with practiced ease.

Susan took an enormous bite of toast and mumbled something through her mouthful.

Amy laughed. "I didn't catch that."

Susan leaned in and stage-whispered in her ear. "Chris and I are going to get detention today."

Amy raised her eyebrows in disbelief. "Say what now?"

Susan licked honey off her fingers. "Chris says his brother is in detention all the time, and he thinks it'll be super fun!"

Amy rolled her eyes. "Sue."

Susan's gaze flitted to the clock on the microwave. "Amy, we should—"

"Detention isn't fun. It's a punishment."

"Sure it's fun! Chris says—"

"Sue, just because Chris's brother thinks detention is cool, that doesn't make it true."

Susan puffed out her cheeks, then blew out the breath. She darted another look at the clock. "Amy, don't you think—"

Amy slapped the table, her frayed patience wearing thin. "Susan, I mean it. Stay out of detention."

"Amy, the time!"

"Why aren't you listening?"

"Because," Susan drew the word into three frustrated syllables, "our bus leaves in less than two minutes!"

Amy sprang to her feet, toppling her stool to the floor with a tumbling wooden clatter. "Why didn't you tell me?"

"I tried. You were too busy lecturing to listen." Susan ran to the closet to fetch her coat.

"Come on! We have to hurry!" Amy snatched her jacket off the living room floor and galloped past the still-snoozing Rex.

"Amy!" Susan panted as they flew down their front steps.

"What now?" she said, already halfway down their driveway.

"You're working tonight, right? What about your uniform?"

"Crap! I'll meet you at the bus." Amy tore past her sister, her boots skidding on the icy asphalt.

"You'll never make it!" Susan shrieked with more drama than an actress in a Broadway musical.

Amy crashed headlong through the door and tore up the stairs to her bedroom. She snatched her unflattering orange uniform off a shelf in her closet and crammed it into her backpack in a bunched-up, wrinkled mess. She careened back downstairs, nearly tripping in her haste.

Rex bellowed like a foghorn from his place on the sofa. "Shut the hell up!"

"Enjoy sleeping it off." Rex drank almost as much as her dear alcoholic mother.

She and Susan only made the bus because a frantic blond boy chased it down. Susan waved an exuberant greeting to Frank, their friendly bus driver, and the two chattered happily as the bus merged with rush hour traffic. Amy stared out the window and fought to keep her eyes open. Once upon a time, she had been as positive and sunny as her little sister. Then she grew up.

Amy and Susan disembarked with a herd of little kids in tow. Her mother had entrusted her with getting Susan to school safely, so Amy had taken responsibility for the others as well. She had assumed the unofficial position of crossing guard, shepherding groups of tiny kindergartners through the busy intersection every morning.

Susan's school, Parsons Elementary, had a lush, sprawling lawn and wide, welcoming front doors. A secure chain-link fence wrapped around its entire perimeter, and two majestic oak trees framed the gate onto school grounds. Scores of happy children played on a large jungle gym, monkey bars, and swing set.

Susan hugged Amy goodbye and raced to join her friends on the swings. The rest of her charges dispersed, except for little Bobby Price, a particularly shy kindergartner.

The sweet-faced five-year-old clung to Amy's hand and gazed up at her with his big blue eyes. "Don't go. Come to class with me."

She gently patted his shiny black hair. "I'm too big for kindergarten. You'll have more fun with your friends."

He dropped his gaze and scuffed the ground with the toe of his sneaker. "I don't have friends."

Amy placed a sympathetic hand on his shoulder. When she was five years old, she had had millions of friends, but one of her closest playmates had been quieter than Bobby. "Hey, Cole!" She waved another little boy over.

The Hispanic first grader glanced up from playing in the sandbox, smiled at her, and scampered to her side. "What's up, Amy?"

"Do you know Bobby? Want to show him what you're building in the sandbox?"

"I'm making train tracks!" Cole flashed a proud smile. He was missing a front tooth. "Wanna come see?"

The boys trotted to the sandbox just as their first bell rang. Amy winced. She was going to be late for class again. She sprinted for the gate against a tide of children heading the other way.

She dashed across the street on a green light, disregarding every last warning she had ever given to children. She acknowledged the horns with her middle finger, rushed into school, and made it to homeroom seconds before the last bell. She dropped into a spot in the back-left row and blocked out the world.

Three

ZACK DONNELLSON AWOKE to an obnoxious ringing. "Stop it. It's too early," he mumbled into his pillow and pulled his blankets over his head to muffle the earsplitting noise.

"It's your phone," a far-off voice said.

"Hello?" he croaked.

"Still ringing, bro. Swipe to answer."

Zack poked his head out of his blankets and blinked blurrily at his nine-year-old brother. Chris was standing in his doorway, clad in jeans and a navy T-shirt depicting Superman. His blond hair was slicked back exactly like Zack wore his. Zack grimaced. Why did his brother insist on swiping his gel?

"Like my hairdo?" Chris's sky blue eyes sparkled with mischief.

"How are you so awake this early?" Zack fumbled for his phone and accepted the call.

Chris rolled his eyes. "I'm not hung over."

"Hey honey!" His girlfriend's loud, chipper voice made his head throb.

He winced and put her on speaker to increase the distance between her shrill tones and his ear. "Chelsea? Why are you calling me so—" He groped for his alarm clock, forgetting to check the time on his phone. He accidentally sent the clock careening across his room. The back popped off, and batteries rolled across his hardwood floor. One collided with a dirty sock. The other vanished beneath his bed. Zack gave it up for lost, far too tired to go searching for it. He instead steadied the precarious stack of sports magazines and comic books that cluttered his table.

"Hello?"

Zack scrunched up his face. Chelsea desperately needed a mute button. He settled for adjusting the volume on his phone. "Chelsea, what time is it?" His voice had a grumpy, sleep-deprived edge to it.

"Are you still in bed?" she asked, annoyance etching her falsely cheerful voice.

"Yeah, why …" Chris switched on the light. "Ouch, stop it!" Zack squeezed his eyes shut against the excruciating glare.

"Stop what?" Chelsea demanded.

"Just a sec. Chris?" He dragged himself and most of his blankets out of bed.

"What?" Chris said from the hall.

"What time is it?"

"Six."

Zack's eyes bulged. "Six a.m.?"

"Yep." Chris giggled, rudely amused at his brother's plight.

Zack snatched his phone. "Chelsea, why the hell are you calling me at six a.m.?"

"Honey." She drew out the word into three whiny syllables. "You promised you'd drive me to school early so I could get Jessie to finish my homework."

Chelsea's best friend, Jessie Davis, had a sunny disposition and loved to help others a little too much. Jessie did more of Chelsea's homework than Chelsea herself.

"Right." Zack sighed wearily and cradled his aching head. "When do I have to pick you up?"

"Ten minutes. You promised." He hated her smug tone.

"Relax, I'll be there."

"Thanks babe!" She abruptly ended the call.

Zack grabbed jeans, a T-shirt, and a hoodie off his floor, the first semiclean clothes he stumbled upon in his disaster of a bedroom. He caught a glimpse of himself in the mirror on his closet door and laughed out loud. Zack was a solid six foot two with just the right amount of freckles and an unruly mop of copper-colored hair. Girls swooned at the sight of him with his chiseled features and bright crystal blue eyes. He usually dressed casually in sport shirts, jeans, sneakers and liked to painstakingly slick back his messy hair with gel. This morning he had dull eyes, wild hair, and wore a sickly grimace, compliments of his killer hangover. THS's student population was finally about to experience an unattractive version of their star quarterback.

He staggered across the hall to the bathroom and put in his contacts in a hungover haze. Zack stared at his silhouette in the glass door to the shower stall. He squinted longingly at the pristine white tiled interior. A hot shower was just what he needed to bring him back to life. Damn his too-hot-to-refuse girlfriend. He at least had to brush his teeth. He squeezed out too much toothpaste and slimed the marble countertop. Zack shoved the toothbrush into his mouth and sprinted from the bathroom. He stumbled down the spiral staircase, still brushing his teeth.

The Donnellsons' sprawling, three-story home had cream-colored paneling and polished oak floors. Family portraits adorned the walls with special emphasis placed on a row of baby pictures in the entrance hall. The photos were interspersed with expensive paintings and other works of art. His parents had a tendency to combine the extravagant with the sentimental.

His mother, Tatiana Donnellson, was sitting at the kitchen table with a cup of coffee and her laptop. She was dressed for work in a starched white blouse, pleated black skirt, and heels. Her wavy blonde hair was pulled neatly into a bun, and her pretty face was artfully made up with painstaking precision. Her ocean blue eyes gazed sympathetically at him as he staggered into the kitchen in extreme disarray. Early morning perkiness ran in his family, but Zack had missed out on those genes.

"Morning, honey." His mother smiled softly.

He frowned. Why did all the women in his life insist on calling him honey? "Hey," he gargled around his toothbrush as he rummaged through the fridge for something to grab and go.

"Your dad and I are leaving for our business trip this afternoon," she reminded him for what had to be the twentieth time. "You'll have to fetch Chris from school, and he's having a friend over."

Zack spat his toothpaste in the kitchen sink, tossed his toothbrush onto the counter, and sprinted from the kitchen. "Got it!" The door slammed on his shout. He'd receive a lecture later for not saying a proper goodbye but after being out of town for a week, she'd forget to be upset. He burned rubber as he sped down his street. His bad-tempered girlfriend was not as forgiving.

He rubbed sleep out of his eyes as he pulled into Chelsea's driveway. She was waiting on her front porch, a bad sign. She stalked toward his car in black heels, figure-hugging jeans, and a preppy cashmere cardigan.

Chelsea Brookes was the hottest girl in school, head cheerleader, and future Beverly Hills trophy wife. She was model fit with a thick mane of cascading honey blonde hair and a flawless, creamy complexion other girls would kill for. She had a sexy rosebud mouth and pouty red lips he could kiss all day. Her lively green eyes twinkled merrily when she lied.

"You're late. I've been waiting for, like, five minutes." He bit his tongue and glared at her. "And you look terrible." She tossed her bag into the back seat and settled herself in the front.

He pressed his lips into a thin line. Would it kill her to show some gratitude? He reversed out of her driveway and cruised toward THS.

Zack pulled into the school's mostly empty parking lot and waved a sleepy hello to Jessie. Chelsea flounced from his car without so much as a thank-you. Zack leaned against the steering wheel and accidentally on purpose blared the horn.

He slouched into school and flopped on the floor in front of his locker. The tile was cold and hard, but he was too dead inside to care. He woke to hushed voices discussing whether or not to wake him up. He opened his eyes, and a group of freshman girls scattered.

"Hey man." His best friend, Ken Richards, was ambling toward him through the flock of giggling girls.

Ken was lean and athletic with naturally tanned skin, an open, smiling face, and perfect bleached blond hair. He wore a cherry red leather jacket over a white muscle shirt and black jeans.

"Late night?" Ken quirked an eyebrow at Zack's disheveled appearance.

"Yeah. I got home around two in the morning, and I had to drive Chelsea here early."

Ken chuckled. "But you still made it to school in all your messy-haired glory. Bet you had no clue what you were in for when you started going out with that chick."

"You have no idea." Zack stood to stretch his legs. "Does Jessie give you a hard time too?"

Ken was dating Chelsea's drop-dead gorgeous best friend, a brilliantly smart cheerleader whom everyone loved. This union had cemented the four teens' standing as the social powerhouse of their grade. Jessie offset Chelsea's bitchiness and the jocks' entitlement with genuine, caring charm. She let sad freshmen cry on her shoulder at the state of their nonexistent romantic lives and gently let down the hopelessly smitten nerds who fell prey to her beauty and brains. There wasn't a soul at THS who hated her. People envied her, sure, but disliked her? Never.

"Nah, she's great!" Ken smiled dreamily.

Zack grimaced. Jessie was always great. Ken had been seeing her for two months. Two long, agonizing months for Zack. He loved Jessie like a sister, but he wanted his best friends back to normal. Ken claimed Zack and Chelsea had a different type of relationship. Zack agreed. Ken and Jessie's relationship was equivalent to high school marriage.

"Seriously though, aren't you sick of her yet?" Ken threw an imaginary football for a long pass down the deserted hall. "Chelsea's a pain."

Zack raised his eyebrows and blurted what was expected of the guy with the sexiest girl in school. "Are you kidding? She's hot as hell!" His words sounded as hollow as their echoing footsteps.

"No one's here," Zack said, dropping into a chair near the back of their empty classroom. "We look like idiots."

"No one ever thinks we look like idiots," Ken said, flopping into the seat next to Zack. "We're cool, and whatever we do becomes cool."

Zack was opening his mouth to protest Ken's flawed logic when the school's resident gang filed into the classroom and claimed seats in the row behind them. Two of these guys were on his and Ken's football team, but both were only alternates, and no one ever saw them play. Zack refused to call them by their self-appointed name, even though Assassin's Honor ironically fit them well. They were known for unpredictability, equally likely to blackmail your enemies as sell you out to the highest bidder. But the lowlifes didn't deserve the cool rep their name implied.

Nathan Johnson, the gang's obnoxious leader, thumped Zack on the back with a lot more force than necessary. "Dude! We had the best night."

Zack glanced over his shoulder. "Yeah?" He arranged his face into a mildly interested expression.

"We met college chicks." Alex leered.

"Sweet," Zack said in a dismissive monotone and turned back to Ken. "What's wrong with them?"

"Who cares?" Ken barely glanced in their direction. He was busy eyeing every girl who passed the open classroom door. Had he studied which seat made the best location to wave at every female in the school? Ken assumed girls needed only to know him to love him. Zack had never been as confident but had always done well on the dating front. Girls threw themselves at him almost as often as Ken hit on them.

"Are you even listening?" Ken punched Zack's shoulder.

"Huh? No." Zack was having what he had termed a stupid day. He was too tired and hung over to function. He stretched in an attempt to clear the cobwebs from his head.

"Let's have a party tonight! We can host it at your place. It's Friday, and your parents are out of town. It'll be perfect! Why didn't we think of it before?"

Zack frowned. He hadn't suggested it because post-party cleanup was a waking nightmare from hell. It was much more fun trashing someone else's house. "Who would we invite?"

Ken's eyebrows formed a high arch. "Everyone, obviously!"

"Can't." His stomach churned at the idea of more alcohol. "Chris is supposed to have a friend over."

"Even better! Your brother will have someone to chill with while we party."

Zack was out of excuses. He nodded reluctantly to shut him up. His friends would never let him forget it if he turned down a legendary party in favor of some aspirin.

"See, your day's looking up," Ken said with a chuckle. Chelsea had arrived and glued her lips to Zack's. He kissed her back with little enthusiasm. His girlfriend loved public displays of affection but cooled off significantly once they were alone. The girl drove him insane.

Chelsea busied herself exchanging flirty notes with Alex. Zack ground his teeth against a burst of righteous anger. Alex, of all people? Seriously? The guy had the worst personality known to man, but Chelsea found his shady rep attractive. Zack clenched and unclenched his fists under his desk, imagining Alex's stupid face when he punched his lights out. He hated how often Chelsea flirted with other guys.

Four

SNOWFLAKES FLUTTERED PAST the window of Amy's pre-calculus classroom. Her teacher's voice droned on in the background, the endless struggle of quadratic equations making her mind wander and her eyes heavy. She had given up note-taking to day-dream, as had half the class. The blond football jock in the row in front of her had fallen asleep on his desk.

Stifling hot air was blowing from a vent in the wall near her feet. She leaned to the side in an effort to stay awake and choked on a cloud of perfume. The girl next to her had doused herself with half her bottle of Daisy by Marc Jacobs. Its cloying floral scent made Amy nauseous.

She scowled at the clock ticking seconds away with agonizing slowness. She longed to ditch the rest of her classes, but she'd have to come traipsing back to fetch Susan at 3:15 anyway. And after that, she had work at 5:00. There was no point in going all the way home to relax for a few painfully short hours.

No one ever liked their minimum wage job, but Amy had a special hatred reserved for working Friday nights. The popular diner where she waitressed attracted everyone under the sun and was overrun on Fridays with a zoo of her peers. Spending seven hours a day with her classmates was bad enough. It added insult to injury when they followed her to work.

The lunch bell saved her from certain suffocation. She swung her backpack over her shoulder and strode confidently from the room. Amy tried to beat the stampede to the cafeteria in an effort to escape outside without trudging through her classmates toxic soup of stupid. This meant she had to rush through the halls with a stack of books balanced precariously in her arms. Her strategy worked better on some days than others. She was bulldozed by a chubby, blond senior halfway across the congested cafeteria. Her books, her calculator, and her iPhone cascaded to the ground. She gave the moron the finger as he swaggered away. Amy released a weary sigh and stooped to gather her things.

The chilly November wind was refreshing, but she was still too nauseated to eat. She lobbed her lunch over a crowd and into the trash, stomped to a corner of the courtyard, and took refuge on a low wall overlooking the football field. She put in her earbuds, cranked Bon Jovi, and stared moodily into space.

The icy wind sliced through her winter coat, and a sprinkling of fluffy white snowflakes blew into her face. The temperature was hovering around minus five degrees Celsius. Amy was originally from Vancouver and had yet to adjust to Toronto's harsh winters. No self-respecting autumn afternoon on the west coast dared get this cold. She wrapped her arms around herself and huddled deeper into her jacket.

A group of athletic guys surged onto the muddy field, disrupting her quiet refuge. She released a disgruntled huff and brushed snowflakes from her hair. The scene took her back to a similar field in a distinctly different time and place. The boys' voices faded as the landscape blurred.

It was a beautiful, warm day in June. Half of Amy's eighth grade class was lounging on the soccer field to soak up the sunshine. She and the girls had gathered to plan their year-end party. As queen bitch, every decision rested squarely on her shoulders. Her best friends picked apart her choices and waited eagerly to destroy her. Everyone wanted a turn in the limelight.

"Look out!"

The shout jolted her back to the present. A tan football was hurtling toward her face. She reflexively put up her hands and caught it before it broke her nose.

"Sorry about that. You okay?" A redheaded jock jogged toward her.

She tossed him the ball and stood to leave. She preferred her face in one piece.

Her afternoon classes dragged at a snail's pace of impending doom. She trudged across the street to collect Susan beneath a thick cloud of dread at the mountain of homework she had to do.

The playground swarmed with little kids welcoming the weekend with noisy gusto. A group of younger children were playing a fast-paced game of tag, little Bobby Price among them. She smiled to herself. *Good job, Cole.*

"Amy! Hi!" A blur of curly blonde hair zoomed toward her at lightning speed and a petite fourth grader joyously tackle-hugged her.

"Hi." She returned the girl's hug. "Where's Sue?" Sarah Matthews was one of Susan's best friends. The crazy bundle of energy never failed to make Amy smile.

"She's gone already," Sarah chirped, brushing sun-kissed curls out of her chubby-cheeked face. "She went to Chris's house."

"She did?"

"Yes!" Sarah laughed at her bewildered expression, her big green eyes dancing with light. "I have to go, but tell Sue I'm coming over soon, okay?"

"You got it. See you later, Sarah."

"Bye!" She flashed a gap-toothed grin and trotted across the playground to her mom's waiting minivan.

Amy gazed heavenward. How had she forgotten about Susan's playdate with Chris? Worse, she had forgotten to get his address. How was she supposed to pick Susan up? She turned toward the road. She'd cross that bridge when she came to it. First, she had to survive Friday night at Pete's. She rubbed her tired eyes.

Amy plodded the six blocks to work through thickly falling snow. She'd arrive an hour early but might score some chocolate cake.

Warm air scented with cinnamon and nutmeg enveloped her the second she stepped into the diner. Pete's was a homey, comforting restaurant. It had wide front windows and a sweeping veranda for outside dining. Its walls were painted a soft baby blue, and checkered linen tablecloths adorned every cozy booth.

The diner was deserted except for Hal Jacobs, a grizzled Vietnam veteran in his midseventies. He was contentedly eating an early steak dinner in a booth by the large front window. Amy met his crinkled green eyes and smiled. Hal had dinner at Pete's five or six nights a week. He had made his way through the menu at least a dozen times but kept coming back for more. He was by far Pete's number one customer and Amy's favorite patron.

Amy removed a slice of apple crisp from the display case and plated it for him. The elderly man's wrinkled, weathered face split in a delighted grin as she delivered his favorite dessert. "You're going to make some young fellow mighty happy someday, missy."

"It's on the house." She smirked. Hal knew she'd sworn off boys. "Will you keep an eye on things while I go change?"

"Young Steve already put me on the job," he said, his eyes sparkling with mischief. "That boy is mighty sweet on you."

Amy made a derisive noise in her throat. Steve Araya was a slacker. A lovable, good-natured slacker, but a slacker nonetheless.

"Thanks, Hal." She retrieved her uniform and ambled to the washroom, discreetly slipping a five-dollar bill into the register as she passed. She decided what was and wasn't on the house by paying for treats herself.

She changed into her uniform and returned to the dining room for a vivid war story from her wise, old friend. She dragged herself to the counter after Hal left, deeply despising her invisible boss. The owner had never set foot in the diner, yet he always knew what went on. She theorized he had cameras watching them while they worked. A nap was out of the question. She yawned for what felt like forever. How was she going to make it through the next five hours?

Amy regularly worked evenings with three other young employees. She, Steve Araya, Andrew Reyes, and Katie Summers were a tight-knit group of co-worker friends. Andrew and Steve were roommates, and she and Katie were often mistaken for sisters.

Steve Araya was stocky but short with cinnamon hair, dark skin, and a bit of a mustache. His moss green eyes crinkled cutely at the corners, giving him a boyish, joyful look.

Andrew Reyes was a sweet, shy, Latino kid with soft onyx hair and kind brown eyes. He worked in the kitchen to avoid talking to the public and had an enormous crush on Katie.

Most girls hated Katie Summers for her stunning good looks. She was a tall, slender bottle blonde beauty with perfect, straight white teeth and fair, flawless skin. She had a fabulous sense of style and a hilarious, confident personality. Girls loathed her on sight, but Amy adored her. Katie radiated positivity whenever she worked.

Andrew and Steve were both nineteen. They had dropped out of high school in their junior year without any plans or goals. Katie, in contrast, was on the fast track to success. She was a freshman at the University of Toronto and had a social calendar the size of a phone book.

"Hey Amy!" Steve sauntered out of the kitchen with his hands deep in the pockets of his too-baggy jeans. She ignored him. It would take too much energy to respond, and if she did, he would never shut up. Steve waved a hand in front of her face. "Hello? Anybody home?"

She slumped forward onto the counter and rested her head on her arms. "No. I'm curled up at home with popcorn and Netflix."

"Wow." He mimicked her emotionless tone. "That's interesting, because somehow I can hear you all the way from work."

"Ha-ha."

"All set for another five hours of fun?"

Amy sat up and brushed hair out of her face. "I need coffee."

She headed into the spotless kitchen with Steve trailing in her wake. Andrew stood scrubbing pots at the sink.

"Must. Have. Coffee," she announced by way of a greeting as she zombie-walked to the counter.

Andrew smiled. "Just made a fresh pot. Help yourself."

The coffee addict in her danced a jig. "Oh my God, I love you!" She poured a cup with reverence and held it out to Steve. Andrew made the world's best French press. They sat across from each other at the stainless steel island. "Now we're going to sit here and watch you work." She and Steve clinked mugs.

Andrew rolled his eyes. "By all means, make yourselves comfortable. There's cake in the fridge."

"Chocolate?" She clutched the island and held her breath.

"Of course."

She raced to the fridge like a five-year-old and held the round chocolate mousse cake aloft like a prized spoil of war. "Andrew, will you marry me?" Anyone who knew her knew how much she adored chocolate cake.

"Sorry. I'm saving myself for Katie."

Amy raised a cake knife high into the air. "I'll challenge her to a duel." She cut generous slices.

"How was school?" Steve passed her plates and accepted a mountainous slice of cake.

"It sucked." She shrugged. She had cake, and cake made everything better.

Pots clanged together as Andrew loaded the dishwasher. "You ask her that every day, and every day you get the same answer. Why keep asking?"

Steve beamed. "Because one day she'll drop out like us and work here full-time."

"Aha, the plot thickens. You *want* me to suffer." She took a bite of moist chocolatey heaven.

Steve regarded her with a lopsided grin. "No, I just want to see more of you. Come work with us full-time."

Amy screamed with a mouthful of cake and nearly choked on it. She swallowed through a coughing fit. "I love you guys, but you would drive me insane."

"You act as though you're sick of me. But you're not, right?" Steve faked a wounded, doe-eyed expression. The effect was ruined by the forkful of cake halfway to his mouth.

Katie burst through the door with donuts for everyone, saving Amy from the impossible task of trying not to crush Steve's heart. Customers flooded the diner with the hectic certainty of impending disaster. The afterschool rush had begun.

Amy feebly waved goodbye to their last group of customers and sagged against the counter with an exhalation of relief. It was already after ten. The last five hours had battered her, body and soul.

"Have fun hanging out with Katie," she stage-whispered to Andrew as she stuffed her uniform into her backpack. It was Andrew and Katie's turn to close. Amy felt bad for not staying to help but not bad enough to follow through with her guilt.

Andrew's brown eyes widened in shock. "Katie's closing with me? What will I say? What will I do?"

She giggled. "How about asking her to turn out the lights and lock the back door? That's usually what you do when you close."

"It's also what you do before other things." Steve guffawed.

"Shut up, you." Amy jabbed him in the ribs. "Don't worry, Andrew. Katie thinks you're adorable."

"And dorky." Steve snickered. Amy gripped his arm and towed him toward the door.

"No! Amy, wait!" Andrew's eyes were wide with panic. "Don't leave me!"

Katie sashayed from the kitchen and gawked at the trio. "What'd I miss?"

Steve grinned. "Welcome to the soap opera starring Amy Christiana Evans!" Amy dragged him out the door. "Andrew needs you!" Steve faded out his voice as if she had dragged him into oblivion.

"You shouldn't tease him," Amy said. "And how the heck do you know my middle name?"

Steve brushed his hair out of his eyes and grinned, unashamed. "You started it. And you mentioned your middle name a while back." Amy rolled her eyes. Steve remembered the details of her life better than she did herself. They walked through the dimly lit parking lot together, their hilarity fading as post-Friday night exhaustion set in.

"Need a ride?" Steve unlocked his ancient, flame red pickup truck. Amy had always admired its flashy coloring.

She shook her head regrettably. "I have to pick up my sister." Steve's apartment was in the opposite direction. She couldn't ask him to drive that far out of his way.

"Okay, another time." He clambered into his truck. "Have a good one, Amy."

"See you Sunday."

She adjusted her scarf and trudged to the bus stop through the thickly falling snow. She had searched Chris Donnellson on the internet during her shift and dug up his address and phone number. She needed to have a chat with him about his social media privacy settings.

Amy nodded off during the bus ride and woke in another world. The high-class neighborhood she found herself in boasted block after block of enormous, fancy houses. They were the pretentious, in-your-face kind with perfectly manicured lawns and swimming pools in their backyards. She disembarked onto a pretty, poplar-lined street where full-fledged mansions rose up toward the night sky. Each breathtaking structure had extensive, sprawling grounds and a garage half the size of her house.

She checked Chris's address and scanned the row of beautiful estates. The Donnellson residence was the fanciest home on the block. The Victorian-style mansion was three sprawling stories of wide, curved windows and ornate, little balconies. Its wraparound front porch was lit up like a Christmas tree, and an expensive array of cars lined its circular, sweeping driveway. Obnoxiously loud music was blaring from an open window on the second floor.

She stared, mothlike, at all the lights in the windows and reluctantly approached the front porch. Even the doorbell's rich tones screamed money. She scowled. Wealthy people were judgmental and snooty and had looked down on her all her life.

Moments passed. No one let her in. She pressed the doorbell again. Still nothing. The porch vibrated with the thrum of the bass. She cursed and turned away. She'd have to call the house.

The door swung open behind her. "Hello?" Amy rotated on the spot and cringed. The jock who had nearly taken her out with his football earlier today stood framed in the doorway. He was THS's star quarterback. "You just can't get enough of me, huh?"

She flushed a deep shade of crimson. He thought she wanted to attend his party like some sort of stalker-groupie. "I'm here to pick up my sister." She set her jaw and scowled, hoping to dispel all thoughts of stalker-groupieness.

He arched an eyebrow with a condescending smirk. "I doubt your sister is here."

She raised her chin and glared at him. "Her name is Susan Evans. She's nine years old, and it's past her bedtime."

"Why didn't you come get her sooner, then?"

She skewered him with a scathing gaze. "I was at work, a concept that's obviously foreign to you."

"Must pay pretty bad." He looked down his nose at her wrinkled blue jeans and faded gray T-shirt.

"Is my sister here or not?" She expected rude comments from girls, but guys rarely criticized her wardrobe. They liked to focus on suggestive comments that made her want to punch them out.

The jock grinned as if thrilled he was annoying her. "What was her name again?"

"Susan," she hissed.

His crystal blue eyes sparkled with mirth. "She's upstairs. I'll go find her." He vanished into the party.

Amy stepped into the entrance hall to escape the bitter cold. The house was incredible. Its open-concept design gave her a view of the entire first floor. High schoolers lounged on burgundy velvet couches in a spacious living room. Their feet were propped on a hand-carved cedar coffee table that was laden with beer and a tall stack of pizzas. A set of French doors opened into the kitchen where refreshments and snacks were piled high on the marble countertops, and coolers of booze lay strewn about the polished oak floor.

Crowds of teens milled about, dancing, drinking, and shouting over the music. Everyone wore designer labels and five-hundred-dollar shoes. She made a disgusted face. Half her high school had turned out for this party. The loaded half. Amy folded her arms across her chest, daring any rich, drunk loser to hit on her.

"Amy!" Chris shot from the crowd and rushed in for a hug.

"Hey Chris!" She mustered a smile. His reply was drowned by the music.

Football Jock returned with Susan in tow and motioned them outside. Amy stared. How did he know Chris?

"We have to …" The music obliterated the rest of Susan's sentence. She and Chris disappeared into the party.

"So, you're Amy." Football Jock lounged against the door-frame, beer in hand.

She curled her lip. He thought he looked so cool. "You don't listen especially well, do you? Chris just screamed my name." Disgust tangled in her stomach with a knot of unease. Where were his parents? How long had Susan been exposed to her stupid, drunk classmates?

Football Jock took a long swig of Budweiser. "Chris never shuts up about you and Sue. According to him, you're supposed to be awesome."

"I am." She rested a hand on her hip.

"I've seen you around school." He offered her his Budweiser.

She waved the drink away. She hadn't had a sip of alcohol since the summer before freshman year. Pain spiked in her chest at the smell of his beer. She swallowed the familiar blades of grief and forced a lighthearted smirk. "Yep. I've seen you too. You like to throw things at me."

"You nearly took me out with your lunch."

"Guess we're even."

Chris and Susan raced past, and Amy followed them out. Football Jock stepped out after them and shut the door with a snap.

"Phew!" Susan held her ears. "Zack, your music is too loud."

Football Jock snorted. "At least it's good music."

Susan sucked in a dramatic gasp. "What do you have against Ariana Grande?"

He made a derisive noise. "She sucks."

"She does not!"

"Does too."

Amy laughed. They were acting like they were five.

Football Jock smirked at her. "I didn't catch your name in there. Annie, was it?"

Amy narrowed her eyes. She knew he knew her name.

"She's Amy," Chris corrected him helpfully. "Amy, this is my brother, Zack."

Amy scowled. "We're leaving."

Susan's eyes widened at her abrupt tone. "Already?" Amy gave her a look that barred all protest. "Fine. Bye Chris. Bye Zack."

"Bye!" they said as Amy turned on her heel and marched down their steps. The front door opened and blasted music into the night.

Susan scrambled to catch up. "Why'd we have to leave so fast? I was having fun." Amy winced. Awesome, her nine-year-old sister was a party animal.

"Because it's almost eleven, silly." She ruffled Susan's hair. "We have to be up early tomorrow."

"No we don't." Susan's eyes gleamed with triumph. "Tomorrow is Saturday."

"That's right!" Amy pumped a fist, her heart leaping with joy. She had the day off and planned to spend all of it in bed.

The girls arrived home to a messy kitchen and a living room filled with cigarette smoke, the remnants of their mother's day. Amy soaked some pans, cracked the window, and headed off to bed. She'd deal with the mess in the morning. Procrastination was her middle name.

She did her best to keep their house tidy, but it seemed hellbent on staying in perpetual disarray. The roof had loose shingles, the front porch had rot, and the lock on the front door had broken a week ago. She wasn't even confident in its foundation. Their house perched precariously halfway up a hill and leaned ever so slightly toward the home on their left.

Amy giggled into her pillow at the irony of it toppling to the ground someday. It was a metaphorical reflection of the state of her life. She sobered quickly, her laughter fading into lonely despair. What would Zack say if he saw her house? Rich people imagined themselves as better than the rest of the world simply because they had been blessed with money. Her sorrow sizzled over hot coals of anger. Chris was going to morph into an entitled jerk. He couldn't help it with a family like his. Susan was best friends with a soon-to-be rich snob who was going to break her heart. Hot tears stung Amy's eyes. How was she supposed to stop the world from breaking her sister the way it had broken her?

Five

ZACK SLUMPED INTO a large leather armchair as his friends' partying rose in drunken volume. His guests, half of whom he hadn't even invited, were trashing his house.

"Hey, Zack." Lila Chung staggered to his chair and toppled gracelessly into his arms. "Great party."

Lila had an unhealthy obsession with the football team. She was a social-climbing sophomore with a mission to overthrow Chelsea as queen bee. She was petite and curvy with silky chestnut hair and deceptively innocent chocolate brown eyes. Her slinky, low-cut dress accentuated her curves and left little to the imagination.

"Hey, Lila. Where's your boyfriend?" Zack shifted her to one side to avoid a full frontal of her ample cleavage.

She pressed her front against his chest and wrapped her arms around his neck. "Out of town with Dominic's slut. Where's your prissy girlfriend?"

Zack frowned. Dominic's so-called slut was a sweet little homeschooler who adored her boyfriend and would never think of cheating. Ken had struck out with her enough times to prove her loyalty. Dominic Carter had not been known for the same trait, himself, until meeting his girl. He had earned his stripes by hooking up with a series of seniors in his sophomore year. He was captain of the football team and king of their school. Girls flocked to him like bees to honey, making Lila's jealousy routinely boring.

"I'm not sure where Chelsea is. I haven't seen her in a while."

"Great," Lila purred and wrapped her legs around his waist. Her dress slid up to reveal a creamy thigh and a lacy black thong.

A series of jarring smashes punctured the air. Zack stood, freed himself from Lila, and followed the smashing into the kitchen. Nathan, Ash, and Dominic were chucking empty bottles at the wall. Zack gaped. Why was Dominic Carter hanging with Assassin's Honor? He hated Alex's crew even more than Zack did.

Zack plucked a bottle from Ash's hands. "Knock it off."

"Zack, come back." Lila swayed unsteadily in the kitchen doorway.

Ash threw a drunken punch, which Zack easily blocked. Ash ducked under Zack's arm and scooted to the other side of the room. Nathan threw a bottle at the microwave, cracking its small, square window.

Dominic's amber eyes sparked in alarm. "Guys, that's enough. Let's—" He broke off as a can of tomato soup whizzed past his head. Ash stood next to the pantry with a new supply of ammo. Zack gaped in horrified disbelief. Alex's friends were drunken lunatics.

"Come on, let's have some fun!" Lila launched herself into Zack's arms, impeding his efforts to get at Ash and put a stop to the soup tossing.

"What the?" Peter entered the kitchen and narrowly ducked a flying beer bottle, this one still full. The bottle sailed out the kitchen door and collided with a vase on the cedar coffee table. White peonies flopped limply to the floor amid a flood of broken glass and lager.

Zack cringed. He needed to make them quit trashing the place, and fast! If not, he'd be paying for damages until graduation … from college. First, he had to lose Lila. "Have you met Peter?" He pried the vivacious brunette loose and propelled her toward the befuddled gangster. "He's on the football team too. Peter, Lila. Lila, Peter. Have fun."

Lila pouted. "I've never seen you play."

"He's our secret weapon." Zack smirked, neatly catching a can of vegetable broth Ash had chucked at him with surprisingly good aim.

"Zack, I think you should go upstairs," Peter muttered out of the corner of his mouth as he feebly held Lila at bay.

Zack raked his gaze over his partly destroyed kitchen. "I think you and your stupid friends should leave."

"What's happening upstairs?" Dominic deftly blocked a pair of beer bottles with one muscular arm. He had the classic football player build, tall with broad shoulders and a rock-hard chest. He was half-African Canadian with jet-black hair and interesting amber eyes.

Lila was intrigued by Peter's lack of interest. She stood on tiptoe to kiss his neck as a can zoomed straight for the back of her head. Peter barely managed to snag it out of the air before it cracked her skull. "Dude, stop it. You're going to break something, or someone." He shuffled toward Ash, Lila hanging off his arm like an oversized leech. Her six-inch heels scraped through a pile of broken glass.

Ash's eyes gleamed. "That's the idea!" He scooped up a sixteen-ounce can of black beans and hurled it at the kitchen window. Dominic made a wild grab for it, slipped on a pile of glass, and landed on his rear. Zack winced. Glass shards to the butt. The can smashed through the window and landed in his mother's prized rosebush.

"Dude! Oh my God! My dad's not paying for that." Peter grabbed Ash's shirt and hauled the smaller kid into the center of the room. He held him there, far away from anything that could morph into flying projectiles of death. "You're going home before you get yourself arrested." Peter dragged him off.

"Zack!" Jessie rushed past the boys, her auburn hair in a flustered tangle. "Someone puked—What on Earth happened in here!" She skidded to a screeching high-heeled halt, no easy feat, and surveyed the demolished kitchen with horrorstruck dismay.

"Ash." Zack winced. "Who puked?"

"Where's your pretty-boy boyfriend?" Nathan grabbed a handful of Jessie's azure party dress.

She tugged her dress from his grasp with disgust in her emerald green eyes. "He's passed out upstairs."

Zack's quick temper flared. He slammed Nathan against the fridge, causing a tall stack of Tupperware to topple to the floor. They ricocheted off Dominic's head like a gentle plastic rain. "Do you want to go to prison earlier than expected? Because that's what will happen if you touch her again." Zack had been close with Jessie since the third grade, and the kindhearted beauty was like a sister to him.

Jessie smoothed her dress. "Raquel puked in the hall upstairs, and Chris is trying to clean the mess."

"Gross. I'm on it." Zack propelled Nathan from the kitchen.

"I'll take care of the glass," Dominic called. "I just need a second to …" He retched.

"And another one bites the dust," Jessie said and sighed, trailing Nathan and Zack through the overcrowded living room.

"I'm not leaving! The party ain't over until I say it's over." Nathan slammed a meaty fist into Zack's jaw.

Jessie gasped theatrically. "Oh my God! Why is Lila taking her dress off on the front lawn?" The boys turned as one to look. Jessie shoved Nathan out the door. "Psych."

"Nice one!" They high-fived.

"It's like we're performing an exorcism of Assassin's Honor." She snickered.

"Three down, one to go. But first, the puke upstairs."

She cringed. "Guess that leaves me with the vomit in the kitchen."

"I have faith in you." He gave her a double thumbs-up.

She saluted him and strutted across the living room, her slender hips swaying sexily as she went. Jessie in stilettos turned more than a few heads.

Zack sprinted upstairs and found Chris in the hall with Raquel Nickels, a pretty blonde cheerleader who hung around with Chelsea's friend group. She was leaning against the wood-paneled wall with a hand pressed to her mouth. Chris had taken care of most of the mess but looked about to hurl himself.

Zack sighed. "Thanks, bro. I'll take it from here. You should go to bed. It's almost one a.m."

Chris lifted his eyebrows in an incredulous scowl. "You think I'll be able to sleep with all this noise?"

"Hum along with 'Party Rock Anthem,'" Zack said. He took the mop from his brother and screwed up his face at the puke.

"S-sorry," Raquel stammered, her too-pale cheeks flushing crimson. "I was trying to find the bathroom." She gazed at them with tears shining in the corners of her sad cornflower blue eyes.

"It's okay." Chris gave her a sympathetic smile. Zack shook his head. His brother had way more patience than he did.

"Go sit outside for a while. The fresh air will help you feel better." He wouldn't have to clean it up if she puked on the lawn. She nodded mutely, her stick-thin frame trembling beneath his gaze. Chris guided her downstairs. "Make sure no one takes her home.

And go out the back." He had to keep them both away from Nathan and his lunatic buddies.

Zack mopped up the rest of the mess and carried the cleaning supplies to the broom closet. A faint glow caught his eye as he neared the end of the dim hall. Light was shining from under the door to his parents' bedroom. He cursed under his breath. He was as good as dead if someone made a mess in there. Making them move was a necessary chore. He rapped on the polished wood, expecting squeals of alarm and the speedy exodus of a naked girl or two. Instead, his knock was met with silence. He waited a beat, knocked again, and gave up on being polite.

He swung open the door and stared, disbelieving, at the scene before his eyes. Chelsea and Alex lay naked in his parents' bed. They had kicked the mink comforter into a heap on the floor and lay tangled together between the silky sheets. Alex smirked at Zack and kissed Chelsea's neck.

Blood roared in his ears. He strode into the room and threw a punch, doing his very best to break Alex's nose. "Get your filthy hands off her!" How dare this lowlife steal his girl in his own house!

Chelsea watched their exchange like it was a riveting movie. Her lips curled into a grin, and her eyes sparkled with self-satisfied excitement. She loved being the center of attention.

"Chill out, Zack. We're only having a bit of fun. Right, babe?" Alex stroked a hand down Chelsea's bare back.

Bile rose in Zack's throat. His eyes blazed with hate. "I don't believe this!" Chelsea's grin evaporated. "You filthy—"

"Watch what you say about her." Alex swung his legs out of bed and threw on his pants.

Chelsea pouted. "You're leaving?"

A dull blade twisted in Zack's gut. "You're history." He turned to go. "You're the biggest mistake I ever made."

"Alex, do something!" Chelsea struggled into her dress. Her hair bunched around her shoulders in frizzy disarray. "My life will be over if I lose him."

Alex's upper lip curled in disdain. "Such a sweet sentiment for a guy you only use for popularity."

She impatiently shoved her hair out of her face. "My social life will be over. It's not like I'll have a broken heart. He's spoiled and douchey, but he's my ticket to the fast lane."

Zack's jaw tightened. Was that all he had meant to her? He stumbled toward the door with the room spinning around him.

"Alex! Please!"

Alex grabbed Zack's shirt and hauled him into the bathroom. He was stone-cold sober, and Zack was suddenly wasted. Alex shoved him into the wide porcelain tub. "Chelsea, get in here and help."

She straddled Zack and pinned his wrists to the sides of the tub. He struggled against her but was unable to shake her off. Disbelief and panic rioted within him. She should not be this strong. He should not be this weak. He had just finished dragging a six-foot-two gangster through his living room. Why couldn't he shake a 110-pound cheerleader?

Alex was mixing powder into a glass on top of the vanity.

"What's that?" Chelsea pointed a slender finger at the drink in his hand.

"This will ensure your boyfriend forgets what he saw."

"Are you going to kill him?" She leaned forward, fascinated by the idea.

"If I should be so lucky." Alex held the glass to Zack's lips. "Drink up, Zack."

The amber liquid reeked of rubbing alcohol and burned his nostrils. He yanked one of his hands free and knocked the glass aside. Vodka splashed across his chest. Chelsea scrambled off of him with a high-pitched squeal.

"Yuck! That'll stain!" She grabbed a cloth off the counter and dabbed frantically at her chest.

"Hold him still." Alex's words rang with authority.

Zack half scrambled, half fell out of the tub. His pulse pounded painfully in his ears, scattering his senses and making him dizzy with anxiety. He crawled toward the door, his instincts screaming for him to run.

Alex mixed a new concoction, pinned him to the floor, and forcibly poured it down his throat. Zack gagged and fought to spit it out. He wound up swallowing most of it.

Alex's stormy blue eyes glinted with glee. "One more glass ought to do it." He shook three brightly colored pills into his hand and dropped them into a second amber drink.

A distant shout made all of them freeze. "Everyone out! A neighbor called the cops!" Zack recognized Jessie's strong, clear soprano. He guessed she was lying to end his nightmarish party.

"We have to get out of here!" Chelsea scrambled toward the door. Alex cursed under his breath, booted Zack in the stomach, and followed her.

"What if he tells them what happened?" Chelsea's voice echoed in his head.

"Trust me, he won't." The bedroom door slammed, and Zack was left alone on the cold marble floor.

He heaved himself onto his elbows and inched toward the door. The floor stretched out in front of him, an impossibly long distance. The room dipped and swayed, and a wave of nausea made him gag. His palm grazed something sharp. More glass? Why was his house full of broken glass? He closed his eyes and saw cans of tomato soup the size of footballs. He tried to think calming thoughts. Alex and his friends were gone. Chelsea was gone. Everyone was gone. Jessie? His head came to rest on the bath mat.

Zack floated in and out of consciousness on a misty sea of tranquility. The noise from downstairs ebbed and faded into nothing. He heaved a contented sigh. He liked his ocean of quiet.

Someone was calling his name. He tried to answer, but the words wouldn't come.

The bathroom door was flung open, and light flooded the room. A blurry figure rushed to his side. He strained to see around the splotches of dark that were blotting his vision.

"Zack, what happened?" Chris's voice was shrill with panic. The dark splotches expanded, and Zack sank into blackness.

Six

A MONOTONOUS RINGING dragged Amy from sleep. She checked her watch, pulled her blankets over her head, and prayed for it to stop. It did for half a minute before starting up again. She stumbled out of bed and staggered downstairs to answer the house phone. Why was someone calling at two o'clock in the morning? She gritted her teeth against a burst of sleep-deprived rage.

"Hello?" The caller was about to receive a serious talking to.

"Amy!" Chris said her name in a shrill, panicked tone. "Is that you?"

"Yeah. Do you realize what time it is?" She propped her elbows on the kitchen counter and yawned into her hand.

"I'm sorry! I need help!"

"I'm listening." Amy sighed.

"Zack is passed out in my parents' bathroom. I guess he had too much to drink, but I've never seen him this wasted before."

"Wake your parents." She yawned again. "They'll know what to do."

"They're both away!" His voice shot up another two octaves. "It's only me and Zack here until next Friday."

Amy held the phone a few inches from her ear. "Chris, take a breath. Try to calm down."

Chris inhaled sharply. His words tumbled out, rapid and scared. "I don't want to call an ambulance if he doesn't need one. He'll get in so much trouble!"

Amy blew out a breath. "How about I come over and check on him? Sue and I can stay with you until he's better." She didn't care one bit if spoiled Zack Donnellson got arrested. But she did like Chris, and he needed someone.

"You will? Thank you!" His voice cracked with unshed tears.

"We'll be there as soon as we can." She sent him a mental hug.

Amy climbed the stairs and woke Susan with a stream of curses running through her head. How could Zack have let this happen? He was forcing his nine-year-old brother to take care of him when it ought to be the other way around. She bundled a confused and sleepy Susan in her jacket with gentle apologies and reassurances that everything was fine. She hated to ruin her little sister's sleep on account of Zack but with her mother working the night shift, the only option was to bring her along.

The buses had stopped running, so the girls wound up taking an appallingly expensive taxi to Chris's neighborhood. They climbed from the cab and gaped at the wreckage of the Donnellson's lawn.

"Check out their kitchen window," Amy said.

"Look!" Susan raced up the Donnellsons' drive and across to a battered rosebush. She scooped something off the ground and trotted back to Amy with a can of black beans in her hand. "Guess we know what smashed the window."

"Come on, let's go inside and check on Chris."

Chris threw open the door. "I'm so glad you're here!"

"It's okay." Amy patted his shoulder and strode into the entrance hall. Bottles and cans lay strewed about on every available surface; some empty, some on their sides with their contents spilled around them in sticky puddles. A shattered vase lay next to the cedar coffee table, its gorgeous flowers scattered across an expensive-looking rug. The kitchen looked like a war zone. Broken glass, dented walls, a cracked microwave, and for some strange reason, an army of soup cans littered across the floor. It was as if a cyclone had exploded outward from the pantry.

Amy cautiously stepped forward, and something crunched beneath her shoe. A baby picture in an ornate frame was lying on the polished floor. She stooped to pick it up and came face-to-face with a laughing baby Zack. Amy recoiled and went to toss the portrait aside. Letters scratched into the picture's frame caught her eye. *A + J.*

"Oh no, Zack fell off the wall." Susan took the picture. "Aww, he's cute!" She turned to Chris. "What happened after we left? Is Zack okay?"

"Let's go find out." Amy led the way up the Donnellsons' spiral staircase. The second floor looked less like a battlefield. The hall was clean apart from a single painting lying face-down on the carpet. Amy bent to prop it up, and the canvas ripped in half. "I didn't do that!" Dollar signs with scary amounts of zeroes flashed in her peripheral vision.

"Don't worry. It was like that when I found it. My parents' room is through here." Chris showed them into a spacious master bedroom with thick maroon carpeting and silky bedding the color of jade. Amy gazed around in awe. Zack lived in a palace.

She headed into the attached washroom and grimaced in disgust. Zack lay on his back in a pile of broken glass with sweat and alcohol soaking his shirt. She smirked. It looked like he was sweating vodka. She knelt at his side. His eyes fluttered open but lacked all focus. His lips moved soundlessly as he strained to speak around the barricades in his mind. Panic filled his gaze. Amy placed a comforting hand over his. "It'll be okay. Lie still." His palm had a jagged line of crimson across his skin. He had cut himself on the glass. She checked his breathing and snatched her phone. She dialed 911 with a surreal feeling of detached concern.

Zack's breaths were quick and shallow, and his pupils had shrunk to the size of needlepoints. This was worse than a case of alcohol poisoning. Zack had dabbled in harder narcotics.

The operator answered as Zack began to choke.

"What's happening to him?" Chris cried, fear flitting across his face.

"We need an ambulance!" Amy struggled to roll Zack onto his side. Her phone slipped and clattered to the floor. It landed with a splash in a puddle of vomit. "Chris, talk to them for me."

He snatched up her phone and rattled off his address. Amy shot him a grateful look. The kid was impervious to puke. If only she had his skills. She clamped her mouth shut, battled her gag reflex, and scooped a glob of vomit from Zack's mouth. Who knew getting up close and personal with a football player would be this disgusting? She heaved Zack into a sitting position by propping him against the bathtub. A stream of puke dribbled from his mouth. She wrinkled her nose and wiped his face with toilet paper. She was never going to look at THS's star quarterback the same. He was the most repulsive sight she had ever seen.

"The ambulance is on its way." Chris wiped Amy's phone with a washcloth before handing it back to her.

Amy took it between two clean fingers, placed it on the vanity, and rinsed her hands in the sink. "Okay. Now we need to get him outside." She took his shoulders, the kids each grabbed an ankle, and they dragged him unceremoniously through his demolished palace.

An ambulance wailed up the street, and EMTs zoomed Zack onto a stretcher. "Where are your parents?" a brown-haired medic demanded, narrowing her ice-blue eyes at Amy.

She bristled. They thought this was her fault? "His parents are out of town." She jerked a thumb toward Zack. "My sister and I are their friends." She drew a line in the air to exclude herself and Susan from the wreckage behind them and made air quotes around the word *friends*.

The EMT made a derisive noise in her throat. "Hope the party was worth it. You kids better come with us."

The trio piled into the ambulance. Amy clenched her jaw against a burst of indignant rage. Zack had better take full responsibility for any trouble with the law.

Chris called his mother on the way to the hospital to get parental permission for them to treat his brother. The trio took seats in a crowded waiting room as Zack was rushed to an OR to have his stomach pumped. Amy shook her head. Friday night in an ER. Zack had picked the worst possible time to OD. She sat between the two kids with an arm tight around each of them. Susan dozed against her shoulder, while Chris tried not to cry.

Amy squeezed his shoulder. "He'll be fine. You did everything right."

"If I had called nine-one-one right away …" He blinked back tears.

Amy pulled him into a hug and gently rubbed his back. "You did your best. Zack's going to be super proud of you when he wakes up."

Susan rubbed her eyes. "Are your parents coming home?"

Chris hung his head. "They can't catch a flight until the morning. They only just landed in Beijing."

In the end, with his parents out of town and his brother in a coma, Amy brought Chris back to her house for an impromptu sleepover. He dozed for a few hours and woke her at dawn begging to visit Zack. The exhausted trio trooped back to the hospital a mere three hours after leaving.

A nurse in her early twenties was manning the front desk, typing feverishly at her computer with a frantic gleam in her green eyes. She was on the heavier side with frizzy brown hair and a spray of pimples across her chin.

"We're here to see Zack Donnellson." Amy yawned. "This is his little brother, Chris."

"Of course." The nurse had a kind, pretty smile. "Head down that hall to the third door on your right. Room 112."

"Thanks."

Amy led the kids down the hallway. Zack's door was ajar. Chris ambled in without knocking and beckoned for the girls to do the same.

Zack was sitting up in bed, talking on the phone. "No. Mom, I'm fine. I know. I made a stupid decision." He nodded toward a cluster of chairs facing his bed.

Amy sat, hiding a smirk. She hoped his mother gave him the lecture of his life.

"It will never happen again," Zack said. "I promise. Don't let it ruin your trip. Yes, really. Stay in Beijing. I'll ground myself until you're back and after that you'll ground me for even longer. Love you too." He hung up and face-palmed.

Chris grinned. "You are so busted."

"Grounded until I'm thirty." Zack cringed. He shot Amy a questioning glance. "No offense, but why the hell are you here?"

"I saved your grounded ass. Do you not remember puking on me?"

"Now you mention it, sorry about that."

She narrowed her eyes. "You owe me money for the taxi."

"Right." He pulled a thick wad of twenties from his wallet.

"We don't live on Mars." She handed half his money back.

"It's the least I can do." He pushed it into her hand.

She accepted the bills with the ghost of a smile. "Suit yourself, but you can't buy me off. Those pictures I took of you dribbling vomit are already on Instagram."

"What!"

She giggled. "Calm down, football freak. I'm kidding."

Seven

CHARLES WOKE AT dawn on Monday to a raging storm outside his window. Sheets of rain obscured the faint morning light. Wind shrieked mournfully through the sodden trees. The branches of an oak scraped against his windowpane like fingernails on a chalkboard. He tossed and turned for a while and wrote off sleep as a lost cause.

He stepped from his bedroom and breathed deep. The salty tang of frying bacon gently mingled with hints of something sweet and chocolatey. He followed the tantalizing aroma to the kitchen. His mom stood at the counter mixing a bowl of pancake batter. Zoe Banks was short and plump with a young, welcoming face and a beautiful smile. She was casually clad in sweats and a T-shirt with her dark brown hair pulled back in a messy bun. A pan of bacon sizzled on the stove, and a pitcher of fresh-squeezed orange juice sat ready on the kitchen island.

"Hey, hon. You're up early." She wiped her hands on her flour-dusted apron to give him a quick morning hug. Her kind caramel eyes brimmed with loving concern.

He quirked an eyebrow. "And you're ambitious. Why are you making pancakes on a Monday morning?" He took a seat at the kitchen island and snuck a peek at her years-out-of-date laptop. A photo of him at seven was set as her screen saver. He pressed a key to make his beaming face disappear, and a nearly finished news story appeared in its place.

"I have writer's block," she said, pouring a dollop of pancake batter into a second frying pan. "I decided to spend my thinking time making something nice to begin your week." She smiled, smoothing the worry lines around her mouth. She knew how much he dreaded Mondays.

"Thanks, Mom." Grateful affection hummed beneath his words. He yawned his way through two plates of pancakes and finished up her article for the *Times*.

"My seventy-two hours in labor has paid off." She beamed, reading the ending over his shoulder. "I knew one day you'd come in handy." She fact-checked his work as she bustled around in preparation for her busy day. The pancakes had put her behind schedule. "Please be safe." She pecked him on the cheek and flew out the door.

Charles dressed casually in jeans and an admiral blue sweater and completed his outfit with black Nikes and a matching black belt. He shaved, brushed his teeth, packed a lunch, and even had time to do the dishes before facing the tumultuous outdoors.

Though the worst of the storm had subsided, the dreary sleet-gray sky still had a somber border of violent storm clouds. Several small branches littered his lawn, and lakelike puddles had formed in the street. Cars speeding down the narrow road sent freezing, opaque droplets spinning in all directions. Charles was repeatedly splashed with cold, dirty water as he plodded to the bus stop. He squelched up to the thankfully dry bench, huddled under the shelter, and began a game of Tetris on his phone.

He squeezed into a seat on the bus and avoided eye contact with everyone as he wiped mud off his jeans. He would have been dryer traipsing to school through a car wash.

"Nice look, Banks," a senior on the hockey team sneered.

Charles sank down in his seat, took shelter behind his math book, and engrossed himself in a practice problem.

He spent his first couple classes in peaceful but lonely solitude. Conversation ebbed and flowed around him in streams of happy chatter. He watched his peers with detached pain, an island untouched by the sea of humanity.

He found a quiet spot in the back of third period study hall and started in on a practice chem quiz. No one else was doing homework. They all had a life. *One day*, he vowed as he balanced a nasty equation. *One day that'll be me.*

A loud conversation between two girls in the row in front of him broke his concentration. "How'd you get home Friday night?" Chelsea Brookes, the bitchiest blonde in school, asked her equally blonde friend. Charles made a face. When had THS become blonde Barbie central?

Chelsea's friend giggled. "Peter drove me home. I think he had to carry me to the door. I was so wasted I don't remember."

"Raquel!" Chelsea rapped the girl's knuckles with her ruler.

"Ouch!" Raquel snatched her hand off the desk and cradled her fingers against her stomach. "Geez, woman, what's your problem?"

"You went out with her ex? You broke the code." Jessie Davis, the beautiful redhead Charles had had a crush on since the beginning of time, turned in her seat to join in the blondes' conversation. She was holding a pencil. Had she been doing homework as well? His heart leapt with joy. They were clearly meant to be!

"I did not go out with him!" Raquel covered her face as if repulsed by the idea. Charles grinned. Finally! A girl in this school with some sense. "I only said he drove me home. He was a perfect gentleman." Charles stifled a laugh, turning it into a cough. Peter Jenkins, the gentleman gangster? So much for someone having sense.

Jessie grimaced. "I can't believe you went out with him in the first place, Chels. The guy creeps me out."

Raquel giggled. "You should see who she's dating—ow!" Chelsea had kicked her friend in the shin.

Jessie raised a questioning brow. Chelsea's green eyes twinkled. "Raquel's a teensy bit hung over still."

The bell rang. Charles ghosted from the room before his classmates flooded the halls. He was ambushed the moment he took a seat in biology.

"Here. Get started." Ash slid him a sheet of paper with a few illegible phrases scrawled in messy, lopsided cursive.

"Get started on what?" Charles gaped.

Ash jabbed him in the ribs. "My homework, freak."

Charles groaned. Ash had named himself his lab partner a few months back with the less than articulate threat of "get me through this class or you're dead." He shook his head. How was Ash planning on getting through college? More carefully crafted threats? He stifled a snicker at the thought of Ash in a university classroom. *Yo, professor. Give me an A or you're dead.*

"Sure." Charles hid his amusement. Cooperating with the gang kept him on their radar but prevented a lot of pain.

"Have it done by the end of today," Ash said and smirked, his hazel eyes gleaming with glee.

Charles's mouth fell open. A flood of anxiety swept his humor aside. "It's not due until Friday. I have classes. How am I supposed to finish this by then?"

"Not my problem. But I'd find a way if I were you. The guys and I have been bored lately." He cracked his knuckles.

Charles threw him a withering look. Ash acted like a big shot but was only part of the gang because Alex owed Ash's girlfriend. Charles sighed and skimmed what little notes Ash had written. The assignment required a five-page report on last week's experiment. He was never going to finish it by the end of the day. He ground his jaw and imagined how great it would feel to send Ash hurtling through a wall with the snap of his fingers.

He researched in the library over lunch and scribbled in a feverish haze throughout his afternoon classes. He managed to knock out three pages and prayed it would appease Assassin's Honor. He was not holding his breath.

He shuffled to last period in a swiftly narrowing funnel of doom. Should he leave now? Make a run for the bus? No, avoiding them would only make it worse later on. Maybe if he told someone, perhaps a teacher? Nope, he had tried that in fifth grade. Big mistake.

Three thirty arrived with the sick certainty that he was about to die. He headed for the exit with mounting dread. He was out of school, walking through the parking lot, almost at the corner.

"Banks."

The single word sealed his death. He ran for it.

Alex caught him easily and threw him to the ground. Pavement scraped his palms. Several students ambled past on their way out of school, but none stopped to help. They had more important things on their minds than the well-being of a student they cared nothing about.

Alex held Charles still with inhuman strength as Nathan and Ash closed in on either side. Peter was nowhere to be seen. He avoided gang beatings as though they were a blot on his nonexistent honor.

Alex's blue eyes burned with hate. He bared his teeth as they locked eyes. Darks took sadistic pleasure in others' suffering, and Alex's love of blood made him creepier than most.

Every Dark had an animal half and was able to transform into that animal at will. The type of animal they became partly defined their personalities. Alex shifted into a shark, which explained his thirst for blood and violence. Charles smirked. Would girls still find him attractive if they knew they were making out with a slimy sea creature?

Alex's fist collided with Charles's jaw. He had forgotten the Dark could read minds.

Eight

A CRASH OF thunder jolted Amy awake. She checked the time and groaned. Her alarm was going to blare in fifteen minutes. Monday mornings were never pleasant, and this one promised to be miserable. She had lost precious sleep and faced a rainy walk to school.

She seized the opportunity for self-care and indulged in a long hot shower. She left her blow-dried hair down to flow gently over her shoulders and dressed in formfitting jeans and a burgundy crop top sweater. Since moving to Toronto, her style had transitioned from imitation chic to comfy cute. This was partly because of the plunge in her family's income and partly by choice. Amy no longer lived life to impress her peers. She was simply existing to survive.

She looked in on her mom before waking Susan. Mrs. Evans lay curled on her side like a child, her careworn face restful in sleep and her wispy salt-and-pepper hair trailing gently across her pillow. Relief unraveled the knot of tension in Amy's chest. Her mother was a full-time alcoholic and a part-time intravenous drug user. Amy constantly worried about her and the problems she created. What would she do if her mother disappeared one night or wound up unconscious in the morning after a drinking binge? She and Susan had no family to help them apart from a brother back in Vancouver. Foster care would be a genuine concern if anyone learned of her mother's neglect. She pressed a palm to her forehead and closed her mom's bedroom door. It was time to wake her sister.

The girls found Rex making a mess in the kitchen. He stood with his back to them in nothing but baggy crimson boxers and a too-tight orange T-shirt. He stirred something foul in a pan on the stove, while already burnt toast continued to char in the toaster.

Amy cleared her throat. Rex turned around with a dripping whisk in his meaty hand. Filmy droplets of uncooked egg white splattered the linoleum floor. "What do you want?" He shook his slimy whisk.

"My new sweater!" Susan squealed, ducking behind Amy to avoid the spray.

"We need to make breakfast before going to school," Amy said, resisting the urge to pluck the whisk from his pudgy fingers and smack him on the nose with it.

"Wait your turn. Papa's gotta eat." He patted his bulging stomach. His T-shirt rode up to reveal a pale layer of flab.

Amy made a face and towed Susan from the kitchen. "Come on. We'll go out for breakfast."

"Really?" She clapped her hands in delight. "I'll get ready super fast. Time me!" Susan careened upstairs to brush her hair and grab her schoolbooks.

Amy smiled to herself. "One, two, three," she counted obediently.

They strolled into Starbucks a full half hour before they had to catch their bus. Susan ordered a breakfast sandwich and a double chocolatey chip Frappuccino, and Amy coaxed down a slice of whole wheat banana bread. They spent a soothing twenty minutes people-watching through the window.

The girls arrived at their bus stop with time to spare. A lone high school student was slumped beneath the shelter with his pretty blue eyes locked on his phone.

Susan perched on the bench and flashed him a bright smile. "I like your glasses."

He shot her a perplexed look. "Thank you?"

The girls found seats near the front of the bus. Susan and Frank exchanged cheerful greetings and chatted away the ride. Amy settled into her seat and stared blankly out the window. Her sister had never used to be outgoing. It had all begun a few months ago at the beginning of fourth grade. Susan had wiped out on the merry-go-round during recess and scraped both her knees. Chris had played her knight in shining armor and helped her to the nurse's office. The incident had sparked a fast friendship, and Chris had taken it upon himself to introduce her to everyone he knew. Amy smiled softly. Most cute boys made Susan giggly and awkward. Chris had turned her shy little sister into a chatterbox who never shut up. She had been happier, braver, and more confident since meeting him.

Amy bit her lip, her thoughts fixating on the Donnellson brothers. They had status, and with status came snobbery and entitlement. Did she really want Susan around people like them? Did she really have a choice? Even if she went all 1960s on her sister and forbade her to see him, the kids would still hang out at school. Amy would come off looking like an overbearing helicopter parent and have absolutely nothing to show for her strictness.

Amy drifted through her day on autopilot. She was tired and cranky and wanted to be left alone. She departed through the school's side exit in an effort to avoid the worst of the crowd.

A throng of students had bunched up near the sidewalk that led off school grounds. They trickled past three hulking guys who had surrounded a familiar-looking teen. He was the quiet guy from the bus stop, the one whose glasses Susan had complimented. Amy struggled to channel ignorance and made to walk away. She had a mountain of her own problems and didn't need any more.

One of the hulks raised his fist and punched the kid in the face. They laughed as he raised his arms to protect his head.

A swift rush of anger sizzled through her veins and electrocuted her into action. Amy dropped her pack and sprinted toward the group. She was forty feet away. Thirty, twenty, ten.

"What do you want?" The leader loomed over the kid with his chunky fist raised.

"Leave him the hell alone." Amy stood with her back ramrod straight, her shoulders squared, and her mouth pressed in a firm line.

They looked at her and laughed. She stood her ground. She had been raised in one of the toughest neighborhoods in Vancouver and knew how to hold her own.

"Leave him alone?" A brown-haired guy chuckled softly. The sound raised the hairs on the back of her neck. "Who's going to make us?"

"I am," Amy declared with more bravado than real confidence. She reached into her purse and grasped the first object her fingers found. Her iPhone 6S. She brandished it like a weapon having no idea what else to do. "See this?"

"You gonna attack us with texts?" The leader's mouth curved into a smirk.

Amy narrowed her eyes. "I will call nine-one-one right this second and have you arrested for violence on city property."

Their gazes traveled from Amy, to her phone, to the kid on the ground, and back again. Their dumbfounded expressions would have been comical if the standoff had been less tense.

"You have five seconds." Amy stabbed the nine. "Five, four, three."

They scattered before she got to two. Elation whizzed through her like a breath of spring air. She, Amy Evans, had done something right.

The short kid leapt to his feet and brushed dirt off his jeans. He avoided meeting her eyes.

"You okay?" she asked gently, her voice laced with concern.

His pale cheeks flushed crimson. "I'm fine. I don't need help from a girl." He rushed away without a single backward glance.

Amy clenched her jaw against a shock wave of blistering anger. "Fine." The anger crumbled into something worse. Her eyes burned. "Fine. You're welcome." A single hot tear rolled down her freezing cheek. Furious with herself for the outward sign of weakness, she brushed her sleeve across her burning eyes and marched to Parsons Elementary. How did she always manage to mess everything up? She had been cursed with the gift of total destruction. Everything she touched went catastrophically wrong. Tight bands of loneliness constricted her chest.

She rushed to her room the second they got home, threw herself onto her pillow-top mattress, and fell apart in a sea of tears. Amy had never dealt well with rejection. It had always been a trigger for self-hate and the toxic guilt that lived like a parasite within her. Her breathing accelerated as hot tears stained her face.

She pulled a knife out from under her mattress and rolled up her long sleeves. Her world was out of control. Cutting was her only escape. Cloying fingers of shame tangled around her soul as sharp needles of regret pierced her bleeding heart. Life was a suffocating nightmare from which she would never wake.

Amy lost herself in the physical sting and let it numb her emotional torment. Her sobs subsided; her breathing slowed. The world narrowed to the rhythmic certainty of the blade against her wrist. She let her pain crystallize into calm. This control was all she had left. No one was going to save her because she was always alone.

Nine

ZACK WADED THROUGH the chaos of THS's lunch line, his spirits in the toilet at the demise of his too-short weekend.

"You seriously don't remember anything from Friday night?" Ken asked as they purchased the cafeteria special, some sort of mystery meat.

Zack made a face. He vaguely recalled the ambulance's flashing lights and Amy's pissed-off looks. "Not a thing," he lied. Friday night made no sense. He'd had two, maybe three, beers. That was it. How had he wound up in the emergency room? "The doctor said I was drugged," he said in an undertone.

Ken's blue eyes widened in shock. "That's messed up."

"What's worse is the drugs they found in my system were similar to ones used for date rape."

"Some crazy girl date-raped you?" Ken gasped way too loud. A group of sophomores in the lunch line behind them turned to stare.

"No!" Zack cringed, his cheeks heating. "I said the drugs were similar, not identical." This conversation had become catastrophically embarrassing. Zack blurted the first new topic that popped into his head. "Did you go to Dominic's party Saturday night?" He squeezed his eyes shut, painfully aware of how obviously desperate his attempt at changing the subject had been.

Ken failed to notice. "Yeah, but it was tame compared to yours. Too bad you missed it."

Zack shrugged. "I thought I'd better give my liver a little break."

Amy entered the cafeteria with several books under her arm. She looked unusually cute, all ass-hugging jeans and soft ebony hair. He flashed her a smile. He liked her hair down.

Ken elbowed him in the ribs. "You checking out loner chick?"

"What? No." He hurriedly averted his eyes.

Chelsea scooted along the bench and snuggled against his shoulder the instant they joined the girls at their table. She snaked an arm around his back and rested a hand on his thigh. He narrowed his eyes. She was trying too hard.

The group spent their lunch period discussing the eclipse scheduled for Friday and making plans to watch it together. The eclipse looked super cool. It turned the full moon red. Bloodred.

"So, Zack. How's life as a single dad?" Jessie giggled as they composted their lunch scraps.

"Horrible. I have to find Chris a sitter for tonight, and I don't even know where to start."

Jessie lifted one sculpted brow. "You're cutting it kind of close."

"Oh, come on. Babysitters are twelve-year-old girls with no lives. I just need to figure out how to find them."

"Let's see how well that works out for you." She blew Ken a kiss as they went their separate ways.

Zack texted his mom on his way to class. *Hey, sorry if this wakes you up, no clue what time it is there. What's the number for the sitter? I have a game tonight for some stupid reason.*

His phone buzzed a few minutes later. He hid it behind his textbook to read her message undetected. *A football game on a Monday? Strange.* Her skepticism was obvious even over text. *I've attached the sitter's contact info, but we've never had to have her watch Chris before. She was recommended by a friend.* Zack rolled his eyes. His mother disliked inviting strangers into their home unless they were as wealthy, or wealthier, than they were.

Thanks. Don't worry, I'll make sure she doesn't run off with the good china. ;)

Ok. And Zack, you might not know what time it is in China, but even halfway across the world, I am well aware of when you are in class. Put away your phone and pay attention.

Zack stifled a chuckle. *All right, disturbingly psychic mother. Good night or good morning or good whatever word best fits your time zone.*

He called the sitter between sixth and seventh period. She answered on the second ring. "Hello?" Her words were barely audible above a background of clamoring voices.

"Hey. You babysit, right? I need someone to watch my brother tonight."

"Can't help you." Her tone was clipped.

He was distracted by Amy hurtling toward him at speed. She was also talking on her phone and ignored him as she passed. He returned his attention to his call. "But it's important. I have a football game."

Amy screeched to a halt and whirled to face him with her gray eyes blazing. "Because high school football games trump everything else in the world," she said, both in person and in his ear.

He lowered his iPhone, his jaw going slack. "You're the sitter?"

"No!" She scowled and folded her arms. She looked impossibly cute, like a fluffy-tailed squirrel squaring up to an angry bulldog. "I can't watch Chris. I'm working tonight."

"Oh." He deflated. "Okay, I'll find someone else."

"I'm sure you will," she huffed, disappearing into a classroom to his right.

The babysitter saga continued as Zack ran through a list of names in his head. Jessie would've been his first choice, but she had gymnastics Monday evenings. Chelsea was free, but he refused to inflict her upon Chris. She was notoriously terrible with children, and his brother hated her guts. Zack finally texted Chris himself to see if he had any ideas. His brother would do anything to avoid an evening with Chelsea.

Chris responded within seconds. *I'll hang out at Jake's, no worries. Good luck tonight. Rose Lake won't know what hit 'em.*

Zack typed a speedy reply. *You're the best, bro. I'll pick you up afterward.*

Zack and Ken trudged to detention the moment the last bell rang. Their homeroom teacher, Mr. Fields, had caught them whispering during class and sentenced them to an agonizing hour of staring at the wall.

Mr. Fields had no interest in decorating, or no life, or both. His office reminded Zack of a hospital room with its off-white walls and its disturbing lack of personal effects. The only thing worth looking at was the clock above his fastidiously organized desk.

4:28, 4:29, 4:30. The clock slowly ticked away the last minutes of their detention. Mr. Fields released them at 4:31.

"Come on," Ken said and whooped exuberantly as they raced from the school. "Let's rock this game!"

Their football team, the THS Tigers, was playing their worst rivals, the Rose Lake Wolves, across town in half an hour. The boys were guilty of a streak of late arrivals to practice but had never missed a game. They leapt into Zack's Lexus, surged forward, and screeched to a halt at the exit to the street. A steady stream of traffic blocked their path. "Coach is going to kill us if we're late." Zack stepped hard on the gas. His Lexus shot forward and clipped the mirror of a 2019 Corvette. "Oops."

"Be careful with that beautiful car!" Ken shrieked, clinging to his armrest. "Slow down!"

Zack gripped the steering wheel and cut in front of a red SUV. "If I slow down, we'll be late."

"If we die, it won't matter!" Ken's eyes bulged as the driver laid on his horn. "Zack!"

He zoomed through a yellow light. "Why are we playing Rose Lake on a Monday?"

"Something about needing to do maintenance over the weekend." Ken nervously checked his watch.

They arrived with five minutes to spare. Zack strutted into the locker room and came face to face with their fuming football coach. Coach Coleman was a huge African Canadian in his early forties. He had black hair, dark brown eyes, and a stern, square face. His nose was slightly crooked from a college football accident. He had played for the pros in the nineties and coached the Tigers like a military drill sergeant.

He crossed his arms and scowled at Zack. "If you are late one more time, I'll suspend you. Playing on this team is a privilege, and if you guys treat it like a joke, I'll treat you the same."

Zack glowered at Alex, who was smirking at them behind Coach Coleman's back.

"Ignore him," Ken muttered. "He's just hoping we'll get kicked off the team so he'll actually get to play."

Zack flipped Alex off and focused on the game, imagining every member of the opposition had Alex's sneering face.

The THS Tigers obliterated the Rose Lake Wolves 34 to 10 and headed to Pete's for a victory celebration. The team claimed the diner's two best tables and ordered their usual. Burgers, fries, and shakes all around.

The waitress placed a giant bucket of complimentary fries in the center of Zack's table, Pete's way of mimicking fancy restaurants' bread baskets. Zack grabbed a handful and checked her out. She had a great ass and silky, straight ebony hair. He choked. It was Amy. Her orange uniform was unflattering and blinding, yet she still looked seriously hot. He stared as she swept away and returned a few moments later to take their orders. How did she pull off that uniform so damn well?

Amy barely said two words to him. Zack pretended they had never met. Ken beamed at her as if they were old friends. "Sup, locker buddy?"

She stared at him, dismissed him with her eyes, and moved on without comment. Zack snickered. Ken's charm had no effect on her either.

Zack elbowed his friend as Amy walked away. "That's Susan's sister."

Ken stared at him. "Diner chick is your brother's friend's sister? Why do we care?"

Zack shrugged. "She's hot."

"Really?" Ken turned in his seat to check her out.

Zack chuckled nervously. "What the hell, man! Don't stare." Ken smirked. "So, like, you know her?"

"Nope, but we see each other every day."

"The hell? How?"

"Her locker is right below mine. Hence the locker buddy reference." Ken's eyes crinkled at the corners. He was getting a kick out of the interrogation.

"Have you talked to her before?"

"Nope."

Zack shook his head. He had never understood Ken's insufferable need to flirt with every girl he met. "Do you ever see her with friends?"

"Not really. She likes to keep to herself." Ken stuffed his face with fries. "What's with all the questions? You got the hots for loner chick?"

"Of course not. I'm curious about her is all. She's a mystery."

Zack watched Amy out of the corner of his eye. She kept pacing to the window to discreetly wipe her face. He got up to get napkins and passed her as she brushed a tear from her cheek. He bit his lip and averted his gaze. Despite his ladies' man reputation, he was laughably out of his depth when it came to comforting a hot, crying stranger.

It all happened so fast, Zack felt sure he would have missed it if his eyes hadn't been glued to Amy. Alex slipped a hand down her shirt as she leaned in to refill his glass. Amy reeled backward and dumped her entire pitcher of water over his head. Shocked gasps and a smattering of laughter rippled through their teammates. Amy slammed the pitcher to the table with a dull, muffled thud, turned on her heel with a murderous look in her eyes, and marched away with her back ramrod straight.

Zack's temper flared, along with a protective instinct he hadn't known he had. "Asshole." He glared daggers at Alex. Was this a good enough reason to punch him? Coach Coleman had to agree Alex deserved it.

"Piss off." Alex grabbed a wad of napkins and wiped at a stream of water dribbling from his mocha hair. Beside him, Peter fought a smile. Alex slouched off to the bathroom.

Zack got up to check on Amy. He glimpsed a flash of ebony hair as she whipped around the corner into the kitchen. A dark-skinned guy in a Pete's uniform emerged to take her place.

Zack cursed under his breath. He had blown another chance to talk to her. This girl had seriously thrown him off his game.

He tossed and turned all night, his mind replaying conversations with Amy. Her adorable snark and hilarious bad temper made him want to kiss her, half to shut her up and half to find out if she would kiss him back. Amy was unaffected by everything that attracted girls. Money, popularity, and flirting repelled her. He had never had to work to make someone like him. The challenge was fun, and the pretty brunette more than fulfilled his fantasy of a mysterious conquest.

"What's up with you?" Ken yawned as Zack searched for a parking space in front of THS Tuesday morning. "All you'll talk about lately is diner girl."

"Her name's Amy. I don't understand why you won't introduce us."

Ken waved good morning to Jessie. "Because you've already met her. And what's wrong with Chelsea?" He chuckled. "Okay, don't answer that. But you could easily dump her and date someone more in your league. What about Raquel? She's hot."

"I'm not interested in Raquel." Zack pursed his lips. "I'm not even interested in Amy. I just want her to know she'd be lucky if I was." He found a tight space and cautiously parallel parked. "You're locker buddies." He smirked. "You know her. Put in a good word for me?"

"I don't know her, though. If she was a serial killer or a saint, I wouldn't be able to tell you which!"

"Why are you so crabby this morning?" Ken was usually Mr. Cheerful, even at school.

Ken clenched his jaw. "You're always whining about how I treat girls. Then you turn around and do the same thing." He slammed his car door and shouted through its closed window. "Don't expect my help messing around with bonus chicks."

Zack's mouth fell open. "Chill out!"

"You have a girlfriend! Remember that before you cheat!" Ken scowled over his shoulder and marched off with Jessie.

Zack goggled after them. The auburn-haired beauty had turned his player best friend into a stand-up dude.

Zack's morning went steadily downhill. Jessie surmised that Zack was cheating and ran straight to Chelsea with the news. Both girls began giving him the silent treatment, and Ken followed suit upon orders from Jessie. Zack's classes were even worse than the state of his social life. Mr. Fields gave him another detention, he took a dodgeball to the face during PE, and he incurred hefty late penalties for forgetting to write his English essay.

His friends had all disowned him so he entertained himself by looking for Amy. Zack hesitated halfway across the cafeteria at lunch. Did Ken have a point? Was he becoming her stalker? He shook his head. When had Ken ever been right? Amy was a phase. He just had to get her out of his system. Like a junk food craving or the urge to binge-watch *Friends*, his fascination with the beautiful brunette would quickly run its course.

He found her outside on a concrete wall near the football field. She was sitting with Charles Banks, a nerdy kid Zack had gone to school with since kindergarten. The two sat side by side, their interaction stiff and forced. Amy looked even more pissed than usual, like she was preparing to punch him out. Zack's lips curved into a smirk. He'd love to watch that spectacle, but years of ingrained politeness made him turn away to let them talk. He wandered back inside with another piece of the puzzle that was Amy's confusing life.

Alex Cardelle and Peter Jenkins, the two members of Assassin's Honor on the THS football team, stood a few meters from the exit. Both wore anxious expressions as they peered through a foggy window.

Zack crept up behind them to see what warranted such rapt attention. They were staring at Amy and Charles. His gut curdled with unease. "What ya doin'?" he said with a singsong edge of mockery.

They whirled to face him, Alex puffing like a hornet protecting its nest. "That's none of your business."

Zack's hands curled into fists. Alex had already made an inappropriate move on Amy, and now he was ogling her like a creeper? "If you have something to say to her, say it to her face."

"I don't care about the chick. It's the company she keeps whom I have a problem with."

Zack rolled his eyes. Alex had launched a campaign against Charles back when they were kids. Anyone who hung out with him was bullied until they stopped. Charles had never done anything to warrant such abuse, and Zack was appalled Alex's hatred had persisted into high school.

Zack gave the gangsters a narrow-eyed glare. "When are you losers going to grow up and find a new hobby? Guess spying on chicks is all the action you get."

Alex advanced with a murderous look of fury. "I think you want to take that back."

"Zack, I need to talk to you!" Ken rushed up and skidded to a halt at Zack's shoulder. "Hey guys. We having a team meeting or something?"

"God you're stupid." Alex threw Ken a withering look and stormed from the cafeteria.

Zack frowned. It wasn't like him to let things go. "What's he up to?" he said, turning his glare on Peter.

"Couldn't tell you even if I knew." Peter joined his friends at a nearby table.

"Picking a fight with those guys will get you in trouble with the coach," Ken said.

Zack made a derisive noise and brushed past him on his way to the lunch line.

Ken kept pace with him. "I know how you can talk to Amy."

Zack cut him a doubtful sideways glance. "Yeah? How?"

"Go to Parsons Elementary. Amy has a little sister in Chris's class, right? Casually drop by to scoop your brother. He'll be with Susan, and Susan will be with Amy."

Zack offered his friend a lopsided grin. "You have a brain after all."

Ken's blue eyes twinkled. "Let's just say I understand why you want to dump Chelsea."

Zack shut his eyes, praying for patience. "I don't want to dump Chelsea."

Ken pretended not to hear him. "She's a babe, but annoying as hell. Now, Jessie, she's—"

"She's the center of your universe, I know." Their magic or whatever needed to die, but he had only himself to blame. His matchmaking had turned two quality friends into lovestruck idiots. "I can't talk to Amy today. I have detention again."

"So go for it tomorrow!" Ken thumped him on the back as if he had scored a touchdown.

Zack was half-asleep in history when his name was announced over the school intercom. He jerked upright. "Zack Donnellson and Amy Evans, please report to the principal's office. Once again, Zack Donnellson and Amy Evans are needed in Principal Cook's office. Thank you." Zack gaped. What had he done now?

Ken laughed. "It's fate, man."

Ten

AMY CLENCHED HER pencil in her fist and silently cursed out Zack. What cruel twist of fate had landed her in the principal's office with him of all people? A sharp snap made her look up from her seat at the back of her English classroom. The girl in front of her was rubbing the back of her neck and glaring over her shoulder. Amy's pencil tip lay on the floor between their desks. "Sorry," she mouthed.

She gathered her things and stood to leave. Charles glanced over his shoulder from his seat in the front row. She shot him an icy glare and strode out the door. He had found her at lunch to apologize for Monday. His introduction had come with a shock. He was the son of her mother's former rehab counselor. She had sworn him to secrecy and promised to ignore him in future. They each had their own problems to deal with and they were better dealt with alone.

The first problem on Amy's list was freaking Zack Donnellson. She marched to the office, cursing him with every step. He beat her there.

"Kind of you to join us, Ms. Evans," Principal Cook commented dryly.

"Uh-huh." Amy folded her arms. So what if she had arrived last? The principal was scowling at her as if she had committed a crime. Amy sat next to Zack in the only free seat.

Principal Cook's office had cream-colored paneling, elegantly trimmed with mahogany crown molding. A collection of family photos decorated one wall, and a vast array of awards and degrees adorned another. The woman sitting behind the imposing oak desk was as elegant as her office. She had a trim figure, perfectly shaped eyebrows, and luxurious chestnut hair. She was dressed like a lawyer in a crisp navy blue pantsuit that brought out her aquamarine eyes.

"I'm tired." Principal Cook leaned back in her beige leather chair. "Are you growing sick of this office, Mr. Donnellson?"

"Absolutely!" Zack flashed her a grin. "I can't imagine how you must feel. Maybe you should hold meetings somewhere else every once in a while, like the football field or a buffet?"

"Idiot," Amy muttered under her breath.

"Ms. Evans, do you have something to share?"

Amy forced a bright smile. "Nope." Zack scowled at her.

"Do either of you know why you're here?" Principal Cook folded her hands on her desktop and regarded them with stern disappointment.

Amy and Zack exchanged a puzzled glance. "No," they chorused.

Principal Cook swept some files aside. "Let me clear it up for you. Your younger sister," she nodded to Amy, "and your younger brother," she pointed an accusing finger at Zack, "also got detention this afternoon. They told their teacher you guys enjoy it and purposefully got into trouble to try it out." Her lips twitched. "Do you enjoy detention, Mr. Donnellson? Because we can arrange many more after-school visits if you desire."

Zack's jaw dropped. "I never said that! What lunatic would like detention?"

"I can't imagine why either of you would say such a thing."

Amy's temper flared. "I have never told my sister anything that stupid. Who knows what he told his brother, but it's not my fault if Chris got my sister into trouble because of Zack's bad example."

Zack scowled. "This isn't my fault. Kids that age copy their older siblings."

"That's right, and which of us is the one always in trouble?" Amy raised her voice above Zack's indignant protests. "This has nothing to do with me. This conversation is a waste of my time."

"Enough!" Principal Cook slapped a hand to her polished desktop. "I want the both of you out of my office. Do not return to class," she added as they bolted for the door. "Go over to Parsons Elementary and sort things out with Susan and Chris's teacher."

Amy accidentally slammed the door on her way out. A clatter echoed within. Had a family portrait taken a tumble?

"Temper, temper," Zack said. "Anger issues much?"

"Oh, I'm the one with issues, am I? Look in the mirror."

"What's that supposed to mean?"

Amy tossed her ebony hair. "You're a spoiled rich jock who drinks too much. At our twenty-year high school reunion, you'll be sending a postcard from your state-of-the-art rehab center."

His eyes narrowed. "Well, you're pretty much trailer trash so you won't have to send a postcard. You'll just show up in your orange uniform."

"Now I'm going to prison?" Amy laughed despite herself and flounced past him down the hall.

"I meant your Pete's uniform, but prison works too." He smirked and opened the outside door for her.

Zack headed for his car. Amy walked straight across the street to Parsons Elementary. She smiled sweetly as she forced him to stop while she crossed the road.

Chris, Susan, Principal Castello, and their teacher, Mrs. Peters, were all crammed into Mrs. Peters's tiny office. The rectangular space was painted a soothing spring green. A bouquet of yellow daffodils rested on her narrow, cluttered desk next to a framed photograph of a beaming Mrs. Peters with her two grown sons.

"Amy!" Mrs. Peters flashed her a smile. "Sorry to pull you out of class, but we felt this matter required immediate attention. Is Mr. Donnellson also attending?"

"He's on his way." Amy flopped into the empty seat next to Susan. Zack arrived and sat beside Chris.

The adults stood to face them like an alarming knockoff of the Spanish Inquisition. The two women made a funny pair. Mrs. Peters reminded Amy of a super fun aunt with her round figure, girlish smile, and quirky style. She was the type to bake cookies for dinner on a weeknight or stroll through the park with dog treats for all her four-legged friends. Principal Castello gave off strict grandmother vibes. She had a stern face, graying hair, and penetrating arctic blue eyes perfect for unraveling childhood schemes. If Amy were nine years old, she'd cross the street when she saw the woman coming. Susan's teacher adored her because Amy escorted half her class to school. She expected leniency from Mrs. Peters but had little hope for the hard-assed principal.

"So." Zack guiltily drew out the word. "I guess this is my fault." Amy gaped at him, thrown by his attitude change. Rich kids never accepted the blame for anything. Zack raked a hand through his messy red hair. "I accidentally implied to Chris that I don't mind detention, and I guess he thought that meant I enjoyed it."

"But you said—" Chris shut up as Zack nudged him to be quiet.

"I accept full responsibility. Don't blame Amy for this." He caught her eye and smiled.

Amy's expression softened. This was the first unselfish thing she had ever seen him do.

Principal Castello fixed her with an icy stare. "Ms. Evans. Do you have anything to add?"

Amy forced a relaxed smile, resisting the urge to squirm beneath the principal's penetrating gaze. "Nope. Zack covered it."

Susan broke into silent giggles.

Principal Castello set her mouth in a thin-lipped frown. "Susan says she told you what she and Chris intended to do, and you did nothing to dissuade her."

Amy scowled at her sister. "You never said anything about this."

"Yes I did. Remember on Friday?"

Amy cringed, recalling their ridiculous conversation before Friday's mad dash to school. "You mean right before we almost missed the bus?"

"Yeah." Susan beamed. "We were talking about it before we noticed we were late."

"So, it appears we are correct." Principal Castello puffed like a spider who had succeeded in capturing a particularly juicy fly. Amy shriveled on the inside. She was sixteen, and this lady freaked her out. The poor children!

She threw up her hands. "Come on! This is ridiculous."

"We know you're right," Zack cut in. "Great work by the way. You must be talented to get this much info out of them. These two love secrets."

"Yes." Principal Castello allowed her face a smug smile.

"We have lots of experience with secretive fourth graders." Mrs. Peters twinkled.

Amy tried to picture Zack in fourth grade. He was probably just as obnoxious back then.

"How about you leave it to us to explain our mistakes to our siblings and let us off with a warning?" Zack beamed at the women.

"All right, you're free to go." Mrs. Peters shared an amused look with the principal. "But Susan and Chris, you'd better stay out of detention. We won't be so understanding if this happens again."

"We will! Promise!" Chris said with a hand over his heart.

"Phew," Susan said as the foursome fled the school. "I thought we were toast."

"What did you do to get detention?" Zack asked.

"Toilet papered Caleb's desk!" Chris said.

Zack and Amy shared a glance and struggled not to laugh. "What criminals!" Amy snickered.

"They'll have to join you in prison." Zack mimed handcuffing Chris.

Amy gave him the finger and sauntered away. She paused at the curb and tossed a smile over her shoulder. "Later you two."

Eleven

AMY'S HEART RACED as she peered around her darkened bedroom in search of what had woken her. She sat paralyzed in bed with her gaze locked on her window. Had it been a clatter from outside? Was someone spying on her house? Headlights passed her window, accompanied by the steady whir of cars on the highway. Calm spread from her thundering heart and relaxed her tense muscles. Everything was normal. A sudden crash from downstairs sent her scrambling out of bed. She darted into the hall and hovered at the top of the steps.

She tiptoed forward like every hot blonde extra in a horror movie. Her muscles were tighter than the strings of a guitar, and her heart thrummed in her ears like the boom of a too-loud bass. She gazed at her front door with its broken lock. It was shut tight against the still, silent night. Everything was so quiet. Too quiet. Amy crept across her living room, rounded the corner into the kitchen, and screamed. She leapt backward, tripped on the narrow step, and fell gracelessly onto her rear.

Her mother rushed to her side. "What are you doing up?"

"Mom, it's you!" Relief flooded her chest.

"Who else would it be?"

"I thought someone had broken into the house."

Amy surveyed her mom with a troubled frown. Her salt-and-pepper hair hung limply in ratty tangles. She reeked of cigarettes and booze. An open bottle rested on the countertop, and she clutched a half-empty wineglass in each hand.

"Go to bed, honey," she slurred, swaying where she stood.

"I thought you were working tonight. Did you call in sick?"

Tears filled her mother's cloud gray eyes. "Rex is g-gone." She engulfed Amy in a smothering embrace, sloshing red wine onto Amy's tattered T-shirt. "All men ever do is leave."

Amy nodded sadly. Her dad had split shortly after Amy's fourteenth birthday, and every other deadbeat boyfriend her mother had brought home since had done the same. Amy was thrilled to have seen the last of Rex, but it broke her heart that her mom was upset by his leaving. Didn't she know she deserved a million times better?

She guided her mom to the couch and pried the wine from her hands. "Come on, you're going to be wicked hung over tomorrow as it is." Her mom relinquished her glass with a sour look. "I'll be right back." Amy trudged into the kitchen and dumped the wine down the drain. She made a pot of strong coffee and brought her mom a steaming mug.

She took the mug with shaking hands. "He didn't even tell me in person. I woke to a text, and all his things were gone."

Amy's heart soared with joy. No more stinky Rex clothes! She kept her expression sympathetic and put an arm around her mother. "That's awful, Mom. I'm so sorry he treated you that way."

"I thought he loved me!" she wailed into her coffee. Hot liquid sloshed over the rim and dribbled onto her white uniform. Amy took in her mother's outfit with a deeply troubled frown. She had paired her 7-Eleven shirt with jeans and black Sketchers. She must have dressed for work, seen Rex's text, and ditched her job for a drinking binge. A knot of anxiety tangled in her gut.

"I know you thought he loved you, but you can do about a billion times better." She had shared this sentiment after every painful breakup, but it had never been truer than in regard to Rex Kastel.

"You think?"

"Of course!" Amy plucked a tissue from the box on the coffee table and handed it to her mom.

She blew her nose with an explosive hoot. "It's so hard to date as a single parent. No one wants to deal with kids."

Amy's heart sank slowly into the pit of her stomach, guilt weighing it down like a block of cement. She looked away from her mother's tear-streaked face. She and Susan were a burden. Message received. "Sorry, Mom. One day you'll find the right guy. It just wasn't Rex."

"What would you know?" She hiccupped and sipped her coffee. "You should go to bed. I'm fine." More tears shimmered in the corners of her cloud gray eyes.

Amy bit her lip. "Are you sure?"

"Yes. Go to bed."

Amy returned upstairs, knowing her mom would reach for the wine the moment she was out of sight. She was far from fine. They both knew it.

Susan stood in the doorway to her room, clad in pink pajamas and clutching her favorite stuffed animal, a plush koala bear. "Amy? What's going on?"

"Everything's fine. Go back to sleep, it's the middle of the night." She towed Susan to her bed and tucked a floral-print quilt around her.

"Will you sleep in here with me?" Susan gazed up at her with worry clouding her gentle eyes.

Amy's heart twisted, responsibility weighing heavy on her shoulders. She leaned against the wall and longed for her pillow-top mattress. "Why do you want me to stay?"

"Because Mom's not okay."

"I'm taking care of it. Stop worrying so much." Amy wrapped her in a hug. Susan refused to release her. Amy flopped into bed, resigning herself to a night with her pillow-hogging sister.

The burgundy walls of Susan's eight-by-eight bedroom closed in around her as she lay awake while her little sister slept. Susan was growing up without a mother who cared about her, never dreaming that that, too, was all Amy's fault.

She woke to Susan elbowing her out of bed. Amy opened her eyes, came face-to-face with Susan's alarm clock, and screamed. "Oh my God! Sue, wake up!" She shook her sister's shoulder.

"What?" Susan groaned into her pillow.

"Our bus leaves in twenty minutes!" Amy raced from her sister's room and tore around the house in a cyclonic frenzy of morning chores.

"Wait!" Susan squealed as the girls chased after their fleeing bus. "Wait for us!"

Frank let them on at the light. Twenty-five pairs of eyes gawked at them as they took their seats. Amy stared out the window with her cheeks on fire.

"What happened to you?" Zack's football friend stared as she charged up to her locker.

"Slept through my alarm." Why did this jock insist on talking to her? Zack sauntered toward them, looking hot in jeans and a T-shirt that showed off his well-toned arms. Her heart gave a traitorous flutter. Amy stuffed books into her bag and fled in the opposite direction. She was way too tired to deal with him.

The rest of her day was a sleep-deprived blur. Amy had never been a morning person, and her middle-of-the-night adventure had furthered her chronic exhaustion. She plodded through the parking lot on her way out of school, fantasizing about a cup of French press and an enormous slice of cake. Andrew was going to make her day all better. She was going to power through her shift, hitch a ride home with Steve, and sleep for a year.

A burly junior in a black leather jacket appeared out of no-where and physically blocked her path. Amy halted midstride, narrowly avoiding a collision.

"Hey." He snarled. "Watch where you're going."

Amy scowled. "You watch where you're going."

His expression darkened. She went to step around him. This guy was bad news. He was decently attractive except for a jagged scar that disfigured his face. He spoke with a thick, Southern twang that made everything he said come out in a slow, menacing drawl.

She caught a flicker of movement out of the corner of her eye. Two more guys had appeared, each of them wearing a black leather jacket. One grabbed her roughly and twisted her arms behind her back.

"Hey!" She struggled to wrench free. "What do you think you're doing?"

"I don't like your tone." The burly junior sneered. He appeared to be the group's leader.

"What is this? What the hell do you want?" She bit her lip to keep from wincing as the guy behind her twisted her arms tighter.

"No one messes with us, Evans. No one. Certainly not little girls."

Her gaze flitted between the three huge guys. "I have no idea what you're talking about." She kept her voice level, determined to stay calm. "What the hell did I do? I don't even know you."

"You know what you did." The leader glared. "And soon enough, you'll regret it."

"Wait! Seriously!" She giggled and his glare deepened. Amy had a bad habit of laughing when she was terrified. Her responses to danger had been screwed up from a young age. "You're confusing me with someone else."

Her pleas were met with laughter. The leader shook his fist in her face. "Are you ever stupid? I got two words for you, Evans. Charles Banks."

Her stomach lurched as if she had left it at the top of a ninety-degree drop. These guys knew exactly who they were talking to.

"We checked the bylaws," Ash chipped in. "This parking lot isn't city property like you said the other day. It's school property. We're all students, so anything we do here goes."

Amy glowered. Ash had been her chemistry lab partner last year. She had caught him stealing from the supply closet and had chosen not to turn him in. Now she wished she had.

"Exactly," the leader said, agreeing with Ash's idiotic reasoning. He raised his fist.

Amy had met plenty of bullies in her day and arguing with them had never changed their minds. She closed her eyes and braced herself for pain.

"Hey!" Running footsteps announced someone else's arrival. Amy cringed internally. More of their friends? "What the hell do you think you're doing?" She opened her eyes to identify the newcomer. The leader blocked her view.

"Fancy meeting you here, Donnellson," the guy holding her in place said with blasé nonchalance. "What's up, man?"

Zack? Zack had come to her rescue? Heat crept up her neck. She laughed when terrified and blushed while being rescued? She'd make one hell of a weird Disney princess.

"Let her go," Zack ordered in a tone cold as ice.

"This does not concern you." The leader's brown eyes narrowed into two dark slits. "Piss off and walk away."

Zack strode forward into Amy's line of sight. His crystal blue eyes briefly met hers. He clenched his fists, and muscles bunched beneath his navy sweatshirt. "Let her go. Or I promise you'll go down for it."

Her heart fluttered with gratitude, even as her gut clenched with nerves. What the heck was he doing? They were never going to release her just because he asked them to.

Zack stood his ground and held the leader's chilling gaze. Their stance reminded her of a hockey face-off moments before one team won the puck. She winced. Did that make her the puck?

The leader motioned for his lackey to release her. He shoved her toward Zack so hard she lost her balance and hit her knees. Pavement tore through her jeans and sliced into her skin. Amy barely registered the pain. She was held captive by the look in Zack's eyes.

Twelve

ZACK STRUGGLED TO keep his cool. How dare Alex hurt her! Who were these creeps to push around a girl a foot shorter than them? And on top of that, three on one? He grabbed Amy's arm and pulled her to her feet. Alex looked at them with a firestorm of hate in his eyes. Zack turned and marched her away. His stomach clenched with tension. His muscles screamed for action. He wanted to do something. Get Amy out of there fast, pick a fight with Alex, anything but walk away passively. But he had never been crazy enough to cross Assassin's Honor before and had no idea what psychotic infamy came next.

"Donnellson," Nathan shouted at their backs. "You got lucky today. But don't ever try pulling something like this again. You won't get off so easy next time."

Zack ignored the empty threat. His connections had already saved them. He had three lawyers in his family, two uncles and a cousin. None of the gangsters fancied a lawsuit.

He glanced over his shoulder. "They're gone," he spat with contempt. He gentled his tone as he turned back to Amy. She looked pale but furious. "Are you okay? Did they hurt you?"

"No. I'm good." They stood awkwardly for a moment before Amy met his eyes. Indifference clouded her gaze, but emotion swam just below the surface. She cleared her throat. "Uh, Zack? You can let go of me now."

"Right." He dropped her arm. "What did they want with you?"

She took a breath as if about to explain, then shook her head and shut her mouth. "Nothing." She lowered her eyes and scuffed the pavement with the toe of her boot.

"Nothing? Really? Looked like something when you were about to have your face smashed back there."

"It's not your problem." She shifted from foot to foot. "I have to go, but thanks for what you did. It was cool of you to help." She raised her misty gray gaze and met his eyes. A jolt of electricity rushed through him, along with that same absurd instinct to protect her.

"Don't mention it." He waved off her gratitude. "You should tell me what they wanted." If this escalated into something he brought to his relatives' attention, he needed to understand the situation as clearly as possible.

Her eyes skittered away from his. "It's not important." She straightened her shoulders and strode away.

Concern spiraled within him as the distance between them grew. Amy obviously knew something else, something she was refusing to share. "Hey, Amy!" She whipped around, her eyes wide with panic. She saw it was only him, turned on her heel, and marched away at an even faster pace. "Amy, wait!" He jogged to catch up with her. "You go that way to pick up your sister." She raised her eyebrows. He winced internally and flailed for a way to undo his stalker-like comment. "I mean, you usually head in that direction."

Amy pressed her lips together. He struggled to work out whether she was amused or annoyed. "I do. But Sue has a playdate, and I missed my bus. See you around."

That stupid protective instinct spiked his concern. He didn't want her walking anywhere alone. "Want a ride?" He held up his keys.

"Oh, no. No, that's okay." A strong fall breeze blew strands of hair into her face. She took a flustered swipe at them. "It's thoughtful of you to offer but seriously, I'm fine. I'm heading to work. It's close by."

He resisted the urge to tuck her hair behind her ear. "Come on. Let me drive you. It's going to rain." The gray sky was blanketed with ominous storm clouds. If she refused his offer, he was going to have to follow her to make sure she made it to Pete's in one piece. He was already late picking up Chris. He tried a different tact. "Afraid to be seen with me? In my fancy new car?"

Her brows snapped together. "What? No," she said, swiftly defensive.

"So, what are we waiting for?"

"Wow!" she said with reverent delight as they halted by his Lexus. "Is this seriously yours?"

"Yeah. My parents bought it for my sixteenth." He pressed a button on his keyless remote to unlock the doors.

Amy rested her hand on the shiny black hood. "A 2019 Lexus LS!" Awe transformed her face. She climbed into the front seat and examined its sleek black leather interior.

"You know cars?" Pretty girls who liked cars were a rare commodity in Zack's world.

"Yeah." Amy smiled and played with the radio. "My brother thought about becoming a mechanic. I used to hang out with him in his friend's garage."

His eyes widened a fraction. Amy on her back beneath a car, clad in nothing but a tank top and shorts. That was one hot mental image. He swiftly changed the subject. "You have a brother?" Neither Susan nor Amy had mentioned another sibling.

"Yeah. He moved away to go to university." She settled on a hard rock station and leaned back against her seat.

"Where does he go to school?" He finally had her talking, and this was a better topic than the weather.

"Vancouver." She tucked a lock of hair behind her ear. "Justin is studying criminal justice."

"Savage!" Zack flashed an impressed smile. They pulled into a parking space in front of Parsons Elementary.

Chris appeared at Amy's window. She rolled it down. "This why you're late, Zack?" He smirked.

Zack grinned, unashamed. "Yep. We're dropping Amy off at work before heading home."

"Where do you work?" Chris scrambled into the back seat with a happy-go-lucky smile.

"Pete's," Amy and Zack said in unison.

"Oh, right." Amy sighed. "You were there with your team a few days ago."

"Yeah, we celebrate there on the reg." He cruised out of the elementary school parking lot and hit the gas as a good song came on.

Amy's ebony hair swirled around her face in the wind from her open window. She looked at him bobbing his head to the beat and burst out laughing. His breath caught in his chest. Laughter transformed her like a flower opening to the sun. Her defenses fell away, leaving her simultaneously beautiful and vulnerable.

"What?" Zack chuckled. "My team wins a lot!"

"I know." More giggles burst from her lips. They painted the car in shades of shimmering sunlight. "I'm surprised you jocks party it up with such family-friendly style."

"Babe, our after-parties are too lit for your loner mind to handle. Come watch us play this Saturday and maybe you'll score an invite."

"I'll pass." She chuckled. He never wanted her to stop laughing. "My kid-friendly restaurant needs me."

"Did you just start working at Pete's?" It was weird he had never seen her there before.

Her eyes danced with mirth. "I've been there over a year."

"Oh." Heat crept into his cheeks. He was an oblivious idiot.

Chris leaned forward to tell Amy about his day. She gave him her full attention, truly listening to everything he said. They acted like siblings, joking, laughing, and teasing each other mercilessly.

He insisted on walking Amy to the door, and from the moment they entered the diner, he regretted his decision. Every last person in the place turned to gape at them. Two employees at the counter waved hello to Amy and continued staring openly at Zack.

"Hey Amy." The shorter of the two greeted her with narrowed eyes and pursed lips. "Who's your friend?"

"Steve, Andrew, this is Zack." Amy did her best to ignore the attention they were receiving. "He's also a junior at THS."

A grizzled old guy waggled his fingers at them. "What'd I tell you, Amy? I knew you'd make some lucky fellow's life a little brighter."

Amy cringed. "Hi, Hal." She looked like she wanted to melt into a puddle and never solidify again.

Steve mumbled something under his breath and stalked into the kitchen.

"Nice to meet you." Zack shook Andrew's hand and waved hello to the old guy. "Hi, sir." He crossed the diner to shake his hand as well. "I'm Zack."

"Good to meet you, son. The name's Hal." He had a firm handshake but a welcoming smile. "You be sure to treat our Amy right."

"Oh God." Amy's cheeks flamed. She buried her face in her arm.

"I'll be sure to do that." Zack winked. A gagging sound from the kitchen doorway signaled Steve's return.

Hal looked Zack up and down. "You seem familiar. You eaten here before?"

"Yeah, my football team drops by all the time." Steve screwed up his face. Zack suppressed a chuckle. Amy had a college dropout love interest? He ought to free the loser from his delusions. "I'd love to stay and chat, but I'm late for practice right now. Later, hon." He blew Amy a kiss and sauntered out the door with his hands in his pockets.

He and Chris blared Amy's rock station on the drive home while Zack mulled over the sensation he had created at Pete's. Either everyone working with her had as bad a crush as he did, or his and Amy's class difference had prompted the staring. Was she not supposed to associate with rich kids? Or did Amy seriously have no friends at all? Had it been that weird for her co-workers to see her with someone from school? He shrugged. Befriending unpopular kids was out of the question, no matter how addictively attractive they were.

Thirteen

CHARLES BREEZED INTO homeroom Thursday morning with a smile on his face and a spring in his step. Assassin's Honor had ignored him since their run-in with Amy on Monday afternoon. He grinned to himself and took a seat with the nerds. Chem jokes were a hell of a lot less painful than Alex's fists.

A light knock at the door interrupted his homeroom teacher midsentence. All heads turned as Amy slipped into a seat in the back row. Mr. Fields scowled, his hazel eyes shooting sparks of annoyance. "Kind of you to grace us with your presence."

"Sorry, sir." Amy gazed demurely at her desk.

Mr. Fields huffed out an annoyed breath and resumed class with his usual blustering rage. Zack and Ken shared a look. If either of them had arrived this late, they would have gotten a week's worth of detention. Their bitter, old teacher must dislike some of his students marginally less than others.

The next time Charles saw Amy, she was hurtling toward him through the cafeteria at lunch. He tried to move out of her way, but a crowd of chattering freshmen blocked his path. She smashed into him with a lot of force for a small person, and their books exploded in all directions.

"Damn it! Sorry." A flush crept up Amy's neck.

"No problem." He bent to retrieve his stuff. She gathered her things and rushed outside.

Charles sat with the nerds and began cramming books into his bag. He hesitated with a pair of identical history texts in his hands.

He opened one to check the name on the inside cover, and a scrap of paper fell onto the table in front of him. His stomach lurched. The slanted handwriting was horrifyingly familiar. It spelled his doom just as surely as Nathan had misspelled the word 'invincible.' How had he missed seeing this message? When had he received it? Assassin's Honor was the furthest thing from stealthy. His gaze flitted back to the book, and a rush of relief loosened the knots in his gut. That wasn't his name scrawled across the inside cover. It was Amy's.

His relief evaporated. His eyes stretched wide, his stomach doing a sickening flip of horror. Amy had received a note from Assassin's Honor. Charles smoothed the paper with shaking hands.

Evans,

You have crossed a line. Not once, but twice. Do you truly expect to get away with this? Do you honestly think you're invinsable? Are you relying on that boyfriend of yours to protect you? Because news flash, he can't. Anyone who messes with us pays a painful price. Everyone has a weakness, and it will be our pleasure to exploit yours. You better watch your back, because we're watching you.

Nathan had signed his note with an *X* in the bottom left corner. Charles stared at the paper, his stomach churning with queasiness. Were they targeting Amy because she had helped him on Monday? Guilt snaked through his gut and tangled with his dread. *You have crossed a line. Not once, but twice.* His blood turned to ice. What other encounters had she had with them?

His chair scraped against the floor as he shakily stood and pocketed the note. He had to put a stop to this. A human was helpless against a Dark. He was helpless against a Dark, as well, but that was beside the point. This was a supernatural conflict, and it was his duty as a mage to keep Amy safe.

Charles summoned his nonexistent courage and went looking for the most dangerous super he knew. Alex spent his lunch periods seducing girls in the soundproof music room. Charles peeked through the little, round window in the door and found Alex making out with a curly-haired blonde. He was going to have to wait until after she left. He leaned against the wall, his heart pounding in his ears and his muscles rigid with tension. His thoughts tumbled over one another as he tried to imagine surviving the lunch break.

The blonde slipped from the room, and Charles's jaw dropped. She was Chelsea Brookes, the girlfriend of popular football jock, Zack Donnellson.

Her eyes widened a fraction. She licked her lips, opened her mouth, and swiftly snapped it shut. He had been deemed unworthy of an excuse. Chelsea assumed, rightfully so, that he had no one to tell. She smoothed a hand over her hair, dismissed him with an imperious jerk of her head, and floated down the hall like an addict on ecstasy. He glanced up to the ceiling. Chelsea was in way over her head.

Darks possessed a creepy ability to enslave their victims by kissing them, a process they had termed bonding. Darks' saliva contained hormones that relaxed the mind and body and invoked a drug-like sense of euphoria. This caused addicted victims, like Chelsea, to crave attention and validation from their Dark, doing anything and everything to win their favor. Bonds were characterized by every aspect of unhealthy relationships. They encouraged physical and emotional dependence, loss of identity and self, and abusive tendencies bordering on BDSM behavior. Darks often created entire armies of bonded victims for their unflinching, blind loyalty and zombie-like acceptance of whatever the Dark did and said.

"What you looking at?" Alex stalked from the music room, straightening his leather jacket. "You so starved for attention, you spy on people making out? Go home and watch some porn."

Charles's heart leapt into his throat at Alex's sudden appearance. "I'm not here to discuss Chelsea." Doubt slithered into his mind as he met Alex's cold blue eyes. Was Amy worth risking his life? He barely knew her and what he did know, he didn't much like.

Alex bared his teeth. "Spit it out, loser. I don't have all day."

Yeah. You've a whole list of cheerleader conquests to enslave before the lunch period ends. Disgust chased away his doubt. Charles pulled Nathan's note from his pocket and waved it in Alex's face. "What's with this?"

"Nathan gave that to her." Alex leaned against the music room doorframe, a smirk playing at the corners of his mouth.

Charles crossed his skinny arms over his chest and scowled. "Cut the crap, Cardelle. We both know you control everything they do."

"That's right. I do control them. I control anyone I want."

"Leave Amy out of this. I barely know the girl."

"You two dating? This chick must dish it out like candy."

Charles grimaced. "God, no!" He would never, ever go out with someone as bitchy as Amy. "I'm only saying targeting her is pointless. She means nothing to me."

"And yet here you are, begging me to leave her alone. Amy must have considered the consequences before she got involved."

"End this." Charles shoved him with pure magical energy. Alex's mocha hair stood on end.

He outright laughed at the flimsy attempt at force. "Look who thinks he's a big man now. Stay out of our way, and the next time we chat, Amy might still have all her teeth." He sauntered away, whistling.

Charles blanched at the vivid image of Alex punching out Amy's teeth, or worse, him operating a dental drill. His stomach roiled at the pictures Alex had placed in his mind. He hung his head. Standing up to the Dark had made him even more psychopathic.

Fourteen

"HEY."

Smash. Amy's beaker of chemicals slipped from her hand and shattered on the laminate countertop.

Her chemistry lab teacher motioned for her to clean up the mess. Amy held her breath for a second and shrugged free of her clinging terror. Her startle response had shot through the roof since the note had appeared in her locker. Assassin's Honor had a gift for crafting creepy phrases. *We're watching you. Everyone has a weakness.* Their threats echoed in her mind, poisoning her thoughts and choking her with unease. The girl leaning across the aisle, the one who had spoken, took in Amy's deer-in-the-headlights expression and gaped at her in openmouthed dismay.

"Sorry? Didn't mean to startle you." The girl was several inches taller than Amy with long, wavy auburn hair and enough style to impress Hollywood. She radiated cheerleader popularity.

Amy flushed with embarrassment. "It was my fault."

"Are you going out with Zack Donnellson?" The cheerleader skipped straight to the point and pierced her with a chiding look.

"Not again," Amy groaned. "Everyone's been asking me that all day." She gratefully accepted the rag her lab partner passed her.

"Because he has a girlfriend. You know that, right?"

"No and yes." She wrinkled her nose and mopped up the spill.

The cheerleader narrowed her emerald green eyes. "Yes, you are going out with him, but no one told you he had a girlfriend?"

"No." She threw the pushy cheerleader an exasperated scowl. "No, I'm not going out with him, and yes, I know he has a girl-friend."

"Good." The cheerleader smiled, dazzling the room with a row of perfect white teeth. "I just wanted to check, because I'm friends with his girlfriend."

"Whatever." Amy shrugged. "Good talking to you."

"My name's Jessie." The cheerleader shook her hand with a surprisingly genuine smile.

"Amy," she mumbled. She had been going to THS for two entire years and had had less conversations in all that time than in the last week alone. She hated the attention with an intensity that rivaled her alarm on a Monday morning or people who still used the word 'retarded.'

Jessie was the one person who confronted her to her face. Everyone else was much less polite. People stared at her wherever she went. Conversations broke off the second she grew near, and hushed whispering followed her through school. Angry frustration simmered silently within. So what if Zack had dropped her at Pete's that one time, and so what if he had driven her and Susan to school that morning? A few rides meant nothing. Zack was just being para-noid after what he had witnessed with Assassin's Honor.

Amy was in a foul mood by the end of the afternoon. She marched to her locker to retrieve her jacket and once again got ambushed.

"Hey!"

She spun on the spot and slammed her locker shut with a bang. She had enough stress in her life between raising her kid sister and avoiding a bunch of psychopathic gangsters without the whole school accusing her of dating a football star.

"No!" she yelled, planting her fists on her hips. "I am not going out with Zack Donnellson!"

"I was only going to ask if you had notes from precalculus yesterday." Zack's friend raised his hands in mock surrender.

"Sorry." She deflated, heat searing her face. "I've had a rough day."

The chatty girl from chemistry galloped up and greeted Locker Buddy with an enthusiastic kiss. Amy shook her head in confusion. Could this day get any weirder?

Locker Buddy smiled as he unglued himself from Jessie. "Amy, this is—"

"Jessie, I know." Amy shoved her hands into her pockets. Why was this rando introducing her to his girlfriend when she didn't even know his name?

"Hey." Zack ambled up and rested a hand on her shoulder. "How's it going?"

Amy swept her gaze over the group and raised an eyebrow in skeptical disbelief. Had the three of them planned to ambush her here? They kept multiplying. She shook her head, a string of snarky retorts leaping to her lips. *Oh yeah, I'm fantastic. I've got half the school hating my guts for stealing some poor girl's boyfriend, the other half gossiping about you becoming my personal chauffeur, and a group of hulking gangsters leaving threatening messages in my locker.* "Great," was all she said aloud. She stepped away from Zack and his hand. "You?"

"Good." Zack glanced at Jessie and her boyfriend, who were once again making out. "Either of you want a ride home?" He dangled his keys in front of their smooching faces. "Look, shiny."

"This looks fun." A leggy blonde stalked over and slid her arm through Zack's. "Who's this, honey?"

Honey? Amy struggled to keep a straight face. She caught Zack's eye and grinned. He cringed. Laughter bubbled inside her like a golden spring of joy. Why did this guy make her happy? Uneasy butterflies fluttered through her mirth. Zack was an ass who had called her trailer trash. She jerked her gaze away from his, refusing to be charmed.

"Amy, this is Chelsea. Chelsea, Amy." Zack shifted uncomfortably and darted a glance between the two girls.

Chelsea shot Amy a glacial glare. "I'm his girlfriend."

"Never would have guessed." Amy smirked.

"Want a ride home?" Zack flashed her a sexy smile.

Her insides swirled like water. She cut her gaze to Chelsea in an effort to break his spell, and the other girl shot her a look worthy of Medusa. Amy rolled her eyes. Chelsea fixed her with a death glare that Zack pretended not to notice. Amy shook her head. This was a volatile situation, one she needed to escape before it blew up in her face. She stepped away from the couple. Distance was what she needed, physical and emotional. "No thanks. I'll grab the bus."

"The bus." Chelsea laughed derisively as Amy strode away. "Too bad you can't afford a car. Or better clothes."

Amy clenched her fists. She'd be damned if she let Chelsea's poison affect her. She squared her shoulders, lifted her chin, and marched down the hall with her head held high.

Susan and a dozen of her friends were waiting to ambush her at Parsons Elementary. "Ready to go?" her sister called over the din of clamoring children.

"We're all going to your house!" Sarah cheered from the middle of the mob.

Amy gaped. "What? Susan, you never said anything about this." First the detention incident, now a surprise party? She and her sister were having serious communication issues.

"Really? Oops. Can we please still have my party? Please!" Susan's soft gray eyes begged her to allow it. With one sorrowful look, she brought back all the times she had come home crying because she didn't have any friends at her new school.

"All right." Amy put a hand to her head in anticipation of a migraine.

She led a parade of fourth graders up her street after a long, chaotic bus ride. She quickly counted heads and breathed a sigh of relief. Everyone had survived.

"Hey, did you guys get a new car?" Sarah asked over her shoulder from the bottom of their driveway.

Susan giggled. "Half the time we can't even afford Froot Loops. How would we buy a car?"

A sleek new Mercedes sat majestically in front of their house. Amy halted next to Sarah and stared at it in wonder. "A 2019 Mercedes-Benz," she said in a breathy voice.

"It's pretty," Sarah agreed.

"With over two hundred and fifty horsepower and a new nine-speed automatic transmission, the turbocharged C three hundred can accelerate to one hundred kilometers per hour in under six seconds!" she crooned.

"Huh?" Sarah tilted her head.

"Ignore her." Susan laughed. "I never understand her when she speaks car."

"That's Chelsea's dad's ride," Chris chimed in.

"What?" Amy recoiled, her Mercedes lust forgotten.

"You snapped her out of it!" Susan high-fived Chris.

"Let's toilet paper it!" Chris beamed, his eyes alight with mischief.

"No!" Amy gasped. As pissed as she was at Chelsea, she shuddered at the thought of defiling the Mercedes's flawless exterior.

As if sensing the impending danger to her car, Chelsea stepped gracefully from the Mercedes and regarded the group imperiously from the top of the driveway's gentle slope.

"Crap, she's in it," Chris whispered. "Amy, you distract her while we get the toilet paper." His flock of friends giggled and nudged each other forward.

Amy strolled up to Chelsea with a confident grin. Screw her imperious tallness and screw her fancy car. Amy thrived on intimidation. "Hey girl, you lost? This neighborhood don't look too kindly on outsiders." She played up the trailer-trash, tough-girl act.

"No." Chelsea smiled. Her tone dripped sickening, syrupy sweetness. "I thought I'd take a trip down memory lane and revisit my humble roots." Amy blinked at her in confusion. What was she blabbering about? "You'd know what I mean if you had the slightest chance at prosperity. Poor Amy Evans, doomed to live life in financial ruin. Now you don't even have your rich boys to buy you pretty things."

Amy studied Chelsea from her honey blonde hair to her new designer shoes and belatedly made the connection on a cold ripple of shock. "Long time." She met the other girl's sly green gaze. No wonder Chelsea had been unfazed by her tough-girl talk. She had grown up down the street from Amy in the heart of Vancouver's downtown east side. "I see your acne has cleared up." When Amy had last seen Chelsea, she had been a freaky eighth grade loser with frizzy hair and horrible skin. She used to follow Amy and her friends around like a dog begging for scraps.

Chelsea curled her lip. "My dad made it big in the oil industry. We moved to Toronto around the same time you did. Guess that's karma, hon."

Disconcerted whispers had broken out behind them. She tossed Susan her keys. "You guys go inside. I'll be there in a minute."

"Aww, is this little Susan?" Chelsea turned her malevolence on the nine-year-old. "You look just like Amy, before the drugs. Where's the other little brat?" Chelsea lazily drifted her gaze over the ragtag group of kids. Her green eyes sparkled as they settled upon Amy. "Oh, that's right. She died, didn't she? Poor sweet Katie."

A giant fist squeezed Amy's heart. It constricted her chest and made it hard to breathe. "Susan, take your friends inside." Her sister fled up the steps with tears in her eyes.

Chris glowered at Chelsea. "You're a bitch. I don't care if you tell Zack I said that."

Amy waited until the door had closed behind Susan and her friends. "Don't ever speak to my sister again." Her voice was deadly calm, her words tense with fury. "Get back in your stupid fancy ride and never set foot on this street again." Her fingers flexed with the urge to claw out the other girl's eyes.

Chelsea held her ground but rested a protective hand on her Mercedes. "I'll leave her alone when you leave Zack alone."

Anger bubbled inside Amy like a pot of boiling water. All this was over her nonexistent relationship with a football star? "This is about Zack? He's almost as stuck up and pretentious as you are. How many times do I have to tell you people? I am not interested!" She shook her fist at Chelsea, something she had only seen done on TV.

"Well, good." Chelsea stomped the two steps to the driver's side door. "He just wants a hookup, anyway. Don't flatter yourself. It wouldn't mean a thing, even if he did waste his time on you." She slammed her door and fumbled with her keys.

Amy marched to her open window. She gripped its edge to keep from punching Chelsea in her smug little mouth. "Girl, you don't mean anything to Zack either." She forced the fakest smile she could muster and leaned into the car. "I'll let you in on a secret. You might have learned how to brush your hair since eighth grade, but you sure as hell haven't learned much about boys. If a guy spends this much time obsessing over someone else, even if it's just to hook up, he's far from happy. It's only a matter of time before he dumps you."

"You bitch!" Chelsea raised a manicured hand to slap her.

Amy stepped back in the nick of time. "Have a nice ride home alone. You'd better get used to it. It's how you'll be spending the rest of your life." She strolled into her house.

A dozen anxious little faces peered down at her from the staircase. They had been listening in and hadn't fled fast enough to avoid being detected.

"Guys, this is supposed to be a party. Go have fun!" She waved her hands in a shooing motion. Everyone scattered but Susan. "You okay?" Amy swept to the landing to hug her sister tight.

"That girl was mean." Susan's voice was thick with tears.

She stroked her sister's hair. "I know. I was mean to her in middle school so now she's being mean to us. It's okay, she's gone now." Susan stared at the floor. Amy gently cupped her chin. "Do you want to talk about Katie?"

"No." Pain flashed in her sister's gentle eyes. "Not with my friends here."

"Okay." She gave Susan a squeeze. "I'm always here if you change your mind." Susan nodded and scampered upstairs.

Thorns of grief pierced Amy's heart. Susan had been old enough to remember Katie, yet too young to understand her death. She blinked back tears of her own and wandered into the kitchen in search of a snack to cheer everyone up. Chocolate chip cookies ought to do it.

The cookies did it all right, and more. She soon had twelve sugar-high children charging manically through her house. They were demolishing the place with enthusiastic gusto. She needed to contain them with an activity.

"Hey, you guys, I have an idea." A dozen kids stampeded toward her. "Do any of you know how to dance?"

"I know how to break-dance," Chris said.

"Amy knows ballet," Susan piped up.

"Are you going to show us?" Sarah whooped.

Amy smiled at their infectious enthusiasm. "We're all going to dance. We'll have a prize for whoever pulls off the best or craziest moves." She dragged the furniture out of the way and cranked the music on a thunderous cheer. "Okay, everyone! Three, two, one, dance!"

Complete pandemonium ensued. The boys were outnumbered three to one, so they formed rings of girls and slid around in giggling groups. Hooray for the timeless entertainment of socked feet on a slippery wood floor.

Chris bounded up to Amy. "Want to dance?" He bowed.

"Why, of course, fine gentleman." She took his hands and twirled him onto the floor.

Fifteen

ZACK, JESSIE, KEN, and Chelsea stood in a shocked cluster by Ken's locker as Amy stalked away with her head held high. She had a brave type of honesty Zack had never even glimpsed in anyone else. She didn't give a crap where she came from. It was part of who she was, and she was proud of it. Her spirit was unquenchable, her soul alight with fire. Amy drew people in without even trying. He and his friends were the four most influential juniors at THS, and she had them staring after her in awe. He was jealous of her jeans and the way they hugged her butt. He was even more jealous of Dominic Carter, who checked her out as she passed. Zack shook his head to clear it. What the hell was happening to him? He didn't get jealous. He was with someone else!

"Chels, she heard you," Jessie murmured as Amy disappeared around the corner.

"So?" Chelsea refused to lower her voice. "Bitch needs to learn her place. She's nothing but a sneaky little slut."

"She is not." Jessie held up her hands, placating her friend. "Amy doesn't even like Zack."

Zack huffed out an indignant breath and shot Jessie a reproachful look.

Chelsea jutted out her hip and scowled at her best friend. "She hit on my boyfriend, and she's not even that pretty." The boys exchanged a doubtful look. Chelsea lived in denial.

Jessie crossed her arms. "Will you please stop calling her names? You're making a scene over nothing."

"I'm making a scene?" She puffed with fury. "I'm making a scene? I have the right to be upset when some slut makes a play for my boyfriend! You don't understand. You don't know what she's like." Her high, shrill voice was strained and filled with tears. "I went to middle school with her. I know what she's capable of."

"Oh my God, Chelsea! The girl is not out to get you." The crowded hall quieted as their classmates turned their attention to the arguing queens.

"She's nothing but a bitch!" Chelsea shrieked, her voice raw with pain. "Why do none of you see what she is? Amy manipulates people into thinking the way she does. She plays with your emotions for the fun of breaking you down." Tears filled her eyes.

"Chelsea, you're acting crazy." Zack slipped an arm around her waist, trying to calm her. "Amy's just a friend. There's nothing going on." Except that he had been fantasizing about her all week. He shoved the guilty thought into a box in his mind and padlocked it shut. He was not a cheater. He wasn't Ken.

Chelsea shrugged free of his arm. Her eyes narrowed into furious green slits. "Have you slept with Amy yet?"

"What? No!" He staggered back a step and gaped at his girl-friend.

Her face twisted into a sneer. "Well, when you do, you'll probably get an STD."

Zack opened his mouth to speak up in Amy's defense, but Jessie beat him to it. "Oh, shut up!" Her emerald eyes blazed. "You're just jealous that everyone's talking about Amy instead of you. Everything's not about you!" She shook a manicured fist for emphasis.

A gawking circle of prying eyes had surrounded the foursome. Ken and Zack looked on, unable, and a little unwilling, to break up the chick fight.

"I never said it was!" Several strands of Chelsea's curly hair had escaped their elegant twist and clung to her forehead and flaming cheeks. "Why are you on her side? You're supposed to be *my* friend."

Jessie drew herself up to her full height of five foot six. "Right. I'm your friend when you want your homework done, or when you need to borrow money, or when you're itching to start a rumor about someone who disses you. I overheard you talking about Amy with Claire and Raquel in the washroom. You're so insecure, you made up tons of lies about her. You told people about her old school. You called her a whore and said things I never want to repeat. You should be ashamed of yourself." Jessie resembled a righteous goddess, heaping condemnation upon a sinner. It was a welcome change from Chelsea bossing her around.

Chelsea held up both hands to silence her. "I am not ashamed of telling the truth."

"God!" Jessie furiously tossed her auburn hair, nearly whipping Zack in the face with it. "That's half your problem! You never, ever know when to shut your mouth. Come on, Ken." She grasped his arm and towed him down the hall. "Oh, and Chelsea," she screeched from twenty feet away. "I also heard what you said about me!"

"High school drama at its finest," a student said to her friend and giggled. "Go, Jessie!"

Chelsea had been rendered temporarily speechless. "We're leaving." She shouldered her designer handbag and beckoned Zack with a finger. He skewered her with an icy glare and stayed rooted to the spot. "Hello?" Chelsea tugged on his sleeve. "You coming or what?"

"No." The word sliced through the tension in the hallway like a sword through a paper shield.

"What did you just say?" Lightning bolts of rage shot from her eyes.

He pressed his lips together in a hard, unyielding line. "I said no, Chelsea. It's over." The chatter that had begun with Jessie's dramatic exit died away. All heads swiveled back to the arguing couple. Dominic caught his eye and made a run-for-it gesture toward the fire doors.

"What? What's over?" Chelsea's green eyes were pools of skittering panic.

"Us." As if she didn't already know. He stared at her with no emotion.

"I knew it!" She cut the air with one narrow hand. "This is about *her*, isn't it?"

"This has nothing to do with Amy. This is all because of you." He snatched his arm from her grasp. Her acrylic nails dug painfully into his skin before her hand fell away. "I'm dumping you because of your annoying personality, your selfish attitude, and your the-world-revolves-around-me mindset. I'm sick of it, *honey*, so find your own way home." He strode to the end of the hall and slammed the door on her apology. A smile split his face. He was free! Chelsea

Brookes was dead to him, and he felt nothing but relief. No girl was worth the continual drama she put him through. He ought to have listened to Chris sooner. His kid brother hated her, and he liked everyone.

He parked in front of Parsons Elementary and scanned the crowded grounds for Amy. He was worried about her after yesterday and wanted to drive her home. Amy needed someone, and he wanted that someone to be him.

Chris's teacher told him that his brother had gone to Susan's for the afternoon. Keeping tabs on a nine-year-old was harder than it looked.

He blared the radio, Amy's hard rock station again, and cruised home in a state of smug delight. Two girls had made an enormous scene. Over him. People were going to be talking about it for weeks. He puffed out his chest and played the guitar solos against his steering wheel. A chick fight raised anyone's popularity, and his had reached an all-time high. Even Dominic Carter would be impressed.

What if he invited Amy to watch the eclipse with him tomorrow? There was nothing more romantic than a lunar event. Her frosty exterior would melt beneath its mystical glow.

Sixteen

CHARLES HAD PULLED a stalker-like move. He had wanted to speak with Amy in person, so he had sifted through his mother's client files and found Amy's home address with alarming ease. His mom really ought to quit using his birthday as her password.

He climbed the steps to Amy's shabby front porch and stopped to work up the courage to knock. The rickety boards vibrated beneath his feet with the thrum of thunderous hip-hop music. Shadows flitted to and fro behind thin, ratty curtains. Was Amy throwing a party? Should he ditch her history book and run? The door was thrown open before he had the chance to flee.

A miniature version of Amy stood in the doorway to a dimly lit living room where a swarm of grade school kids bobbed and weaved to Ariana Grande. The little girl was cackling at her friends. "Hi!" she said, clutching her stomach.

"Hi. Is Amy here?" His voice squeaked on the word *here*.

"Amy!" the little girl bellowed. "Your boyfriend's outside!"

Amy stalked from the kitchen, her eyes blazing with rage. Her expression shifted to confusion at the sight of him. "Charles? Why are you here?" She plucked an iPhone off the table and silenced the deafening hip-hop. A clamor of protest rose from the crowd. "There's more cookies and milk in the kitchen. Help yourselves, but don't make a mess." The herd of children stampeded from the room. The mini Amy waved goodbye and ran after her friends.

Charles handed Amy her history book. "I accidentally mixed this up with my stuff."

She flipped it open and held up the note. "You didn't read this, did you?"

He ducked his head. "I did."

Amy snapped the book shut. "Okay, thanks for bringing it by." She opened the door and motioned him out.

"What? I'm dismissed?"

"In a word, yes!"

"What are you going to do?"

"I have a few ideas," she said and shrugged. "It's my problem. I'll handle it."

"You have no idea what they're like." He clenched his jaw against a burst of frustration and worry. Alex and his gang could kill her without issue. Discounting their threats was a fatal mistake.

"I've got this. I don't need help from you." Amy threw his own stinging comment in his face with a toss of her ebony hair.

"Are you going to tell anyone?" He put a foot in the door to stop her from slamming it in his face.

"You never did."

He frowned. "Yeah, but—"

"Okay then." She raised her chin, her eyes flashing with triumph. "I have nothing more to say to you. Get out of my house."

"Why are you mad? Besides the fact that I got you mixed up and involved with the most ruthless gang in Toronto."

"Besides that? No reason. I'm not in the mood to chat, and I have a lot going on."

"Your big evening plans are to throw a party for a bunch of fourth graders?"

Amy's gaze turned steely. "Says the kid who's best friends with his mother."

He jutted his chin at her and rolled his eyes. "Great insult. Real original." His neighbor's rottweiler was his best friend, but he doubted telling Amy he was tight with a dog would reduce her ridicule. She looked like she was getting ready to slam the door, so he moved his foot out of the danger zone.

"They aren't the most ruthless gang in Toronto," Amy said and scowled, returning to their original argument. "They're a bunch of bullies. Trouble, not the end of the world."

"You're underestimating them. They'll do anything to settle the score. These guys are sick, Amy. Alex's favorite game is exploiting others' weaknesses. They'll hurt you, and they'll have fun doing it."

"Oh no," she said in a mocking tone. "I'm scared now."

"Has anything weird happened to you lately?" Alex's vendettas never developed this fast. Amy had to have done something to exacerbate his rage.

"Yeah. This weird kid from my class followed me home and refused to leave."

"I mean has anything weird happened that was unexplained or dangerous?"

Her expression grew serious. "I got locked inside the walk-in freezer at work."

Charles shivered. "What? When? How did that happen?"

"Monday evening. I was grabbing some fries and the door slammed shut. It was no big deal. Someone's idea of a joke."

"No big deal? People don't just get locked in freezers. How long were you stuck in there? How did you get out?"

"A while, maybe an hour. My co-worker Katie found me after we closed."

He stared at her, mouth agape. "Did you go to the hospital?"

"No. What's with all the questions? You trying to tell me it wasn't an accident?"

"The more 'accidents' you avoid, the worse they'll get," he muttered darkly. "Don't you think a life-threatening calamity that happened the exact same day you stood up for me is a tiny bit suspicious?"

Amy tugged at a lock of her hair. "It was a joke. You need to lighten up. This is high school, not *How to Get Away with Murder*."

"Amy, you have to listen." He reached for her hand. She snatched it away and plucked at her long sleeve. A flicker of unease flashed in her misty gray eyes. He blinked, and it was gone.

"I have a dozen nine-year-olds in my kitchen. I have to go." She slammed the door in his face.

Charles kicked the wall. No one ever listened to him.

"Banks?"

His heart leapt into his throat. Assassin's Honor was here for Amy. He started with fright, teetered precariously on one foot, lost his balance, and toppled backward into Amy's hedge.

"Why is it whenever I see you, you're either about to get punched by a tiny chick or stuck upside down in her hedge?"

Charles struggled to his feet. Several strawberry blond tufts parted company with his scalp as he feverishly brushed shrubbery from his hair.

"What are you doing here?" Zack chuckled. He was standing on Amy's front steps, his blue eyes pools of mirth.

Charles scowled. "Why does everyone keep asking me that?"

"Maybe it's because you keep getting stuck in hedges."

"Very funny." Charles kicked a pebble underneath Amy's porch. Zack and Peter had once found him beat up and bleeding behind Peter's house in the second grade. Charles had sheltered beneath the Jenkins's hedge to try to get away from Alex and had been in too much pain to hobble home on his own. Zack and Peter had been nice about it in the moment and walked him to his street. This was years before Zack became a popular ass and Peter joined the gang hellbent on destroying Charles's life.

"No, seriously, why are you here? How do you know Amy?" Zack strode down her steps to join him in the front yard.

"Our moms know each other." Charles provided the simplest explanation possible and marched down Amy's drive with what was left of his dignity.

"Ah." Zack fell into step beside him.

"How do you know her?" Zack had to be interested in Amy if he was making this much of an effort to talk to him. Charles hadn't had this long a chat with a classmate since the sixth grade.

Zack raked a hand through his messy red hair. "It's complicated. Her little sister is friends with my brother, she's a server at the restaurant where my team goes to celebrate, and after school yesterday, I caught some guys about to beat her up." He clenched his jaw. "It was pathetically unfair, three on one."

Charles halted midstride and stared, horrorstruck, at Zack. The threats were spiraling out of control.

"Hey. Bro. Why you turning white? You guys aren't dating, are you?"

"No. It's just ..." He waved his hands in a feeble let-it-go gesture.

"Just ...

"It's my fault, okay? What's going to happen to Amy, it's all my fault."

"What does this have to do with you?"

"She stopped those guys from beating me up," he blurted, his cheeks burning with shame. He waited for the staring, the mocking laughter, all the usual crap.

Zack shocked him by taking it in stride. "How did she stop those guys from beating you up? She's even smaller than you. Sorry, no offense."

"She said she was going to call nine-one-one and get them arrested for violence on city property."

"You're kidding." Zack snorted. "They bought that?"

Charles shrugged. "They're even dumber than they look. But now …"

"Hold on." Zack held up a hand. "You said something was going to happen to Amy. It already happened. I stopped it."

"Of course!" Charles snapped his fingers. "You're the boyfriend!"

"What are you talking about? What's going to happen to her?"

"Chill for a second." Charles launched into the story before Zack could interrupt. He recounted everything from Monday's near beating to the note in Amy's book.

"Let me see it," Zack demanded the moment he had finished.

"I can't show it to you."

"Why the hell not?" His voice was low and threaded with anger.

Charles pressed his lips together and eyed him uneasily. Was Zack about to join the other jocks in beating him to a pulp? "I can't show it to you because I already gave it back to Amy. That's why I came here tonight." Zack turned on his heel and sprinted back toward Amy's house. "Where you going?"

"To get that note!"

"Good luck," Charles muttered.

Seventeen

ALEX TOOK A deep breath and dove into the cool, clear water. The luxurious indoor pool was the one good thing about inheriting his dead parents' mansion. The vast expanse of tranquil blue calmed him like nothing else. Swimming was a rhythmic release of pent-up energy and a mental stimulus that organized his thoughts.

The encounter with Charles had put Alex on edge. Mages had creative ways of tipping the odds in their favor, and he had too much at stake to risk Charles screwing things up. He decided the mage's fate in less time than it took to blink. Taking him out was the safest path forward.

"Alex!" A muffled shout shattered the peace.

He choked on a mouthful of chlorinated water that burned his nostrils and made him gag. He surfaced with an explosive splash and searched for the person who had dared to disturb him. If his sister had followed him down here, she'd miss more than a few meals.

"Behind you," a girl said and giggled.

Alex whirled around and stared in shocked contempt at the raven-haired beauty standing near the deep end. She resembled a fairy with her petite features and wide-eyed, falsely innocent gaze. He had never met this girl before but knew exactly who she was. Her aura of darkness screamed her identity to the world. Darkness was the physical source of every Dark's powers, and she controlled it with an iron fist. She even wrapped herself in it like a pretentious royal cloak.

This teenager, the supposed queen of all Darks, was an ancient and powerful wolf. She was the very first Dark to permanently escape hell, making the throne hers by default. Though her wolves revered her, most other Dark kingdoms did not. Why let her lead simply because she clawed her way up first? Many whispered she was clinically insane and unfit to rule, yet no one had managed to seize her throne. Not yet, anyway.

Alex pierced her with an icy glare. "What the hell are you doing here? Go back where you belong, you flea-bitten fur bag!"

"Is that any way to address your leader?" She gave him a wounded look from beneath her thick, dark lashes. He scrunched up his face. No one had mentioned she was such a talented actress.

He curled his lip and repeated his question. "I have no time for your games. What are you doing here?"

She twirled a lock of hair around her index finger. "Who said anything about games? I'm simply here to talk."

"You've traveled an awfully long way to speak with me." The queen's castle was in Vancouver. Had she come clear across the country just to address him? Warning bells rang in his ears. Darks lost their grip on reality as they grew more in tune with the darkness, and she was the embodiment of Darkness itself. She was one hundred percent insane, and she wielded a massive amount of power. Unease pricked his skin.

"Don't even think about doing what you're thinking," she ordered, failing to grasp how tangled her words were.

He pressed his lips together in a disconcerted frown. "How the hell do you know what I'm thinking?" He was used to being the only one in the room with mind-reading powers. The idea of her snooping around in his head made his gut clench with tension. He focused all his energy on ripping her free of his mind.

"Alex, try to understand. Whenever you use the darkness, you just reflect the abilities I bestow upon you. You are unable to hurt me with my own power."

Boiling hot rage surged through his veins. "Tell me what you want so I can laugh in your face and do the exact opposite. You will never control me, you senile old bitch!" Alex held his breath and braced himself for an explosive queenly meltdown. Maybe he had gone too far. Maybe he hadn't gone far enough. How far was it safe to push her?

She ignored his outburst entirely. "This plan of yours, don't do it. You underestimate the Blood Moon's power. *It* strives to control you, not I. Do you truly wish for that fate? The Blood Moon is a fickle master to serve. I expected you to have learned that much by now." Her penetrating sapphire gaze bored relentlessly into his soul.

Pain lanced through him like the briefest of lightning strikes. He shot a volley of excuses at her to mask his emotion. His best defense was a brilliant offense. "I serve no one. The decisions I make are my own. Besides, why should they matter to you? You love chaos. The Blood Moon's curse is probably something of your invention. One more desperate attempt to maintain your hold on the minds of all Darks."

"You're full of accusations today." Her nostrils flared. At last he had hit a nerve. "Has it never occurred to you that there are other evil forces out there besides you and I? That curse is the devil's work."

"So what? We were created to serve him anyway."

"Wrong!" Her sapphire eyes blazed with rage and glowed bloodred for an instant. "You serve me. *Only* me. Satan has no power over us except that which we allow him. Is that what you want? To fall for his traps? If you do it will cost you."

"Oh really? Well, guess what? I have nothing left to lose." A familiar stab of agony pierced his heart. "What do I have to fear from a hundred-year-old, half-crazed Dark with an overblown ego? You're only saying this to frighten me into submission. That's all your power relies on, fear. I am not afraid of you!"

Her eyes narrowed into furious slits. "Oh, no, Alex, you need not fear me. If you continue on your current course, it will be the Blood Moon's fury you shall face."

He snorted. Did she have any idea how demented she sounded? Queen of the Darks? Try Queen of the Crazies. He opened his mouth to make a snarky retort, but she vanished before he so much as took a breath.

Fury surged deep within him, and a tidal wave of pool water crashed over the place where she had stood. He took a deep, steadying breath. He refused to acknowledge how much their meeting had rattled him. A frosty flood of calm spread from his heart and through his veins. He would simply have to put his plan into motion before she had time to stop him. The note had only been the beginning. In twenty-four hours, Amy would be dead.

He toweled off, changed into his spare clothes, and checked his phone for messages. A text from Chelsea caught his eye. *Baby,*

I know all about Amy's weaknesses and would love to help you take her down. I beg of you, let me prove my loyalty.

His lips curled into a smirk. Chelsea's desperation to prove herself reminded him of a lapdog. No, that was insulting to the dog. He doubted her usefulness but was curious what she had to offer. He slipped into her mind. She sensed his presence and opened her thoughts to him. He sucked in a breath as her knowledge sank in. *Good work, baby.* He caressed her mind. She shivered with pleasure. He broke the link, his lips parting in a feral grin. This was beyond perfect. When he was finished, Amy would wish she were dead.

He texted Nathan, eager to put his plan into motion. *Isn't it time we had a gang meeting?*

Alex's phone vibrated within seconds. Nathan had sent a group text to the members of Assassin's Honor. *Gang meeting at Jenkins's house. 6:00 sharp.*

Already there. See you in 20 ;) Ash replied.

His response made Alex laugh. Nathan kept forgetting that Ash lived with Peter. Ash's parents had kicked him out after finding his stash of heroin, and Peter had been stuck with him ever since.

Peter lived in a shabby neighborhood, the sort women tried to avoid walking alone in at night. His house was a square, two-story structure, a plain, dilapidated box with no creativity or charm.

Alex sauntered through the door without knocking and glanced around the messy living room in distaste. Beer bottles and empty soda cans covered the coffee table, and a stack of empty pizza boxes rested on the chipped tile floor. The room had an overwhelming aroma of weed and unwashed socks.

Peter lounged on a stained cerulean sofa, watching his favorite TV show, *The Walking Dead.* Ash sat in a nearby armchair, busy sorting through several tiny bags of dark powder. Alex made a face. He hated drugs. They clouded the mind and made controlling the addict near impossible. Sifting through a druggy's thoughts was like drowning in a murky whirlpool.

Ash's girlfriend, Lara Tzadik, was glaring daggers at Alex from where she perched on Ash's armrest. She was a cat Dark with distinct feline characteristics even in her human form. Lara was tall and slim with sleek blonde hair and piercing jade green eyes. She sat with her slender legs curled beneath her as she leaned seductively into Ash.

"Have a nice swim?" she asked with mock politeness. He flicked water droplets from his hair. She flapped her hands and screwed up her face. "Ew! Get away. You're dripping everywhere!" Lara had an irrational aversion to water. Typical cat. He strolled into the kitchen to raid Peter's fridge.

Wrappers littered the counter, the sink was overflowing with dirty dishes, and the trash can by the door was oozing brown liquid. He grimaced in disgust. These people were slobs.

"What are you and Nathan up to?" Lara had followed him into the kitchen like an obsessed feline fangirl.

"Who says we're up to anything?" Why was everyone questioning him today?

"Oh, please. Don't play dumb." She fastened her gaze to his. "Ash told me all about that note of yours."

Alex groaned. Ash couldn't keep a secret if his life depended upon it. "You're as irritating as that mangy mutt," he grumbled under his breath.

Lara perked up. "Mangy mutt?"

He winced. He had forgotten about her heightened cat hearing. "None of your business."

"God, Alex, you're getting grumpier by the day." She rested her hands on the counter and gazed at him with a fake look of concern. "Are you PMSing?"

"Piss off, Lara. I'm sure you and Ash have better things to do."

"Better than annoying you? Never." She studied his face. He found it hard to look away from her brilliant, jade green gaze. Alex turned his back on her and pretended to examine the sticky countertop. "What are you hiding? You look freaked, and you mentioned a dog. I only know of one mutt who scares you this much."

He turned on the tap and filled a glass with water. He refused to discuss the queen's visit with Lara. She'd call him weak and pathetic and shame him for showing fear.

Lara tugged on his sleeve. "What did she say to you? Whatever it was, I hope you heed her advice."

"You support her?" he roared, forgetting his decision to avoid the subject. "After all the stupid things she's done, you're going to roll over and submit to her will?"

"The Dark is a powerful enemy. It's easier to follow her than oppose her." The Queen of the Darks had nicknamed herself The Dark as if she embodied their entire race. She was as arrogant as she was crazy.

Anger scorched through him like an out-of-control forest fire. He slammed his glass onto the counter. It shattered in his hand and soaked his shirt. Superior strength sometimes sucked. Lara bit back a giggle. He fixed her with a burning glare. "You're pathetic for serving her. You fear a crazy lunatic. She's a control freak, that's all. She wants everything to center around her and as soon as it doesn't, she tries to steal the limelight. Well, she has never scared me, and she sure as hell won't stop me. I bow down to no one, especially the Queen!"

Lara took a hasty step away and bumped into the fridge. "Listen, Alex, I obey her because I've seen what happens to the people who disobey. I'll stop arguing with you, but don't expect me to stick around and clean up the mess you are making."

"I never asked you to."

"She destroyed my family," Lara whispered, her lower lip trembling with the force of her grief. "She and her wolves slaughtered them all. I watched her kill them." A tear rolled down her cheek, leaving a glistening streak across her alabaster skin. "She found me hiding after the massacre. I was the last one left, only six years old. The rest of my people had surrendered or been killed. She thought about killing me too. But in the end, she let me live. Do you have any idea how awful it feels to have your opponent turn their back on you? As if you're too pathetic and worthless to even waste their time on?"

He beat back a twinge of sympathy with years of practiced callousness. "Did I ask for your life story? If your family was defeated by a pack of dimwitted dogs, they deserved to die."

"Alex, please." Lara rushed forward and grasped his arm. She held him tight, forcing him to meet her mesmerizing green gaze. Fear swam in her eyes. "If you have any self-preservation at all, you will not cross her."

He blinked at her in confusion, uncharacteristically lost for words. He had expected her wrath, her ridicule, or at the very least, a cold shoulder. He had never expected her to plead with him as if she truly cared what became of him. He shrugged her off and headed back into the living room. Nathan had arrived. They were ready to begin.

"Amy's not taking our threats seriously," Nathan said as Alex sat on the sofa across from him.

"That's why we're kicking things up a notch." He smirked.

Nathan smiled, twisting the ugly scar on his face. Alex had briefed him on the plan through a mind link, a useful darkness power that allowed him to implant his own thoughts and schemes into other people's heads. The stupid human believed Alex's plan was his own idea. He smiled. Let Nathan think what he liked. He was going to take the fall for anything he screwed up. "We take her tomorrow." Nathan nodded.

Ash grinned with mindless eagerness. Peter shifted in his seat, his green eyes flicking from face to face. He was looking for support and finding none. Alex speared him with a narrow look. Peter had better not mess this up. He had always been the most reluctant of the group because he was there against his will. Peter's father had founded Assassin's Honor when he was in high school and had grown the gang into an infamous arms dealing business. As Peter was his only son, Mr. Jenkins expected him to follow in his footsteps. Forcing Peter to join the junior division of Assassin's Honor had accomplished nothing except to plant an enormous thorn in Alex's side. His shark's grin widened. He had his own special plans for Peter.

Eighteen

AMY CLENCHED HER fists so hard her nails broke the skin. Charles was wrong. He had to be wrong, because if he was right— The doorbell chimed, and Amy leapt out of her skin. She shook herself and wrenched it open. Mrs. Matthews stood smiling on her doorstep.

"Sarah, your mom's here!" Amy called over her shoulder. Relief swept through her at having Susan's party over with. Hosting a gathering of fourth graders at a house targeted by a gang was a recipe for disaster.

Zack was the last to arrive. She opened the door and bit back a string of grumbling complaints about him having nothing better to do than inconvenience her. "Hey. Chris will be ready in a minute."

"You got—the note—Banks said," Zack spluttered. She took in his red face and rigid expression and slammed her door for the second time that evening. "Amy, open up!"

She took a deep breath and let him in. "I don't want to talk about it, okay?" She turned toward the kitchen. Zack grasped her arm. "Hey!" She tensed at his touch.

"Where is it?"

She huffed out a breath. This was like a badly rehearsed robbery. "You people are obsessed." She yanked the crumpled piece of paper from her pocket and slapped it into his palm.

His expression darkened as he read. "How dare they! Who do they think they are? Why aren't you freaking out?"

"Been there, done that."

He raked his gaze over her face. "When did you get this?"

"It was in my locker before homeroom."

His expression softened. "Is that why you were late?"

He genuinely cared? Warmth spread from her heart and trickled through her veins. "It wasn't the best start to my day," she said.

"You and Sue could stay with us for a while." Zack gave her a tentative smile. Sparks of heat zipped between them.

Amy blinked, unease and affection twisting together in her gut. This took helping her to a whole new level. Why was he offering? Why was she tempted to accept? "Your parents would hate that idea. Not to mention your girlfriend."

"My parents aren't even in the country right now. No one will care. Chris and Sue will love it."

Prickles of annoyance crept up her spine. Why was he acting as if she had already agreed to stay with him? She erected a swift emotional boundary to safeguard her heart. "Thanks, but no thanks." She had learned the hard way to rely on no one but herself.

His expression hardened. "What's your plan, then?"

Amy took a deep breath and let it out slowly. "Zack, I appreciate your concern, I really do. But this is on me, okay? Trust me, I know what I'm doing. I was hanging out with gangsters while you were busy playing Farmville."

"You were in a gang?" Skepticism laced his tone.

She laughed. "Of course not. I dated a few guys who were."

His mouth twitched. "You dated gangsters in middle school? What were their crimes? Did they rip off candy stores for you?"

"One was a small-time drug dealer, but that's just my point! It's the same difference, whether we're talking middle school drug dealers or high school gangster wannabes. They walk around in groups, acting all macho and tough with nothing but their egos to back them up. These guys live for intimidation. Hiding from them just lets them know they're getting to you."

Zack gave up and took Chris home. Amy made a late dinner of mac and cheese and spent the evening watching ancient reruns of *Buffy the Vampire Slayer* with Susan. She drowned her worries with innumerable mugs of hot chocolate and firmly steered her thoughts clear of Assassin's Honor. Focusing on the kickass teen vampire slayer and the bowl of buttery popcorn at her elbow was better than spending the evening in a state of debilitating panic. But try as she might to keep calm, the walls closed tighter around her with every bit of daylight that leeched from the darkening sky. Night had always brought a certain dread to Amy's heart. Something about being unconscious for the darkest hours of the day made her nervous. Now, more than ever, she wished she were able to sleep with one eye open.

Distant ringing clashed with a fight scene. She dug her mother's cell phone from between the couch cushions and checked the caller ID. It was their landlord, a compassionate soul with a heart of gold. She jabbed the accept icon. "Hello, Mr. Davis."

"Hello," he replied, exhaustion thick in his voice. "That you, Amy?"

"It is." She smiled affectionately. Mr. Davis was a kind man, too kind for real estate. They were three months behind on their payments, yet he was still patient with her mother. Mrs. Evans had gotten him to lower their already reasonable rent in exchange for passing on routine upkeep and maintenance.

Mr. Davis cleared his throat. "Is your mother there?"

"Sorry, she must have left early for work. I haven't seen her all afternoon." Unease knotted in her stomach. How had her mom forgotten her phone? And why had she left so early?

"Okay, she's at work." Skepticism saturated his words. "Will you pass along a message?"

"Of course." Amy opened a note on her iPhone.

"Please tell her this is your thirty-day eviction notice."

Her heart took a sickening nosedive into her shoes. She stared at the phone in her lap, then at the one in her hand. "W-why?"

"She missed the rent deadline again. I am truly sorry, Amy. I can't afford tenants who are unable to make their payments."

Her mouth felt impossibly dry. She cleared her throat and choked out words. "Of course. I, I understand." Her thoughts tumbled over one another. What would she do now? Where would they go? The streets? A homeless shelter? Fists of fear clenched her insides. They were going to transfer Susan into foster care.

"Do you have any relatives who might help you?" Mr. Davis was grasping at straws, giving her every chance to save their home.

She considered Justin, across the country in Vancouver. He might be able to support Susan if he worked two jobs while going to school. Susan would have to leave her new friends behind, but at least she would escape the foster care system.

Amy spoke, her words coming out dull after a painfully long silence. "No one can help with the rent." The image of a bulging, cream-colored envelope skittered across her mind. Hope raised her heart back to its proper place in her chest. "I swear Mom withdrew the money. Maybe she forgot to bring it to you. Will you stay on the line while I check?"

"Absolutely," he answered on a relieved sigh.

She muted the call and raced up the stairs two at a time. Her mom had withdrawn the money, she was certain of it. There had been an envelope of cash in her top dresser drawer when Amy had put laundry away a few days ago. Rex dumping her had thrown her into a tailspin, causing the rent to slip her mind. It was lying there, ready for the taking, buried beneath a pile of her mother's ankle socks.

She yanked open her mother's dresser drawer and riffled through her piles of folded clothes. She searched the drawer three times before admitting the money wasn't there. Dread tugged at her heart, even as hope urged her onward. She repeated the process with each drawer of her mother's dresser, flinging garments over her shoulder as she methodically trashed the room. When the drawers were bare and she had failed to find a single bill, she tore them from the dresser itself on the off chance the money had fallen behind them. She only stopped her frantic flinging when faced with a hollow, empty wooden shell.

Amy stood frozen in the center of her mother's ransacked bedroom and bit back a sob of annihilated defeat. The money had been there two days ago. Where had it gone? Her gaze fell upon a sweat-stained, canary yellow shirt. "Rex Kastel!" she roared. He must have swiped the cash the night he dumped her mother. Her anger melted into nothing, and despair slithered into the hollow cavern in her chest. They were never going to see that money again.

She grabbed her mother's phone and unmuted the call. "Hey, Mr. Davis, you still there?" Her voice came out pinched and raw.

"You didn't find the money." His words were heavy with regret.

"Yeah, sorry to keep you waiting. I'll tell Mom about the eviction notice." She ended the call before he could apologize again. It wasn't his fault the world sucked.

Notifications on the lock screen caught her eye, a missed call and voicemail from her mother's work. She listened to the message with a tightness in her chest that made it hard to breathe. It was there, perched atop a pile of her mother's crumpled clothes, that her last shred of hope slipped away. Her mom had been fired. She was late for the fourth time that week, and she had missed three full shifts that month alone. It was a wonder they hadn't let her go sooner.

A floorboard creaked. Susan was hovering in the hall, her face pinched with worry. "I heard you yelling. What'd Rex do now?"

"Nothing," Amy lied. "I'll sort it out, don't worry." She wanted to curl into the fetal position and die. Instead, she tucked Susan into bed and sat with her sister until she fell asleep.

Amy wandered through their tiny house, imagining the walls bare, the rooms empty. She had never liked the place much, but it had sheltered her and Susan for two mediocre years.

She sat in the kitchen to think through her options with a mug of cream earl grey tea. If she dropped out of school and worked full-time? No. Susan needed an adult guardian. If she and Susan moved to Vancouver to be with Justin, Amy dropped out of school, and worked full-time? That could work. But what about their mom? She and Justin couldn't support her in addition to Susan, and her drinking created instability that social workers frowned upon. She set her jaw and squared her shoulders. If the choice was between her mom or Susan, she'd choose Susan every time.

With that decided, Amy moved on to more immediate problems—the gang of lunatics intent on killing her dead. She marched up the stairs to her bedroom, locked the door, and stood on tiptoe to reach her closet's top shelf. She pushed aside some ratty linen sheets and removed her dad's pistol, the only thing he had left behind when he ditched. Amy loaded it with a grim nod and tucked it deep into her backpack. Assassin's Honor had another think coming if they thought she was going down without a fight.

Amy had a restless sleep. Her dreams were haunted by piles of bills and tiny paychecks, when they ought to have centered around hulking gangsters in black leather jackets. Her mother returned home around three in the morning, and Amy slept easier after that. At least she was okay. Useless and self-absorbed, but okay.

Amy woke Susan twenty minutes ahead of schedule. They caught the early bus to avoid a surprise meeting with Assassin's Honor. She flopped into a window seat and rested her forehead against the cool glass pane. Charles's dire warnings ran through her head for the billionth time, and the pistol tucked safely in her pack was all that kept her calm. It had to put an end to the gang's antagonism. No sane person picked a fight with the crazy chick who brought a gun to school.

The bus squealed to a stop to let some more kids on, a tall, shady-looking guy among them. A jolt of electric fear nearly stopped her heart. The shady guy was the member of Assassin's Honor who had held her arms behind her back on Wednesday. She thought his name was Alex. He headed for the back of the bus, passing within inches of her and Susan. She risked a glance over her shoulder and met his piercing blue eyes.

Her stomach lurched and churned like it had been stuffed with wriggling snakes. She darted her gaze away and struggled to calm her racing pulse. Alex couldn't do anything on a crowded bus. Showing up out of the blue was a scare tactic, nothing more. Still, she had woken up early to avoid this very thing. How had he known where to find her?

Susan and Amy got off at Parsons Elementary. She rushed her sister to class and warily crossed the street to the high school. Alex was waiting near the entrance, his muscled arms crossed over his chest and his blue eyes glinting like chips of ice. She approached him with her heart pounding in her ears and every muscle tensed to run. Why had she stuck her pistol in her backpack? What lunatic part of her brain had imagined that was a good idea? She needed to clutch the pistol in her pocketed fist and be ready to defend herself if he made an aggressive move. But with her weapon buried beneath her school supplies and zipped securely within the bookbag on her back, it might as well be collecting dust on the top shelf of her closet for all the good it would do.

She drew level with Alex and held his penetrating gaze. They stood like that for a long, potent moment, each of them sizing the other up with mingled wariness and disdain. It took everything she had to stride past him into the school. His eyes bored into her back, but she resisted the temptation to glance over her shoulder. She would not give him the satisfaction. She marched forward on jelly legs, bracing herself for a blow with every shaky step she took. An attack never came. Alex's goal had been psychological warfare, and he had achieved that simply by standing still. Amy sped to her locker and hid behind its metal door. She dug her hand into her backpack's inside pocket and slipped the pistol into her purse. A forceful breath escaped her lips, a visceral reaction to surviving the encounter.

"Hey."

"Ouch!" she squeaked as she knocked a thesaurus onto her shoes. She looked up and nodded to Zack's blond football friend.

His eyes widened at the sight of her. "Wow! You look terrible. Sleep through your alarm again?"

Why was he keeping track of her life? "Nope, didn't sleep much at all." She brushed a tangled lock of hair out of her face.

In sharp contrast to her disheveled appearance, Zack's friend had perfectly styled blond hair and dazzling, china blue eyes. He magnetically attracted girls, laying the charm on thick and breaking hearts with a single pretty-boy smile.

Locker Buddy's girlfriend was prancing straight toward them. Amy gazed heavenward. When had her locker become the new cool kid hangout?

"Hi, Amy!" Jessie flashed her that kind, genuine smile she had. "Rough morning?"

Amy frowned. Was that a dig? "Yeah," she mumbled. "Have to get to homeroom." She had the sinking suspicion Jessie's dad was her landlord. They had the same last name, and they both came from money. They would have a juicy something to discuss at the dinner table when she fled Toronto in disgrace.

"Amy, wait." Jessie grabbed her arm before she could escape. "Are you going out with Zack? Because it's cool with me if you are. Chelsea is a total bitch. I'm super sorry for the way she treated you yesterday. She's awful, mean and selfish to the point of narcissism. That's why Zack dumped her." Amy stared at Jessie. Information overload. "Sorry, I didn't mean to babble. Sometimes I do that. I'm going to stop now." Jessie clamped her mouth shut.

A loaded silence followed her words. Amy shifted from foot to foot. "They broke up? When?"

Jessie toyed with a lock of her auburn hair. "Yesterday afternoon. Right after you left."

"You've got to be kidding me!" Amy wailed.

"Don't worry. No one thinks it was your fault. Chelsea made a huge, dramatic scene. Pretty much threw a temper tantrum in the middle of school. It must have been awful for Zack."

"Why are you cool with this? Aren't you guys best friends?"

Jessie's pretty smile dimmed. "Not anymore." She rushed on after an uncomfortable beat. "I hear Zack was over at your house last night."

Amy felt her mouth part. Rumors spread like wildfire. Did cheer squad girls know everything? Was the whole school spying on her? She pictured gossip-obsessed cheerleaders peering through her living room windows in the dead of night and fought an insane fit of giggles.

Zack's friend blinked in surprise. "Zack went to your place? He told me he had to scoop Chris from a friend's."

"Yes." Amy threw up her hands. "Chris is friends with my sister, Susan."

"Oh." Jessie face-palmed, giggling. "Now it makes sense."

"And we're not dating, I swear!"

"Okay, but he's been talking about you a lot lately. It's Amy this and Amy that. We're loving teasing him about it because he makes fun of us for the same behavior."

Amy's heart soared. Zack had ditched his annoying-as-hell girlfriend and might have a thing for her? She was dying to quiz Jessie but didn't want Zack's best friend passing her interest along.

The bell rang. "Want to head to class with me, Amy?" Zack's friend asked with an easy smile.

Sitting with him would make her less of a target and distract her from her financial woes. "Sure." The word popped from her mouth before she had a chance to consider Jessie. What if this cheerleader freaked like Chelsea had?

"See you in chemistry!" Jessie flashed a grin over her shoulder. Amy smiled. This girl had a heart of gold.

She waved goodbye and fell into step with Zack's friend. "You do realize I don't even know your name."

"Really? I never told you?" The corners of his eyes crinkled.

"Nope." She smirked. "I know you only as Locker Buddy."

"It's Ken," he said and chuckled. "No wonder you acted weird whenever I said hello."

They chatted all the way to homeroom and sat together by the window. Amy was surprised to find herself enjoying Ken's company. He was easygoing and hilarious.

"Wonder where Zack is," Ken whispered. "He's usually here by now."

The mention of Zack Donnellson was a bucket of freezing water thrown onto the tentative embers of her mildly good mood. What if he had tried to confront Assassin's Honor on his own? Her gut clenched at the thought. Surely he wasn't that stupid. Or was he?

Nineteen

ZACK WOKE EARLY Friday morning with a gnawing feeling of unease in the pit of his stomach. Assassin's Honor had it out for Amy, and they were not going to leave her alone until and unless the score had been settled. Worry niggled at the back of his mind until sleep became impossible. He dressed quickly and went to wake his brother.

Chris was grumpy at being dragged out of bed before his alarm. Zack wound up telling him about ending it with Chelsea and that made him so happy, he agreed to leave early.

They drove to Amy's and found her house silent, the blinds shut and the lights off. "You sure you have the time right?" Zack anxiously checked his watch.

Chris nodded. "Sue said they catch the seven fifty bus."

Amy's front door opened, and a middle-aged woman stumbled out onto the porch. She looked like a walking skeleton, pale and scarily thin with wispy salt-and-pepper hair and tired cloud gray eyes. Her sweatpants were old and faded with an obvious rip near the knee, and a faint brown stain ran the length of her baggy T-shirt. A light breeze carried cigarette smoke toward Zack's car as the woman swigged straight from a wine bottle.

Zack frowned. "Who is that?"

"Susan's mom." Chris goggled at her.

Zack poked him in the shoulder. "Quit staring or she'll notice us."

"Too late. She's already coming over."

Zack swore and jammed his keys into the ignition. The last thing he wanted was a parental chat.

The lady staggered to his car and tapped on the driver's side window.

"We're in trouble now." Chris sank lower in his seat.

"You're acting like we're being busted by the cops." Zack snickered.

"I'd rather the cops."

Zack rolled his eyes and lowered his window. Mrs. Evans removed a cigarette from between her colorless lips. "Are you boys lost?"

He raised his eyebrows. Why was Amy's mother talking to them as if they were five? He shifted in his seat. "Uh, no, we're waiting for someone."

Mrs. Evans squinted through the window. "Hey, I know you from somewhere."

Chris squirmed in his seat and nodded. "I'm Susan's friend."

"That's right." She tapped her fingers against her wine bottle. "Kyle, is it?"

"Chris," he corrected, his cheeks turning red.

"Of course, dear. And who are you?" She pointed a finger at Zack, her pale hand shaking with the effort.

"Older brother." He suppressed a stab of pity. What had she been through to end up like this, alone and frail and drinking at 8 A.M.?

Mrs. Evans bobbed her head to a song no one else could hear. "Are you waiting for Susan? She and Amy already left."

"They did? Where did they go?"

"School, I think." Mrs. Evans tottered back to her porch.

"Okay, we'll be on our way then." Zack watched to make sure she reached her door without falling. He started his car and reversed out of Amy's driveway. What had he gotten himself into with this girl? Every time he talked to her or anyone who knew her, he uncovered more and more facets of her complicated life. And every time he tried to help her, she either wound up hating him or pulled a disappearing act.

A disturbing thought crept into his mind. What if Assassin's Honor had visited Amy's house last night, beat her senseless, and left her unconscious on the bathroom floor? Would her alcoholic mother even notice? He took a deep breath and tried to ignore his overactive imagination. Amy had to be at school. In homeroom. With Assassin's Honor. He pressed down on the gas.

"Phew." Chris relaxed after Amy's street was a good two minutes behind them.

"What's wrong with her?" Zack drummed his fingers against the steering wheel and cursed the morning traffic. He was never going to make it to class on time.

"No clue. Susan doesn't talk about her much. She says her mom's sick a lot."

Zack made a derisive noise in his throat. "Try hung over a lot. You think she's mental? Explains Amy and Sue."

Chris scowled. "That's not funny."

"Chill out, bro."

Chris sat in stony silence for the rest of the ride. Zack blasted the radio in an effort to ignore his sour looks. When had he stopped seeing the world the way his little brother did? He struggled to recall the last time he had believed the best of someone. Had high school ruined the illusion? Was it a natural part of growing up, or was he, Zack, becoming brainwashed and bitter?

The school was quiet, the halls deserted. He peeked around the door to Mr. Fields's classroom and checked the back row for Amy. Icicles of dread slid down his spine. She wasn't there. Alex was lounging in her seat. His stomach lurched, and his heart pounded at twice its normal speed. He scanned the rest of the room and found her sitting with Ken. A wave of relief threatened to sweep him away. Amy had harnessed him to an endless emotional roller coaster. He snuck into class and searched for an empty seat.

"Mr. Donnellson." Mr. Fields barked his name like the crack of a whip. "I don't see a hall pass. That'll be detention, yet again."

"But sir." Zack raised his hands in protest.

Mr. Fields clenched his jaw, making his square, sallow face resemble a cube with a nose. "No buts. Sit down and shut up."

Zack hesitated. He had to drive Amy home or she'd be a walking target.

Mr. Fields scowled at him over the top of his horn-rimmed spectacles. "Mr. Donnellson, do you wish to teach this class?"

"No sir."

"Will you take a seat and allow me to teach this class?"

Three straight years of loathing bubbled over and spilled into his insolent tone. "There's nowhere to sit."

His teacher's eyes narrowed into furious hazel slits. "Enough with the disrespect. Detention on Monday. And there's a seat free next to Mr. Johnson."

Zack gritted his teeth. He had to sit with Assassin's Honor? He stomped to the seat and scowled at the clock. It was only eight forty-five, and he already hated his life.

He glanced at Amy and caught her looking at him. She averted her gaze but her eyes darted back to him a few seconds later. He winked at her. She grimaced. Zack smiled. This girl was adorable, but the way she avoided people made him nervous. If Assassin's Honor caught her alone, they could easily make good on their threats. He was grateful to Ken for sitting with her.

He joined them after class. Amy was cramming books into her bag with frantic, manic urgency, while Ken smiled goofily at all the girls as they passed. The pair made seriously unlikely friends.

Ken greeted him with a cheerful slap on the back. "Hey man. How's it hanging?"

"Super," he said and sighed, surveying Amy with concern. There were dark circles under her eyes, her silky hair was in a hopeless tangle, and her clothes were wrinkled as if she had slept in them. Her soft gray eyes had an eerie, haunted look. "You okay?" he asked with tentative concern. He wanted to touch her arm but doubted she'd welcome the comforting gesture.

"Sure." She shrugged placidly. "It's another wonderful morning at THS." Chelsea pushed past them on her way out the door. Amy glanced between her and Zack. "So, I'm off." She made a hasty escape.

Ash broke away from his friends and followed her. Zack cursed under his breath. How was he going to keep her away from them? He and Amy had entirely different schedules.

"Wonder what's up with her?" Ken mused as he and Zack ambled down the hall together. "She said she was up late studying. Usually she ignores me. Except this morning …"

A strange buzzing filled Zack's ears. Nathan and his friends knew he had detention after school. His head spun with the implications of what that meant. They were going to get their revenge that afternoon, while he, Zack, was conveniently out of the way.

Twenty

"CHARLES!" SOMEONE BELLOWED from halfway down the hall. "Wait up!"

Charles jumped and lost his grip on his ever-present stack of books. A flurry of loose papers fluttered to the floor around him as he scrambled to retrieve his stuff.

Zack emerged, smirking, from a throng of snickering students. "What'd I tell you? Every time."

"Shut up." Charles clenched his jaw.

Zack handed him a few papers. "I've got detention this afternoon."

"I know. I was there."

"You're in my homeroom too?"

Charles shut his eyes, praying for patience. "So what if you have detention?"

"So." Zack shifted from foot to foot. "Something might happen."

"Something might happen to Amy, you mean."

"Exactly."

Charles raised his eyebrows. "Have you met Assassin's Honor? What do you expect me to do about them?"

Zack clenched his fists. "So you're going to sit by and do nothing? After she stood up for you, you won't even think twice about doing the same for her? You're pathetic." He thrust the last few books into Charles's chest and stormed away. "No wonder everyone thinks you're a loser. It's 'cause you are!"

Charles shuffled through the rest of his classes under a heavy blanket of guilt. Alex had Amy trapped in a checkmate before the game even began, and there was nothing Charles could do to save her. If he raised the alarm, Assassin's Honor would take it out on Amy. If he stood with her, they'd beat him up as well. If he did nothing, they would hurt her, and he would hate himself as much as Zack hated him.

Charles stopped by his locker to retrieve his paperback copy of *Hamlet*, the play he had to read for English. He shifted his textbooks around, making a jumbled mess of his fastidiously organized collection. A low voice behind him made him freeze.

"Cut class with me."

Charles snatched his math textbook, raised it like a club, and pivoted on his heel. Peter Jenkins was leaning against the locker next to his. He had ditched his leather jacket, and his thick arms were at his sides. The gangster was doing his best to appear nonthreatening, but Peter looked way too much like a nightclub bouncer to pull it off. Girls described him as tall, dark, and handsome. He more closely fit tall, dark, and shy. Most people labeled the guy brooding because he hardly ever smiled. Charles knew better. Peter never smiled because he was clinically depressed.

"That's your weapon of choice?" Peter eyed the textbook with a smirk.

"What do you want?" Charles scanned the hall for the rest of Assassin's Honor.

Peter held up his hands. "Relax. I'm alone, but we're short on time. Cut class with me, and I'll explain once we're out of here."

"You seriously think I'm that stupid?" He had thought these guys at least respected his intellect. Why else would they force him to do their homework?

"The others are up to something, but they won't tell me what."

"Feeling left out?"

Peter scowled. "Nathan and Alex ice me out when their plans get violent. I think it's about that girl."

"Her name's Amy." He resumed his search for the elusive novel.

"Whatever. I want to help you and Zack help her."

Charles froze. Had Peter witnessed his confrontation with Zack? How else would he know Zack meant to protect Amy? "Go away."

"You don't understand. Alex—" Peter darted his eyes around the now deserted hall. He lowered his voice. "I've seen him like this before. It's all a game, and he's a sore loser."

"You're the one who doesn't understand. I trusted you once before, and look where that got me. We're not doing this again." Charles was pleased to see a telltale flash of guilt in Peter's sea green eyes. He slammed his locker door and stormed down the hall. Peter Jenkins genuinely wanting to help someone? Yeah right.

Peter reached to grasp his forearm, thought better of it, and dropped his hand. "You know I'm sorry about what happened between us, but this is important." Guilt soaked his tone. "You know I'd never ask if I had anyone else." Charles sighed. He was everyone's last resort. Peter kept pace with him as he strode down the hall.

"Quit following me!"

"If you don't listen, you'll regret it."

Charles stiffened. "That a threat?"

"No man, it's the truth."

Jessie emerged from a classroom on their right. She waved her hall pass and smiled at him. A million butterflies swooped in his gut. "Why are you guys lurking out here? Don't you have class?"

Charles opened his mouth to explain, met her gorgeous emerald green eyes, and was immediately paralyzed. The only comments that sprang to mind were nonsensical compliments of her hair, her outfit, and her smile. Shakespeare himself would be proud.

"Who died and made you hall monitor?" Peter said rudely.

Jessie narrowed her eyes and turned her attention to Peter. "Shall I report you?" She smirked and waved her hall pass again. Charles breathed a sigh of relief. At least he hadn't recited his soliloquy out loud.

"I was just leaving." Peter threw Charles a frustrated scowl and trudged toward the exit.

"Thanks." Charles ducked his head. He used to wonder if Jessie knew he existed. Now she would remember him as the sketchy nerd who hung out in deserted halls with Peter Jenkins.

"No problem. I seriously have to run though, or I'm going to pee my pants." She flashed him a grin and dashed down the hall. He gazed after her in openmouthed awe. She was gorgeous, smart, and handled enormous gangsters as effortlessly as directing a cheer squad.

Daydreaming about Jessie calmed him down and helped him think. He had a solution by the end of the period. He would follow

Amy, but from a safe distance. Assassin's Honor never had to know, and he'd be able to get her help when she needed it.

The last bell rang in his ears like the start of a boxing match. He hurried to the parking lot to stake out the exit. Droves of students streamed past him, segregated by grade, clique, and status. They babbled mindlessly about their rivals, friends, and weekend plans. Charles watched them wistfully, an island in a sea of peers who were never going to accept him.

Ash and his girlfriend exited the school holding hands. They parted after a brief but heated argument, Lara heading for the bus and Ash crossing the street toward Parsons Elementary.

Ten agonizing minutes dragged by without any sign of Amy. He checked his watch for the millionth time, his heart pounding in his chest and his stomach clenching with nerves. Had he missed his chance at playing the hero? Had Assassin's Honor trapped her inside? His palms grew slick with sweat.

A slim, dark-haired figure slipped out a side exit. Amy marched across the parking lot like a soldier ready for war. Charles wished he had her confidence. But ready or not, it was showtime.

Twenty-one

AMY HAD BECOME a sensation overnight. Half the school hated her, the other half worshiped her, and four of her classmates wanted to kill her. Drama aside, she was having an awesome day. Jessie had asked her to eat lunch with her and her friends, and Ken had invited her to watch the lunar eclipse with them that night. She declined both offers, claiming she needed to work on an overdue paper. She had to limit her time with Zack until everyone quit gossiping about his breakup with Chelsea.

Lunch in the library made a pleasant change from sitting outside in the cold. She spent a relaxing half hour flicking through magazines and was positively cheerful throughout the afternoon.

Amy swept out of her last class, strutted confidently through the halls, and slipped out a side exit in the middle of a gaggle of loudly gossiping freshmen. She kept one hand in her pocket with her fingers clamped around her pepper spray and the other in her purse with a firm grip on her pistol. She crossed the street without even having to press the signal and arrived at Parsons Elementary in under two minutes. Unease fluttered in her stomach, even as the tension left her shoulders. Why had they let their opportunity slide?

"Hi Amy!" someone chirped from behind her.

Her heart rate accelerated to three times its normal speed. She whirled to face the speaker with adrenaline roaring through her veins. Chris leapt back with a comically shocked expression. "God!" Amy gasped and clapped a hand to her mouth. "I'm sorry. Didn't mean to startle you." Her cheeks burned. At least she hadn't pulled the gun on him.

Chris giggled. "I startled you first. Why you freaked?"

"No reason." She dismissed her weird behavior with an unconvincing shrug. "Do you know where Susan's hiding?"

"She left. Your brother picked her up."

A chill ran down her spine. "My brother is in BC."

"He must be back."

The chill spread over her shoulders and down her arms. The noisy playground faded until all she heard was her own pounding heart. "What did he look like?" She hardly dared to breathe.

Chris furrowed his brow. "Um, I didn't really see. Don't you know what your brother looks like?" Her phone began to ring. She pulled it from her purse and stared at the blocked number. "Aren't you going to answer that?"

She accepted the call with mounting dread.

"Step away from the kid," a male voice commanded.

Goose bumps pricked her skin. "Who is this?"

"Do as I tell you, or something unfortunate will happen to your sister," the cold voice drawled. She recognized Johnson's thick Southern accent.

She backed away from Chris with her eyes stretched wide and her heart in her throat. "Amy? What's wrong?"

"Go out onto the street and turn left," Johnson ordered. She obeyed, her blood roaring in her ears. She was being crushed between anger and panic, the warring emotions making it hard to breathe. "Listen carefully." Johnson spoke in slow, precise sentences, his drawling tone assaulting her ears. "Stay on the phone. Avoid talking to anyone. Don't draw attention to yourself in any way, shape, or form. If you do, we will know. Wave goodbye to the kid. Do it now!"

"Okay." Her voice trembled with choking rage. She waved to Chris and forced a sickly smile.

"Walk to the corner." His acidic tone burned her skin.

"All right," she answered through clenched teeth. "I'm here."

He cackled. "I know, good girl. Cross the street and head north along Twenty-second Avenue. Don't forget my rules."

"Wait." The word came out in a barely audible rasp. She took a breath to steady her voice. "How do I know you have Susan?"

"So that's her name. She wouldn't say."

"Amy! What's happening?" Susan's words were shrill with panic.

Amy's heart twisted at the terror in her sister's voice. "Sue, it's okay. I'm coming to find you."

"Shut up, Amy." Johnson had the phone again. "That enough proof for you?"

She clutched the phone to her ear in a clenched, trembling fist. "Don't you dare hurt her."

"You're awfully demanding for someone in your position," he crooned sweetly.

"I'll do whatever you want. Just let her go." Her words vibrated with molten fury even as hot tears of shame pricked her eyes. Susan was scared and alone because of her.

"No way." He chuckled, relishing in her powerlessness. "Not until you arrive. We warned you, Amy."

"Where are you?" She strode in the direction he had indicated earlier.

"You must think we're pretty stupid." The sharp edge had returned to his voice. "We're gonna take this one step at a time."

She followed their directions block by block and walked for what felt like forever. Her eyes blurred with tears of rage, but she refused to make a sound. She trudged down abandoned, trash-littered alleyways, passed shabby houses with darkened windows. She left the possibility of help further and further behind with every painful moment that passed and every instruction she was forced to follow. She hated herself more with every single step she took.

"You better hurry, Amy. We're getting bored." There was laughter in the background.

Her stomach clenched. What were they doing to Susan? She quickened her pace and struggled on. She had to reach her little sister. The instinct to protect her ran deeper than her bones. It coursed through her veins with every breath and every beat of her aching heart.

Her silent sobs became too much to bear. She collapsed against a chain-link fence and quietly fell apart in the mud. The rain mixed with the tears pouring down her face as suffocating despair dragged her down. She had to get help. But like always, she was alone.

"On your feet," Johnson said in a voice colder than ice.

Susan needed her. She pushed up from the mud and battled on.

"Stop crying, Evans. People will notice," a different voice snapped. This one held more authority. Alex. His businesslike tone was far more chilling than Johnson's glee.

Amy choked down a sob and wiped her eyes with her sleeve. "How much farther? Where's my sister?"

"Five driveways down at the end of the road."

Amy squinted down the street through the sheets of pouring rain. The muddy road sloped steeply toward the edge of a marshy swamp. Rickety shacks dotted the slope in no particular order, many leaning to one side or turned at odd angles. They looked like toy houses a child had thrown around in an angry tantrum.

She squelched through the mud, counting the dirt paths Alex had generously termed driveways. Her heart plummeted at her first sight of Assassin's Honor's hideout. The desolate structure squatted at the end of the shabby street, a good two hundred feet from the nearest dwelling. No one would hear them when they screamed. Trash littered the overgrown lawn, graffiti decorated the tiny front window, and the four-foot-wide porch sported a lopsided sign that read Keep Out.

"I see it," she said. "Now what?"

The line went dead. She jolted as if electrocuted and plunged toward the shack through the swiftly darkening evening. A sixth sense urged her to hurry. She had to get to Susan, and she had to get there now. She tore through overgrown bushes that threatened to rip out her hair. She splashed through lakelike puddles and nearly slipped in the mud. She smashed her way through a flimsy wooden gate and shrieked her defiance to the night.

The door flew open the moment she reached the porch. "Glad you decided to join us." Alex sneered. "Took you long enough."

Twenty-two

ZACK HACKED AT his partially dissected frog with more force than strictly necessary. If Charles wouldn't help Amy, it was her versus Assassin's Honor. The thought made his stomach churn. He had to help her. He needed to escape detention. He racked his brains for an excuse and accidentally decapitated his frog. His lab partner pulled their mangled dissection to the other side of the table to rescue it from Zack's erratic stabbing.

He ditched his friends at lunch to pay Principal Cook a visit. She greeted him with an amused smile. "Mr. Donnellson? You're here early. Looking forward to your third detention of the week?"

"Not exactly." He dropped into the straight-backed chair across from her. "I have to pick my brother up after school because my parents are away. I tried to explain this to Mr. Fields, but he semihates me and wouldn't listen."

She steepled her slender fingers. "You're the only one able to pick him up?"

"Yeah," Zack lied with an easy smile. Chris could easily chill at a friend's house, but his principal didn't need to know that.

"And it's pure coincidence that it's Friday?" She arched a brow.

He gazed earnestly into her aquamarine eyes. "It is! I have to make sure my little bro makes it home okay."

"All right, Zack." She spread her hands, a faint twinkle in her eye. "You may complete your detention next Tuesday, since you already have one booked for Monday. Does that comply with your schedule?"

"Yes." He breathed a sigh of relief. "Thanks for being so accommodating."

"You're welcome." She graciously inclined her head. "But try putting forth more effort in class, okay? You'd avoid detention and possibly prevent certain homeroom teachers from how did you put it? Semihating you?"

Zack flashed her a grin. Teachers had been telling him to put forth more effort since the fifth grade. Thanking his lucky stars females of all ages found him charming, he sauntered from her office with a spring in his step. He was going to catch Amy as she left school and escort her home like the hero that he was.

He was one hundred percent confident until seconds after the last bell. He strode purposefully out of class and froze in the middle of the hall. Where was he going? Where would Amy be right now? Unease fluttered in his stomach. What class did she have last period? Why hadn't he thought to ask her? His apprehension grew as he wandered the school without finding her anywhere.

"What's up?" Ken joined him in the nearly empty parking lot.

His heart leapt. Ken's locker was next to hers. "Have you seen Amy?"

"Yeah. She left ten minutes ago. Hey!" Ken shouted after him as Zack charged for his car. "You're losing it, man! She's just a girl!"

An eternity, or ninety seconds later, he squealed to a halt in front of Parsons Elementary. The grounds were crawling with clamoring little kids and their stressed-out parents.

"Bro!" Chris leapt into Zack's Lexus before it reached a complete stop. "It's the weekend!" he whooped, thrusting a fist into the air.

Zack raked his gaze over the grounds, worry spiraling within him like an expanding Slinky of doom. "Chris, where are Amy and Sue?"

Chris shrugged one shoulder. "They left."

Zack's eyes bulged. "I can never get you to shut up, and now you give me two words? They left? When? Where did they go?"

"Susan got picked up by her brother. Then Amy came looking for her. I guess she didn't know her brother was going to get Sue because she didn't know where she was."

"Wait. Slow down. Start from the beginning." He zoomed away from the school with a screech of tires.

"You're relentless." Chris rolled his eyes. "Susan got picked up by her brother."

Zack reflexively slammed on the brakes. The driver of a gray pickup laid on his horn and swerved to avoid rear-ending them.

"Look out!" Chris paled.

Zack pressed the gas. They flew forward with a gut-wrenching jolt. "Their brother is in Vancouver. How would he pick up Susan?" Thick bands of anxiety knotted tightly in his chest.

"I have no idea." Chris gripped his armrest. "Stop speeding or you'll get us killed."

"What did Amy say when you saw her?" he asked, trepidation lacing his tone.

"Not much. She asked me where Sue was, got a weird phone call, and ran off."

"That makes no sense. You sure that's all she said?"

Chris thought for a minute. "I don't think she knew the person who called her."

A chill ran down his spine. His thoughts raced faster than his speeding car. "Chris, I need you to remember exactly what happened."

"I told you three times already."

"Please, this is majorly important." His words vibrated with desperate urgency. "You have to help me."

Chris heaved a long sigh and started from the beginning. "Me and Sue were hanging out on the swings, just waiting for you and Amy. You were both late. You're always late." He paused to scowl at Zack. "A teacher came over and told Sue her brother had come to pick her up. She got super excited and ran off to meet him. Amy showed up a few minutes later, and—"

"Wait. What did Amy's brother look like?"

"I'm not sure. His car was on the other side of the playground."

"Anything else?" Zack asked as they neared their street.

Chris slowly shook his head. "I don't think so. Amy just seemed confused when I told her their brother had showed up."

"Okay, thanks bro. I'm going to be out for a while. Sit tight at home and make sure you lock the doors."

Chris twined his fingers together, a nervous flicker in his sky blue eyes. "Where are you going?"

"To find Amy and Sue. There's something weird going on."

"What do you mean, weird?" he asked as they pulled into their garage.

Zack furrowed his brow, considering what to tell the younger boy. "Their brother lives in Vancouver, and the girls didn't expect him home."

Chris smiled and slid from the car. "Maybe he surprised them."

"Yeah, maybe." Zack pursed his lips in a doubtful frown. He reversed out of their garage and backed toward the street.

Chris chased after his car, motioning for Zack to roll down his window. "Dude! I remembered something. Susan's brother had a scar on his face." He traced a finger down his right cheek.

That cute nine-year-old kid had hopped into a car with Nathan Johnson's gang? Zack broke half a dozen traffic laws as he tore through his neighborhood. His pulse pounded in his ears, his thoughts whirling like a tornado. Had Assassin's Honor kidnapped Susan to bait Amy? Had Amy learned of their plan and tried to stop them on her own?

He took a deep, calming breath. Amy knew what was going on. He had to call her. She had given him her number when he had driven her to school the other day. Did he still have it? He whipped out his iPhone and ordered Siri to call Amy. Siri informed him in her detached way that he had no one in his contacts with that name. He slammed a fist into his padded dashboard. The one time he had forgotten to save a girl's number.

It started to rain. The drops pinged against his roof and cloaked the world in thick, uncertain mist. He parked in an empty lot behind a high-end furniture store, dumped out the contents of the glove box, and sifted through a multitude of fast-food wrappers, Chris's comics, and Ken's lost homework. Amy's number was nowhere to be found. He punched the dashboard again, and a light bulb flicked on in his mind. He had called Amy without realizing it was her to ask her to babysit Chris. He skimmed his recent calls and selected her number on a rush of elated relief. It rang a few times and went to voicemail. He stabbed the end icon with a frustrated groan.

Zack covered his face with his hands and squeezed his forehead in an effort to think. What if he contacted Amy's brother and proved he was still in Vancouver? He'd have enough shady info to bring their case to the police. They'd put out an Amber Alert and find the girls.

He plucked the phone book his mom made him cart around from the pile of debris once contained within the glove box. He called Amy's house, told her mom he was an old friend of Justin's, and asked for his new number. She dictated it to him after a quick, slurred chat.

Zack held his breath and dialed Justin's number with mounting dread. He longed to be wrong about everything and for Susan to be safe.

Someone answered on the second ring. "Hello?"

Zack froze. What was he supposed to say? "Uh, hey. Is this Justin Evans?"

"You betcha," a cheerful voice replied. "Can I help you?"

"I think. I hope so. I'm a friend of Amy's, and she's in trouble."

"What kind of trouble?" His tone instantly grew serious.

"I'm not sure. I think …" How was he supposed to tell this guy that his nine-year-old sister had been kidnapped?

"If my sister is in trouble, I need to know about it right now." Justin had gone from serious to glacial in five seconds flat.

Zack winced. Hadn't Amy said something about this guy being a cop? "Someone scooped Susan after school, pretending to be you. I'm pretty sure she was kidnapped, and that Amy took the bait."

"I'm on my way."

"What? But you're in Vancouver, right? You're coming all the way here?"

"Yes. I'll make the next flight if I hurry. I know someone who can help. She's the absolute best in her field."

"But how—"

"Bring me up to speed when I arrive. Don't call Amy's phone. Don't involve anyone else. We don't want them to know that we know something's up. Meet me at the airport at ten p.m."

"You want me to wait for six hours?"

"I know." Justin sighed, irritation pricking his words. "But you won't be able to convince the police of foul play until I arrive. There's a chance you could make the situation worse. Meet me at the airport." He hung up.

Zack clenched his jaw and tossed his phone onto the passenger seat. It bounced and fell to the floor. Cold realization doused him like a bucket of ice water. Justin had warned him not to call Amy. Zack already had.

Twenty-three

THE PUTRID STENCH of rotting garbage assaulted Amy's nostrils as Alex dragged her through the shack's front door. The living room was dimly lit with matted carpeting the color of mud and paneling that had gone out of style in the midseventies. Johnson and Ash were lounging in a pair of overstuffed, ripped armchairs. Susan lay tied up on the floor next to an insanely buff, dark-haired guy Amy had never seen before.

Amy rushed to her sister and fell to her knees on the dirty shag carpet. Was brown its natural color, or was it that disgustingly filthy? She took Susan's small hand and squeezed it between both of hers. Her sister's skin was clammy and cold. "You okay?" Amy whispered. Susan nodded. Amy stood and faced Assassin's Honor with one hand on her hip. "I'm here. Let her go."

"It ain't gonna be that simple," Johnson sneered. He stared at her and Susan as if assessing their weak points. "Cardelle, Jenkins, you take Amy here and show her some Assassin's Honor hospitality. Ash and I will deal with the little one."

The guy sitting on the floor with Susan, the one called Jenkins, blanched at his leader's words. "Ash, I'll switch with you."

Amy clenched her teeth against a burst of white-hot rage. Jenkins preferred to torture a nine-year-old? What sick bastard liked torturing a child? Hatred simmered in her soul.

Ash shook his head. "Johnson said I was supposed to go with him."

Alex grabbed Amy by the hair and dragged her toward a dark doorway. She kicked and clawed at him in an effort to get back to her sister. He yanked on her hair, and she fell to the ground. Alex hauled her across the threshold, her knees scraping painfully over an uneven plywood floor. He released her and slammed the door to the living room.

This second room was even less attractive than the first. It was empty apart from a rickety table and chairs situated in the center of its unfinished floor. The walls had once been painted either a watery blue or a pea green. It was difficult to tell in the fading light. The room had a single slit of a window high up on the far wall, and a door in the corner that appeared to lead outside. Amy made a mental note of the possible escape route.

Jenkins flopped into a peeling leather chair. "What now?"

Alex forcefully turned her in a circle as if cataloging her weaknesses. He seized her wrist, and she bit back a yelp of pain. Last night's cuts were still open and raw.

He rolled up her sleeve. "Look what we have here? This one's a cutter."

Amy winced and tried to shove him away. He held her wrist in a death grip. She ducked her head, her cheeks burning with shame. She cut when life was hard to take, and this past week had been one long nightmare.

"How about we help you out." Alex smiled amicably as if offering to pay for a movie ticket she couldn't afford. "You stay with her while I find a big enough knife," he told Jenkins and strolled from the room.

Jenkins picked up a remote and flicked on a tiny TV she had failed to notice. It was tucked away in a corner, crammed precariously on a narrow shelf. Jenkins channel surfed with military intensity and refused to meet her eyes. Alex's idea was bothering him. Why?

Alex pranced through the door with a butcher knife in his fist. "This is going to be awesome!" Unbridled joy danced in his eyes as he sliced a jagged gash from her elbow to her wrist. The throbbing sting of pain was achingly familiar. She set her jaw and fought to feign indifference.

"Your turn," Alex crowed, passing his knife off to Jenkins.

"No thanks."

"Come on, dude. Everyone gets to participate."

"No." Jenkins shook his head, his brow shiny with sweat. He rose from his seat like a mind-controlled zombie and reluctantly pressed the blade to Amy's arm. He ran it lightly across her skin, barely leaving a mark.

"That's what you call torture?" Alex grabbed the knife's handle and pressed down hard as Jenkins moved to make another light scratch. This gash went even deeper than the first. Amy scrunched her eyes shut, silently riding the wave of pain. Metal clattered against wood. Jenkins had dropped the knife. "You're such a baby." Alex laughed.

He seized the knife and slashed at her skin with feverish delight. Amy tried to predict where the blade was going to strike next. Alex moved too fast. Fear unfurled within her like a kite on a gusting breeze. Alex was wielding the knife with practiced efficiency. How many others had received this same torture? What had become of them? She scrambled backward to huddle against the wall and raised her arms to shield her face. Alex tore into them, reopening old scars.

She stumbled into a corner, seeking protection from the knife that was everywhere at once. Alex pinned her against the wall, pried her arms away from her face, and forced her to meet his feral gaze. Alight with happiness, like a child's on Christmas morning, his cold blue eyes were far more terrifying than his knife. Alex enjoyed seeing others in pain.

He pressed the butcher knife to her neck. She held her breath, her pulse beating wildly beneath its sharp steel blade. She was no murder expert, but slicing open someone's throat was a surefire way to kill them.

"Alex!" Jenkins lunged forward and wrested the knife from his friend. "We're not supposed to kill her!"

"Who says? She's a problem and she needs to go." His gaze was locked on Amy's throat, his stormy eyes smoldering with passion. His look made her physically ill. She was cornered like a cow in a slaughterhouse.

"She's not a problem. Are you, Amy?" Jenkins grasped her arm and yanked her away from Alex. She hated being grabbed but welcomed the distance from the knife. "You'll forget this ever happened, right?" Amy nodded mutely. She'd promise anything to get Susan out of the mess she had created.

Alex's lips drew back in a snarl. "Whose side are you on? You're with us, remember? That X tattooed on your arm is a permanent symbol of your loyalty. You chose this. Suck it up!"

Amy glanced down. A small, bold X marked the inside of Jenkins's right forearm. It was identical to the one concluding

Johnson's note, except that his tattoo more clearly depicted two crossed daggers. She flicked her gaze to Alex. He had the same tattoo.

"Excuse me for not wanting to spend the rest of my life in prison. With you." Jenkins tightened his grip on her arm and pulled her close against his side. His gentle green eyes sparked with anger.

"You're right." Alex's cruel mouth twisted unpleasantly in a sneer. "Good thinking. We'll make her death look like an accident."

"That's not what I meant!"

Alex grabbed her arm and wrenched her toward the outside door. Jenkins held her close and refused to let her go. Amy winced at being the human center of a bone-crushing tug-of-war. She threw her weight toward Jenkins, the lesser of two evils.

Alex dragged them both outside into a ferocious Ontario storm. They sloshed their way across a muddy yard to an old, run-down toolshed, Amy thrashing like an animal in the grips of a snare. Alex dragged her into the ten-by-ten space, calmly handed her off to Jenkins, and busied himself removing tools from an old cedar chest. Fear solidified within Amy as if the musty air had frozen her core.

"What are you going to do to her?" Jenkins closed the door, plunging them all into darkness.

The storm beat against the shed's lone dusty window like a wale in the background of a grisly horror film. Alex pulled on a cord and a dusty bulb flicked on above his head. The dim light illuminated a large, square room. The walls were lined with shelves, and every shelf was piled high with a myriad of tools. Amy swallowed hard. From the nail gun to the handsaw to the innocent-looking broom, everything could be used as a torture device. As if on cue, Alex lifted a power saw from the bottom of the chest.

Amy tried to run, but her legs were useless pegs that refused to move. She tried to speak, to use her words to shame them, condemn them, but her tongue was heavy, her mouth impossibly dry. An unnatural blanket of blinding terror had wrapped her in its smothering embrace.

"Okay, Amy." Alex gave her a twisted smile. "Your coffin is ready." He grabbed her shirt collar, swung her into the chest, and slammed the lid with a bone-jarring crack. Total darkness surrounded her once more. "How long do you think it will take for her to suffocate?" Alex's voice vibrated with elation.

Jenkins did not reply. Amy clenched her fists and counted the rapid beats of her heart. A rising tide of panic threatened to sweep her away. The airtight wooden chest was as good as a vacuum-sealed coffin. She was going to suffocate. She became acutely aware of her racing heart pumping precious, oxygenated blood through her veins. Panicking was a waste of her valuable air. She needed to calm down and fast.

Amy curled up on the bottom of the chest and pictured her sweet little sister curled safe in bed beneath her floral-print quilt. Her breathing slowed, and her heart tried to follow suit. She took deep, careful breaths, holding each one for as long as possible before releasing it into the musty box.

Her lungs cried out for air and her heart pled for oxygen. The air had thinned like a bowl of watery ice cream left on the counter to melt. She was lightheaded and woozy. She knelt on the chest bottom and pushed up on its lid with all her might. She refused to die at the hands of these lunatics! Susan still needed her.

"This is boring." Alex yawned. "I'm going to check on what they're doing to the little one."

The shed door slammed, and the chest was flung open. Strong arms helped her sit up.

"Thanks." Amy gulped a lungful of the cool, damp air and pressed a trembling hand to her throbbing chest.

The shed door flew open, and Alex stormed back in. "What is with you tonight?" He fixed Jenkins with a hate-filled glare.

"What's with you?" Jenkins exploded, his arm tightening around Amy's shoulders. His toned body was an unyielding wall of iron at her side. "You're going to kill her because she's smarter than you? That's insane."

Alex snatched a large metal wrench and clonked Jenkins in the forehead. He stumbled and Alex, taking advantage of his temporary imbalance, shoved him backward into the chest alongside Amy. Alex slammed the lid shut, sealing them both in the dark, coffin-like box.

"Hey!" Jenkins pounded on the wood. "What the hell do you think you're doing?" He strained against the lid. His triceps rippled, but the lid refused to budge.

"I already tried that." Amy was pleased at how calm she sound-ed. The limited space was squeezing her way closer to this buff gangster than she ever wanted to be.

A roaring mechanical racket drowned out Jenkins's response. Alex had fired up the power saw.

Her heart beat a wild tempo of terror in her ears. "What's he going to do now?" she shrieked, her calm gone in an instant. "Chop us up?"

"Don't give him any ideas." Jenkins grimaced. Amy joined him in his efforts to lift the lid. It rose a centimeter and caught on the latch. "He locked us in," Jenkins said.

"Let us out!" she screamed. Ice-cold certainty froze her heart in her chest. Alex was going to kill them.

A deafening crunch sent vibrations through the wood. Strong arms wrapped around her waist. Jenkins had pulled her tight against his chest, as far away from the saw as possible. Amy stared in horror at a tiny sliver of light and the bottom of a deadly metal blade.

Twenty-four

ALEX SAWED THROUGH the soft wood, delighting in their terror-filled screams. He licked his lips to taste the air. The dizzying aroma of Amy's blood filled him with euphoric pleasure, and the anger and dread humming around Peter got him high. Their desperate cries and rising horror quickened his heart and heated his blood with a heady rush of power. He was a fearless hunter, about to slaughter his cornered prey.

Peter Jenkins was weak. Killing him would make Assassin's Honor stronger. The others would eventually see things his way. Their gullible minds were delighted to accept his thoughts and directions. Peter was not. Alex had to fight him for every ounce of control, and Peter still managed to rebel against his influence. Having to force him to hurt Amy had been the last, annoying straw. Alex was sick of it and wanted him gone.

He pushed the chest closer to the saw and sliced through the lid above Amy's legs. His lips parted in a lurid grin as he eyed them through the slit. They were huddled against the far wall, Amy cowering in Peter's lap. Alex grinned as he shredded the chest, inching the saw closer and closer to their toes. The humans were trapped in a shrinking tomb with the spinning blade blocking their only escape. They could either wait to get chopped into mincemeat or risk diving under the jagged metal blade. Both options would result in death.

Peter struggled to shove Amy behind him, but the chest was too narrow for them to switch spots. He would have to watch the girl die before greeting death himself. Alex smiled. That ought to mess with his head. Peter had a major problem with violence against women.

Alex shaved leather off the ends of their shoes. Amy readied herself to jump the blade. He suppressed a mirthless chuckle. Her death would be faster than Peter's, but much messier.

An unseen force wrenched him backward and hurled him into a wall. The saw landed inches from his face with a clanging whirl of sharp metal teeth. Alex scrambled to his feet and turned to face the idiot who had dared oppose him.

Charles Banks stood framed in the doorway, his skinny frame shaking with terror. Alex bared his teeth in a feral grin. He had been planning to kill the mage tonight, as well as Amy, Peter and Zack. He got to his feet with a lighthearted chuckle. Charles had delivered himself like a willing sacrifice. The Blood Moon would be pleased.

Alex swept a cool look over the terrorized trio. He had to lose the humans before he offed Charles. They would go insane if they witnessed a supernatural battle. As much as he would love to put Peter in a psych ward, Alex couldn't risk his powers going public.

He glowered at Peter. "Go tell Johnson we have an intruder. Take that with you." He jerked a thumb toward Amy.

Peter grabbed Amy's hand, and they bolted from the shed. He halted out in the torrential downpour and glanced over his shoulder at Charles. What was he doing? Waiting for the smaller kid to follow him to safety? Peter and Charles had been friends for a time. Was the fool still loyal? Alex curled his lip in disgust.

"Go, you idiot!" Charles shouted as Alex influenced the humans to run.

They tore across the yard holding hands as if the forces of hell were after them. They were like frightened little rabbits fleeing their burrow. His lips formed a malevolent smirk. "Yes, flee little humans. Flee for your lives. I'll finish you later."

A bright flash of lightning bathed the shed in red. Rage far more powerful than his own roared through his veins and set his blood ablaze. The storm had better not dim the Blood Moon's night of glory. He peered through the window at the violent night sky, longing for its arrival with every taut nerve and every pounding beat of his heart. He must kill, and soon.

He turned his attention to the mage. "So, decided to man up and face me, eh? If I had known pretty girls made you grow a pair, I would have set you up ages ago."

A disturbing thought crossed his mind. Charles never stood up for himself, let alone others. Was someone manipulating him? He shook his head to dislodge the silly notion. Surely The Dark had more efficient ways of stopping him than manipulating fragile mages.

"You've lost your mind." Charles hit his knees as Alex broke into his mind in as brutal a way as possible. "They're human. They're of no concern to you." Charles's face contorted in pain. "How come you never pick fights with other Darks? You too weak to face anyone more powerful than a defenseless high school junior?"

Fury ripped through him like a red-hot bolt of fire. He squeezed Charles's mind with darkness, intending to crush it like a grape. The darkness acted as a ring of razor blades, slowly slicing into and pulverizing his brain. Charles was surprisingly resistant. He blocked the darkness with barriers of magic and shoved Alex away with sheer willpower alone. Alex bit back a roar of molten rage. Charles's fragile body presented an easier target. He hooked the power saw with a fine, dark tendril and flung it at the mage's head. Charles dove out of the way on a magical swoop of luck.

Alex couldn't breathe. He gasped for air like a fish out of water. Charles had removed the oxygen from Alex's side of the shed. The remaining gases, nitrogen and carbon dioxide, made him sick to his stomach. He retched on the molecules he had nearly swallowed and expelled them on a choking breath.

"Fitting, isn't it?" Charles struggled to his feet. "It's time you got a taste of your own medicine." He hurled the power saw at him atop a glowing burst of magical energy.

Alex deflected the tool with a hand and received a jarring stab of pain as the blade scored his arm. An unpleasant sensation churned in his gut. Fear? He pushed past it with a thunderous rush of rage. The mage needed to learn his place, and fast. Nathan was going to arrive at any moment and could not find them dueling with supernatural powers. Worse, he could not find him losing to Charles Banks.

His throat burned and his lungs throbbed. His body fought to breathe the poisonous gas. He scrambled to the other side of the shed, gasped in a breath of oxygenated air, and sent an array of tools flying at Charles. None hit him. The drill lodged in the wall above his head, the hammers and mallets clattered harmlessly to the floor, and a barrage of nails sprayed from the nail gun merely decorated the ceiling. Alex let loose a stream of curses. The infuriating mage had used magic to alter his chances of being hit.

A suffocating pressure slammed into his chest. Charles had done something different to the air. Alex clutched at his ribs and struggled to breathe. The pressure tripled. His lungs were on fire. His chest threatened to explode. Was he having a heart attack? Fear careened through him. The room spun in wide, dizzying loops. He fell to his knees as his vision flickered. He clawed at his shirt in a wild frenzy of panic. The pressure was coming from within. Charles had forced an air bubble into Alex's chest. It was crushing his lungs and making it impossible for him to breathe.

He lassoed Charles's ankles with darkness and yanked his feet out from under him with a vindictively vicious jerk. Charles crumpled backward, his skull hitting the concrete floor with a satisfying crunch. The pressure in Alex's chest evaporated. He gulped a relieved breath and clutched his head between his hands. The little mage had horrifying powers. Payback time. He spent the next thirty seconds beating Charles to a pulp. He had to look messed up for the humans' benefit and Alex wanted him awake when he murdered him slow.

Peter and Nathan crashed through the door, drenched from the rain and reeling from their latest trauma. Nathan's skin had a sickly green hue, and Peter's eyes were wild as if he was living through a nightmare. Alex regarded them with a satisfied smile. Susan's torture had gone as planned.

Nathan gaped at Charles. "How did he find us?"

"Relax." Alex influenced him to stay calm. "The kid followed Amy without her knowledge and tried to play the hero."

"This is so messed up." Peter's green eyes blazed.

Alex frowned. Had Peter told Nathan about his near-death experience yet? "Where are the girls?" he asked before Peter had the chance to sell him out.

"With Ash." Peter cut his steely gaze to Alex.

"Ash is higher than a kite! You think it's a good idea to leave the girls alone with him?"

"Jenkins, go help Ash guard our prisoners," Nathan said as if the idea had been his.

Peter crossed his arms over his chest. "Fine. But I'd stay away from cedar coffins and power tools if I were you." Nathan gave him a dumbfounded look. Peter left without explaining.

Alex jabbed the mage with the toe of his boot. "How about I stick Charles in the cellar?"

Nathan brightened. "Sure. If we drug him, he might forget this ever happened."

Alex shook his head. He hated drugs. They twisted the mind into a confusing labyrinth of distorted reality. This made manipulating the users unpredictable and dangerous. "Charles is a Goody Two-shoes. I doubt anyone would believe he'd do drugs willingly. Let's handle this like we always do. We'll promise him a few days of peace and make sure he knows what'll happen if he snitches."

"Whatever. You deal with it." Nathan stumped back to the house.

Alex dragged Charles through the mud and down into the cellar, letting his head clunk on every concrete stair as they descended. Charles wouldn't wake for some time and when he did, the worthless mage would wish he had never been born.

Twenty-five

AMY GLOWERED ACROSS the living room at Ash as he pulled a needle from his pocket and filled a syringe with heroin. He was treating their abduction like a boring Tuesday afternoon. She looked away in disgust that melted into heartrending concern. Susan was sitting beside her on the floor, staring into space with anguish in her eyes. Amy's stomach twisted with mingled trepidation and guilt. What horrors had her sister endured? Did she even want to know?

Susan's vacant expression morphed into a murderous mask of fury. "You didn't stop him." Her soft gray eyes blazed with hate. Amy recoiled, shock lancing through her at her sister's transformation. Ash shifted uncomfortably beneath Susan's unblinking gaze. "You should have stopped him!" she shrieked and lunged at Ash with the ferocity of a jungle cat. She pummeled him with her tiny fists and howled her rage through an unintelligible sob of hurt. Ash simply gazed at Amy over the top of Susan's head as if her sister was a badly trained pet she ought to contain. Susan bared her teeth in a startlingly vicious snarl and doubled her wild assault.

The wheels spun in Amy's mind. She and Susan were no longer restrained, and Ash had put himself at a major disadvantage by taking those drugs. His reflexes would be slow, his mind in outer space. This was their best and only chance.

Amy sprang at Ash and karate kicked him in the groin. He howled in pain as she shoved him to the floor and knelt on his skinny chest. She wrapped one hand around his neck and bashed his face with her other fist.

"Amy, stop!" he shrieked, his eyes bulging. "He told me to help you."

"Let us go," Amy said with a snarl, squeezing his throat in a death grip.

"Go! Please!" His hazel eyes welled up.

She grudgingly released him. He lapsed into a coughing fit and pressed a hand to his flushed face. He had a split lip and the start of a nasty black eye. Amy got to her feet and pushed Susan toward the door.

"Amy, look." Susan pointed with a trembling hand.

Amy's purse lay dumped in a dusty corner. She blinked in elated surprise, sure it hadn't been there before. She dove for the pistol and trained her weapon on Ash's chest. He froze. "If you follow us, I'll shoot you." Ash nodded, his eyes wide with fear.

The girls raced out the door and tore down the flooded street, Amy clinging to her sister's hand and dragging her headlong through the dark. Their sneakers pounded the pavement like the drumming of a giant heart. They ran until their breaths came in great, gasping gulps, each gust of autumn air a punch to their burning lungs.

"Are you okay?" Amy panted as they stopped to catch their breath.

"Fine." Susan avoided meeting her eyes.

"Did they hurt you?" Amy hugged her, but Susan kept her arms rigid at her sides.

Her small hands squeezed into fists. "No."

Amy snatched her phone from her purse and dialed 911. Someone needed to help Charles, and Alex needed to be committed.

A 2008 Tata Nano cruised up beside them. The driver's side window rolled down, and for one heart-stopping moment, Amy saw Assassin's Honor. She gripped Susan's hand and slid the pistol from her purse. Instead of Alex or Johnson leering like psychopathic murderers, a middle-aged man gave them a friendly wave. "You girls lost?" His voice was gravelly like a dirt country road.

"Yes!" Susan whimpered. "Some creepy guys are after us. They're trying to hurt us. I want to go home!" Tears sprang to her eyes.

"You're being chased by someone who intends to harm you? You must call the police."

"I was about to." Amy slipped the pistol back into her purse.

The man tapped on his phone and put it to his ear. "I have two young girls here at the corner of Harris Avenue and James Street. They say they are being followed by a group of young thugs. I am going to get them to a safer location. No, ma'am, I will not bring them back to their house. Yes, I understand." He made eye contact with Amy. "Where are these guys now?" he mouthed.

"Three two three four Holly Tree Road," Amy spat, hoping Assassin's Honor spent the rest of their miserable lives in prison.

The man repeated the address. "I'll take them to twenty-two hundred Magnolia Crescent." He thanked the dispatcher and set his phone aside. "Climb on in. You're welcome to stay at my place until it's safe for you to go home."

Amy stiffened. "Thanks, but no thanks." She had trust issues on a good day. She and Susan were not going anywhere with a stranger on a night like this.

Susan ignored her and climbed into the back seat. "Come on, Amy! He's going to take us home!"

"Sue, get out of that car." Amy reached for her wrist. Susan jerked away as if she couldn't bear to be touched. Amy's unease grew. She followed through with her own 911 call. Her phone lasted for half a ring before its battery died.

"I'm trying to help you." The man looked heavenward as if praying for patience. "What will you do if those boys come back?"

Amy frowned. He had a point. She had to get Susan out of there, and she had her pistol in case things went south. She would rather face one potentially dangerous stranger over four definitely dangerous gangsters.

She climbed into the front seat and placed her purse on her lap to keep her pistol close at hand. The car stank of beer, but the man himself seemed sober. He was over six feet tall with the build of a wrestling champion. He had thick chestnut hair and deep-set eyes the color of a stormy sea. He wore work boots, faded black jeans, and a paint-splattered long-sleeved shirt. His expression was relaxed, but his big hands gripped the wheel with such force his knuckles had turned white. Was he angry? Nervous?

The man drove them through the suburbs and turned into the driveway of a shabby, sketchy-looking house. Loud music blared from the home next door. A banner hung in its wide front window. It depicted a large, bloodred moon and the words *Umbra Mortis*. The Latin phrase sent a shiver down Amy's spine.

Their driver opened the garage and stepped hard on the gas. They shot forward, and he slammed on the brakes. Susan screamed. Amy's purse flew out of her lap and landed with a thump on the floor.

"What the hell?" She bent to retrieve her bag. The man dragged her from the car. "Get your hands off me!" She smashed her foot into his knee. Her ankle throbbed as if she had kicked a brick wall.

"Now, now, stop struggling." He twisted her arms behind her back and secured them with a thick, scratchy rope.

"Susan, run!" Amy screamed. Her sister sat frozen in the back seat, her face white with fear and her eyes as round as saucers.

Their abductor gave the rope a vicious jerk, and Amy fell onto her rear. He took care to tread on her fingers as he hauled Susan from the car.

Flames of fury burned her skin. "You're insane. The police will be here any minute."

"You still believe that?" He laughed as he secured Susan's wrists. "I only pretended to call the cops."

Amy clenched her jaw so hard her teeth threatened to crack. She was an idiot, dumber by far than the football jocks she mocked. Their captor dragged them into the house, towing them along as if they were lighter than air. Amy screamed as if she was already being murdered. The music from the block party drowned her cries. The man slammed and locked the inside door to the garage. Amy bowed her head beneath the weight of her despair. She and Susan had been taken prisoner for the second time that night.

Amy peered around their new jail cell, another darkened living room. Rough, stained carpet covered the floor, fast-food wrappers and beer bottles decorated the coffee table, and thick, faded brown drapes veiled the windows. The muted TV offered the only light in the room.

Amy threw her weight against the rope, hoping to unbalance their abductor. He jerked the rope to his chest, forced her to her knees, and followed up with a brutal kick to her gut.

"Sit," he ordered Susan. She dropped to her bottom. He tied them to the legs of the couch. "Stay." He smiled to himself and left the room.

Susan scooted close and huddled against Amy's side. She was shaking from head to toe and her eyes were filled with tears.

"It'll all be okay. We'll be fine, I promise." She had no idea how she was going to keep her word.

The stranger was talking on the phone in the next room. Amy eavesdropped on his side of the conversation. "Your incompetence is astounding. Do you have any idea what would have happened if they had gone to the police? Guess I'll have to finish your dirty work myself."

Fear spiked, thick and hot, in her chest. Their abductor was linked to Assassin's Honor. It all made a sickening amount of sense. He returned with a beer in hand and a leer on his unshaven face.

Her hands balled into fists. "Who are you? You work for Alex?"

He roared with laughter, making Susan jump. "That stupid kid? Hell no! Alex works for me."

"Who are you?" Amy repeated through clenched teeth. She needed his name for the police.

"Oh, did I forget to introduce myself? My apologies." He set aside his drink and untied her. She whirled, fists raised, and came face-to-face with the barrel of a .45. Her stomach dropped into her shoes. "Untie her." The man pointed his gun at Susan. "March," he said the second her ankles were free.

He herded them through his dark, gloomy house and out into the dismal night. An icy November wind blew drops of drizzle into their faces. They tromped across the muddy yard to a large toolshed. A chill knifed through her. Was their abductor picking up where Alex had left off? The door swung shut behind them, plunging them into darkness.

Amy blindly searched for a makeshift weapon. Her hand grazed a shelf, and she identified objects by touch. Wrenches, screwdrivers, a tape measure. She closed her fingers around a hammer.

A spark of light caught her eye. Their captor had lit a candle. The flame cast eerie shadows across his bearded face and glinted off the cold metal of his gun. "Allow me to lend you some light." He placed the candle on a narrow, rickety table and lifted a large plastic can from a nearby shelf. He splashed its contents onto the floor. Her heart skipped several beats as the unmistakable smell of gasoline filled her nostrils.

"Well, ladies, it was nice knowing you." He waved a hand in farewell and knocked the candle into the puddle of gasoline. Greedy flames leapt into the air and illuminated his speedy retreat. He had blocked the exit with a blazing wall of fire.

"What do we do?" Susan said, her voice raw with fear.

Amy gaped at the flames in paralytic horror as the fire consumed the wooden structure. They backed into a corner to escape the choking smoke. "Cover your face with your shirt," Amy screamed over the roaring inferno. She crouched low to the ground and pulled Susan down with her.

"I'm scared!" Susan wailed.

Glass shattered nearby. Amy sprang to her feet on a jolt of hope. Her eyes widened in shock. A teenage girl was perched on the windowsill to her right. "Grab my hand!" she shouted.

Amy herded Susan toward her. "Take a big breath and hold it until you're outside." She boosted her sister up to the sill. The girl helped her down and extended a hand to Amy. She struggled through the window and dropped to the ground with a flicker of stinging pain. Her shirt was torn, and a trickle of blood ran down her side. She had nicked a piece of glass. She skimmed her eyes over Susan and breathed a sigh of relief. Her sister looked okay.

Amy gasped in a breath of much cleaner air and snatched up Susan's hand. The shed creaked like it was about to topple over. Or explode. "Run!" the girl screeched. They took off as something inside blew up.

"That was close," Amy breathed as they watched the blaze from two houses down.

The girl shoved thick raven hair out of her soot-streaked face. "Why were you locked in a burning shed?"

"That's a long story. It involves an insane phone call, a gang of lunatics, and a madman." Amy chuckled. "We've had one hell of a night. Thanks for getting us out."

The girl waved away her gratitude. "I saw the smoke from two blocks down. I like playing the hero."

Amy lifted a brow. The tiny girl looked nothing like a hero with her elfin features and her vibrant, sapphire blue eyes. She seemed as fragile as a rose, and yet she had hauled them from a blazing shed. She was a total badass.

"You two okay?"

Amy nodded. "I'm fine." Susan tried to answer and lapsed into a coughing fit. Amy slipped an arm around her shoulders and rubbed her sister's back. "We need a safe place to crash. Going home is not an option."

"You're welcome to stay with me. I live just down the street. You both need water, a shower, and a nice long nap." She held her nose but softened the gesture with a smile.

A strange sensation drifted over Amy. She felt overwhelming-ly tired and unusually calm. Distant alarm bells rang in her mind. They were swiftly silenced and swept away on a sparkling river of tranquility. "That sounds awesome. But my purse is in that dude's car. I need it back."

"Sure thing." The girl's eyes twinkled with mischief. She passed Amy a flashlight trimmed with a glass breaker.

"Cool!" Amy grinned. She sprinted to the Tata Nano and smashed the passenger side window. She snatched her purse, drew the pistol, and marched into the house. Their abductor had passed out on his vinyl couch with an empty beer bottle in his hand.

"Whoa, wait, what are you doing?" The girl rushed after her with her arm wrapped around a stumbling Susan, guiding her. "If you shoot him, you'll go to prison too."

Amy narrowed her eyes. "Dead men never get to prison. They go straight to hell." But the girl did have a point. Zack was not allowed to be right about that prison-issue orange uniform. She snatched the empty beer bottle and smashed it over their abductor's head.

"I like your style." The girl smiled appreciatively. "By the way, pardon my manners and let me introduce myself. My friends call me The Dark."

"Weird name." She and Susan followed her outside.

"Everyone says that." The corners of her mouth twitched.

The dark girl led them down the street to a cozy one-bedroom apartment. The place was tastefully decorated in soft pastels that complemented the rich maple brown of its hardwood floors. Its spacious kitchen sported stainless steel appliances, and the living room furniture was upholstered in cream-colored silk. Satin throw pillows lined the armchairs, couch, and ottoman, and a massive sheepskin rug lay in front of a miniature woodstove. A single framed photograph hung on the living room's pale blue wall. A boy and girl of about sixteen stood atop a snowy mountain, holding hands as they beamed at the camera. The boy had dark red hair and melt-your-heart caramel eyes. The girl in the photo was The Dark.

"That your boyfriend?" Amy took a stab at conversation. "He's cute."

A jolt of pain rippled across The Dark's pretty face. "No." Her tone barred all further questions.

The girls each took a turn in her wonderfully hot shower, while The Dark whipped up a snack of cookies and hot chocolate. The drink was warm and comforting and made it hard for Amy to think. She sank deeper and deeper into a soothing ocean of calm. The tranquil sea cradled her in a cocoon of gentle warmth and swept all her doubts away. The girls soon fell asleep on The Dark's silk ottoman.

One last worry niggled at the back of Amy's mind. She was supposed to be helping someone. A fuzzy image of a boy with pretty eyes and strawberry blond hair floated in and out of focus.

She woke to an angry shout from the other side of The Dark's front door. "Found you. Come out and play." She recognized Alex's glacial glee. Panic ripped through her like a jolt of electricity. She fumbled for her pistol.

The Dark hefted a shotgun. "Go back to sleep. I'll deal with these pests."

Twenty-six

PETER STORMED FROM the shed with a dull throbbing in his head. There was nothing more he could do for Charles. At least Susan and Amy ought to be free by now. Peter had ordered Ash to help get them out. As long as Ash listened to him, which he usually did, the police might find Charles before things got bad. And if he, Peter, got arrested in the process? He shrugged. Alex had escalated this thing with Amy way further than it needed to go, and the rest of them had sat back and allowed it. His stomach roiled at what had happened to Susan. The little girl was going to be scarred for life, and it was one-fourth his fault. He clenched his jaw against a burst of blinding self-hatred. He ought to have pushed harder to stay with the kid. He deserved whatever punishment came his way.

Peter opened the shack's door to total destruction. Ash was sitting on the floor, propped against the wall with a hand pressed to his left eye. A nasty bruise marred his cheek, and his lower lip dripped blood onto the dirty shag carpet.

Peter gaped. "You sure made this look convincing."

Ash hung his head. "The little one went crazy. She flipped out, and Amy took their stuff. I wanted to go with them, but they said they were going to shoot me!" He was close to tears. "Alex will shoot me anyway!" He stared at the floor like a dog about to be hit. "What are you gonna tell them?"

"You did good, man. Sorry they beat you up, but can you blame them? I'll help with the others, I promise."

Nathan crashed through the door and froze at the sight of the hostageless room. "What the hell did you do?" His dark eyes narrowed into slits. "You had one job, guard the prisoners, and you somehow messed it up? You stupid, useless piece of—" Nathan punctuated each insult with a blow to Ash's face.

Peter rushed to block Nathan's warpath of rage. "It's not his fault. We left them both alone with him and they weren't even tied up."

Alex burst into the room with his hair dripping from the rain. "You let them escape?" His face grew splotchy with rage. Peter pictured steam pouring from his ears and suppressed a chuckle.

"Well, I didn't exactly let them," Ash said from where he lay sprawled on the floor. "I didn't have any rope, and there were two of them. I tried to stop them, but Amy had a gun!" Peter silently cheered his friend as he babbled. Ash was too good for Assassin's Honor but had peer pressure PTSD.

Alex loomed over him, his blue eyes chips of ice. "You expect me to believe two little girls beat you senseless? You're saying they retrieved their weapons from the other side of the house and wandered back to threaten you before they walked out?" His voice was deadly calm, anger boiling just below the surface. Peter tensed. Alex wasn't buying it. He braced himself for a fight.

"Their stuff was over there," Ash said, feebly waving a hand toward a dusty corner of the room. "I'd never help them, I swear!"

"Yeah." Peter nodded, glimpsing an escape route. "And if he had helped them, he would have left with them instead of waiting around for you guys to beat him up."

"Whatever! You let two tiny girls overpower you! You're a wimpy, little, lying retard." Alex looked about to join Nathan in beating Ash senseless. He raised his fist but thought better of it at the last second. "Come on, let's go." He stormed from the room.

"Go where?" Peter asked with a knot of unease in his gut.

"To find them before the police find us," Alex hissed through clenched teeth.

Nathan released Ash and followed Alex outside. Ash scurried after them like a faithful puppy. Peter trailed in their wake with a weighted hopelessness in his chest. "Where do we even look?" he asked, dreading the answer.

"Shut up and follow me." Alex led the group in the opposite direction from which Amy had come that afternoon.

"Wouldn't she go home?" Ash opened an umbrella, and a gust of wind nearly ripped it from his hands.

"No. She's smarter than you." Alex stalked down the street like a bloodhound following a scent.

They wandered the deserted, flooded streets with aimless abandon. Peter wiped raindrops from his forehead and hoped Alex was lost. "How do you know they even went this way? They could be anywhere. Heck, they could have called the cops by now!"

Alex's nostrils flared. "You got a better idea?"

"Yeah, I do. Split while we have the chance."

Alex halted at a street corner and scanned the wet pavement. "If we kill them, no one will be around to tattle to the police."

Peter suppressed an involuntary flinch. "Why is it so important that we kill them? Amy has learned her lesson." Anxiety knotted in his chest. Amy's little sister was only nine.

"We kill because I say so!" Alex thundered. Jagged red lightning split the sky.

Ash and Nathan gaped stupidly at each other. Nathan nodded first. "We can't risk them ratting us out."

Thick black fog swirled in Peter's head. His will eroded, crumbled, and dissolved. He followed Alex through the storm and clung to the hope that Amy and her sister were somewhere safe.

"We've passed that house three times already," Ash said.

"Shut up!" Alex rounded on him. Ash scrambled backward and crashed into Peter.

Peter's phone rang as he opened his mouth to point out Ash was right. He checked the caller ID, grimaced, and shoved his phone into his pocket. He rarely accepted calls from his father. They usually resulted in a rant about what a giant disappointment he was. His dad tried calling once more and gave up.

Alex's phone buzzed. He accepted the call with an irritated groan. "What?" He listened for a moment and smirked. "Jenkins, your dad's been trying to reach you. He says you're a real screwup. I have to agree." Peter scowled. What else was new? "What?" Alex said. "They are? How did you—" He broke off midsentence. "First, it was Ash's incompetence, not mine. Second, I understand perfectly what will happen if they call the cops. That's why I tried to get rid of them. But your idiot son kept interfering. He's too soft. I doubt he's cut out for this line of work."

"Give me that!" Peter snatched the phone from Alex. "Hello, Dad." He braced himself for a lecture.

"Hello, Peter," his father answered coolly. **"Guess I'll have to finish your dirty work myself."** Peter cringed. Amy and Susan had escaped Alex only to wind up with the one person in the world who might actually be worse. "I warned you hostage situations were tricky business. You never listen. You think you know it all."

"It was Alex's idea." Peter cheerfully threw him under the bus.

"I don't care who came up with it. It was stupid." His dad hung up on him.

"He thinks you're stupid." Peter smirked at Alex.

"So wait, they're at your place?" As usual, Nathan was confused.

Alex snatched his phone. "No, they're at the Magnolia clubhouse. Let's go."

"It'll take over an hour to walk there." Ash clung to his battered umbrella.

"Fine, I'll hail a freaking cab." Alex flagged down a taxi.

Peter joined Ash and Nathan in the taxi's back seat, a heavy cloud of doom pressing hard upon his shoulders. How the hell was he going to get the girls out of this one? Ditching now would earn them all a place on his father's blacklist. The leader of Assassin's Honor took betrayal seriously. Fleeing from the gang might get them all killed. Sickening dread knotted in Peter's stomach. Facing the police would have been a million times easier than his dad.

"Here's good." Alex indicated for the driver to let them off at the corner of Magnolia Crescent.

"Nasty fire there." The driver pointed down the street. Peter followed his gaze to a plume of thick gray smoke billowing toward the black night sky.

"Come on," Alex said. They sprinted down the street toward the fire's orange glow.

"What happened?" Nathan gasped.

The fire was raging in the backyard of the Jenkins's gang clubhouse. Peter sprinted for the main structure, dreading what he might find. His dad lay on the cheap vinyl couch with broken glass in an arc around his head and a large welt between his brows. Had Amy knocked him out with his own beer bottle? Peter suppressed an elated grin. He kind of loved that girl.

"So much for disposing of them." He poked his dad's thick shoulder. "Guess they disposed of you instead."

"Where are the girls?" Nathan darted a panicked look around the living room.

The backyard shed had burned to the ground, and the flames were devouring the overgrown lawn. The blaze was about to reach the house, the buckets of torrential rain doing nothing to slow the greedy tongues of fire.

Alex paced the room like a dog who had lost a scent. He froze midstride and darted a nervous glance toward the door. "Grab him." He jerked a thumb toward Mr. Jenkins. "We need to split."

Sirens wailed in the distance. Cursing energetically, Nathan tossed Mr. Jenkins over his shoulder like a limp sack of potatoes. Peter wished he had time to snap a photo. His macho, gangster father being carried off like a damsel in distress had him in silent stitches.

They sprinted the two blocks to Peter's house as dusk gave way to night. Peter ran along at the back of the group with his heart soaring high above the clouds. His luck had at last chosen to turn. Amy and her sister were going to be fine, and Alex and his dad were both headed to prison.

Nathan unceremoniously dropped Mr. Jenkins on the kitchen floor. Peter happily doused him with a pitcher of ice water.

"The hell!" Mr. Jenkins spluttered, swiping water off his dripping beard.

Peter leaned against the counter. "You let them escape. And you say I'm incompetent? They would've burnt you to a crisp if we hadn't come along and saved your ass."

"Nah, the fire was my idea. They went up in flames." He sat up and put a beefy hand to the welt on his forehead.

"Nope, but your clubhouse did." Alex threw him a contemptuous scowl. "Where are they?"

"How the hell would I know?" he slurred. He must have downed a few drinks before Amy knocked him unconscious.

"He's useless," Alex said and knocked him out with a swift punch to the temple. Mr. Jenkins sagged to the floor, out cold. "Stop smirking, Peter, unless you're proud of your inherited stupidity."

"Now what?" Ash worried his lower lip. "Do you think the cops are onto us?"

Alex shook his head. "If Amy was going to call the police, she would have done it by now. She has nothing on us. We have her address, her class schedule, her work schedule, and her bus routes. We'll track her down anywhere she goes. It's only a matter of time."

Peter gaped at Alex in openmouthed horror. "How much research have you done on this chick?"

"I like to understand my enemies."

"So, we're waiting until they go home?" Ash asked.

"No." Alex slammed a fist into his palm. "I told you, she'll avoid going home because she knows we will find her there. She's found herself a cozy place to hide. We'll wait until after the storm to track her down."

Peter flopped onto the sofa, praying Alex was wrong. "Wake me when you're about to punch out my dad again."

He closed his eyes and pretended to doze. Ash and Nathan wandered back into the kitchen to raid the fridge. Alex paced the living room floor and muttered maniacally to himself. "You clever bitch. Where are you hiding them? I will find you, and the Blood Moon will have its sacrifice." Peter sighed. It was just another day with his deranged associates.

He woke to Ash shaking his shoulder. "We're leaving." He nodded to Alex and Nathan, who were heading out the door.

Peter groggily followed them outside. Though the rain had stopped and the wind had calmed, thick gray clouds still obscured the night sky. It looked like someone had pressed an enormous pause button, temporarily halting the raging storm.

Alex led them confidently through town, straight up to the plain white door of a ground-floor apartment. "Found you!" he bellowed. "Come out and play."

The door flew open. A tiny, dark-haired chick stepped out with a shotgun clutched in her petite, little hands.

"Holy crap!" Peter hit the ground as a deafening blast echoed through the still night air.

Alex stood his ground. "Cut the drama. We both know you won't kill us."

"It's not too late to walk away." The girl fixed him with a steely glare.

Peter backed up with his hands in the air. He refused to get shot over some stupid obsession of Alex's.

The dark-haired girl raised the shotgun and took aim. Peter dove behind a dumpster. Ash scrambled behind a parked car. Nathan crashed to the asphalt. Alex stayed put. He grinned cockily at the girl as if he had already won the showdown. She shrugged and pulled the trigger.

The subsequent bang was more deafening than a thunderclap. A bolt of red lightning struck the girl in the chest, leaving nothing but a smoldering crater in its wake. The filmy clouds parted to reveal a large, bloodred moon.

"Umbra mortis," Alex whispered reverently.

Twenty-seven

AMY WRAPPED AN arm around a trembling, pale-faced Susan, and hoped with all her heart their rescuer was okay. The Dark had risked everything to help them. Gunshots echoed through the night, and an elated cheer confirmed the worst. The Dark had failed. This night had become one long, inescapable nightmare.

Amy tightened her grip on her pistol and stared grimly at the door. Johnson burst through first. She shot him, and he collapsed to the floor with a howl of agony. She moved on to Alex, but he dove forward and she missed. Susan screamed a warning as bullets sprayed the wall behind them. Alex was returning fire. She shielded Susan with her body and pointed her gun at Jenkins. Her heart twisted with indecision. He had saved her from Alex. Alex took advantage of her hesitation and tackled her to the floor, knocking the pistol from her grasp.

"Enough!" He smacked her across the face with his gun.

She thrashed wildly and managed to elbow him in the throat. Alex recoiled, and she scrambled free. Hope unfurled within her as she lunged for the gun. Johnson blocked her path. She threw all her weight into tackling him out of the way. He barely even moved. She cringed. She had not thought that one through. He was built like a rock, and she was five two.

Alex pressed his gun to her temple. "Give me one reason to shoot." His breath was hot against her neck.

Jenkins squinted out the rain-splattered window. "Ash is here with the car."

"Guess I'll wait until later." Alex lovingly tucked his gun into his jacket. He dragged the girls out the door while Jenkins helped a still-howling Johnson. Disappointment left a bitter taste in Amy's mouth. Her bullet had only grazed his thigh.

Ash sat in the driver's seat of the same Tata Nano their abductor had driven. He looked decidedly worse for wear with a bleeding lip, a bloody nose, a bruise on his cheek, and two matching black eyes. She cocked a brow. She hadn't pummeled him that badly. Someone else must have taken a turn after she and Susan had escaped.

Alex hurled her into the back seat and took shotgun himself. Jenkins and Johnson piled in on either side of her, Johnson dragging Susan in after him. She flinched at his touch, slid to the floor, and cowered at his feet. Jenkins reached across Amy and pulled Susan to the opposite side of the car. He placed her on the seat between them. Susan peeked at him from under her lashes, her body trembling with fear.

Alex glared at her over his shoulder. "We don't have enough seat belts, and we're not giving the cops an excuse to pull us over. Get down on the floor."

Susan slid off the seat and crouched in front of Jenkins. Amy buckled her seat belt and sat in stony silence as they drove straight back to the shack from earlier. Their nightmare had come full circle.

Ash and Johnson stumbled inside in search of a first aid kit, while Alex again plundered Amy's purse. He produced her phone and frowned. "Why did you let the battery die? Now how will your boyfriend call you?" He tossed the gun to Jenkins and strolled into the shack. "Get them inside."

Jenkins darted a quick look over his shoulder. Amy followed his gaze to the swamp and dense foliage surrounding it. He sighed. "Come on. Let's not give him an excuse to come back."

Susan stared at the dilapidated shack, her dove gray eyes glazed with horror. "I can't! I can't go back in there. Amy, please don't make me." Her face paled. "I'm going to be sick."

Jenkins scooped her from the car and set her at the edge of the dirt driveway. The broad-shouldered gangster gently held her hair back as she was sick on the grass. Amy gawked at them, open-mouthed. Jenkins had more sides to him than a Rubik's Cube.

She climbed from the car and cautiously approached the pair. Susan's shoulders heaved. He pulled her into an awkward hug. "I won't let it happen again," he said with quiet intensity. "Ever."

Susan nodded, blinking back tears. He tucked her close to his side and guided her toward the shack. Amy followed, unease and confusion knotting together in her stomach. Jenkins led them past the rest of Assassin's Honor and tied them up in the smaller room with a deep look of pain in his sea green eyes. He sat next to the TV. Either he thought it too risky to leave them alone, or he imagined his presence helped Susan.

Amy's stomach clenched with guilt. She had to make them let Susan go. The problem was they knew hurting her little sister was the best way to hurt her.

Alex burst through the door with Amy's pistol in his fist. "Someone's been trying to call you. Did you slip up on your way here?" His blue eyes simmered with rage.

She lifted her chin and scowled. "No. I was on the phone with you guys the whole time."

He fixed her with a glacial stare. Her entire body tensed under his penetrating gaze.

Jenkins stood, crossed the distance between them in two long strides, and leaned against the wall to her right. He was a solid burier of muscle protecting her from Alex. "She couldn't have tipped anyone off. She's telling the truth."

Grateful relief swept through her. She released the breath she had been holding. "It's probably our mom," she lied, knowing her mother would never check in on them in a million years. She squared her shoulders and switched to the offensive. "I've done everything you asked. It's time you let my sister leave."

Alex sneered. "Not a chance. We're just getting started." She darted a swift glance to Susan, and her insides tangled with unease. The rest of Assassin's Honor filed into the makeshift prison.

"On your feet!" Johnson glowered at the girls. Amy struggled to stand, but it was difficult while bound. "Not you." He shoved her to the floor. "You." He pointed at Susan. Alex twirled Amy's pistol in his hands.

Panic fluttered in her gut. What if they used her own gun on Susan? "You can't. You—" Amy struggled to speak, her words solidifying within her in a pit of frozen dread.

"Oh yeah?" Johnson sneered, delighted with her reaction. "Wanna bet?"

She met the unflinching gazes of Johnson's followers, pleading with each in turn to stop their leader. They were treating this like a joke, as if her sister was merely their evening entertainment. Only Jenkins appeared surprised.

"What are you going to do to her?" He shifted closer to Susan as Alex yanked her to her feet.

"Relax." Alex grinned, his eyes glinting with sadistic pleasure. "The kid will only suffer a little pain before it's all over."

Amy fought frantically against her restraints. Alex shoved her to the floor. "Don't worry, Amy. We'll even let you watch."

Jenkins scowled. "Cut the crap, Alex."

Alex dragged Susan into the center of the room. Amy held her breath. He wouldn't actually kill her, would he? She was just a child. His threats were nothing more than bravado. Like the tool chest and the power saw. Bile rose in her throat.

Alex flashed her a toothy grin. "By the way, sweet gun. I'm looking forward to testing it." He flipped the G19 in his hand and aimed it at Jenkins. "Check it out!"

"Holy crap!" Jenkins leapt aside. "Get that thing away from me!"

Alex laughed and turned the pistol on Susan.

"Stop it!" Jenkins's hands curled into fists.

Alex waved the gun at him. "Shut up."

Jenkins strode forward and stood directly in front of Susan. "Guys, this has gone on long enough."

"Shut up." Johnson glared at Jenkins from where he leaned unsteadily against the wall. The color had drained from his face. Amy smiled with grim satisfaction. He deserved a world of pain.

"Leave the girl alone," Jenkins said with sudden authority.

They stared each other down until Jenkins looked away. His broad shoulders slumped.

"Right then." Johnson rubbed his hands together. "Let's do this."

"I'm not watching." Jenkins stormed into the living room and slammed the door behind him. The window rattled in its frame.

"You sure about him?" Alex arched a brow.

"He's okay," Johnson grunted, raising one shoulder in a half shrug. "Better than you two, anyway. At least he thinks for himself. You and Ash do exactly what I say like a couple of well-trained dogs." Alex's mouth twitched as if he was itching to argue. Johnson turned his attention back to Susan. "Have you ever experienced true pain?" Susan nodded, too frightened to speak. "Well, you're about to define pain on a whole new level."

"Wait!" Amy pleaded, her voice choked with terror. "Hurt me instead. Don't touch her."

"Don't worry, Amy. We're not going to hurt your precious sister." Alex patted her head. "We're going to torture her instead."

She jerked away from him. "My pistol doesn't have a silencer. Someone will hear it and call the police."

Alex curled his lip. "Unlikely. We're pretty far from the neighbors. Still, it never hurts to play it safe. Arms out," he told Susan, an excited twinkle in his eye.

"Huh?" The strange command shocked her into speaking up at last.

He grabbed her wrist and placed her hand palm down on the table.

"Stop it! Leave her alone!" Amy strained against the ropes. Her face heated from exertion, her jaw clenched so hard her teeth threatened to crack, and her raw wrists wept tears of red where the rope had worn away her skin. And still, her bonds refused to break.

Alex spread Susan's fingers and pressed a butcher knife to her pinky. The blade was crusted with Amy's dried blood.

Jenkins burst into the room with Amy's iPhone in his hand. "You're going to want to take this."

"You answered her phone?" Johnson roared, spittle spraying from his lips. "You idiot! If it's the cops they'll have traced it by now."

"It's not the cops. It's Zack Donnellson."

Amy gaped. Why the hell was Zack calling her? He needed to lose this obsession. It had become life-threatening. Realization hit her like a fist to the gut. Her stomach lurched and her breath caught in her throat. She had been talking to Chris when she had gotten Johnson's call. What if Chris had said something to Zack? "Hang up," she blurted. "Zack's not your problem."

"He is now. Since Jenkins was stupid enough to answer your phone." Johnson glowered as Alex laughed.

"Please." Amy struggled for a beseeching tone. "Leave him out of this. He doesn't know anything." The thought of any harm coming to the surprisingly kind football jock made her heart ache.

Twenty-eight

ZACK RAKED A hand through his hair and anxiously scanned the airport parking lot. Where the hell was Amy's brother? He blew out a breath, worry spiraling within him. He had texted Justin a picture of his car and even dropped a pin to mark his location. Why hadn't he shown up? He stared at his silent phone and willed it to ring.

He drummed his fingers against the steering wheel and scanned the parking lot again. A dark-haired guy in jeans and a UBC sweatshirt broke from the crowd and made a beeline for his car. He was about five ten with thick onyx hair and smoky gray eyes. He had a friendly smile that made Zack think of Susan, and he was the only passenger without luggage. He rapped on the window, and Zack rolled it down.

"Zack Donnellson?" The guy extended a hand.

"Yeah." They shook.

Justin skirted the front bumper and joined Zack in the car. "Explain everything you know and make it fast."

Zack launched into the story, relaying everything from Nathan's death threats to Susan's disappearance.

"You did the right thing when you called me." Justin scrubbed a hand over his forehead. "So, you called Amy before I told you not to. But no one answered, right?"

"Yeah." Zack raked a hand through his messy hair. "Guess I wasn't thinking."

Justin nodded and closed his eyes. A crease appeared between his brows. "Okay, call her again."

"But I thought you said not to."

"Since you already called her, there's no harm in trying a second time. Chances are no one will answer, but if someone does, we might pick up background noises that help identify where they are." Zack shot him an admiring look. He snatched his phone and dialed Amy's number. "You have my sister's digits memorized, eh?" Justin teased with a twinkle in his eye.

They waited, tense and silent, as the phone rang once, twice, three times. "They're not going to answer," Zack said with his finger on the end icon.

The line crackled as someone accepted the call. Zack froze. Justin hadn't told him what to say. "Um, Amy? You there?" The line sputtered, went quiet, and picked up muffled shouting. "What do I say?" he hissed out of the corner of his mouth.

"Stay calm," Justin said, not the least bit calm himself.

A taunting voice spoke in Zack's ear. "Well, well, well. Have a date with Amy tonight? I'm afraid she has other plans."

"Who is this?"

Justin pointed to his phone and mimed putting it on speaker. Zack pressed the button and placed the phone on his knee.

"Now we're gonna have to mess you up too. You people need to learn to stay out of our way." Zack recognized Nathan's twangy Southern drawl.

"Let me talk to Amy."

"As I told your little girlfriend, neither of you are in any position to make demands. I suggest you shut your mouth and listen to someone else for a change." His voice dripped smug, sadistic glee.

Rage simmered deep in Zack's chest. His hands curled into fists. "I won't do anything you say until I talk to Amy."

Fabric rustled against the phone. Her words tumbled out rushed and breathless, but her voice was strong. "Zack, don't listen to them. We're at three two three four—" Amy screamed, and the phone clattered to the floor. Shock lanced through him, swiftly followed by a red-hot bolt of rage. What had they done to her?

"Okay, Donnellson." Nathan was breathing hard. "Since you're so keen to rescue your Amy, sweet Amy, how 'bout you join us?"

Zack forced an offhand tone, fighting to calm the storm of hate raging within him. "Sure. Tell me where you're at, and I'll cruise on over."

"Cute," Nathan said in a mocking tone. "But you'll have to try harder than that if you ever want to see Amy again. Alive, at least."

Justin flinched. Zack gripped the edge of the seat to avoid putting his fist through a window. Anger hummed through his veins as his gut twisted with fear. "Come on, man. You're not serious."

"That you will never know until it's too late." Zack imagined Nathan's stupid, sneering face and longed to punch his lights out.

He gritted his teeth and looked to Justin for help. "Ask to talk to Amy again," he mouthed.

"I need to talk to Amy."

"He's gonna need more convincing." Nathan chuckled.

"No." Justin made a grab for the phone. Zack held it out of his reach.

"No, leave her alone." He clenched his phone in his fist so hard he feared he'd crack the screen.

"Relax, Donnellson," Nathan drawled. "This is for your own good. Give her the phone."

Amy struggled to speak. Her words were muffled as if there was a hand over her mouth. There was a thump and a terrible, bone-crushing crack. Amy screamed, a piercing, heart-wrenching wail of agony. She whimpered once and gasped for air. Zack's knuckles had gone white from crushing his phone. His muscles tensed with the instinct to do something, anything to help her. His heart thudded against his ribs, as adrenaline with no outlet rushed through his veins. He needed to get to Amy. He had to keep a clear head.

Justin was half out of his seat, staring at the phone as if it was burning him. "Say something," he hissed. "Anything!"

Words poured from Zack's lips like vile-tasting acid. "Okay, stop, that's enough. I'll do whatever you want. Tell me what you want, you bastards!"

"Watch your mouth." Nathan chuckled. "Get into your car and drive north toward the outskirts of the city. We'll call you back with more instructions. And Zack, if you bring company, or if you fail to arrive within twenty minutes, Amy's dead."

Zack's hands shook with rage as he jammed his keys into the ignition. "Get out."

"Huh?" Justin's face was a mask of wild-eyed shock. Even his calm had limits.

"They don't know you're here. Get out and call the cops while I find out where they're keeping Amy and Susan."

"Take this." Justin produced a tiny speaker and thrust it into Zack's palm. "Put it in your shirt pocket, and I'll hear everything you say. Maybe even what people around you are saying if you're close enough."

"Okay. Now go." Zack jerked a thumb toward the passenger side door. "They're going to call at any second."

Justin hesitated. "How well do these guys know you? Would they be able to tell the difference if I went instead?"

Zack started his Lexus. "They'd know. I go to school with them." He shot Justin a sympathetic look. He had only met Amy a few days ago, and he was so worried about her and Susan it made him sick. How awful must Justin feel? "I'm sorry, man. It has to be me."

Twenty-nine

AMY FOUGHT TO breathe, struggling to think through the pain in her side. She had never experienced such agony. Her chest caught fire with every shallow breath and every throb of her heart. Noises were distorted as if she lay under water, and the room warbled in nauseating loops whenever she tried to focus. She strained for another agonized breath, and the room dipped and swayed. The cobwebs of pain cleared for an instant. Susan was crying. Amy had to reach her. She gritted her teeth and struggled to stand. Big mistake. One white-hot bolt of pain from her ribs and she crumpled to the floor again.

"On your feet. Shut the girl up."

Susan's screams grew muffled and drifted off. Someone yanked Amy to her feet and carried her after her sister. A crippling spasm made the world go black. She struggled blindly and received a slap across the face. He deposited her in a corner of the living room next to Susan and slammed the door on his way out. The floor dipped so violently, she feared she would slide away.

"Amy," Susan sobbed. "Oh God, the blood. Please tell me you're okay." Amy tried to answer but only produced a strangled moan. An avalanche of words poured from Susan's lips. "This is all my fault. They told me Justin had come to my school. I thought he was here to surprise us. I was so excited, I just jumped into the car. I'm sorry. I'm sorry!"

"It's not your fault. It's mine. Explain later." Amy clung to the shag carpet as the floor rose and fell with her shallow breaths. Her world went dark.

Someone was shouting. She tried to cover her ears, and fire scorched her ribs. She bit back a yelp of pain and lay still. The voices were coming closer. A gust of icy wind made goose bumps rise on her skin.

"Zack!" Susan exclaimed.

Thick white fog swirled in Amy's mind. Zack? Zack wasn't there. Was she hallucinating? Why would she dream of Zack? Bad subconscious. Bad, stupid subconscious. She willed him to disappear.

"What's wrong with her?" Zack asked in a demanding tone. Amy made a disgusted noise. He was rude, even in her hallucinations.

"I don't know. I think she's unconscious." Susan whimpered.

Amy opened her eyes to reassure her sister. Zack was crouched beside her, his crystal blue eyes deep pools of concern. From this angle, he looked almost cute. Her insides went all squishy. "Hi," she rasped. "Miss me too much to stay away?"

He stared at her like she had lost her marbles. Amy lost herself in the deep blue of his eyes.

"Okay, enough chitchat. Now you've seen her. You happy?" Johnson's grating voice made Amy's head pound.

"No." Zack stood to face him. Amy gazed blurrily up at Zack. Up and up and up. He was so tall. How had she never noticed his buffness?

Johnson chuckled. "I doubted you'd be pleased. Will you cooperate now, or do you need more convincing?"

Zack cocked an eyebrow. "Sure, what the hell. What's next? Do I get to be tied up too?"

"Lose the sense of humor, or his finger might slip."

Amy raised her head off the floor. Alex had her pistol trained on Susan. Amy pouted resentfully. Why did he have to use her own weapon against them? They had other guns.

"Okay. Just chill." Zack backed down immediately. "I'll do whatever you say."

"That's more like it." Johnson's mouth twisted unpleasantly. "We wouldn't want anyone to have to hurt the sweet little child." His tone made Amy's skin crawl. "Jenkins, tie Zack up with the girls."

Zack sat between Amy and Susan and placed his hands behind his back.

Alex pointed at Zack's chest. "What's that in his pocket?"

Zack spun away from Susan and Amy and clutched the object in his fist. They tied him up after a blurry, violent struggle.

"What the hell is this?" Johnson held up a tiny speaker.

Alex took one look at it and flinched. "It's a bug!"

"The cops will be here any second." Zack grinned.

They moved so fast, it made Amy's head spin. Alex clocked Zack in the jaw. Ash and Jenkins raced for the front door. Johnson turned to run, thought better of it, and grabbed Susan.

"Stop, stop!" he roared. "You go out that way, you'll be arrested. Get back here." He snapped his fingers, and they scampered to his side. "Here's what we're going to do. You and you." He pointed at Ash and Alex. "Take her." He thrust Susan into Ash's arms. Ash gave a startled yelp and nearly dropped her to the floor. "Get her to the car." They sprinted for the back exit. Johnson glared at Amy and Zack. "Move."

Move? She could barely crawl. She tried to sit up. Bad idea. She collapsed to the floor on a crippling spasm. Jenkins lifted her into his arms and carried her out to the car. He did his best not to jostle her. She still blacked out.

When she next opened her eyes, Jenkins was setting her down in the trunk of a 2015 Audi A7 sedan. She gaped. Which one of these lunatics was rich enough to afford a luxury vehicle? Maybe they had stolen it. The trunk was dark, dusty, and housed the three prisoners with room to spare. The spacious compartment had a carpeted floor, tinted windows, and strangely, a back wall where the seats ought to have been. Amy frowned. Most Audis featured large, luxurious interiors, but they never had entirely enclosed trunks. Assassin's Honor had modified the car so they were able to keep illegal things, like hostages, out of sight.

"Jenkins, watch them and take this." Johnson passed him the .45. Jenkins clambered into the trunk, and Johnson slammed the hatchback.

Zack helped Amy over to the back wall. She leaned against it and sagged onto his shoulder. Susan cuddled up to his other side. Amy closed her eyes and fought to stay conscious. She focused on Zack's even breathing and tried to match her breaths to his.

Doors slammed as the gangsters piled into the sedan. Amy clenched her fists so hard her nails broke the skin. Where the hell were the police?

A rumble shook the floor, and the sedan's engine purred to life. They sped down the street and around the corner. The skies opened up and drenched the city once more. Police sirens were painfully, deafeningly absent.

Thirty

CHARLES CLAWED HIS way up from unconscious oblivion. He opened his eyes to inky blackness and shivered in the cool, damp air. His ears were ringing and his mouth was full of the metallic taste of blood. He was covered in bruises and scrapes with a swollen eye and a nasty lump on the back of his head.

He staggered to his feet to explore his surroundings. Slimy rock walls, sticky cobwebs, and a muddy concrete floor. Alex had imprisoned him in an underground cellar. His lips curved into a smile. What better place to stash a prisoner than in a giant hole in the ground? He smirked. There was no better place unless that prisoner controlled the elements. With a little magical manipulation, he'd have a dirt tunnel to freedom. *Nice try, Alex.* Charles pumped a fist and set to work. Finding flaws in a Dark's plan was akin to locating the Holy Grail.

His tunnel opened into the middle of a rain-soaked yard. Charles crawled onto the muddy grass and warily looked around. The shack was eerily quiet, the night dismal but still. Tendrils of fear snaked through his gut. The silence unnerved him more than terrorized screams. At least screaming would prove Amy was alive.

Charles had followed her to the elementary school and then halfway across Toronto, sure Assassin's Honor was seconds from an illegal act. Their long, muddy trek had ended at a dilapidated shack, which Amy had rushed to like her life depended on it. Charles had lurked outside in the shadows and waited for her with mounting dread. He had watched from the bushes as Alex dragged her across the yard and dialed 911 before hanging up in a panic. What if Alex found out with his mind-reading powers and murdered Amy before human help arrived? Charles had faced Alex in a desperate and illogical attempt to keep her safe. He hoped nothing worse had happened while he had been unconscious.

A car careened up the driveway, its tires sending mud in all directions. Charles dove behind some dripping foliage and bumped the overgrown shrub in his haste. Ice-cold droplets cascaded onto his head. He held his breath and peeked through the shrubbery, expecting to see Assassin's Honor surrounding him. Instead, Zack Donnellson leapt from his expensive car and charged inside as if his ass was on fire. Charles cringed. The gang had another hostage.

He hid behind the shrubbery and waited for an opportunity to surprise Alex. The gusting wind built to a shrieking howl, and thunder rolled closer with every flash of jagged lightning. He bit his lip, unease fluttering in his stomach. He was never going to hear them if Amy and Zack called for help.

Charles slunk toward the rotting, squat structure to get a closer look. The front window was obscured with graffiti so he stole around back in search of another. The only window on that side was high off the ground. He needed something to stand on.

A shadow darted behind the glass. The back door burst open, and light streamed into the yard. Charles hit the ground and rolled into the crawl space below the house. Panic scattered his senses. What if they had seen him? Two people streaked across the muddy grass to a shiny gray sedan. They loaded something into the trunk and scrambled into the front seats.

Charles darted to a tree, then to some bushes twenty feet away. A nasty, spitting rain had begun to fall. He glanced up at the sky and winced. The bloodred moon glared down at the earth like the un-blinking eye of a mythical monster, its glowing red pupil ringed with an iris of anthracite storm clouds.

He dropped his gaze to the yard with a shiver of foreboding and gaped in horror as more of his classmates charged into the night. Peter tore across the yard first, carrying an unconscious Amy in his arms. Charles curled his lip. So much for him wanting to help her. Zack and Nathan were close behind Peter. Zack's hands were tied, and Nathan had a gun to his back.

Charles squinted in concentration, focusing destructive magic-al energy on their gun. He altered the likelihood that its bullets would hit their marks, cursing the weapon with inaccuracy. If anyone pulled the trigger, the bullet was sure to miss. He nodded with grim satisfaction. That ought to throw a wrench into their plans.

Charles turned his attention to the car. He had to get their license plate for the police. He squinted through the rain, but his glasses had fogged up and the numbers were illegible through the dark, stormy night. Anxiety swirled in his gut. He had seconds left to act.

The car purred to life and careened up the muddy street. Charles sat frozen in the dirt, too terrified and too powerless to stop them. His heart plummeted into a churning pit of nausea. The sedan's taillights faded into the blackness, and he hung his head in shame. Zack was right. He was a pathetic loser.

He thumped a frustrated fist into the muddy ground. His hand smashed a rock, further bloodying his bruised knuckles. Anger surged within him and lent him courage. He leapt to his feet and charged the nearest shack. Alex had taken his phone, but he was going to get his hands on another. He could describe the car to the police if nothing else.

"Hey!"

The shout startled him and he slipped in a puddle. Cold, dirty water oozed into his sneakers and soaked his socks.

"Who the hell are you?" Someone shined a flashlight in his face.

"Uh." Charles wiped slimy mud off his jeans. "I'm Charles Banks."

"I'm Justin Evans." The guy narrowed his eyes, studying him closely from battered head to muddy toe.

Charles grasped Justin's arm. "Some friends of mine are in trouble. Do you have a phone? We have to call nine-one-one."

"Do you know my sister?" Justin shined the light in his eyes again. "Who did you say you were?"

Police radios crackled and voices barked orders. Relief swept through him with the force of a hurricane. Someone else had called the cops. Charles blinked rapidly in the glare of the flashlight as Justin's last name registered. "You're Amy's brother?"

His brows snapped together. "Tell me everything you know."

Charles dropped his hand from Justin's arm, leaving a muddy brown streak across his gray sleeve. "That's basically nothing." Jagged red lightning split the sky in two. The heavens opened up at last.

"Tell me where Amy, Zack, and Susan are," Justin shouted above the storm.

"Susan? Who's that?" Justin glared. Charles struggled to focus through his headache. "Everyone's gone. You literally just missed them. They must have known you were on your way, because they sped off in a gray sedan less than a minute ago. They went that way." He pointed up the flooding street.

Justin called to the officers searching the shack. "They already left. Hurry, we have to follow them." He grabbed Charles by the sleeve and towed him toward the nearest of two squad cars. "Come on, kid. You're coming with us."

"I don't know anything else," Charles said in protest, dragging his feet through the mud.

Justin leapt into the back seat. "You know enough to help. Get in!"

Thirty-one

AMY SAT PROPPED in the trunk with her chest on fire and her thoughts a swirling cocktail of misery. Hours had trickled past since she had been abducted, and no one but Zack had even tried to call her phone. The world was oblivious to the trio's plight, and Amy had only herself to blame. Everyone had tried to warn her. Why hadn't she listened and taken Assassin's Honor seriously? She was reckless with her own life, for sure, but Zack's and Susan's? She ought to have guessed what Alex was planning. She ought to have figured it out sooner. She should have done something, anything to stop this. She should have, but she hadn't, and now her favorite people were paying the price.

Zack had stayed awake for hours before falling asleep with his head on her shoulder. Susan had passed out after five minutes on the highway, the soothing rumble of the damp, warm trunk lulling her peacefully into dreamland. Amy's pain had kept her awake while her mind tortured her with its cloying guilt. Every breath, no matter how shallow, sent burning spasms through her chest and down her left side.

Their guard, Jenkins, had also stayed up. He was leaning against the trunk's hatchback with his gun close at his side. His mouth was set in a grim line, and a five o'clock shadow accentuated his strong jaw. He looked every inch the brooding gangster. A black iPhone rested on his knee with its flashlight app open. This faint glow, together with the occasional pair of passing headlights, was the only illumination in the pitch-black trunk.

"What are you looking at?" Jenkins shattered their suffocating silence.

"Nothing." Amy innocently lowered her lashes.

His gaze drifted cautiously toward the gun as if hoping it had vanished. "How did a nice girl like you get tangled up with Assassin's Honor? Like what did you do to make them hate your guts? Alex doesn't usually try to murder girls he barely knows." He absentmindedly traced his gang tattoo.

Amy gazed at him with bone weary apathy. "You don't know what happened on Monday? They never told you?" Jenkins had been absent when she had stood up for Charles that day.

"Nope." He stretched his arms behind his head. "I was at the gym warming up for the football game."

His absurdly normal response made her giggle out loud. A shooting pain cut her mirth short. Her eyes watered as bolts of fire scorched her ribs. She gasped and clenched her teeth to keep from crying out.

Jenkins leaned toward her, concern evident in his sea green eyes. He reached into his pocket. Amy flinched. "It's okay, take this. You'll feel better." She stared at the red and blue gel capsules he was holding. "It's Tylenol, not poison." A corner of his mouth twitched. "If hanging around with Alex has taught me anything, it's how to prepare for pain."

She tilted her head. "Okay, that might be the most depressing thing I have ever heard. I'm tied up, remember?"

"Right." He fed her a couple pills. She swallowed them fast and prayed for instant relief. "Why did you trust me?"

"Poison or drugs would at least dull the pain."

They were quiet for several minutes before Jenkins spoke again. "Does he know what happened back there?"

"Zack? No, and I'd like to keep it that way." She narrowed her eyes. "Don't tell him. He'll get pissed and do something stupid."

"Amy, relax." He held up his hands in a placating gesture. "I'll keep it between us."

She startled at the use of her first name. He knew so much about her. How? Why didn't she even remember going to school with him? Assassin's Honor dealt in shady, anonymous secrecy. Amy was sick of it and info was power. "So, Jenkins, what's your name?"

"I'll make you a deal. I'll tell you my name if you explain why you're here."

"Okay, but it's not especially interesting."

"I'm all ears." He folded his arms over his chest and leaned against the hatchback, faking a yawn.

"I stopped your friends out there from beating someone up." She sadly shook her head. Rescuing Charles had not been worth a week from hell.

"Seriously?" His green eyes widened. "No one's ever done that before. Was it Banks?"

"Yeah." Her forehead creased as she frowned. "How did you know? You said you were somewhere else."

His shoulders slumped. "I was. But he's their favorite target."

"Isn't he your favorite target too?"

"I guess." Jenkins dropped his gaze.

She threw him a disgusted look and turned away. Why had she wasted her time talking to him? Acting marginally less awful than the rest of his friends didn't make him a good person. He was still a member of the gang who wanted her dead.

"It's Peter."

"Huh?" Her eyes flicked back to his face. The flashlight's faint glow illuminated the sorrow in his eyes.

"Peter Jenkins. That's my name. I promised to tell you."

"Right." Amy tilted her head to one side and regarded him from underneath her lashes. His taut body was all muscle. From his rock-hard chest to his brawny arms, every inch of him was honed for strength. His serious face gave nothing away, but his eyes brimmed with compassion. He wasn't the type to get tangled up with Assassin's Honor either.

"How's the rib?" he asked, his voice laced with concern.

"Better. The Tylenol helped."

"Good."

Amy leaned against the wall and closed her eyes, hoping to fall asleep like Zack and Susan had.

"He adores you, you know."

"Who does?" she mumbled, her eyes drifting open.

"Zack. You two are made for each other."

"How would you know? You don't know us."

"Actually, I know Zack pretty well. He's a good guy, great team player." Peter averted his guilty gaze.

Amy took pity on him and did what she usually did when conversations grew uncomfortable, changed the subject. "It doesn't matter. He has a girlfriend."

"Had a girlfriend." Peter brightened. "He dumped her ... for you."

"He did not. Jessie said they had a meltdown or something."

"Yeah." Peter smirked. "Over you."

"They were not fighting about me." Football jocks did not have arguments with their cheerleader girlfriends over weird loner chicks.

"They were. I was there."

"They were not." She laughed.

"Were too."

"Were not."

"Were too."

"No, they weren't."

"Yes, they were."

"Okay, stop." Amy smirked.

"I won." Peter grinned.

"Did not."

"Did too."

"Did not."

Zack jerked upright, startling them both. "Sorry. I must have fallen asleep."

"No problem." Amy smiled indulgently. Did he remember falling asleep on her shoulder? Why did she care? Peter winked. Amy threw him a dirty look. Zack once again stared at her as if she had lost her mind.

The sedan slowed, pulled over, and stopped. The comforting thrum of the engine cut out, leaving a cold, jarring stillness in its wake. Peter picked up the gun, and Zack flinched as if he expected him to open fire.

The wall Susan had been sleeping against slid to one side, and Ash's freckled face appeared in the gap. "Dude, you're wanted up front."

Peter gently lifted Susan out of the way and disappeared through the hatch. Ash closed it behind them.

"Wow!" Susan's eyes popped open. "I had no idea that was hidden there!"

"Amy." Zack swiftly turned to her, urgency flashing in his crystal blue eyes. "What happened during that phone call? Are you okay?"

"I'm fine," Amy lied, irritation pricking her words.

"Did the Tylenol help?" Susan asked with an innocent smile.

Amy narrowed her eyes at her sister. "I thought you were asleep."

"What Tylenol?" Zack said, his brows shooting upward in alarm. "Where did you find Tylenol?"

Susan smiled brightly. "Peter gave it to her. He's sweet."

"You were talking to him?"

"Yes." Amy jutted her chin at him. "Got a problem with that?" Zack was cute only when he was silent.

His eyes flashed. "Amy. These guys are dangerous. How can you sit there chatting with them after everything they've done?"

"But he gave her Tylenol." Susan intervened on Amy's behalf. "That was nice."

"You took it?" Zack gasped.

Amy lifted her chin. "Yes, I did. And I feel a lot better, thank you very much."

His expression softened as anger gave way to concern. "You said you were fine. Tell me what happened."

"You're so damn pushy."

"They hit Amy with a hammer. Once to her head and once to her side. She couldn't breathe for a while. I thought you were going to die!" Susan fought a sob. Amy's heart ached. Now how was she supposed to get mad at her for spilling the beans?

Thirty-two

RAGE BUBBLED INSIDE Zack like swiftly rising lava. He took in Amy's taut, pained expression and clenched his jaw against a burst of blinding fury. Assassin's Honor had given her a concussion and smashed up her ribs. She had been forced to talk to Peter after he, Zack, had fallen asleep. He was never letting that happen again. He was going to stay awake until they escaped … Or were killed.

The sedan had been still for an anxious five minutes, and the tension in the trunk had built into a clenching hyper alertness that made every sound into a threat and every movement a reason to flinch. Zack's mind leaped from question to question like a kid with ADHD who was unable to hold still. Had the gang stopped to torture them? Had they reached the end of the line? Were they waiting outside a second gang clubhouse? Were they going to kill Susan and make Amy watch? Were they calling his own parents and demanding a million dollars? Amy gazed at him over the top of Susan's head, many of the same questions flickering in her misty gray eyes. She had Susan tucked behind her, shielding the smaller girl from whatever happened next. Her first instinct was to protect her sister, no matter the cost to herself. Zack held her gaze and vowed to do the same for Amy.

The hatch slid open and Peter clambered through. Zack curled his lip. "Great. You're back."

Peter sat cross-legged against the side window. The sedan's engine rumbled to life, and they coasted back into traffic. They turned onto a twisting, windy road and began bumping along rough terrain.

"Where are we going?" Amy asked, her shoulders tense.

Peter yawned. "Nowhere in particular. We're trying to find an out-of-the-way place to stop for the night, but we might have to keep driving until morning."

Zack pursed his lips and exhaled through his nose. At least Peter was being straight with them. His mind continued to batter him with questions. How long would it be until they stopped? What fresh horrors would that bring? The wondering was what got to him. He wished Assassin's Honor would just get the torture over with and dump them at the side of the road.

Amy and Susan had fallen asleep back to back. They had managed to clasp hands despite the ropes that bound them. Susan's hair was splayed around her face in a silken onyx halo. The little girl wore an angelically peaceful expression as she slumbered. She was still young enough to dream of leprechauns, rainbows, and fairy-tale castles in the sky. In contrast to her sister, Amy looked troubled, even in sleep. She worried her lower lip as she slept, and her eyes darted to and fro behind their pale lids. His heart squeezed. Was she having a nightmare?

Zack looked up to find Peter contemplating the girls. He clenched his jaw, fierce possessiveness gripping him. Zack took a deep breath and tried to rein in his anger. He had to behave, or they would hurt Susan or break another of Amy's ribs.

His composure lasted for all of five minutes. "What are you staring at?" He pierced Peter with a hate-filled glare.

"Nothing." Peter wrenched his gaze away. "Look, man. I'm truly sorry about this." His green eyes clouded with sorrow.

Zack snorted. "Which part? Leaving threatening notes in Amy's locker, stalking her at school, using Susan to threaten Amy, or using Amy to get to me?"

Peter bit his lip. "I had nothing to do with that."

"Nothing to do with what? The note?"

"I had nothing to do with using her." Peter gestured at Susan. "I told them they were way out of line."

Zack's short temper simmered just below boiling point. So Peter had a conscience, but what good was a conscience if he refused to listen to it? "And yet you used her anyway."

Peter flinched. "She reminds me of my sister."

Zack furrowed his brow. A lifetime ago, he and Peter had been best friends. They had stopped hanging out in fifth grade, around the same time Peter began slumming it with Nathan Johnson. Zack hadn't seen Peter's sister much since they were kids. She had died in a car accident last year.

Zack raised an incredulous brow. "Amy reminds you of Julia?" Peter's sister had been happy and sweet. Amy was many things, but she was not sweet.

"No. Susan."

Zack blew out a long, irritated breath. Peter had a point. Julia Jenkins had been a year younger than them. She'd had starry blue eyes, bouncy butterscotch curls, and a light-up-the-world smile that made you want to smile too. Five minutes with her made your day. She and Susan looked nothing alike, but both girls had the same bubbly personality and charismatic bounce.

His heart gave a feeble twinge of loss. He bulldozed past it on a surge of frustrated blame. Why had Peter brought her up? Julia's death had nothing to do with what his stupid gang had done to Susan, Amy, and him. "Save it for your therapist."

They passed the next few hours in taut, angry silence. Peter stared out the window; Zack stared at Amy. Soft ebony hair framing her delicate face. Thick, dark lashes resting against fair, creamy skin. She was beautiful and he had never noticed her. Was his field of view really that narrow? Was his hot girl radar so damaged it only picked up snobby, rich bitches? He stretched out a hand to touch the top of hers. Her chest rose and fell with the regularity of gentle, lapping waves. Her breathing was even but shallow. Was she still hurting? Concern for her flooded his chest.

Susan was sleeping fitfully as well. Her fingers had curled into small, ineffectual fists, and she whimpered softly as she dreamed. Her once tranquil smile had been replaced with a tense frown. The rough ropes chafed against her tiny wrists as she tossed and turned. Peter bit his lip and untied her. Susan mumbled something in her sleep and rolled onto her side, her head almost in Peter's lap. He stared at her and didn't move.

Zack pursed his lips. "Untie Amy while you're at it."

Peter nodded and cut them both loose. Shock lanced through Zack at the reckless decision. He rubbed his wrists and swept his gaze around the trunk. Could he get ahold of the gun?

"Why are you doing this?" He stretched his arms out in front of him. His fingers were millimeters from the weapon. "This because of your dad?" Peter had nothing on Alex or Nathan. He had avoided conflict at all cost when they were kids.

Peter moved the gun to his other side and propped it against the hatchback. Zack's heart sank into his shoes. His plan ought to make history as the world's fastest fail. Peter avoided his question by staring out into the night. He and Amy had a lot in common. Both built walls so high, they iced out the world.

The car bounced over a bump, and Amy jolted awake. Her hand flew to her side, a breath catching in her throat. Zack wanted nothing more than to take her in his arms and will her pain away.

"You okay?" he asked and brushed his fingers against her arm.

"Why am I untied?" She ignored his question but didn't pull her arm away.

"Was it more comfortable with your hands behind your back? I could always tie you up again." Peter smirked.

"No thanks." Amy cringed, touching two fingers to her wrist. Her gaze fell upon Susan. "Do you want me to move her?"

"Nah, it's fine. She looks comfy."

"Okay, I'm going back to sleep." Amy leaned her head against the wall and shut her eyes.

Zack gently turned her so her head rested in his lap. A lock of her soft dark hair fell into his hand, and he fought the urge to run it through his fingers. Peter hid a smile. "What?" Zack scowled.

"She thinks you don't like her."

"We're friends, if that." Amy was never going to want anything more, and lying about his feelings was growing old.

"Yeah. You're in denial."

Thirty-three

GENTLE HANDS LIGHTLY shook Amy awake. "Amy, you have to wake up now," Zack said.

"Why?" She opened one eye and let it droop shut again. "I'm tired."

Peter nudged her shoulder. "Come on, bathroom break."

"No thanks. I want to sleep." She tucked her knees up to her chest, curling into a comfy ball of warmth.

"You sure it was Tylenol you gave her?" Zack said accusingly.

The trunk's hatchback opened, and Susan scooted closer to Peter. Amy blinked open her eyes. She had expected Susan to look to Zack for protection.

Ash, Alex, and Johnson stood in a row by the sedan's open trunk. Alex glared at Peter. "Why the hell are they untied?"

"Did you expect them to walk in there with their hands behind their backs? Don't you think that would look a tiny bit suspicious?"

Johnson nodded and shoved Alex's shoulder. His expression darkened as his eyes circled the group. "This is how things are gonna go down. Jenkins and I will stay with the car. Cardelle and Ash will get them in and out. Don't let them talk to anyone or call attention to themselves in any way."

Peter and Susan climbed out of the sedan. Zack stayed close beside Amy. She cuddled up to him and drew strength from his steady presence.

"Out of the trunk," Johnson snarled.

"Amy?" Zack slid an arm around her shoulders. "Can you walk?"

"No."

"Just let her stay here." Peter scraped a hand over the stubble on his cheek.

"Forget it." Johnson slammed a fist against the side of the sedan, making Amy jump. "Amy, we'll drag you if we have to. Get your butt out here."

"Fine." She shakily crawled from the trunk and stood, swaying, in a 7-Eleven parking lot. The storefronts to either side were dark, the area deserted except for a homeless teen sleeping soundly on a park bench. The sedan was tucked in a secluded corner by a grove of tall, slender oaks. Eerie crimson light filtered down from the sky and bathed the scene in a disturbing shade of scarlet. She gazed up at the moon. It glowed a dark bloodred. A clammy, creeping sensation slid into her mind. Hate bubbled in her soul and begged her for violence. The world tilted until it was laid out below her, billions of insignificant termites that needed to be exterminated. Amy wrenched her gaze away and clutched at her pounding heart. Nausea rose up within her, cold terror making her weak. Her head spun as she met Alex's chilling gaze. His eyes were as red as the moon above. Her stomach lurched, fear careening through her like a runaway train. She staggered backward and tripped. She blinked, and Alex's eyes were stormy blue once more.

"People are going to notice something's wrong." Zack put a hand under Amy's elbow to steady her. His touch was warm through her thin cotton sleeve. "Let her stay with the car."

The more they argued with him, the more determined Johnson became. In the end, he made her go. Zack half carried her the thirty feet to the store. She stared blurrily at Johnson over Zack's broad shoulder. Why was it so important that they go to the washroom? Shouldn't Assassin's Honor want them out of the public eye? The gang's decisions never made sense.

The group trooped inside 7-Eleven and formed an uneasy knot by the door. The warm, little store smelled of fruity chewing gum and chocolate. An elderly man dozed behind the register with yesterday's newspaper spread out on the counter. The latest loss by the Toronto Maple Leafs and an announced decrease in foreign trade had put him to sleep. Amy had a feeling today's paper was going to spark more interest.

"What do we do now?" Ash muttered out of the corner of his mouth. "We can't go into the girls' bathroom!" Alex cursed under his breath.

"Come on." Susan's eyes flashed. "We've been potty-trained for a very long time."

"Fine. No one will be in here this early anyway." Alex shoved Amy toward Susan. "Make sure she doesn't pass out and get people staring."

"How you doing?" Susan asked as soon as the bathroom door had shut behind them.

"I'm good." Amy straightened, trying to ignore the dull throbbing in her side. "I've got a plan." She snatched a heavy ceramic soap dish and cracked it against the mirror.

"What are you doing?" Susan gaped at her as if she had lost her mind. Amy resisted the urge to roll her eyes. She had been receiving that look a lot lately.

"No time to explain." The soap dish hadn't even chipped the glass. She smashed it into the mirror with all the force she could muster. Nothing happened. She gave a frustrated roar and yanked on the mirror's wooden frame. The whole thing came right off the wall. Susan's mouth hung open, clearly wondering what had driven her sister to a life of crime and vandalism.

Amy banged the mirror against the counter with enough noise to wake the dead. The glass cracked down the middle without a single shard popping loose. Desperation clawed at her insides as time ticked away. She tossed the indestructible mirror aside. "Sue, we need to leave a message. I'm looking for something to scratch the wall."

"What about writing on the paper towels?"

"I don't have a pen."

"I do." Susan produced one with a triumphant flourish. Amy gaped at her in admiring disbelief. Had her brilliant little sister snagged a pen off a convenience store shelf?

"You're amazing!" She snatched the pen and tore a chunk of paper towel.

Susan bounced on her toes. "What should we write?"

A rap on the door stopped them cold. "You two nearly done? Dad's waiting in the car." Alex's emotionless voice froze Amy's insides with dread.

Amy pressed a finger to her lips and gestured toward the door. Susan's eyes grew wide. "What do I say?" she mouthed.

"Tell them I'm feeling sick." Amy snatched up her paper and pen and hobbled into the nearest stall.

Susan's voice trembled with fear as she repeated what Amy had said.

"Let's go." Amy crumpled her note into a ball and closed her fist around it.

She stumbled from the washroom, leaning on Susan for support. Zack, Ash, and Alex were standing by the door, both gangsters looking nervous. Alex beckoned them with a finger. Amy exaggerated her faintness and pretended to trip. She ignored the instinct to break her fall and smashed face-first into the linoleum. A thousand white-hot bolts of pain shot from her ribs and ricocheted through her body. A strangled moan escaped her lips. Tears streamed from her eyes as she fought in vain to breathe.

"Oh my goodness!" The elderly man at the register rushed from behind the counter. "Young lady, are you all right?" He hurried to her side and offered her a large, callused hand. She looked up into a face that had seen years of hard, honest work. His skin was wrinkled and weathered, his blue eyes kind. He was the perfect helpful stranger.

Amy swiftly seized his hand and clung to his fingers like a girl who was drowning. She got to her feet but refused to release him. "I'm sorry, I slipped. I'm such a klutz."

"Quite all right." The man smiled kindly. He opened his mouth to add something more and gaped in surprise as she pushed her crumpled note into his palm.

She shook his hand. "Thank you so much!" She tried to get him to focus on her and ignore the group by the door.

Alex scowled. "Amy, we have to go."

"Okay." She beamed at the cashier. "Thanks again."

"Goodbye, miss." The man released her hand and discreetly tucked her note into his pocket.

Elation flooded her. Amy fought a triumphant smile and hobbled slowly across the parking lot. The more time the cashier had to call the police, the better.

"She gave something to that guy back there," Alex blurted the moment they reached the sedan. "I think it was a note." Amy's good feelings evaporated.

"What?" An angry red flush crept up Johnson's neck. He swore under his breath and screamed at the others. "Get those two into the trunk!" He grabbed Amy's wrist. "You're coming with me."

Frustrated fury surged through her veins. She was so done being pushed around. She raised her free fist and clocked him in the jaw. "You little bitch!" A vein popped out in his thick red neck. He wrapped a hand around her throat and hauled her bodily into the back seat. His fingernails dug painfully into her skin. She kicked his thigh where she had shot him earlier. He howled in pain, and she made no effort to hide her satisfied smirk.

"Next time I shoot you, I'll have better aim," she rasped through his choke hold.

"Great threat." Alex leered as he joined them in the back seat. "But you're never going to have the chance. If I ever let you hold a gun again, you'll be pointing it at your boyfriend." His eyes lit up. "Hey now, that's a fun question. Who would you rather kill, Amy? Your boyfriend or your sister?"

Thirty-four

CHARLES AND JUSTIN had spent the night crammed into the back of a squad car swapping info. Justin had explained how he, Zack, and the police had gotten involved. Zack had grown worried about Amy after talking to his little brother, who knew Amy's little sister, whom Assassin's Honor had kidnapped. Zack had then phoned Justin, who got in touch with a friend who worked for the Royal Canadian Mounted Police. They had trailed Assassin's Honor all night with the second of two tracking devices that Justin had given Zack. The entire tangled mess made Charles's head throb.

Charles had recounted the events that had led to Amy's abduction. It had been downright humiliating explaining how Justin's little sister had saved him from a beating. Charles was sure Justin thought he was an idiot, especially since he'd had to omit the one cool thing he had done, saving Amy and Peter from Alex in the toolshed. It would have prompted too many questions about the supernatural world. He pressed his forehead against the cool glass of the window and shut his eyes. His dreams were plagued with flying power saws and Alex's sneering face.

Justin nudged him in the ribs. "Dude. Wake up!"

He straightened and rubbed his eyes. The squad car was parked at the side of the road. "What's going on?"

"We've got a fix on their position. They stopped at a 7-Eleven about a kilometer from here."

His heart leapt at the news. "Great! Let's go nab them!"

Justin's smile slipped. "We can't, not yet."

"What? Why not? That's what we're here for, isn't it?"

Justin blew out a weary breath. "They have guns. If we corner them, we'll encourage a hostage situation."

"We're already there!" Tension knotted in his stomach and made it clench tight. He shuddered to think what would happen if they missed this chance. Alex would never provide another.

Justin's gray eyes flashed with anger. "Listen to me. If they're desperate enough, they could shoot one as an example and keep the others around as immunity bargains. There's no way we'd save them all."

Charles struggled to keep the bitter edge from his voice. "So we're going to sit here while they fetch snacks?"

Justin glared at him, his brows coming together in a thick, angry line. "No, we're going to do something stupid and get everyone killed." He stormed from the car.

Charles put a hand to his aching forehead. He never knew when to shut up. Bone-weary sadness threatened to smother him as a literal pain knifed his chest. He stared dully after Justin with despair blanketing his soul. He was standing with a slender female officer. They faced off aggressively in a heated debate.

Curiosity nudged aside his despair. Charles scrambled from the car to investigate. The chilly predawn air was a welcome relief from the stifling heat of the squad car.

The female cop was tiny, barely five feet tall. She was young and devastatingly beautiful with hair the color of midnight and eyes so blue they put the ocean to shame. Her perfect face was sculpted porcelain, her long dark lashes like feathered silk. Charles stared at her in awe. She was a real-life, here on Earth, honest-to-goodness angel! Did she have a secret supernatural job bringing justice to Darks? He loved her on sight.

"You're way out of line, Evans!" The angelic cop stood with her shoulders squared and her back ramrod straight. "Sending a civilian into a hostile vehicle is far too dangerous."

Justin speared her with an angry look. "It's the only way to rescue them without risking a firing squad. They'll never notice a random person hitching a ride on the back of their car. People do it all the time! I'll be fine!"

"What makes you think this crazy plan of yours will work?" She planted her tiny hands on her itty-bitty hips and scowled at him with her blue eyes blazing. "Nothing like it has even been attempted before. You'll wind up getting yourself killed!"

"Or I could save their lives." Justin was impervious to her fiery cuteness. "And that's the beauty of it. They'll never expect anything like it."

"Have you ridden a skateboard before?"

"Of course." Justin spread his hands in an I-can-do-anything gesture. "I used to skateboard all the time."

She arched one perfectly sculpted brow. "How many years ago?" He bit his lip and looked at the ground. "That's what I thought." She softened her tone. "Sorry, Justin. I know you're worried about your sisters, but risking your life unnecessarily is a bad call. We would need someone with fresh experience on a skateboard, and none of my officers have ridden one since they were teenagers. It'll be too late by the time we locate someone qualified."

Justin deflated. The officer turned away and strode to her squad car. Justin stared into space with mingled heartbreak and unease.

Charles's heart twisted. Wasn't there something, anything, helpful he could do? An idea crystallized in his mind, and he yelped with the shock of sudden inspiration. "Wait! I skateboard all the time!"

"You do?" Justin turned to him, hope sparking in his eyes.

"No way." The cop vetoed his idea immediately. "No, no, no."

"Yes!" Charles beamed. He was good at this, and he knew it! A surge of excitement sang through his veins. "I've even skateboarded behind cars before. It'll be a piece of cake!"

Having magical abilities was finally going to pay off. His affinity for the elements would allow him to contort the air around him and shape it into steadying walls of energy to help him keep his balance. He could also alter his risk of falling, tilting the odds in his favor. He used a gentle nudge of magic to attract the angel's attention.

She studied him closely, her brilliant deep blue gaze betraying her interest. "How old are you?" She tapped a finger against her chin and assessed his power level.

"Seventeen."

Shadows of doubt flickered in her ocean blue eyes. "You look fifteen. I'm not sending a child to certain death."

Charles huffed out an indignant breath.

"He's a friend of my sister's." Justin swiftly backed him up. "He's in Amy's class. He is seventeen."

Charles held up his hands in a placating gesture. "I can do this. Just give me the chance."

"But what if you get hurt?" Her gaze flicked nervously between the two boys. She was tempted, Charles could tell.

"What if my sisters die?" Justin asked.

Thirty-five

PETER STRUGGLED WITH Zack as Nathan hurled Amy into the
back seat. Her eyes sparked with pain at the jarring impact. Peter
gritted his teeth, barely biting back a protest. Treating a girl that way,
let alone one with Amy's injuries, made him want to slam Nathan
through a wall.

A white-hot streak of pain flashed behind his eyes. He stiffened, his mind rebelling against the invasion. Alex's eyes bored into
his, the warning clear in his soulless, stormy glare. Peter's stomach
clenched. Beads of sweat formed on his brow. He tensed every
muscle in an effort to regain control of his thoughts. The pressure
broke, and mind-numbing calm enveloped him. He smoothed his expression and slowly unclenched the fists he had curled at his sides.
His anger dimmed, doused by swirling rapids of guilt. There was
nothing he could do.

He shook his head to clear it and scooped Susan into the trunk.
Ash struggled with Zack. Alex pulled the gun on Susan and Zack
sprang into the car. Peter had to hand it to him, Alex knew how to
manipulate people. Threatening a nine-year-old would make any
self-respecting person back off. Alex and Ash dove into the sedan,
Alex into the back and Ash to the driver's seat. Peter tore around to
the passenger side.

"Go!" Nathan screamed. "They'll be here any second!"

Tires screeched as they squealed onto the road. Peter glanced
over his shoulder to check on Amy. Nathan and Alex had her pinned
against the back seat. She struggled with the ferocity of a caged

animal. It took both guys to keep her still and cover her mouth at the same time.

"Tried to pull a fast one on us, eh Amy?" Nathan sneered.

"Yep." Her eyes gleamed with triumph. "It was a piece of cake outsmarting you losers." A sharp exhalation of air hissed from her lips as Alex pressed a hand to her injured ribs and pinned her against the seat.

Peter's gut clenched. She had gone too far. Sassing back was as much a part of Amy's personality as total control was a part of Nathan's. Nathan's eyes blazed with fury as he slapped her across the face. She endured the first two slaps without a sound. Nathan swore in frustration and punched her in the mouth. Amy sobbed. She tried to yank one of her hands free, no doubt to throw a punch herself, but Alex held her still.

Peter stared at them, mute and unblinking, as if watching the scene on TV. But he couldn't change the channel; he couldn't turn it off. The violence was real, and he was a part of it. He had caused the angry red marks on Amy's face, the blood at the corner of her mouth. Bile burned his throat with self-loathing.

Alex grabbed Amy's chin and jerked her face toward him. "Maybe that'll teach you to do what we say from now on." He flexed his fingers, crushing her face in his grip. "Next time it'll be your sweet little sister who's punished for your mistakes." Alex waited for Amy to react, but she stayed silent.

"Got that?" Nathan gave Amy's shoulders a jarring shake.

"Yes," she said through clenched teeth. "Please don't hurt my sister."

"Your sister," Alex spat, "is lucky to be alive."

Blood roared in Peter's ears. He ground his jaw so hard it hurt. He turned in his seat to face them, his expression hard, his gaze unflinching. "That's enough."

Alex's eyes widened a fraction. "Shut up, Jenkins." He slapped her this time, leaving another angry mark on her cheek.

Amy was crying now, her tears spilling from her eyes to flow freely down her face. They were beating the strength out of her. Waves of guilt and revulsion battered Peter's soul. "I said that's enough! Leave her alone."

"I told you to shut up!" Alex's face contorted with fury. His eyes bulged as if he had gone mad.

"We were supposed to have been done with this by now." Peter lowered his voice, trying to keep his cool.

"We would be if she stopped messing everything up. We'll have to end it a few hours from here."

"When are you going to let my sister and Zack go?" Amy whimpered.

"Shut up!" Nathan slammed a meaty fist into her temple. The force of the blow sent her sprawling across Alex's lap. He shoved her away, and she landed in a heap on the floor.

The scene played out in slow motion, splitting Peter's vision into several still snapshots. Amy on the floor. The guys laughing above her. Amy raising her arms to protect her face. The dread knotting in his stomach was achingly familiar. It plunged him back into a memory laced with pain.

Amy vanished. His sister cowered in her place. She clutched a doll to her chest as their father loomed over her with a baseball bat.

"Dad, I'm sorry! It was an accident! I never meant to break the vase!" She gazed up at him, her blue eyes misty, her pale lashes wet. After all this time, Julia still hoped for mercy.

"Dad?" Peter hovered in the doorway. His father had had way too much to drink, and their mom was working the night shift. There was no one around to help. Peter was small for ten and no match for the seasoned gangster.

"Go back to bed, Peter!" His father swung toward him, bat in hand.

Panic lodged in Peter's chest. Julia's desperate pleas followed him as he fled. He halted in the middle of the upstairs hall. He had to do something! He considered a lamp, a heavy picture frame. The gun in the safe? No, never again. His pulse pounded in his ears as he wiped his sweaty palms on his pajamas. He tiptoed back downstairs with no weapon and no plan. His dad glared down at Julia and swung his bat.

Her screams echoed in Peter's ears as everything rushed into focus. The speeding car. The gangsters in the back. The girl on the floor. *Crunch.* His fist connected with Nathan's broad nose.

A stunned silence blanketed the group in shock. Amy gazed at him with mingled astonishment and adoration. Nathan sat up with blood pouring from both nostrils. "Jenkins. Outside. Right the hell now." He tilted his head back and pinched his nose to stop the bleeding.

"Are you nuts?" Ash took his eyes off the road to stare blankly at Nathan. "What about the cops?"

"Pull off the highway!" Nathan roared, spittle flying from his lips.

Ash's eyes grew round and wide. He looked like a deer caught in the headlights. "We'll be arrested! Settle this later." Peter gaped at the first sound piece of advice Ash had ever given.

"Are you questioning my leadership?" A vein popped out in Nathan's neck.

"Nope, your sanity."

Nathan's face reddened. He set his mouth in a snarl and wrapped his hands around Ash's throat. "Do what I say, or Alex and I will have a little chat with your precious girlfriend,"

Faced with endangering Lara and the possibility of being strangled, Ash swerved onto the next exit and threw Peter an apologetic look. Peter shrugged one shoulder. Nathan had a volcanic temper that ebbed after an hour or two. Ash had hoped to help by giving him time to cool off. Peter doubted any delay would matter. He had crossed a line, and there was no going back. At least this time he had done something to stop the abuse.

Thirty-six

AMY EYED PETER with concern. He and Johnson were exchanging matching dark looks as if each wished the other nothing but ill. Alex watched them with a satisfied gleam in his eye while Ash drove recklessly down an abandoned logging road. Peter's face was rigid, his mouth set in a grim, determined line. He could take any of the other gangsters one-on-one, but the others would back Johnson. Peter was out of his depth and by the tense set of his jaw, he knew it. Amy's gut clenched, guilt snaking through her stomach. Why had he risked so much over her? The guy barely knew her.

She peered out the window in hopes of finding help hot on their heels. Thick, dense forest closed in on all sides without a single soul in sight. It was the perfect spot for their medieval duel.

"Right here," Johnson said, jerking his thumb toward the roadside. Ash pulled over to the shoulder, and Johnson and Peter climbed out. They stood at the edge of a steep, rocky ravine.

Peter sauntered around the sedan with his hands in his pockets. Amy admired his composure. Johnson was in no condition to fight, but Alex was ready to intervene on his leader's behalf. He was leaning forward in his seat, his eyes tracking Peter's movements like a hawk watching its prey.

Amy shared a troubled look with Ash. Alex had it out for Peter. He had made that abundantly clear since the toolshed. What if he still intended to kill him? Peter's defiance would have given Alex the perfect excuse. Amy sucked in a breath, her heart freezing in the wake of a horrifying thought. Had Alex orchestrated the showdown to do away with Peter? He had an uncanny affinity for warping situations to suit his needs. Nausea swirled in her stomach, rising ever higher in swoopy, lurching loops. Was that the truth bubbling forth or another symptom of her concussion? She shook her head to dislodge the silly notion. It was pure paranoia. Johnson was the one furious with Peter. Alex merely delighted in violence.

The door she had been slumped against was wrenched open, and she nearly spilled onto the ground. Her stomach lurched. She sucked in a tight-lipped breath of icy air and managed to quell her nausea.

Johnson towered over her and shook a meaty fist in her face. "Get in the back with your boyfriend."

"What are you going to do to him?" She pressed two trembling fingers to her bleeding mouth. Johnson's face made her want to retch again.

"Amy, stay out of this," Peter said with quiet intensity. His green eyes sparked with urgency as he darted a pointed look toward the trunk.

Amy crawled onto the seat. Alex slid open the partition and shoved her headlong through the gap. The door slammed behind her with an unnerving clunk.

"Amy, your face!" Zack was instantly at her side. "What the hell happened?"

She beat her fists against the wall. Johnson had stopped her from watching the fight. Her terror tripled in her mind and built into a crescendo of white noise. The worst crimes happened when there weren't any witnesses. She crawled around Zack and squinted through the tinted window.

"Amy?" Zack's voice was low and urgent. "What the hell is going on?"

"Shh." She put a finger to her lips and strained to listen. She pressed her ear to the glass and held her breath.

A gunshot split the silence. A flock of startled birds burst from the treetops. Amy's eyes stretched wide. "No!" she screamed. "No!"

She crouched paralyzed in place, her body rigid with shock. Terror surged through her veins, even as her heart froze in her chest. Her blood thundered in her ears and threatened to deafen her. Her mouth hung open in a silent scream. A single thought pierced her blanketing horror. She had to get to Peter. She shook free of her debilitating terror and scrambled back to the partition. She beat her fists against it and screamed profanities at Johnson.

He appeared, smiling smugly with blood on his shirt. Amy sucked in a breath that made her chest catch fire then let loose another bloodcurdling scream. She couldn't do this again. She had already caused her baby sister's death, now she was responsible for Peter's? She recoiled and smacked her head against the window.

Johnson locked his thick fingers around her wrist. He yanked her toward him and smeared her hand through the blood. "His life is on you, Evans. You got somebody killed." He cracked her skull against the window and slammed the hatch.

Amy stared at Peter's blood. The wet red streak glistened crimson against her skin. Her stomach twisted along with her heart, and her soul splintered on a silent cry. She crawled into a tiny crevice of her mind and shrank from the world. *You got somebody killed.* His words echoed in her head. All Peter had done was protect her, and it had cost him his life. The sedan sped forward, leaving behind the body of a boy who had tried to do the right thing.

Amy's mind reeled as if she had woken in the night to a thousand wailing sirens. She sat crouched on the floor, stunned and bleeding, crying harder than she had ever cried in her life.

Strong arms encircled her and tucked her against a warm, solid something, Zack's chest. Amy choked on a sob. She didn't deserve comfort. All she exceled at was hurting those she loved. Her river of tears soon soaked through Zack's cotton shirt. He held her close as she poured out her grief, his arms a fortress of strength. She came apart in those arms until they were all that kept her whole. Zack cradled her shattered pieces and refused to let her go. She buried her face in his chest and clung to him like he was the only lifeline she had left.

"It's okay, Amy." Zack stroked her hair. "I've got you, I promise. We'll figure this out." His words rumbled deep within his chest, close against her ear. "You need to take it easy, okay? You're making your injuries worse." Callused fingers brushed her cheek as he gently wiped away her tears. "You have to stop crying or you'll cause internal bleeding and die."

That was good. Serenity blanketed her grief. She took a shuddering breath, and agony scorched her heart. Death would be a welcome end.

Thirty-seven

ZACK CRADLED AMY in his arms, anxiety swirling within him like spinning, icy rapids. How was he supposed to keep it together without Amy? She was the toughest girl he knew, and she was falling apart before his eyes. She hiccupped, and a spasm of pain rippled across her pretty face. His heart squeezed. She needed a doctor. He stared at the dark stain of blood Johnson had smeared on her hand, questions battering his mind and sending his thoughts into a tailspin. Had Nathan shot Peter? Had they witnessed a murder? When would this end?

He glanced at Susan, who sat frozen in a far corner of the trunk, her pinched, worried face bathed in muted predawn light. He took in a cut on her chin and harsh red bruising around her lips. Rage coursed through him and boiled his blood. The little girl had gone through more horror tonight than most experienced in a lifetime.

"Sue?" Zack tried to keep his voice calm for her sake. "It'll all be okay."

She nodded numbly, doubt evident in the dove gray depths of her gentle eyes. "What's wrong with Amy?" She wrapped her arms around herself as if frightened at what he'd say.

"She's just upset. She'll stop soon."

"Zack?" Her voice trembled. "What's going to happen to us?" Tears glistened in the corners of her eyes.

He chose his words with care. "I'm not sure yet. But we'll figure it out, I promise. Everything will be okay."

She nodded, determined this time. He turned back to Amy and looped an arm around her waist to help her sit up. The less pressure against her ribs, the better. A squeal from Susan carried over Amy's hysteria. "Zack! Come here, quick!"

"What is it?" He propped Amy between the wall and his shoulder, hoping she would be able to breathe easier in that position.

"It's that kid from the bus stop!"

"Huh?" Zack gently released Amy and crawled across to Susan. She was peering out the back window, her eyes alight with excitement.

Zack stared at the scene below him, his jaw slack and his eyes round. Charles Banks was balancing precariously on a skateboard, clinging to the sedan's rear bumper for dear life. He grinned at Zack and flapped a hand at him.

"He wants you to break the glass!" Susan exclaimed.

Zack motioned for Charles to duck and slammed his foot into the window. Splintered pieces tumbled to the pavement in a water-fall of glass.

"Hey!" Charles shouted. "Got room for one more?"

"Banks!" Zack said. "What the hell do you think you're doing?"

"I'm saving your butt. Now help me up!"

Zack met the shocked gaze of the driver in the silver Subaru behind them. He mimed holding a phone to his ear, hoping the guy would call the police.

"Zack!" Charles said, irritation lacing his tone. "I can't hang around all day!"

"What if he grabbed this?" Susan held up a length of rope that had been used to tie them up.

"Too wiggly. He'd fly into traffic. Will you stay with Amy while I help him?" Susan crawled to her sister's side and slipped her hand into Amy's. Zack took a deep breath and leaned out the smashed window. "Grab my hand."

Charles stretched to grasp Zack's fingers. A foot of empty air separated their hands. "I can't reach! This isn't going to work." Fear clouded his gaze.

His skateboard swerved to the left, nearly sending him flying beneath the sedan's rear wheels. Charles flailed his arms and grasped the bumper with both hands. "That was close," he said, his face white with shock. "I'm going to have to jump onto the bumper. Grab my hand as soon as you can."

"You can do this!" Zack pumped a fist in an effort to instill confidence.

Charles gripped the bumper and agilely leapt aboard. His skateboard careened away. Zack stretched far out the window and clenched Charles's forearms in an iron vise. His sneakers slipped off the bumper. Zack lurched forward, scraping his arm over a spike of glass. Charles was weighing him down, tugging him out the window toward the rushing pavement below. Zack strained to heave him up, but the awkward angle made it impossible. Sweat slicked his palms. His heart pounded a wild tempo of horror. Charles was slipping away. If Zack didn't let go, he'd go down as well.

Soft hands brushed Zack's. Amy had grasped Charles's wrists. She was sitting on the floor, her feet braced against the hatchback to pull strength from her legs and back. She pressed close against Zack's thigh as he knelt on the floor, half out the window himself. Her warmth and strength surged through him and gave him the energy for one final tug. They heaved Charles through the broken window and landed in a heap on the carpeted floor. Amy backed away and sat against the wall with her head in her hands. She was brave when it counted, but inside her lay a wasteland of debris.

"What happened to her?" Charles's eyes brimmed with concern.

"What are you doing here?" Unwelcome jealousy made Zack's words sound more hostile than he had intended.

"Why must everyone demand why I do everything?" Charles spotted Susan and beamed at her. "Hey! You must be Susan." He gave them a lopsided grin. "We're escaping! Let's go."

Zack arched an eyebrow. "We're in the trunk of a car speeding down the highway with three armed lunatics in the front seat. We're not going anywhere." Who did Charles think he was? James Bond's nerdy alter ego?

Charles turned to Amy. "Peter is alive."

"What?" Amy lifted her head. Her eyes were red and her lashes wet.

"Nathan only wanted you guys to think he had killed him."

"That makes no sense." Amy stared at her shaking hands.

"Sure it does." Charles patted her arm. "He fired the gun into the air after clocking Peter in the head. The dude is only unconscious. Nathan just wanted to scare you."

Amy wiped her eyes. "How did you end up here?"

"Your brother. Justin's a great guy!"

Zack nodded in agreement.

"You've both seen our brother, but Amy and I haven't? How unfair is that!" Susan's eyes blazed with indignant outrage.

Amy furrowed her brow. "Wait, Justin did come to visit?"

Zack smiled at her, relieved she was calmer. "No. I called your brother after you disappeared. He gave me a tracker, that thing that looked like a tiny speaker. He was in the car with me when I called you the second time." His heart twisted at the memory of Amy's tortured screaming.

"And I ran into him after you drove off in the sedan," Charles added with a harried grin. "But let's save the chitchat for later."

Amy locked eyes with Charles. "Are you positive Peter's alive?"

"Yes. I saw everything before I got behind the car with the skateboard. Now let's move!"

Zack stared, openmouthed, as Charles pulled gadgets from his backpack and ordered the three of them around. All traces of the shy, nerdy kid he had known since elementary school had vanished. Charles was a man on a mission.

Thirty-eight

AMY WAS OVERWHELMED by the bizarre situation unfolding before her eyes. Charles, Zack, and Justin had pulled off the impossible. Zack had called Justin when she and Susan went missing and willingly became a hostage to keep them both safe. Justin had given Zack a tracker, which he had used to trail them from Toronto. Charles had launched a cop-sanctioned rescue mission, and wound up alone on a skateboard with a backpack full of weapons. Amy wanted to laugh at the insanity, but the Tylenol had worn off and laughing hurt.

"Amy?" Zack asked. "Are you sure you're okay?"

She offered a tight-lipped nod. She had freaked him out with her hysteria. She was never going to live down the embarrassment of those long moments of vulnerability.

Zack exchanged a doubtful look with Susan while Charles raised a skeptical brow. They were far from convinced by her non-verbal response.

"I'm great. What's our plan of action?"

"You act like you're going into battle." Charles snickered.

"Well, we are." Susan folded her arms across her chest and fixed Charles with a defiant scowl.

"Amy, your sister's taking after you." Zack chuckled.

"Good!" Susan puffed out her chest. "Amy's awesome."

Zack smiled indulgently but shared a doubtful look with Charles.

"*We* aren't doing anything," Charles said. "Zack and I will deal with Assassin's Honor. You two girls will stay here."

Amy scoffed. "Yeah right. I got us into this mess. I'm getting us out of it!"

Susan planted her hands on her hips. "You're leaving us out because we're girls."

Charles's eyes widened. "I just meant—"

Zack adopted a reasonable tone. "Sue, you're too young, and Amy has a broken rib. It's better if Charles and I handle this one."

Susan pouted. "That's so unfair. I was here first. I want to help."

Amy narrowed her eyes at her sister. "Susan, you're staying here and that's final." Susan threw her a filthy look but held her tongue.

"You're staying here, too, Amy." Zack's gaze turned flinty.

"Don't tell me what to do. And give me that!" She made a grab for the Taser he was holding.

"No. You're staying here with Sue." His eyes were narrow slits of unyielding crystal.

"Guys!" Charles raised a hand, calling for peace. "I hate to interrupt a fantastically entertaining argument, but we're a little tight on time."

In the end, Amy made them leave her with a Taser. Zack and Charles planned on zapping the gangsters in the back seat, then whichever of them was closer would stun the driver and take the wheel. Amy had the Taser in case she got a clear shot from above. Her insides churned as her eyes circled the group. So much could go wrong. The boys were armed with Tasers and they faced real guns. They were also outnumbered, even with Peter out of the way.

Both Zack and Charles seemed weirdly calm, an attitude that made Amy nervous. She had the creeping feeling they were walking into a trap. Everything they had done to stop Assassin's Honor had backfired. Charles's first interference had gotten him beat up. Zack had been captured when he had come to their aid. Peter's courageous attempt to help had nearly resulted in his death. And Amy had no idea what had happened to that dark girl. She hoped she had escaped with her life.

Charles silently slid open the hatch and aimed his Taser through the gap. Amy peeked through the narrow slit and choked back a strangled cry. Only Alex sat in the back seat. Zack and Charles leapt from the trunk in unison, Charles firing the Taser at

Alex's head. *No!* Amy cursed under her breath. *Aim for the center of the body.* A larger target was harder to miss. Alex ducked and snatched the .45 from the seat next to him.

Amy screamed a warning. A back window shattered, the bullet missing Zack by centimeters. Charles dove for the gun and wrenched it from Alex's grasp. Another shot went off. That one hit Alex's foot. Johnson twisted in his seat and aimed Amy's pistol at Charles. Zack tackled him in the nick of time. They struggled together, dangerously close to Ash, who was driving.

Amy clutched her Taser in shaking hands and struggled to take aim. Her vision blurred and her head throbbed. Her stomach roiled with indecision. Were the gangsters too close to Charles and Zack? She was terrified of hitting the wrong person.

A bullet lodged in the wall by her face. She shoved Susan to the floor. "Stay down and don't move."

A second bullet went off target and hit Ash in the chest. He slumped in his seat, unconscious or worse. The sedan lurched and spun out of control. Amy launched herself off the platform, her tumbling descent punctured by Susan's horrified gasp.

She crashed to the floor in a tangle of uncoordinated grace-lessness, the force of her impact almost knocking her out. She ground her teeth, battled the blackness, crawled to the front, and grasped the wheel in a thick fog of pain. The highway swam in and out of focus, the cars in front of her just splotches of color. Something warm and sticky leaked onto her arm. A ruby stain discolored Ash's pale gray shirt. His head lolled to one side, his hazel eyes stretched wide in an unblinking, unseeing stare.

A terrible scraping jolted Amy from her daze. A grove of pines loomed directly in front of them. She shrieked and yanked the steering wheel to the right. Why the hell were they still speeding? She looked down and screamed. Ash's foot was jammed on the gas. They were careening down the highway at no less than 140 kilometers per hour.

"Don't move." A gun's cold metal muzzle pressed against the small of her back.

She froze, a mistake. They swerved again, and she fought to regain control.

Johnson screamed at her, but his words were inaudible. Half a dozen horns were honking in response to her reckless driving. She risked a glance over her shoulder, and a thrill of fear electrocuted her heart. Alex and Charles were unconscious on the floor. Her gut clenched as her mind reeled. What if Charles was seriously hurt?

"Not another move, Donnellson, or she's dead."

Amy stared at the scene in her rearview mirror. It looked staged, like the sudden reversal near the end of an action movie. Zack had the .45 pointed at Johnson, and Johnson had her G19 trained on her.

Zack glared. "If you shoot her, we'll all die. Are you seriously that dumb?"

Johnson laughed softly, his hot breath tickling Amy's ear. "Are you seriously going to take that chance with her life?"

Amy struggled to keep the sedan from smashing into other cars. She had no idea how to drive. She hadn't even taken her learner's test yet. She was playing a real-life video game and the guys were oblivious, too caught up in their macho standoff of who was going to pull the trigger first. "I can't do this!" Her heart pounded painfully against her ribs. The speedometer inched toward 180 kilometers per hour.

"You're doing fine." Zack tried to calm her.

"Aww," Johnson jeered, his lip curling in disgust. "That's so damn sweet."

"No, I can't do this!" Her panicked voice rose in pitch and volume. Her pulse thundered in her ears. Every muscle in her body was taut with concentration. "I'm sixteen, Zack! I haven't even taken my learner's yet."

"What?" Johnson blanched. "Get out of the way!" He gripped her shoulder as if to toss her aside.

"No!" Amy clung to the steering wheel. "If I let go, we'll crash."

"We've got to turn off the highway!" Johnson's bellow nearly deafened her.

"No!" Zack said, his voice steady. "We're safer on the highway because it's straight, and the speed limits are higher. How fast are we going, anyway?"

Her heart leapt into her throat. "One-ninety." The silence in the car was more deafening than Johnson's bellow. "Tell me what to do!"

"Turn right," Johnson said as Zack instructed her to keep going. Johnson rammed the pistol into her back. "You've got five seconds to turn or you die."

Zack lunged at Johnson and managed to wrestle the pistol from his grasp. But Amy had already begun the turn, and she had no idea how to stop. Zack and Johnson grappled on the floor as they barreled down a steep, winding slope at 210 kilometers per hour.

Tree branches scraped against the windshield. Pebbles ricocheted off the sedan's metal frame. Amy clung to the steering wheel for dear life. Whole groves of trees were blurry green blobs. A thick, low-hanging branch snapped the driver's side mirror, and a hiss and a lurch signaled at least one mutilated tire.

Amy screamed. A vast body of water lay in front of her. The car had zoomed onto a pier. A flimsy metal railing was all that separated them from the drop to the dark water below. She frantically spun the wheel, but they were traveling way too fast. They crashed through the railing. The windshield exploded. The sedan lurched into a sickening ninety-degree dive, and they plummeted toward the pitch-black water of Lake Superior.

Thirty-nine

PETER PRIED OPEN his eyes. His vision was blurry, and his head ached worse than a rum and vodka hangover.

"Stay where you are," someone said.

He blinked, trying to focus. His vision swam, then cleared. He lay by the roadside, face-first on the cold, muddy ground with blood dripping into his eyes from a gash on his forehead. Two people stood in front of him, a tiny woman in police uniform and a dark-haired guy in his early twenties. Both were glaring at him with undisguised contempt.

Two male officers dragged him to his feet and marched him to a squad car. "Get in," the older one commanded.

Peter did as he was told, everything coming back to him in a dizzying rush. Amy tipping off the gas station attendant, Alex flipping out, Amy bleeding on the floor. He had punched Nathan. He would have punched Nathan many more times but had been knocked out before he got the chance. Nathan had taken off and left him to be arrested. How had the cops found him so quick? He dismissed his question with a shrug. He was much more concerned with what had happened to Susan and Amy.

His eyes circled the car. The dark-haired guy had sat next to him in the back seat. The officers who had dragged him to the car had settled themselves in the front with the younger of the two behind the wheel.

"I am Officer Kimmy Wolf, and I am placing you under arrest," the policewoman told him as she scooted into the car on his other side. "You have the right to remain silent. Anything you do or say can and will be used against you in a court of law."

The squad car sped forward, spinning mud in all directions. "Where are we going?" Peter bit his lip. He had no idea how they would use that question against him in a court of law, but with his luck, they'd find a way.

"Where do you think?" The dark-haired guy scowled. "We're following your friends in the Audi." He fixed him with a probing glare. "How'd you get on the scar dude's bad side?"

"Nathan Johnson," Peter mumbled to the floor.

Officer Wolf perked up. "Did he just provide the name of an accomplice? Please repeat that."

"Nathan Johnson." Peter wiped dirt and blood from his forehead.

The dark-haired guy threw him a disgusted look. "He's only giving us information to try and score a lighter sentence."

"That's enough, Justin," Officer Wolf said, her calm blue eyes sparking with irritation. "Shut up and be quiet." She turned to Peter. "How did you end up in the dirt?" She pulled out a pad and pencil, just itching to use his statements against him in court.

"That girl." He hesitated. Assassin's Honor took betrayal seriously and if he sold them out, there would be no going back.

Justin leaned forward. "One of my sisters?"

"Your sisters?" Peter studied him more closely. Justin shared the family resemblance. All three siblings were slim with dark hair and gray eyes, though Justin's eyes were much darker than his sisters'.

Justin tapped his foot impatiently. "What were you going to say?"

Peter blew out a breath. "I hate everything they've done. We were never supposed to involve little girls." He hung his head in shame, guilt swirling in his gut.

Justin studied him for a long moment. "You were defending them."

Emotion flickered in Officer Wolf's deep blue eyes. Sympathy? Admiration? She lowered her lashes before he could tell. When they came up again, her eyes were pools of tranquility.

"I only managed to help Amy." He would have intervened a lot sooner if it had been Susan being smacked around.

Peter studied Officer Wolf's face. Did she believe him? She glanced up from her notepad and met his gaze. His heart lurched in a stumbling swoop that stole all words and for a moment, his breath. The world fell away. Her deep blue eyes saw straight into his soul. He had never so much as glimpsed anyone, or anything, so beautiful.

"I see them!" The driver's shout ended their heart-stopping moment.

Officer Wolf whipped around in her seat and peered out the front window. "Something's wrong. They're out of control. Who the heck is that driving?" Her voice rose in pitch and volume with every new exclamation. The sedan veered across two lanes of traffic and nearly swerved off the road.

"It's Amy," Justin said with his face in his hands.

Officer Wolf pressed a hand to her mouth. "She's only sixteen, right?"

"Yeah, and she never took driver's ed."

"Clearly." Peter winced as the sedan swerved again.

"If the girl's in control of the vehicle, why wouldn't she pull over?" the officer driving wondered aloud. "Surely she knows how to press the brakes."

The sedan zigzagged to the right and made a squealing turn onto a narrow exit. The driver of an off-white minivan slammed on his brakes to avoid a collision. Several other cars blasted their horns in angry protest.

"Turn right," Officer Wolf ordered with a death grip on her armrest. They sped down a narrow, winding road lined with spruces and firs. The officer driving switched on the siren, and the few cars on the road scattered.

They burst from the trees at the bottom of the steep incline, and Peter stared in horror at a sight he would never forget. A short pier lay in front of them with no car in sight. Black water swirled ten feet below with enormous ripples disrupting its calm surface.

They screeched to a jarring halt. "Oh my God!" Officer Wolf clapped a hand to her mouth and stared in dismay at the scene before them.

"We've got to help them!" Peter shoved Justin's shoulder in an effort to get out. His words jolted everyone into action. Justin and Officer Wolf sprinted for the lake. The older officer radioed for an ambulance while the younger one herded a curious jogger away. They had forgotten Peter was supposed to be under arrest. He dove from the car and took two strides toward the trees.

His steps faltered. A nine-year-old was drowning. Would his sister have lived if someone had tried to save her? He took one

205

hesitant step and broke into a run. Not toward the trees but toward the lake.

He launched himself off the edge of the pier in a tumbling freefall that left his insides behind. Plummeting to Earth like a stone without a parachute was exhilaratingly terrifying, like cliff jumping with his friends even though it was against summer camp rules. Not that he had ever been to camp. Every cent of spare cash his mom had made waitressing had been spent on his dad's cheap beer. Peter grinned with unexpected elation. What would his drunkard dad say if he knew what he was doing? Peter hoped he was about to become the biggest disappointment yet.

His focus returned to him atop a screaming rush of wind. He had eluded panic and shock, but reason and logic came calling halfway through his drop. Peter could hold his breath for forty-five seconds, maybe a minute. Would that be anywhere near enough time to rescue Susan? His best attempt at swimming was an ungainly doggy paddle. Lessons had been low on his father's priority list, somewhere between teaching him manners and how to bake a cake. "He can learn like I did when my brothers tossed me in the river," was all his dad would say when his mother asked. Now Peter wished he had thrown him in a few extra times.

Icy water rushed up to meet him, spray slapping his face a split second before the splash. The freezing water hit his body like a thousand steel knives. His head pounded and his mind reeled at the temperature shock. He forced his eyes open as he sank, and a surge of relief sent warmth through his veins. The car rested on the lake bottom in front of him, its headlights miraculously still shining. Finally, a stroke of good karma! It had only taken the universe a solid seventeen years.

Peter paddled to the rear driver's side door and yanked on its handle. It was stuck. He strained to wrench it open, an icy jolt of fear careening through his veins. He was already running out of air. An idea dawned on a jolt of relief. The smashed side window. He battled his way around the sedan and located the hole by touch. He reached through the broken window and fumbled blindly in the dark interior. Nothing. The freezing water was making his head ache. Where was Susan? Still locked in the trunk? Tied up and drowning? Lying unconscious on the soggy carpet floor?

He slithered through the window. Pain stung his shoulders as spikes of glass scored his skin. Something soft brushed his arm. He reached for it and got smacked by a small flailing hand. Susan. He grabbed her and pulled. Someone else held her in place.

Bubbles escaped his lips as he struggled to free her from Alex, the only person crazy enough to drown a little kid. Peter threw a punch, but the water slowed his fist. Alex reached for him and recoiled as if electrocuted. Susan was free!

Peter guided her backward, taking care to keep her away from the jagged broken glass. She had gone limp in his arms by the time he had her out. He struggled for the surface, Susan's dead weight dragging him down. His lungs screamed in protest. His chest burned like a gasoline fire. He gasped for air and choked on water. He was going to drown saving this kid, but he refused to let her go.

He popped into the predawn light and gulped at the crisp lake air. Half a dozen swimmers surged toward him, Justin in the lead. They helped Susan to the beach, and Justin took her from him to rush her to a stretcher.

Peter sank onto the sand and stared at the pier full of strangers. He staggered up to the parking lot, where medics were resuscitating Susan and Ash, and Officer Wolf was dragging Alex into a squad car. Peter smiled at her badassery. The smile froze on his face as he swept his gaze over the half-empty peer. Where were Amy, Charles, and Zack? Nathan could die for all he cared.

"Where's Amy?" Justin echoed Peter's thoughts.

They turned as one toward the lake. A tidal wave of guilt smacked Peter in the face. Susan had only been one of the people trapped underwater.

He stumbled where he stood, his stomach churning with acid shame. The ground dipped and swayed beneath him. He doubled over and splattered puke across the asphalt. His vomit was dark red.

"We need a medic over here!" Justin grasped Peter's arm and towed him toward an ambulance.

"No, go help your sister." Peter choked on a stream of crimson puke. The metallic taste of blood filled his mouth.

"How much blood has he lost?" a female medic asked. Peter collapsed onto a stretcher.

"I'm not sure. Maybe half a cup?" Justin's gaze skimmed past Peter and settled on the lake.

Several blurry seconds later, the ambulance was speeding toward the highway with its siren wailing. The world was wobbly, distorted, and oddly tinted red. The face of the young doctor leaning over him swam in and out of focus. She placed a hand on his stomach. "His abdomen's rigid. He needs surgery right now. What's our ETA?"

"Four minutes," the driver answered, his words vibrating with tension.

"I can't get a pulse!" another voice called, this one shrill with alarm. "She's crashing."

"Who's crashing?" Peter tried to sit up, and a wave of vertigo made his head spin.

"Lie down." The doctor pressed her palm against his chest until he slumped onto the stretcher. "Keep up CPR," she ordered. Peter smiled to himself. Why were all the women he met so dang bossy?

"You picked one hell of a day for a ride along," the driver muttered.

"Tell me about it." The female doctor grinned. "And it's only six a.m." She flicked her gaze back to Peter. "What's your name, dude?"

"Peter," he managed, willing the vomit to stay in his stomach.

"Okay, Peter." She gave him a reassuring smile. "I need to know if you're taking drugs or if you're on any medications." He shook his head, and stars danced behind his eyes. "Try to lie still." She placed a thermometer under his tongue.

They zoomed through the town with lights flashing and sirens blaring. The ambulance screeched to a halt, and he and the other passenger were transferred to gurneys at lightning speed.

"ORs B and C are ready for you," someone called as the ambulance doctors sped them down a sterilized hospital corridor. Peter stared at the ceiling whizzing by, and nausea overcame him. Blood stung his throat as he coughed up more vomit.

A frazzled blonde nurse blocked his gurney's path. The other gurney and its occupant zoomed into an OR to his right. An elderly male doctor stepped from an OR to his left, and the harried nurse grasped his arm. "Doctor Chang. We need this OR for another emergent patient."

Doctor Chang frowned. "His injuries look severe."

"The chief of surgery says to take him for a CT. He says use the next available OR."

"He has a ruptured stomach ulcer," the ambulance doctor broke in.

"He must wait. The other patient will die if all ORs are occupied when she arrives. These are direct orders from the chief of surgery. Besides." The nurse curled her lip in distaste. "The girl on the way is a victim. He is one of the youths responsible."

All heads turned to Peter. His cheeks heated with shame. "I'll wait," he said.

"We are doctors! We do not prioritize medical attention to those who we feel are more deserving!" Peter blinked woozily at the ambulance doctor. She was determined to champion him. Because she found him first, and he was an awesomely repulsive patient? More likely she wanted to scrub in on an interesting surgery.

Doctor Chang scratched the top of his bald head. "We do bump more urgent cases ahead of less serious ones, though. Take him for a CT, and page me if his condition worsens."

The ambulance doctor grumbled under her breath as she wheeled Peter off. "I hate being an intern! No one listens to you, even when you're right."

Forty

DARKNESS SURROUNDED ZACK. The icy lake dragged at his clothes and weighed him down. He gasped for air and choked on water. He kicked off his shoes and paddled in the direction he guessed was up. The last of his air escaped his lips. His ears rang and his heart pounded as panic rioted within him. What if he was going the wrong way? What if he was swimming sideways through meters and meters of water, heading deeper into the frigid lake? Fear clutched at his chest as water filled his burning lungs. His muscles screamed their protest as he thrust upward one final time. A few more seconds and he would give in. A few more seconds and he would surrender his body to the lake's grasping, chilling embrace.

He stretched his hands above his head, and his fingertips grazed the surface. He strained upward on a final surge of hope and exploded into predawn light. He coughed and sputtered and gulped fresh, freezing air. His pounding heart began to slow.

Zack was approximately twenty feet from shore, treading water at the edge of a vast expanse of blue. The lake was cold, still, and silent. Uneasiness pricked his skin as he skimmed his gaze across the too-quiet water. The silence was chilling and hinted at something worse. Ice-cold fear swept through his veins on a surge of electric alarm. He had been so focused on saving himself, he hadn't stopped to consider anyone else. Amy, Susan, and Charles were still down there, trapped or unconscious or worse.

He took a deep breath and dove. The water sliced into him like a million jagged daggers of ice. Mind-numbing brain freeze and a sharp tightness in his chest sank frozen fangs of doubt into his skin. Was he strong enough for this? Who else would save her? Fighting past the pain, he angled himself downward and swam deeper into the lake. The water in front of him had an eerie glow to it. The sedan's headlights! They were still working.

Zack swam to the car on a surge of triumphant relief. There had been an explosion of glass as they had crashed through the fence. Amy ought to be right there in front, likely tangled in a seat belt but still fighting to get free. He would rescue her first and come back for the others. The windshield wasn't smashed, it was just plain gone. His skin prickled with a warning. Something was very wrong. He glided into the sunken wreck and scanned the sedan's dark interior. Panic fluttered in his stomach. He would have to search the car by touch, and he was almost out of air.

The driver's seat was empty. Had Amy and Ash escaped? He shoved aside his creeping feelings of unease and ran his hands over the back seat while searching the floor with his feet. He checked the trunk for Susan and again came up empty-handed. Warm relief flooded his heart. The car was clear. Everyone had escaped without his help. He launched himself from the wreck and kicked up toward fresh air.

Chaotic noise assaulted his ears as he surfaced. Sirens wailed in the distance, police officers shouted orders at the edge of the peer, and Justin and Peter helped Susan toward the shore. Charles was already trudging up the beach toward a waiting ambulance, leaning on the shoulder of a dark-haired girl Zack didn't know.

"Yes!" Zack punched the air. They had made it.

But where was Amy? Tendrils of fear snaked through his gut. She hadn't reached the shore or made it up for air. His heart lurched as panic constricted his chest. Amy was drowning. He dove again. He was not coming back up until he had her in his arms.

He swam straight for the headlights of the sunken wreck. If she wasn't trapped in the sedan or safely back out on the pier, she must have landed somewhere in the water. But where? He paused by the car, paralyzed with indecision. Her chances decreased with every passing second. Zack ground his jaw and searched his memories of the crash. The windshield had shattered, and Amy had not been buckled in. She must have been thrown from the sedan.

Zack combed the lake bottom in a grid pattern. Reason kept him steady, but urgency screamed for faster action. He was racing a clock without knowing how much time was left. His head ached from oxygen deprivation and the agony of the freezing water, but he refused to come up for air. If he did, Amy would be lost. He pressed forward, painfully aware he was traveling farther out into the lake and farther away from help.

His hand brushed hair. His heart leapt with hope. Amy lay face-down on the sandy lake bottom. Was she unconscious or was she dead? Zack wrapped his arms around her waist and pushed off hard from the mud.

He clung to her as he struggled toward the surface. She was chilled to the bone and frighteningly limp. He clawed at the water above his head and tightened his other arm around her waist. His lungs burned. His chest was on fire. He looked up and glimpsed the rippling reflection of light. He strained upward, the dark water threatening to drag Amy from his arms. He screwed up his face and closed his eyes, putting everything he had into a final frantic struggle. He surfaced with a gasping splash and gulped fresh lake air.

He clutched Amy to his chest and fought to keep her head above water. His breath came in short exhalations, misty vapor curling into the frosty morning. Not even the tiniest wisp rose from Amy's colorless lips. His heart froze in his chest. Her skin was chalky white, her chest still. Icy fingers of fear clutched his heart.

No! He hadn't come this far to lose her. He spun her so her head rested on his shoulder and pressed her tight against his chest. He slammed an open hand into her back. Nothing. "Come on, Amy!" He tightened his grip and repeated the motion. Water gushed from her mouth. She coughed, and more streamed from her lips. Zack loosened his grip and held her a few inches away. Her chest rose and fell with painfully shallow breaths. The crushing grip on his heart loosened a fraction.

He tucked Amy in the crook of his arm and battled toward the shore. The welcoming line of sand was forty feet away. His breaths were ragged, each one sending a spiking pain into his side. The glacial water had frozen him to his core. His skin was numb, his insides like ice. His feeble strokes slowed with every push toward the sand. His exhausted muscles screamed their protest.

Police officers appeared on either side of him and took most of Amy's weight. They towed her to shore and rushed her up the beach. Zack clutched her to his chest and looked down into her face as they ran. Strands of sodden ebony hair clung to her pale cheeks, and her skin was ice cold against the warmth of his body. Was it too late? A literal pain knifed his heart.

He skidded to a halt by an ambulance and set Amy on a stretcher. He clung to her hand and couldn't let go. Narrow palm, slender fingers, ice-cold skin against the warmth of his own.

"Come on, kid," a paramedic said. "I need space to do my job."

Zack whispered a promise and released her hand. They moved her to the ambulance, and Justin scrambled in alongside her. Zack tried to follow, but a female officer blocked his way.

She clasped his arm to hold him back. "Only family allowed right now."

"No," he rasped, attempting to shove her aside.

Her expression hardened. "Sir, I need you to calm down." She had a pistol, a Taser, and a pair of handcuffs clipped to her belt.

Zack dropped his hands. "Sorry. She's my ..." His words fizzled into nothing. His gaze trailed the ambulance, as it turned to face the narrow road. "She's something special."

The policewoman tugged him to one side, and the ambulance sped up the road and out of sight. His heart twisted in his chest. Her expression softened. "It's okay. She's in good hands. My name is Kimmy. I'll give you a ride to the hospital if you like."

Forty-one

SUSAN SAT PROPPED in her hospital bed with a pile of pillows at her back and a tray of yucky-looking hospital food in her lap. Justin had a chair pulled up to her bedside, and Zack was sitting across the room by the window. A sliver of azure sky peeked invitingly from between her plain cotton drapes. If only she was outside, lying beneath that cool winter sky in a field of bright white snow. How nice would it feel to escape it all for a moment and breathe the crisp, clean air that smelled of snow and a hint of Christmas. A wistful sigh escaped her lips.

Justin tensed. "Are you okay? Do you need the nurse?"

Susan rolled her eyes. "For the last time, Justin," she said, trying to calm her thickheaded brother, "I'm fine!"

His mouth set in a firm, stubborn line. "You're in the hospital. You almost died! You're far from fine."

"No!" She slapped her palm onto the tray, making the dishes jump. "Amy is dying. I'm the one who's okay." She regretted her words the moment they had flown from her lips. Justin flinched. "Sorry," she whispered and tugged the plain white hospital blanket up to her chin.

"It's okay." Justin took her hand in both of his. "Amy will get better. I know it."

Susan squeezed his fingers, finding comfort in having someone who loved her by her side. She lifted her chin and met her brother's smoky gray eyes. Shadows of doubt clouded his gaze. Did he truly believe what he was saying about Amy? She had been in surgery for eleven hours. That meant she was really hurt.

Susan glanced at Zack. He had sat, unmoving, in the same straight-backed chair for hours. His resemblance to a statue of a meditating monk she and Chris had seen on a field trip made her cringe. She blew out a frustrated breath. Amy meant a lot to him, but he needed to get a grip. He barely knew her! She and Justin were her family, and they hadn't gone all monkish. Amy was fine. Justin said so, and he was the smartest person she knew. But why was Zack upset? Why wouldn't anyone explain? Her heart twisted with fear and doubt.

Susan's eyes burned with unshed tears. She wanted her mother, even though she had never spent much time with her. She longed for the lavender-scented hugs her mom used to give her as a kid. She desperately needed someone to hold her and make everything okay. But that had always been Amy's role. Hot tears trickled down her cheeks.

Justin pulled her into a hug. "Hey. What would Amy say about that if she were here?"

Susan's shoulders shook. She tried to speak without her voice shaking like a baby's. "She'd tell me to stop crying, 'cause there's no point in crying over something that hasn't happened yet."

Justin rubbed her back. "No point in crying over something that will never happen." He wiped her eyes with the sleeve of his sweatshirt. "Amy's tough. She'll pull through this. I know it." Fierce determination burned in his eyes. He acted as though his faith alone was going to make Amy better.

Justin's words woke Zack from his trance. He turned to them and scrubbed a hand over his unshaven face. "Hey," he rasped and paused to clear his throat. "Are either of you hungry? I could grab us some food."

Susan pouted. Zack had gone from a monk statue to Mr. Helpful Man in the blink of an eye. Five seconds ago, she had been handling this better than him, and she was only nine.

"Thanks man, that'd be great." Justin looked around for his wallet, but Zack was already gone. The door swung shut behind him with a hollow thud.

Susan discarded her untouched tray of food and turned her pout on Justin. "Zack better bring back something good. Like burgers or sushi!" Her stomach grumbled.

"He's a good guy." Justin leaned back in his chair and put his arms behind his head. He had puffy bags under his eyes and unkempt stubble on his chin.

"You like him, then?" Susan asked with an innocent tilt of her head. "I do too, but right now he's being annoying."

"He's freaking out over Amy." There was a hum of fear beneath Justin's words. Her skin prickled with unease. Her siblings tried to protect her too much. What if Amy was worse off than he said? Justin gave a lock of her hair a playful tug. "Why didn't you guys tell me Amy had a boyfriend?"

She rolled her eyes and smirked. "Because she doesn't have a boyfriend."

"Oh yeah? What do you call Zack?" He mock tossed a pillow at her.

"I don't know, her stalker?" She laughed. "He only met her last week, and now he shows up everywhere she goes."

"That was me last semester with Kimmy."

Susan lit up with interest. "Who's Kimmy? Your girlfriend?"

"Not anymore." He shrugged one shoulder.

She sat back against her pillows. "You can't be mad at Amy for not telling you about her stalker if you forget to mention whole relationships to us."

"True that. I'll tone down the teasing, I promise."

"Oh no, you will tease her, and I'll help!"

He laughed. "Okay, munchkin, how about you get some sleep while you think of ways to torment our sister."

Susan scrunched up her face. Justin hadn't used his pet name for her in years. She had hoped she had outgrown it. "But I'm not tired." She yawned. "What's Zack getting? I want ice cream!"

"Right." He snorted, ruffling her hair. "You're wide awake, and Amy is single. Now we have that sorted, you go to sleep. I'll bring you ice cream when you wake up." He tucked the hospital blankets around her, ignoring her feeble protests that she wasn't sleepy yet. It was four in the afternoon, but it felt like the middle of the night.

She clutched Justin's hand. "Let's go to Dairy Queen when Amy's better." Dairy Queen was an Evans family staple. From birthday parties to Thanksgiving, no occasion was complete without a hot fudge sundae or a chocolate dipped cone. Katie had been especially delighted with a visit to DQ, sitting in her high chair with a chocolate syrup mustache and ice cream in her golden blonde hair.

Their baby sister had been a messy eater, but a happy one. And after she died, during the year Justin had lived with them in Toronto, they had gravitated to her happy place in search of a little bit of Katie's joy. The three of them used to ditch the house whenever their mom had a boyfriend over and always escaped to Dairy Queen. Susan's favorite Toronto afternoons had been spent in that booth with her siblings and three vanilla milkshakes.

"Okay, milkshakes on me. But seriously, Sue, you've been through a lot. Zack needs to keep busy, and you need to rest. Amy won't recover by both of you acting like you've been turned to stone."

Susan stuck her nose in the air. "Zack was the one acting like a stone guy. I was completely normal."

Justin patted her head. "Sue, I hate to break it to you, but you're never normal. Ever."

"I'll take that as a compliment." She grinned up at her big brother and rolled onto her side. "And I'll even try to sleep. I am a little tired, I guess." She shut her eyes. The hospital room faded into a sunny field in summertime.

Forty-two

CHARLES LAY IN his hospital bed, staring blurrily at the stuccoed ceiling. His mom had stepped out to buy a few things as he was staying in the hospital overnight. He doubted he'd get much sleep because he refused to close his eyes. Images of shotgun-wielding Alexes plagued his dreams whenever he dared. He'd rather stay conscious until Alex was behind bars.

Alex had a nasty surprise awaiting him in jail. The cool angelic cop planned to detain him with holy light, the one supernatural phenomenon able to imprison a Dark. Alex was about to get exactly what he deserved. Charles allowed himself an exhausted smile. Alex's father had gotten away with murder. Alex had been put away for the attempt.

The floor creaked near his bed. A girl with sleek blonde hair and intense, piercing green eyes had teleported to his bedside. She glared down at him with undisguised malevolence. Lara Tzadik, Ash's girlfriend, was an even more powerful Dark than Alex. She was the child of two Dark parents, which intensified her power level as well as her instability. Children of such unions pompously labeled themselves Super Darks. Charles more accurately labeled them super psychotic.

"Hello, Charles," she purred. "How are you feeling?"

"A lot worse since you arrived." He sat up and swung his legs out of bed.

"I'm glad." She gave him a poisonously sweet smile. "I hoped my visit would have that effect."

"What do you want, Lara?" He scrubbed a hand across his forehead, feeling a headache coming on. Would the universe ever allow him to feel safe?

"They say Ash might die," she hissed, her voice raw and filled with pain.

Shock skittered through him. Lara had real feelings for her boyfriend? She wasn't just using him? He blinked and shook his head. No. Darks enslaved humans. They did not fall in love with them.

"I'm sorry." He ducked his head. His apology was genuine. Ash had been annoying but never his main tormentor. He had only done what Nathan and Alex ordered. Dying for a few poor decisions was a tragedy.

"You caused this. You and your pathetic human friends." Lara's slender frame was rigid, her face taut with fury. Animosity rolled off her in waves.

"Hey! No. Alex was the one who fired the gun. He accidentally shot Ash and—"

Claws shot from her fingertips and sank savagely into his arm. "Stop talking." Her green eyes blazed with hate. She jerked him forward so their faces were inches apart. "Shut up and listen, you worthless, pathetic mage. If Ash dies, if you succeed in killing that boy …" Her voice caught. For one horrible moment she looked about to cry. "I will ruin you," she said. "I will delight in crushing everything you love. I will make you experience every miniscule bit of agony you have put me through."

His eyes widened. "Lara, I had nothing to do with his accident. Ask Alex, hell, even ask Nathan!" He swallowed. She did have a point. He had helped Justin with the rescue, and that had resulted in Ash getting shot. Plus, he had rigged the gun to miss, but he had done so to prevent injuries, not cause them. Ash and Assassin's Honor had kidnapped the girls and threatened to murder them. Ash's gangster friends were the ones responsible, not Zack, Amy, and Charles.

"Stop!" Her voice cracked with grief. "You will never dodge the blame on this. You better hope he lives, because if he dies, you will deeply regret it." She sank her claws deeper into his arm. "I will make you regret it."

"Is there a problem in here?" Officer Kimmy Wolf breezed into his hospital room. She was carrying a paper plate with five banana nut muffins stacked in a precarious pyramid. She had a sixth sense for Dark trouble and a major sweet tooth.

"Not at all." Lara smiled serenely. "I was just checking on a classmate." When genuine, Lara's sweet smile could just about melt your heart. But the way she smiled at Kimmy made it clear she'd rather poison her.

"Charles is tired." Kimmy calmly took a bite of her muffin. "Continue your visit when he's more rested."

"Of course." Lara retracted her claws, leaving five angry red welts on his skin. "Get well soon, Charles." She tossed a final venomous look over her shoulder as she stalked out the door.

Charles slumped back into bed. "Thank you," he said.

"You have an unhealthy habit of incurring the wrath of the Darks," Kimmy said and snorted, offering him the plate.

"I don't understand why I provoke them so much." He accepted a muffin. They were warm and smelled divine. Definitely not hospital fare. He peeled away the paper sleeve. The pastry was sweet and crunchy on top, and fluffy and moist within. He glanced at Kimmy to thank her. His cheeks heated with embarrassment as he met her deep blue gaze. This was the second time today she had saved him. She had also pulled him from the lake. He grimaced. He needed to man up and stop girls from rescuing him all the time.

Kimmy placed her hand on his bleeding arm. Warmth spread from the place where she touched him and soothed away the pain. She removed her hand. His skin was healed. He flashed her a grateful smile. Angels were one supernatural creature the world needed more of. His smile grew wistful. If only Kimmy could heal Amy the way she had healed him. Amy's injuries would vanish within seconds. Charles sighed, bone-deep weariness tugging at his heart. Such actions were forbidden. Since Amy had no knowledge of the supernatural world, Kimmy would face serious consequences with the Office of Supernatural Containment if she interfered. The OSC, the government agency responsible for monitoring super-to-human interactions, was supposed to prevent supers from abusing their power. In reality, the OSC existed to ensure humans never learned of the supernatural world. Kimmy healing Amy was a direct violation of their code.

Kimmy released a wistful sigh, silently agreeing with his unspoken thoughts. "Hospitals are tragic places. So many frightened and hurting people that I am forbidden to help." Her eyes were deep blue pools of swirling anguish. Kimmy sharply shook her head as if sweeping aside a painful memory. "I'd better stick around until your mother returns." She settled herself in a chair across from his bed and cast a wary glance at the door.

"I don't need a babysitter." He dropped his eyes to his lap, his face burning with shame.

"That Dark girl was strongly bonded to her human boyfriend. He's in critical condition, and if he dies, you will bear the brunt of her fury and pain."

Charles jerked his gaze to her in surprise. "But bonding only enslaves the humans."

"The bond goes both ways." She leaned back in her chair and hooked her feet around its legs. "If the Dark in question has several bonds at one time, all are weak. But if a Dark stays faithful, as Lara has, they end up strongly attached to their human. The human's well-being becomes as important as their own, and this attachment often evolves into love."

"Love?" His forehead puckered. "Darks have fallen in love?"

"Yes. As unbelievable as it sounds, it can happen." She spoke with an air of intellectual confidence, but her depth of knowledge hinted at firsthand experience.

Charles leaned back against his pillows and put his hands behind his head. Had Alex ever bonded anyone frequently enough to fall in love? He smirked, picturing his archrival head over heels for some poor, unfortunate human girl. He'd pay good money to see that.

Forty-three

ZACK RETURNED TO Susan's room with burgers and fries and a black hole of despair in his gut. Susan was fast asleep in bed, and Justin was staring morosely into space. The boys attempted polite small talk as they ate and eventually lapsed into miserable silence. The White Spot burgers he had bought turned to cardboard in Zack's mouth, and the weight of their unspoken words weighed heavy on his heart. Amy. Her name was a yawning chasm of grief. He and Justin clung to opposite cliffs, together but alone. Time passed, the minutes turning into hours, every passing second leaching them of hope.

A light knock at the door at last ended their suffocating silence. A middle-aged doctor wearing navy scrubs and a weary expression entered the room. She had jet-black hair with a streak of silver down the middle, and wan hazel eyes that had seen more than their share of heartbreak. "I'm looking for Justin Evans?" Her gaze flicked between the two boys.

"That's me." Justin leapt to his feet. "What's happened with Amy?"

A dagger pierced Zack's heart with every word the doctor spoke. Amy was breathing with the help of a ventilator. She was being kept alive by beeping machines, holding to the slim hope that her condition would improve within the next twelve hours. A thick fog of despair blanketed the room. It saturated his pores and soaked into his soul.

"And if she doesn't improve?" Zack cut the doctor off mid-sentence. "What happens to her, then?"

"Who are you, exactly?" The doctor narrowed her hazel eyes, disapproval etched all over her tired face.

Justin gave a dismissive wave of his hand. "He's a friend of the family, and I would like to know the same thing."

"Very well." She sighed, her rigid shoulders slumping. "I avoid giving families and friends percentages and statistics because analytical odds are never concrete. Ms. Evans is critical but stable. She experienced multiple concussions which caused a brain bleed. Though we caught it quickly and have treated the rest of her injuries, Ms. Evans is still in a coma. Surgically, we've done everything we can. The ball is in her court now. If she doesn't wake within the next twelve hours, she will likely never regain consciousness."

Silence enveloped the room like a hopeless black void, the kind of silence that could hold and swallow worlds. Zack's heart dropped from his chest, its dead weight slowly sinking into his shoes. Amy might not wake up. The stubborn, fiery, unreasonable light that was her soul could go out forever. A knife twisted in his gut. How had he gone to school with her for years and never noticed her? Why had he been such a jerk to her all the time? She deserved better. A hell of a lot better.

A sob punched through the dreadful stillness. Susan was sitting up in bed, face ashen. She clenched handfuls of the hospital blanket in her fists. Her dove gray eyes, so similar to Amy's, bored furiously into Justin's. "You liar! You told me Amy was fine! But she's not. She's going to die! You liar!" Susan fell back onto her pillows and hid her face as she cried. Justin tried to comfort her, but she rolled to face the wall. "I hate you," she sobbed into her pillow. "I hate you, I hate you, I hate you."

Her heartbreak slammed into Zack and doubled his own. He rose with the intention of rushing over and hugging her. But no, the siblings needed privacy. He shook his head to dislodge his opaque cloud of sorrow and followed the doctor from the room. He eased the door shut behind them with slow, quiet care.

Zack wandered the hospital corridors, plagued with dread and haunted by regret. His miserable footsteps eventually carried him to the entrance of the main lobby.

A girl shrieked his name as he trudged through the doors. He blinked in horrified disbelief at the tall blonde blur. Why was Chelsea streaking toward him like a missile on route to its target?

How had she found him? Why the hell was she here? Zack braced himself for an explosive impact with what little strength he had left.

The girl's hair swung back from her face and he sagged with relief. "Zack!" His older sister launched herself into his arms. "You are so stupid!" Her long blonde hair had half obscured her tear-streaked face. Even so, her resemblance to his ex was strikingly off putting. Was it just the hair? No. It had been the way she shrieked his name that had thrown him back into the old nightmare.

"Clarisse?" He laughed at her greeting. "What the hell are you doing here?" His sister lived halfway across the country.

Zack held her at arm's length and surveyed her with concern. Clarisse was slender and tall with movie star platinum hair and dancing mint green eyes. She was usually immaculate in dresses, skirts, or the occasional pair of figure-hugging jeans. Today, she was uncharacteristically dressed in simple black leggings and a long, lacy blue blouse that matched her scuffed-up ankle boots. Smudged makeup and travel-knotted hair completed her new look.

Mrs. Donnellson nudged her daughter aside. "We've been so worried!" She clutched Zack in a smothering embrace and burst into tears.

"That looks fun." Chris snickered sarcastically. He and their father stood a few feet back, a safe distance from the crying women. Chris took pity on him and towed Clarisse and his mother away. "Come on, guys. Zack's fine. Let him breathe."

"My poor baby." Mrs. Donnellson dabbed at her face with a tissue. "You really are okay, right? You're not just saying that?" She fluttered her hands around Zack as if shocked to find him whole.

His cheeks heated. "Mom, I wasn't even admitted here. Let's go sit." He nodded to a thankfully empty corner.

Mr. Donnellson took his wife's arm and guided her to a chair. William Donnellson was tall. He had thick red hair like Zack and smiling, sky blue eyes like Chris.

"I'm super glad Zack's okay," Chris blurted as soon as they were seated, "but tell me about Sue. She'll be okay too, right?" His expressive sky blue eyes begged for the answer the doctor had failed to give Justin.

Zack furrowed his brow. "Physically, Sue will be fine. They just want her to stay overnight for observation."

"That's great!" Chris beamed. "When can I see her?"

"Hang on a sec." Clarisse held up a manicured hand. "What do you mean, *physically* she will be fine?"

"Sue's upset because Amy's not doing too well." He ignored the ache inside at even saying her name. When had he started caring about her so much? A week ago, she was just another girl. Now she felt like most of his whole world.

"Amy?" Clarisse cocked her head. "The other girl taken with you and Chris's friend?"

Zack directed his gaze over Clarisse's shoulder, afraid she'd read the turmoil in his eyes. "Yeah. Amy is Susan's sister. She's also in a couple of my classes."

"Their poor mother." Mrs. Donnellson clasped Chris's hand.

"Where's Sue? I want to help if she's upset. She's my best friend." Chris's eyes filled with sorrow. "I like Amy too."

Sympathy pierced Zack's heart. Chris had had to sit at home for hours, knowing his brother and his best friend were in trouble. Zack put a hand on his shoulder. "Good idea, bro. Susan needs a friend right now."

"Great!" Chris leapt to his feet. "Let's go visit her!"

"You sure, honey?" Their mother's brow creased with doubt. "What if she and her family want to be alone?"

"It's only her brother with her right now. I'm not sure where their parents are, and Amy's unconscious." He ignored the hollow feeling he got saying *Amy's unconscious* and led Chris toward the hall.

"Wait. Zack!" His mother put out an arm to stop them. "You can't barge into Susan's room with four extra people. I'll go determine what the visitor regulations here are." She strode to the front desk, her heels click, click, clicking across the floor.

Zack glanced up at the ceiling, praying for patience. He dropped back into his seat and glowered around the group. "Why are all of you here?"

"Please. You and those girls have been the lead news story all across the country," Clarisse explained with a matter-of-fact toss of her platinum hair. "I got the first flight out of Vancouver, and we came straight here. You seriously freaked us out."

Zack snickered. "Such a dramatic recounting of your adventure. Remind me to tell you my story sometime."

Their mom clicked her way back to them, smiling proudly at Chris as if he had won a gold medal. "Your friend has been asking for you."

"Good. Can I visit her, now?"

"Yes. Zack can see her as well, but they want to keep visitors to a minimum. I told them I won't be letting either of you out of my sight for the next fifty years and got permission for one of us to accompany you."

Zack rolled his eyes at his parents. "Which of you wants to come?"

"I do," Clarisse asserted forcefully. "I need to talk to Zack."

His parents exchanged an uneasy glance. His dad was the one who relented. "We'll wait here, but you three better stay together."

"Oh my God," Zack groaned as they entered the stairwell. "They were overprotective before this happened. Chris will be middle-aged before they let him cross the street without holding hands."

Chris giggled. Clarisse gave Zack a hard look. "You don't know, do you?"

"Know what?"

"Those guys from your school. They were also admitted here."

Zack froze midstride. "What the hell! They've got Amy and the people who tried to kill her in the same damn hospital?" Rage bubbled inside him like lava in a volcano.

"I'm sure they'll be arrested as soon as they're discharged. They're under police guard right now, and one is in the same condition as Amy, so not much of a problem there." She clapped a hand to her mouth. "Oh God, I'm sorry. I meant … They're only here to heal. That's the law. Once they improve, they'll be discharged, arrested, and taken back to Toronto. My guess is they'll get at least ten years." She took in his anguished expression and faltered, at last out of words. When Clarisse got nervous, she regurgitated facts as if knowing everything about a situation made it better. Nothing she said could ever make this better. "Zack?" She touched his arm.

"Let's find Sue," he muttered, refusing to meet her eyes. They headed to her room under a dismal pall of silence.

Zack knocked lightly on her door and waited a beat for Justin to open it. "Hey." Zack forced a smile. "Justin, this is my brother, Chris, and my sister, Clarisse."

"Nice to meet you both." Justin smiled at Chris and shook Clarisse's hand. His gaze lingered on Clarisse a fraction longer than Zack liked.

"Chris is here?" Susan popped up in her bed like a spring-loaded jack-in-the-box.

Chris ran to hug her. Susan hugged him back, relief relaxing her pinched, worried face. He perched on the end of her bed, and she energetically launched into her adventure.

Clarisse's eyes twinkled. "When did our little bro get so cute with the girls?" She glanced sideways at Justin and ran her fingers through her tangled hair.

"After meeting Sue." Zack chuckled. "Before her, girls were gross."

"I seriously have to visit more. I miss so much with how little I see you guys." She gave Justin an intrigued look from beneath her long lashes.

"Where you from?" Justin perched on a cot that a nurse must have brought for him to sleep on that night.

"I go to school in Vancouver." Clarisse sat comfortably close to him.

"No way! Me too! I'm studying criminal justice." Justin flashed a cocky smile.

Her eyes lit up. "That's such a coincidence. I graduated with my psych degree in May and got into the law program at UBC. Where in Vancouver are you staying?" She batted her lashes.

Zack grimaced and backed out of the room. "I'm going for a walk." He doubted anyone would notice his absence.

He wandered the hospital once more and wound up staring out a window on the second floor. The full moon shone down upon the earth, no longer the startling bloodred color of the night before. The velvet night sky was speckled with stars. The world was quiet, cool, and still, a stark contrast to the chaotic desperation of the hospital and its occupants.

Zack ached for Amy, alone in an anonymous off-white room. She didn't deserve to die this young. He ached for Susan, so innocent and sweet. She didn't deserve to lose her sister or have her innocence tarnished with pain.

A noise behind him made his blood run cold. It was the unmistakable click of a gun being cocked.

Forty-four

"TURN AROUND. I want to see the look on your face as I blow your brains out."

Zack turned slowly, his hands raised in surrender. Alex stood ten feet away with a semiautomatic pistol in his hand and a gleam of triumph in his soulless blue eyes. He was dressed in full police uniform, a sight that both disgusted and disturbed Zack. "Pull that trigger, and your sentence will go from ten years to life."

A slim young woman dressed all in black slipped silently around the corner behind Alex like a beautiful figment of Zack's imagination. Kimmy caught his eye for the briefest of moments and slid a few feet closer to Alex on silent, socked feet.

"A life sentence, huh?" Alex quirked a brow. "Too bad the cop I just murdered forgot to mention that. Nothing to lose now, I guess." He stalked a few steps closer and pointed his pistol between Zack's eyes.

Zack held his breath. Tension clenched his insides as he tracked Kimmy's soundless, creeping progress out of the corner of his eye. His heart raced. Sweat trickled down his back. He had to keep Alex talking to distract him. "How's your friend?" Zack blurted, desperation leaking into his voice. "I heard he ain't doing too well."

"Heard the same about Amy. She'll join you soon. I'll make sure of it."

Zack stiffened. "Shouldn't you be trying to escape? Going after the girls will make sure you're caught." Kimmy would cart his miserable ass off to jail within minutes, but just the thought of Alex getting his hands on Amy or Susan made his blood boil.

Alex chuckled. "Don't worry. I plan on keeping your pretty little girlfriend as a hostage. She'll be all the insurance I need. Any last words?"

Panic rioted in his mind as numbing certainty settled in his chest. Kimmy was too far away. Alex was too close. These were his last seconds on Earth. Zack's eyes flashed with hate. "Go to hell."

"Only if you go first." Alex curled his finger around the trigger.

Kimmy dove forward with the grace of an angry ballerina. Zack shoved away from the wall and flung himself to the side. A bullet skewered the window frame a fraction of an inch from his face.

Kimmy tackled Alex to the ground and sent his weapon flying through the air. She pinned him to the floor and trained her own pistol on his chest. "Don't move."

"Took you long enough." Zack staggered to his feet as she radioed for backup.

"Are you okay?" She kept her gaze trained on Alex.

"I'm good." Zack wrenched Alex's thrashing arms behind his back. His face was taut with anger, and his wild eyes bulged. He acted as if he was being electrocuted. "Can I cuff him?" Zack asked.

"Knock yourself out. Make sure they're good and tight."

"Don't you worry about that." He snapped the cuffs around Alex's wrists and tightened them as far as they would go.

Kimmy regarded Alex with a smug smile. "I guess there's no point in reading you your rights, as you and I have already gone over those once today."

"You're going to pay for this, you bitch!" Alex howled. Half a dozen officers sprinted around the corner and surrounded him. "One day, I'm going to find you, and I'm going to kill you!" The officers dragged him off.

"All in a day's work." Kimmy smiled serenely and tucked a lock of hair behind her ear.

Zack gaped, stunned by her composure. "How many psychotic death threats do you regularly receive?"

"Oh, none as well crafted as that one." She laughed musically. "They're usually a little more vague. 'I'm gonna find you and you'll be sorry' or 'I'm gonna find you and you'll regret this.' I just say what the hell. I'm safe as long as they never find me."

The corners of his mouth quirked up. "You better never go to prison."

"Do I look like the type to end up behind bars?"

Zack surveyed her from head to toe. She had ditched her police uniform, was dressed entirely in black, and stood there smirking with multiple weapons clipped to her belt. "Yes, you do." He winced internally. What idiot opens his mouth and says a cop belongs in jail? Her reaction was more musical laughter. He smiled. "How come you're still here? Thought you got off duty a while ago."

"I stayed to support Justin." He raised his eyebrows and she giggled. "Also, there were no flights back to Vancouver until morning."

"You're from Vancouver too?"

"Yeah. Justin phoned me right after he received your call. I was a guest lecturer in one of his classes last semester. He knows I'm the best, most amazing tracker the RCMP has."

"And most conceited," Zack quipped.

"Want to take another ride in my squad car, Zack?" Her blue eyes danced with mirth.

"That would be a lot harder to explain to my parents than detention." He chuckled. "I better go check on my friends before I say anything else that could land me in prison."

"Try to avoid getting shot on the way there."

"Don't even joke." He winced, imagining his mother's reaction when she learned what had just happened. "Will you keep this under wraps for a while? Everyone has enough going on without adding my near-death experience to the mix."

Kimmy nodded, her eyes full of understanding. "You'll have to give your statement eventually, but I'll tell my colleagues to hold off until morning."

He smiled. "Thanks. For everything."

Susan's room was packed with guests. She and Chris were snuggled up in bed, exhausted and shockingly quiet for once. His mom and dad had chairs pulled up to Susan's bedside, and Charles and his mother were sitting on the cot by the window. Zack shook his head. So much for keeping visitors to a minimum.

"Any news?" He joined Chris on the edge of Susan's bed.

His dad ran a hand through his dark red hair, an agitated gesture. "Not yet. She's still in a coma."

"Justin and Clarisse went for coffee." Susan forced a brave smile. "Chris and I think they like each other." She made air quotes around the word *like*. "You know, they like, like each other!"

He managed a gentle smile. "Sue, I'm so glad you're okay. Sorry I didn't tell you earlier."

"I know." Her dove gray eyes brimmed with a depth of understanding older and wiser than her nine short years.

His heart swelled with love for her. This little girl would always be important to him. No one went through what they had been through without forming a bond. He had always wanted a little sister. Now he had one in spirit if not in name.

He turned to Charles. "You too, man. You were awesome." Charles had saved his life, risking his own to do so. He was a solid dude.

Charles widened his eyes at Zack's praise. "Thanks. I only wish ..." He broke off. "Does anyone know what her chances are?"

Mrs. Donnellson wearily shook her head. "We have no idea at this point."

Time dragged by, each agonizing minute more painful and hopeless than the last. Charles and his mother retired to Charles's room. Susan and Chris fell asleep side by side. Justin and Clarisse returned with coffee for everyone. Mrs. Donnellson repeatedly tried to convince Zack to leave for a hotel. He repeatedly declined her offers. He was going to be there for Amy, no matter what happened.

A knock at the door sent Justin leaping to his feet. He threw it open to reveal the doctor from before. Zack's heart took a plummeting nosedive. This was it. She had news of Amy.

"What happened?" Justin demanded. "Is my sister okay?"

The doctor smiled. A tidal wave of relief swept over Zack. "Ms. Evans is awake!"

The room erupted with cheers that woke Susan and Chris.

"Amy's awake!" Justin squeezed his sister tight.

The doctor held up a cautionary hand. "As you know, Ms. Evans has been through a lot. She has two broken ribs and had extensive internal bleeding. She experienced several concussions in the space of a few hours, and she nearly drowned. She will need time to recover."

"When can I see her?" Susan crawled to the edge of her bed, ready to charge down the hall in her cream-colored nightgown.

The doctor's eyes twinkled, but her mouth remained firm. "Your sister can have visitors, but only one at a time. It would be best if you went to see her in the morning. You need rest as well."

Susan obediently flopped back in bed. She'd go along with anything now Amy was safe.

Zack had an idiotic smile stuck on his face. Amy would be making snarky comments in no time, no doubt throughout her entire recovery. Justin followed the doctor from the room. Zack suppressed a pang of jealousy that her brother automatically got to visit her first.

Clarisse suggested a walk. They wandered Susan's hospital floor in companionable silence. Zack wanted to tease her about Justin but lacked the energy. Amy was the only thing on his mind. They circled the floor twice before Justin returned.

"How is she?" Zack asked.

"Go see for yourself, man." Justin gestured back the way he had come. "Follow the corridor until you reach the stairs. Go down two flights and her room is the first door on the left. Number 307. Keep it short, though. She's exhausted."

Amy wasn't the only one. Justin's eyelids drooped like it was a struggle to keep them open, and his shoulders slumped as if they bore the weight of the world. The insane events of the last twenty-four hours had caught up to him at last. Clarisse moved to his side, and Zack rushed to Amy's room.

She sat propped in bed, her tiny frame dwarfed by beeping machines. She looked small, fragile even. Zack seethed with anger at Alex and Assassin's Honor. Amy was a natural-born fighter. It broke his heart to see her this way.

"Hey." She managed a weak smile. "You coming in?"

He closed her door and crossed the distance between them in three long strides. "How you feeling?" He took her hand and knelt next to her bed.

"Oh, come on!" She drew out the words on an exasperated groan.

"What did I do this time? I've literally spoken to you for five seconds, and you're already mad?"

Amy rolled her eyes. "You and Justin are acting like I'm made of glass. It's annoying!"

"Sorry." He ducked his head to hide his smile. "How shall I treat you?"

"Like normal," she said grumpily. Nearly dying had not improved her mood.

His smile grew, affection for her making his heart swell. "Drop the attitude, okay? Let's call a truce on annoying the hell out of each other." She took a breath as if about to argue. He cut her off before she had the chance. "I'm insanely worried about you, okay? You're going to hurt yourself if you keep pretending you're fine. You don't have to do that around me." He squeezed her fingers and met her beautiful misty gray gaze. His heart skipped a beat at the tide of emotion he felt for her. This was no longer a game where Amy was a hard-to-win, short-term prize. This was terrifyingly, heart lurchingly real.

The moment fizzled into fiction at a blazing look from Amy. "Seriously, Zack, who do you think you are?" She yanked her hand from his. "Who are you to tell me how to feel? You don't even know me, so how the hell do you think you know what's best for me?" Her words stung. Worse still, they rang with truth. He and Amy had met a week ago. It was a stretch to even hope she felt the same. His heart squeezed with the loss of what never was and never would be. Amy's furious gaze burned holes into his soul. "God! All you people are the same. Money doesn't give you the right to walk around as though you're better than everyone else." Her voice rose as she built up steam. "Take away your fancy cars and your fancy clothes and your fancy freaking mansions and you're just like the rest of us. You're a spoiled jerk, and I hate you."

His mouth fell open. He struggled to undo whatever it was that he had done. "Amy, please." He reached to touch her hand. "I never meant …"

She smacked his hand away. "You made things worse for me and Sue. Charles is the hero, not you. Stop basking in your privileged, fake glory and acknowledge what a spoiled ass you are."

Hot shame burned his cheeks. Her words ripped into him, each one a well-aimed knife to his heart. She hated him? She thought he thought he was a hero? That was worlds away from the truth.

She tried to sit up despite the pain in her eyes. Her blanket slipped, and his aching heart froze in his chest. Amy's side was encased in a bandage that stretched from just below her shoulder to under the blankets near her waist. She followed his gaze and strained to fix her covers. The machines hampered her efforts, and they slipped further down.

"Amy." Her name fell raw and aching from his lips. He wanted to help her but had no idea how. His throat tightened with emotion. His chest constricted with pain. He couldn't bear to look at the place where they had hit her, where they had hurt her because of him.

Forty-five

AMY LOCKED EYES with Zack and struggled to break his heart. She spewed handcrafted hate designed specifically to hurt him, lies specially created to finish pushing him away. He shouldn't care about her. She was a walking, lying, manipulative torpedo. She had shattered her family with one reckless mistake, one moment of stupidity she would regret for the rest of her life. Worse, her family would pay for it for the rest of their lives. And what had Zack gotten for caring about her? A week from hell. She hurt everyone around her, and she refused to hurt Zack.

The football jock was genuinely kind. She knew in her heart he had way more to him than his spoiled rich kid persona. She could grow to care for him, and that terrified her. Every man she had ever loved had ditched her, betrayed her, or learned to hate her. Every relationship she had ever had was laced with pain. Letting Zack in would open up a world of heartbreak. Better to keep him and her heart safe.

She opened her mouth to blast him, to scream lies she had to make real in order to drive him away. The blanket slipped and uncovered her bandaged side. Her anger evaporated at a glimpse of Zack's anguished crystal blue gaze. His eyes held a world of misery. His expression was what Amy faced every morning when she looked in the mirror. Zack had the haunted gaze of someone with deep regrets.

Her next dreadful lie died on her lips. She placed a gentle hand on his rigid shoulder. "Zack? Hey, it's okay." Guilt and shame tangled in her gut. She had never meant to make him feel this terrible. She squirmed uncomfortably and released a slow breath. "Look, I, what I said before." She stumbled over her words. Shouting at him had been so much easier. "I'm sorry, okay? Sometimes I'm a total bitch. I've improved since middle school, but old habits die hard."

"What are you talking about?" His eyes traveled to her face and back to her side. He winced.

"Does it look that bad?" She dropped her eyes, uncharacteristically unsure of herself.

Zack lifted his gaze and noticed her hand on his shoulder. She moved to pull it away, but he caught her hand and tenderly threaded his fingers with hers. "Nothing you can't handle."

"So why do you look so horrified?"

"Because it's my fault!" Zack's expression twisted with anguish. "I'm the reason you're here. If I had paid more attention to what went on last week, I could have stopped this from happening. I should have stopped it."

Amy met his eyes, overwhelmed by the genuine concern in their crystal blue depths. "What? Your fault? The hell it's your fault. I'm the one who refused to listen when everyone warned me about them. I'm the one who tried to handle Assassin's Honor on my own."

His fingers brushed her side. "They did this to you because of me. They wanted me to listen, and they hurt you when I didn't."

"Zack." She bit her lower lip and dropped her gaze once more. "What I said before … I didn't mean it. Justin told me about the lake. You saved me. You are a hero." Her cheeks burned.

"No. I messed up." He pressed a hand to his forehead. "There are a lot of things I want to do over, and most of them concern you."

Amy's heart sank. He was doing it again, acting as though they were more than classmates, maybe even more than friends. But she and Zack were never going to happen. It was a risk to let anyone close to her. It was better to be alone. She softly began to cry.

"Amy? What's wrong?" His voice was laced with concern. "Want me to call a nurse?"

Amy buried her face in her arms. Physical pain was easier to explain than emotional agony.

Zack moved to sit on the edge of her bed and carefully wrapped an arm around her back. Amy buried her face in his shirt. This one goodbye was killing her. "You shouldn't like me so much." Her words were muffled by her tears and the soft cotton of his shirt.

"Why is no one allowed to like you?" he murmured into her hair. "Why do you have to push everyone away?"

Her heart swelled with a rush of affection. It flooded her soul with a tingling, comforting warmth. Zack understood her like no one else. Most people would be angry after what she had said. Most would have stormed out the door and never looked back. Not Zack. He saw through her layers of defenses, straight to her damaged core. He had glimpsed her scars and refused to turn away.

She looked up into his face and tearfully wiped her eyes. "You wouldn't like me if you knew what I did."

"Tell me?" He held her closer. "I'll do my best to understand. I know how it feels to want to change the past." His eyes shone with a gentle, earnest intensity. His arms were a cocoon of strength, wrapping her in a circle of understanding and trust.

She had run out of ways to lie to him. Her walls crumbled and fell away. She let go of the secret that had haunted her life for two and a half years. "I have a sister," she whispered, hardly daring to breathe.

He stared at her like she had hit her head one too many times. "Yeah, I know. Sue's fine, though."

"I had another little sister. Her name was Katie. She was three years younger than Sue." Zack's stunned silence made her second-guess herself, but she took a shaky breath and blindly plunged ahead. She wanted, no, needed, to share her past with him. Telling him the truth might be the only way to save him. "Katie died because of me."

Zack didn't pull away. He wrapped his arms around her and gently hugged her close. She was safely nestled against the warmth of his chest, sheltered from the world and its harsh reality. "Tell me, Amy. Let it out."

And she did. For the first time in years, she went back to the night she had let her littlest sister die. "I was thirteen when it happened. Sue was six at the time, and Katie, Katie was three. Mom and Dad left me in charge. Justin went out with his friends. I was mad I got stuck at home babysitting so I invited my boyfriend over. We told the girls to go play while we made out on the couch. They wanted to swim in the pool we had set up in the backyard. They were gone way too long, but I, I—" Her voice cracked. She paused for a moment to compose herself. "I got distracted. I was getting up to check on them when Sue ran in screaming. Everything blurs after that. I remember flashes of waist-deep water, and Katie's icy hands."

Her heart twisted. She clung to Zack. He squeezed her fingers and ran the pad of his thumb over her knuckles in a gentle, soothing motion.

She inhaled a shaky breath. "Katie wasn't breathing, and I had no idea what to do. Susan kept screaming, and my boyfriend yelled at her not to look. I told him to call nine-one-one while I tried CPR. He took one look at me and Katie and split. I wound up alone, holding my three-year-old sister as she died in my arms. I barely remember calling nine-one-one, but the wait for the ambulance is burned into my mind. Sue was screaming for me to tell her what was happening. Katie's face was turning blue. I felt the moment her tiny heart stopped. I held them both, one alive and one dead and prayed for a miracle. I remember my dad yelling at me in the hospital parking lot, and her tiny, tiny casket. Katie died because I was irresponsible and didn't know how to save her. I didn't know what to do!"

A storm of despair swirled inside her, battering her heart and destroying her from the inside out. But she was not alone. Someone was holding her close, guiding her through the raging tempest of regret, shame, and heartbreak. After all she had told him, after everything she had done, Zack was still by her side.

"There's more," she choked out. He stroked her hair, patiently waiting for her to explain in her own time. "My family fell apart after Katie's death. Mom started drinking, and Dad walked out." She clung to his hand and fastened her gaze to his. "I killed my baby sister and ruined what was left of my family."

He shook his head. "You can't blame yourself for your parents' choices. Your one mistake isn't the sole reason for everything that went wrong. They chose to split up. Your mom chose to drink. They made those decisions on their own. Amy, you shouldn't keep tearing yourself to pieces over Katie's death." He raised his hand and ran his thumb along her cheek, brushing away a tear. "What happened to her was a tragedy, but it was also an accident. You loved your sister. You did everything you could to save her."

"But she died!" Amy shrieked. "She died, and no matter what I do, I can never go back and fix that."

He cupped her chin. "You're right, you can't go back, but you need to move forward. You have to forgive yourself for what happened to her. I'm scared of what it will do to you if you don't."

"How do you not hate me? My old friends did. Everyone back home did. Why don't you?"

"There's no way I could ever hate you," he said, brushing a lock of hair over her shoulder. "I promise. We've all made mistakes, and we're all going to make a whole lot more. The trick is to learn from our screwed-up choices. I know I have." He gazed deep into her eyes.

Amy gazed back at him, his steady presence centering her and soothing her spirit. "Want to be my new counselor?" She smiled through her tears at the clarity his words had brought. "You should seriously consider it as a career path."

He grinned. "It's all my sister's fault. Clarisse has rubbed off on me with her psych major crap. When she comes home from law school, I'll start spouting legal advice. Besides, I don't want to be your *counselor*." A slow blush crept into her cheeks. His grin widened. "Maybe we should go see a movie sometime. How does that sound, Evans?"

Zack had seen the worst of her, and he still wanted her? Maybe, just maybe, he was worth the risk. "I'll have to check my schedule. I've been pretty busy lately." His face lit up. Her heart swelled. Tonight, she had given him a maybe, but tomorrow?

"I'll be here whenever." Zack laid a hand over his heart in a theatrical but solemn gesture. "Right now, you need to rest."

"Okay." She leaned back against her pillows. "Will you stay with me for a while?"

"Absolutely." He took her hand in his. "As long as you want me here, I'm here."

"You better never leave," she murmured, her eyelids beginning to droop.

"Amy?" Zack said her name with sudden urgency.

She blinked open her eyes. "I thought you wanted me to sleep. Make up your mind, Donnellson."

His expression remained serious. "I would never have left you. I would have stayed with you and helped."

"I know," she whispered, entwining her fingers with his. "You're one of the good ones."

Amy drifted off to sleep in the arms of THS's star quarterback. She had only known him a week, but Zack had changed her life forever. Her last waking thought brought a smile to her face. She was no longer alone.

Forty-six

ALEX SWEPT A look of contempt around his jail cell. Enemies, allies, and police officers alike would soon get what they deserved, starting with Peter. Alex had placed toxic darkness inside him after he had rescued Susan from the lake. It was slowly dissolving his stomach lining like a poisonous cleaning solution. Peter was going to drown on his own blood, a fitting end for a traitor. His lips parted in a smirk. Peter was his first in a long line of victims. Death was about to come knocking on many, many doors.

The cops planned to keep him imprisoned until they dumped him in court and tried him for his crimes. He rolled his eyes. As if he'd let that happen. He was going to disappear and leave Nathan to the consequences of his stupidity. Why pay for his followers' incompetence? All of them had made fatal mistakes.

They had snatched the little brat, Susan, expressly to torture her sister, but thanks to Peter and that blasted mage, Alex hadn't gotten much of a chance to torture anyone. He had grown bored of the girls and had influenced Peter to answer Zack's phone call. Zack had long been on his list of sacrificial candidates, and Alex was excited to cross him out. His plan had taken a hit when Zack had showed the police to their door. Even so, Alex had stayed optimistic until the gas station fiasco. He had made Nathan force Amy into 7-Eleven, knowing she planned a bid for freedom. That had given him the excuse he needed to kill her and keep his followers quiet. It would have worked, too, if Peter hadn't again interfered. The night had gone downhill from there, ending with him literally shooting himself in the foot.

Alex had pretended Charles had knocked him unconscious and waited for Amy's erratic driving to kill them all. He had sent darkness to carry Ash to safety after they crashed into the lake but had stuck around to drown Susan and finish his mission. He needed to kill someone for the Blood Moon, and she had been closest. The next thing he knew, the horrifying angel cop was electrocuting him with holy light and dragging him from the car. She had taken it upon herself to keep him imprisoned, going so far as to reinforce his cell with holy light after he had nearly killed Zack. This had made it impossible for him to ghost away as darkness, a useful power that allowed him to tunnel intangibly through solid ground. He shrugged. Ghosting was still how he would dodge a life in prison. The angel had to sleep eventually, and when she did, revenge would be his.

A raven-haired girl appeared in the center of his cell. "I warned you," The Dark declared, her steely gaze pinning him to the wall at his back.

He made a derisive noise. "Yeah, well, I won't be stuck here for long,"

"What is it with you, Alex? You're always wrong."

"What is it with you, Dark? You're always three steps behind. When the angel sleeps, the holy light disappears, and I walk. Understand?"

She smoothed her expression into an unreadable mask. "You disobeyed a direct order. You must be punished."

Alex laughed. "What are you going to do? Ground me for the summer?"

"From this moment forward, you will no longer be granted the privilege of using the darkness."

His stomach lurched. "You can't do that!" He leapt to his feet and pointed a finger at her chest. He waited for darkness to pierce her heart. Nothing happened. He glared directly into her eyes. She simply grinned back at him, unfazed by his influence.

Fear swirled in his gut, rising ever higher as realization dawned. She had reduced him to nothing. Losing his powers was akin to having a limb removed or a sense stripped away. "Wait, hold on." He took a deep breath and forced a cordial smile. "We both agree I've made mistakes, but there's no need to be hasty."

She threw her head back and laughed. "Alex, I'm not being hasty. I'm simply ruling the supernatural world. This is me doing the job you are convinced I cannot handle. You have become a danger to supers and humans alike. You will remain here until you learn your lesson or die. Whichever comes first."

"I'll be your most loyal supporter," he blurted, desperation forcing him to make promises he knew he'd later regret. "You need an advocate among the sea creatures. Let's set this madness aside and work together."

"Madness?" Sparks flew from her sapphire eyes. Darkness rippled in the air. "I am not mad." She stalked toward him, her face a mask of rage. "I have ruled for longer than you have been alive, and in all that time I have made fewer irrational decisions than you have in a single night. If anyone has a touch of madness in this room, Alex, it's you. But I'll tell you what." She leaned in close. "If you manage to escape this prison without the use of your powers, I'll return them to you. That should be easy, right?" She giggled girlishly. The sound made his skin crawl. "Simply escape a maximum-security prison, and I'll give you your life back."

"Please," he whispered, his eyes stretching wide. "The Blood Moon must not find me here."

"The Blood Moon already knows where you are. Have a nice life, or don't. I don't really care." She smiled brightly and vanished.

Alex tried for hours to summon the darkness. An irrational part of his mind clung to the idea that it was going to return to him. He fell back onto his bed and stared morosely at his cracked ceiling. Perhaps sleep would soothe his racing thoughts.

A young girl screamed. His eyes flew open. He peered around his cell at the white concrete walls and the bars blocking the door.

"Alex! Help me!"

He leapt to his feet. The blood rushed from his head and sent him lurching into a wall. Her voice made him shiver and raised gooseflesh on his arms.

An ethereal vision drifted into view. The girl appeared slowly, like mist over the ocean on a cold winter morning. Soft blonde curls framed her kind, sweet face, and her gentle blue eyes brimmed with overwhelming sorrow. The lovely apparition stretched imploring hands toward him. Her lapis blue dress was stained with blood.

"No! You're not real." He shut his eyes and still saw her face. Steel blades of anguish scored his heart.

Tidal waves of pain slammed into him and crashed over his head. Loss, despair, and grief struck one after the other, the latter so intense it made him fall to his knees. Delicate glimpses of memory battered his bruised soul.

She stood, smiling, by a lake at sunset. She giggled as she blew out candles on her birthday cake. She chatted animatedly with a friend as they walked through the mall. She shyly met his gaze across a crowded room. He remained at a distance as they grew up, never allowing himself to grow close to her. His life had no place for the fragile joy of innocence. Memories blossomed behind his eyes, each one a knife to his aching heart.

Their class stood clustered around a duck pond in third grade as their teacher demonstrated how to feed the birds. Alex amused himself by tripping people with darkness. A girl and boy lost their balance. He allowed the boy to slip into the murky water but caught the girl before she fell.

Alex watched with interest as a classmate pulled a gun on his former friend. A girl with curly hair the color of butterscotch rushed to stand between the two boys. His interest switched to ice-cold fear. She must not be hurt.

He glimpsed the curly-haired girl in front of a window display. She gazed longingly at a doll in a frilly pink dress. His lip curled in distaste, but something drew him inside the store. She was radiant when she found the gift in her locker the next morning.

Alex cupped her face as she cried. The purple bruise below her eye looked like an unfortunate encounter with a door. Alex knew better. He ran his thumb along her cheek and used darkness, for the first time in his life, to heal instead of hurt.

The sweet scent of spring lingered in the air as he walked her home at twilight. He pulled her to him at a street corner and gazed deep into her blue eyes. When their lips met, time stopped. He had kissed others before her, but no one else compared. Her silken hair smelled of summer; her soft lips tasted like honey. His heart sped up and adopted a new rhythm, beating in time with hers. He placed her hand against his chest, and her starry eyes widened in understanding. She belonged in his arms. She was his, and he was hers.

Alex was standing on her porch, trying to keep a straight face as she yelled at him. She was cute even when she was pissed.

He lay awake in the middle of the night with her soft, warm body nestled against his. Her head rested on his shoulder with her silken hair brushing his cheek. She smiled faintly as she dreamed. She had given him everything that night. She would always be safe with him; he would always keep her safe. When he pictured happiness, she was everything that came to mind.

Nathan was blundering his way through an Assassin's Honor meeting. Alex was reclining in an overstuffed armchair and daydreaming about her. He was struck with blinding terror as suddenly and as certainly as if he were inches from death. The room swam in and out of focus. Agony clouded his mind. He clawed past his panic and hauled himself back to his surroundings. The shabby living room. The blistering summer day. Nothing was wrong, which meant everything was.

He charged from the room and fought to locate her through their bond. Their link was shockingly weak, a thread so fine it would snap at any moment. She was dying. A lump of terror formed in his throat. He used darkness to ghost to her, not caring who saw or what trouble it caused.

Alex appeared beside her family's totaled car. The street was deserted apart from two smashed vehicles, a beet red station wagon and a Ford F-150. Both drivers were dead. His girl clung barely to life.

The station wagon was upside down in a ditch with the Ford smashed against its passenger side door. He ghosted her from the wreckage and scrambled to her side. Spikes of glass protruded from her chest. Her entire right side had been crushed. He clutched her hand and struggled to heal her, fighting the fear that his powers would fail. Darkness was a far better weapon than a cure. He was fighting a losing battle, but he would not, could not, stop fighting for her.

"Don't die! Don't you dare do this to me!" The words were ripped, raw and desperate, from his core. Crimson covered his hands. She was losing too much blood.

He called an ambulance and held her close, waiting for the shrieking of sirens and the rotund rattle of a big rig rescue. A breeze rustled gently through the trees, a peaceful sound that flooded him with panic. Where were they? Why weren't they here? His love was bleeding out in front of him. His eyes burned. A painful pressure constricted his chest. How long had it been since he had called? Five minutes? Ten? He struggled to stem her blood flow, but her blood just kept coming. He choked on a sob that physically tore him apart. He could not save her. An angel could heal her, but he was powerless even to help. He had failed the only person he had ever dared to love.

Her face twisted in agony as she fought for a labored breath. He was hurting her more by keeping her alive. Alex cradled her against his chest and let her slip away. She briefly focused on his face. He held her starry gaze, trying to memorize the color of her eyes, the kindness in their depths.

"Love you, Alex," she whispered. Her starry blue eyes closed forever. His heart stuttered as hers stopped. It had nothing to keep time with. She was gone.

Alex stood at the back of a crowded church, dressed in funeral black with emptiness in his heart. Everything inside him rebelled at standing on holy ground. But the girl he had loved had passed on to a better place, a place he could never reach. It was ironic that he believed in heaven, yet he would never be granted entrance to its hallowed halls. Darks had no place in heaven. His soul belonged in hell. The afterlife meant nothing but eternal separation from her, and the service at the church was his last chance to honor her.

He wandered the streets all night. He refused to sleep. He barely ate. Life had lost all meaning. He tormented himself by writing letters she would never read. He imagined he glimpsed her smile in a crowd of strangers' faces. He reached for his phone, forgetting he had no one to call. He lay awake at night and longed for one more chance to hold her. Sometimes he grew angry and hated her for leaving him, but he had no one to blame except himself. She was gone because he had failed to keep her safe.

Time passed, but the agony never faded. The pain of losing her never dulled. Her memory remained as both his comfort and his curse. Her absence had left a gaping hole inside that would never, ever mend. He never wished to love again.

Alex came to on the cold floor of his cell. He brushed moisture from his eyes and put a hand to his throbbing head. A wave of misery lifted him and swept him away. He was doomed to relive the worst moments of his life until they thankfully drove him mad. His prison cell had become his personal hell on Earth. So, this was what they called the Blood Moon's fury.

Afterword

ALEXANDER CARDELLE WAS discharged from the hospital after his violent encounter with Zack Donnellson. He awaits trial in Toronto where he is expected to receive a life sentence.

Nathan Johnson was transported to the hospital to have his gunshot wound treated. He was discharged the next morning and arrested for the kidnapping and torture of Amy Evans, Susan Evans, and Zack Donnellson. He, too, awaits trial in Toronto.

The doctors examined Peter Jenkins and were baffled to find nothing physically wrong with him apart from a minor concussion. They transferred him to police custody with disconcerted mutterings of a medical miracle. Peter's case has been separated from Nathan Johnson's and Alexander Cardelle's. He is expected to receive leniency for his defense of Amy Evans and his cooperation with the police.

Ashton Jones died in his hospital bed late Saturday night. His estranged parents held a small funeral and quietly buried their son in the same cemetery as Peter's mother and sister.

Byron Jenkins, Peter's father, managed to disappear before the police tracked him down. He is wanted for several crimes, including illegal arms dealing, drug trafficking, and now, attempted murder.

Officer Kimmy Wolf caught a flight back to Vancouver early Sunday morning. She plans to testify at Peter's trial, but no one knows whether she will exonerate or condemn him.

The Queen of the Darks informed the Office of Supernatural Containment that Alex was to, in her words, "stay where he belonged." She also had an angel reverse Peter's injuries. The OSC believes she offered a lot more assistance than she reported, suspecting she gave Amy easy access to her pistol and put Byron Jenkins to sleep while the girls escaped. The Dark dismissed these accusations with a flippant "you must be mad" and went back to Vancouver where she lives in a castle with seventeen pet dogs. Her subjects still consider her eccentric but grudgingly acknowledge her usefulness.

Susan Evans and Charles Banks were kept in the hospital until Sunday afternoon when they were both discharged with clean bills of health.

Amy Evans was discharged from Thunder Bay General six days after waking early Sunday morning. She is expected to make a full recovery. The tragic death of Katie Evans remains a secret shadow on her heart, but sharing her past with Zack mended a fracture in her soul.

Justin Evans checked his mother into rehab after Amy returned home. Erica Evans has promised to take it seriously this time and has vowed to stay single until she can stay clean. Zoe Banks played a central role in this decision and has offered to assist the Evans family in any way she can.

Bryan Davis, Jessie's father and Amy's landlord, drove his daughter all the way to Thunder Bay to visit Amy in the hospital. He happily informed Amy that an anonymous benefactor had paid their rent for an entire year. No one has the faintest idea how the donor knew of their financial woes.

Clarisse Donnellson and Justin Evans vacationed in Toronto for the holidays. Both were excused from writing final exams. They traveled back to Vancouver together in early January and have spent a suspicious amount of time together ever since.

Witnesses Chris Donnellson and Susan Evans have reported that Justin and Clarisse are not the only older siblings acting, in Susan's words, "all lovey-dovey." Zack and Amy have also spent a significant amount of time together, and as Susan says, "They act so disgustingly cute, it's sickening!"

Chelsea Brookes was horrified to learn of her ex-boyfriend's relationship with Amy Evans. But Jessie championed Amy and Zack, easing the impact of Chelsea's hostility.

Amy, Zack, and Charles have grown close, but each keep secrets that threaten to destroy them all.

Author Note

Thank you from the bottom of our hearts for reading our debut novel, *Blood Moon's Fury*. This book was nine years in the making and co-written by two authors a country and a half apart. The first draft was shockingly terrible. We're not talking bad. We're not talking dreadful. We're talking rip your hair out, chuck your laptop out a window, scream at the heavens awful.

Jenna Faris, a small-town girl from Canada with a worshipful adoration of Harry Potter, wrote the first draft of *Blood Moon's Fury* when she was fifteen. She liked to blare music while jogging on the treadmill, and her music lit the spark of creativity. She began imagining a storyline and embellished upon it to pass the time. A month later, she had an entire novel in her head. The natural thing to do was write it down.

Fifteen-year-old Jenna was in writerly heaven. She had inspiration coming out her ears and words flying from her fingertips. What could be better? Basic knowledge of spelling, grammar, and sentence structure would have been nice. Teenaged Jenna finished writing her then 60,000-word novel in under two months. She went on her merry way and forgot all about its existence.

A year later, Jenna met Heidi Springstroh, an exuberant lover of fantasy novels from the great state of Florida. Heidi had a wild imagination which she expressed in the form of creative short stories, poetry, and songs. The teens became fast friends but did not begin writing together for another six years.

The girls were FaceTiming one blustery March evening when Heidi happened to mention Amazon's Storyteller contest. She lamented the fact that she had a zillion great ideas and no motivation to write them down. For the first time in seven years, Jenna thought of that book she had scribbled with such feverish ease. But her computer had been taken out by a virus that had swallowed her novel whole. The girls bemoaned its fate for a while before remembering Jenna had sent Heidi a copy some three years prior. This did not spark instant hope as Heidi had gotten a new computer and no longer had a saved copy of the book. Still, she refused to give up. She scoured her email and managed to recover the nearly lost novel in an attachment. If it weren't for her, the story you just read would still be living in oblivion.

Jenna had reservations about sharing her work with the world, but Heidi refused to listen to such nonsense. She was convinced her best friend had written a masterpiece. Jenna relented and agreed to Heidi's plan to edit the book and enter it in the Storyteller contest.

The friends examined the horrifying mess of a story and nearly lost their nerve. The novel, lamely titled *The Heroes* at that time, featured the same characters and plotline as it does today. But the book had terrible dialogue and missing quotation marks, atrocious and arbitrary paragraph breaks, punctuation and spelling that would bring you to tears, and thousands of unnecessary rambling adjectives and sentences … like this one. It also lacked visual descriptions of any kind. Jenna and Heidi were both born blind, and describing people and their surroundings with detail, flair, and colorful imagery was an enormous struggle in the beginning. They studied color like a foreign art and gained perception of the visual world through nothing more than words.

Jenna and Heidi spent several months in early 2017 trying to get the disaster of a novel contest ready. Heidi did all of the early edits, proofreading and formatting that first draft into something resembling a book. Jenna read through every draft, eliminating excess words and rewriting entire chapters to achieve better flow. The girls stayed up all night the day before the contest was due to end. It was only as they familiarized themselves with Amazon's self-publishing platform, Kindle Direct Publishing, that they realized they had overlooked something big. Winning depended upon their book being bought while the contest went on. As they were entering their novel on the contest's very last day, they hadn't a hope of winning. The aspiring authors shut their laptops with snaps of finality and retired to bed.

The next morning, they were at it again. They had an entire year to get their book ready for the contest, and they vowed to polish it to perfection, or as close to perfection as novels ever get. Heidi convinced Jenna to write fantasy into the previously realistic story, which sparked an idea for a sequel. They tossed out *The Heroes* as a title and tried out *Take Control* as an alternative. This idea seemed even worse than *The Heroes*, which sent them right back to square one. Hope came knocking in late July when Heidi dreamed up *Eight Days of Hell*. Jenna tried out *Seven Days with Satan* as a title for the sequel she was hard at work writing, and this snowballed into an eight-book series called "Countdown."

The young authors threw out the countdown theme in favor of a series title with more fantasy/thriller vibes, "Curse of the Blood Moon." Up until this point, their book had supernatural creatures interspersed throughout but no overarching fantasy storyline. Thus, the curse was born! In keeping with this theme, they renamed their novel *Blood Moon's Fury*. They still had ideas for seven more books, though. What to do with them? Write seven more books of course!

Heidi happily set to work dreaming up titles, new characters, and cover designs for future books, while Jenna continued to write the sequel to *Blood Moon's Fury*, *Blood Moon's Servant*. Jenna spent the summer of 2017 writing and editing in her stifling studio apartment at the University of British Columbia while retaking advanced biochemistry.

It took a whopping two and a half more years before *Blood Moon's Fury* was ready for publication. Jenna, juggling university, a part-time job, and a social life, edited the novel over and over and over every chance she got. She researched writing and editing tips until her mind ached and reread the book so many times she can quote large chunks by heart. Heidi, going through life transitions and working full-time, reformatted the novel from first person present tense to the more professional third person past tense. She proofread every finished draft and meticulously formatted the paperback and Kindle manuscripts to match Amazon's requirements. She also corresponded with a brilliant cover designer to create an exciting and engaging first image.

Jenna and Heidi dreamed of being published for years. Now they look up their book on Amazon and can hardly believe it exists in the world. Whether you are a published author, an aspiring novelist, or simply have an idea, we encourage you to follow your dreams and bring them to life. If we can do it, anyone can. Feel free to drop us a link to your Author Central or unpublished snippets of writing. We would be delighted to browse your work!

If you enjoyed our first novel, please support us and our writing by leaving a review. There is nothing we love more than hearing from our amazing readers. We read every single review and value your feedback above all else. It is for you we write, and you we want to hear from.

Follow our website www.leahkingsley.com for beyond the book insight into your favorite characters, exclusive deals, and direct conversation with us. Thank you for reading *Blood Moon's Fury* from the bottom of both our hearts.

Printed in Great Britain
by Amazon